The Woman
Who Rode to the Moon

A CORDELIA MORGAN MYSTERY

The Woman
Who Rode to the Moon

A CORDELIA MORGAN MYSTERY

Bett Reece Johnson

Published in the United States by Cleis Press Inc.,
P.O. Box 14684, San Francisco, California 94114.

Printed in the United States.
Cover design: Scott Idleman / BLINK
Text design: Karen Huff
Cleis logo art: Juana Alicia
First Edition.
10 9 8 7 6 5 4 3 2 1

ACKNOWLEDGEMENTS

Special thanks to Syb and Della of Grandma's House for giving me shelter from the storm; to Joy Alesdatter whose veterinarian expertise provided invaluable help, and to feralcat.com for consciousness-raising and mind-boggling statistics; to forensic pathologist Joe Cohen, M.D., for helping out on all my "bone" questions, though mistakes and liberties taken herein are my own; to all my rowdy neighbors at Zapata who wear white hats; and above all to the Goddess who does indeed work in mysterious ways.

LIBRARY OF CONGRESS CATALOGING-IN-PUBLICATION DATA

Johnson, Bett Reece.
    The woman who rode to the moon : a Cordelia Morgan mystery / by Bett Reece Johnson.
        p.   cm.
    ISBN 1-57344-086-8 (alk. paper)
    I. Title.
    PS3560.037184W6   1999
    813'.54—dc21   99-24553
                                                                         CIP

for Virginia

Morgan

"Cordelia," the hanged woman says.

The saints say that visions are a glimpse into the divine. I wouldn't put any money on it. I wouldn't put any money on the divine, either. Any fool knows that visions are a commonplace commodity—snatched from the entrails of thought, revealing a certain coagulate truth. For my money, nightmares are their handmaids, silence their sole and diabolic covenant. It was not those prophetic visions that doomed Cassandra, but her naïve belief that she could communicate them.

The woman does a slow spin at the end of the rope, hypnotic in the shadows of the barn rafters. She turns clockwise, unhurried as the second hand on the face of a clock, pauses, turns back, saying my name as it has not been said in my four years of exile, not until Saturday two weeks ago by the hanged woman's mother:

"Cord."

Claire looks up as I touch my heels to the black horse and emerge from the bank of oak trees. She sits on her chestnut mare, waiting as the horse drinks long and deeply from the pond. A raw, cow-sized patch of water.

So small that even at this distance, on its opposite side, I follow the way Claire's lips move when she says

"I always knew I'd see you again, Cordelia."

She sits straight as a rod on the horse, her blond hair gone to pearl, cut short and chic. Even at seventy-six, she has not the look of an old woman. Not significantly changed from when I saw her last, though most of the world appears antiquated through a seventeen-year-old's eyes. I would have known her even if I had not traced her whereabouts and followed her these last weeks so that I can recite her daily routine by heart. Saturdays: she arrives at the stable at 3:00 on the outskirts of Nashville, takes her weekly ride on the mare she boards here. Always the same trail, stops at the water, lets her mare drink before turning back to the stables.

Because four years is too long to go without hearing your name, and a million miles is too long to travel for it. I have used the indirect route, four years of resorts and tourist holes, galleries and museums and mausoleums and every natural wonder big enough to make the maps on the seven continents. I had thought just hearing it would be enough. It is the seeing that I had not expected.

She looks nothing like my mother, though in my mind's eye that is who I see as I look at her in the Saturday afternoon Tennessee sunlight. See them standing with arms linked, watching me board the Greyhound bound for Chicago, my first semester at Northwestern, the two of them waving as the bus pulls away. Three months before the fire burned the collective where they lived, killing every woman and child who had been there that day.

I touch my heels to my horse, and she follows me toward a path leading into the forest. One I know to be seldom used, ending as it does at a cliff's edge.

As we ride, I sketch for Claire my life in minimalist strokes since the fire destroyed the women's collective—living in Kentucky with my father, recognizing at last the bursts of temper and alcoholism that drove my mother away; living two years in Santa Fe with the man named Cruz; working for the international company owned by my surrogate father, Pasonombre, where my assignments as a Research Specialist during those eleven years were well suited to my particular talents. I have ever hungered for the edge.

"Cordelia," she laughs in her bemused way, as we stop our horses at the edge of a steep cliff overlooking a meandering stream below. "You're telling me you're a hit man?"

"Of course not," I say. "Much too extreme."

"Far-fetched."

"Highly implausible."

Claire turns to me, taking in my hair, which I wear short and combed back, my clothes which are still black as they have been for years, the boots pressed into the metal English stirrups. My horse shakes his head, eyes the precipice. A narrow ledge slopes down one side, leading to a trail of switchbacks and the water below. He paws the ground impatiently, dances in place, rears slightly.

"Nice stallion," Claire says, eyebrows raised. "Handful, looks like." Her face is angular, sharp-chinned, less wrinkled than finely embroidered with lines. Her pupils are pinpoints; a vague smile plays at the corners of her mouth. She tilts her head back slightly, a familiar gesture, and examines me with shrewd eyes the color of my mother's large aquamarine stone she still wears: "So you're running from them."

"Not running. Traveling." My horse pulls at his bit, gnashes it in his teeth. Claire's mare stands quietly, its glossy neck arched, its eyes on the stream below.

"Ah. Traveling, then." Her mare's small ears, which curve inward at the tips, flick forward and back between the cliff and our voices. "Suits you, does it? You were ever one for rushing about."

I meet Claire's eyes, grin slowly at her, loosen my hold on the reins. The horse lunges toward the ledge, edges along the narrow granite lip, then plunges down the steep switchbacks at breakneck speed. He barely pauses at the stream. I feel the muscles of his thighs collect, his shoulders lift, his forelegs leave the ground. We are above the water, airborne, then landing on the opposite bank. At the long, flat dirt road, the animal's body surges forward, and I press myself against his neck, moving with the rhythm of his stride, smelling the musky horse scent of him, the adrenaline singing between my legs.

When Claire arrives, the horse and I are standing at the end of the dirt road on a high grassy promontory. Nashville lies spread out before us in the long rays of afternoon sun. The chestnut mare is dark with sweat, lathered white around the girth; Claire's face is slightly ashen. We sit our *horses, side by side, watch the shadows of the mountains begin to fall across the city.*

She says it again, my name. She leans over to comb my hair with her fingers. A gesture from my youth, in that lost time when the planet creaked so slowly on its axis that I paced our barren meadows wishing for tornadoes on the horizon, wishing for the feel of the silver-blue Stingray's wheel owned by a boy next door. Claire's hand settles across mine, cool over my feverish one.

"Need a Project, dear?" She lifts a brow. Her eyes carry the old foxy look. Claire and I, we are kindred spirits, fellow conspirators. Projects to stem my boredom were Claire's specialty. She makes her familiar opening gambit: "Might have just the thing."

It is her turn. She tells me that she is a real estate investor now, but even before that, before she had met my mother, she had once developed a mountain community called El Gato in the Colorado Rockies. That had been after her own daughter, Camilla, had graduated high school and left home for New York City and art school, during a time when she herself had been bored and at loose ends.

"I would have told you more about Camilla back then if I'd known what to tell. She was such a reclusive child, a stranger to me. She left home the day she graduated, and I didn't see her again until after the fire, after I'd returned home to Nashville. Must have been '76, '77 maybe. Showed up with a baby, stayed awhile, then one day she was off again. Didn't say where."

The sun has set and left the sky orange behind the western hills above the city. Claire tells me about raising the child whose name is Wendy, and that as a freshman in high school, Wendy had become pregnant.

"Married, her and Gerald Crawford. A wild boy, Gerald. Son of a family friend, the boy and Wendy practically grew up together." She shakes her head at the sprawling hills, at the horizon where pinks and oranges and lavenders marble the sky. "Well, seemed like he might do better out of the city, so I dreamed up a little Project for them, figured the best place for Gerald was in the middle of nowhere, thought that property I'd developed and kept a part of back in Colorado all those years ago might be just the place. I sent them out there, him and Wendy and the baby, told them to look it over, build if they had a mind to. Told them it'd be theirs if they made it their home.

"That seemed to work fine. Gerald took to the place, spent all his time building his house from what Wendy said. Then Camilla shows up here again. I don't know where exactly she'd been, she wasn't the type to say much about her past. I knew she'd finished art school in New York, traveled around in Europe. She stayed here awhile, didn't like Nashville much. She was just sad somehow, kind of rootless. I mentioned a visit to Wendy out in Colorado, thought maybe getting to know her daughter might help. She seemed to like the idea, went out there, decided to stay. I thought they were all doing fine. Then..."

Sequins of light begin to appear across the city below. Claire's back, which had been straight, has curved into the shape of an old woman's.

"One night, a year ago last September, I got a call from the sheriff out in Colorado. It's Camilla, he said. She'd hung herself, up in the loft of that horse barn I had built all those years ago."

"Claire, I'm so sorry."

"Sheriff said it was suicide, but I've never quite understood it. Why did she do it? That's what nobody can tell me."

Her back is straight again, and she leans forward, her hands braced on the pommel of her saddle. She turns to me, and her eyes have the foxy look.

"You're looking for a secluded place to light for a while?" Her face is a shifting pattern of intricate lines. *"Well, it just so happens, dear, that I'm looking for somebody to do a little research."*

PART I

The Road to El Gato

1

GARBO WOULD HAVE LOVED EL GATO. It's nested so high in the Colorado Rockies, you can hear the angels sing. You can follow its streams through bright pockets of aspen with trunks neat and straight as telephone poles, their leaves trembling even when the air is still; streams that trickle across high mountain pastures where deer graze in the wet purple dawn, where elk wander in the evening as the sun drops behind the San Juans. It is then, in that last dying light, that the bronze-eyed cougars steal from their lairs hidden deep in the canyons and stalk the night, refreshing themselves in the star-sprinkled waters.

And Garbo loved to walk. She would have followed the central stream, the only one that flows year around, as it weaves an enchanted, serpentine path through the heart of El Gato. It is a narrow stream, yet deep enough for rainbow trout, bordered by cottonwoods so lush they form a circuitous, five-mile corridor of green shade all the way up to the water's source. There, you will find a small natural dam filled by water rushing from above where two immense granite columns rise up to form a towering black obelisk against the sky, leaning their smooth bare shoulders together, and from between them, inside their tall thin darkness—the great cataclysmic roar of a waterfall.

I can see her: Garbo entering this sacred place, using the same smile she wore at the end of *Queen Christina* as she looks around her. With her head up, her shoulders back, and that indomitable smile, she would have pronounced it Eden.

But Garbo aside, for us mere mortals, El Gato's the kind of remote mountain community you could've bought into for the price of back taxes a few years ago. Before the great suburban exodus of the nineties when burned-out, cashed-out, dropped-out yuppies packed it in and moved to the outbacks with enough bucks to build their trophy houses and enough change left over for sleek income-producing investment portfolios. Before the EL GATO sign with the cougar logo went up, right next to the security gate that keeps out anyone without a plastic card to open it.

It was the shank end of a Saturday afternoon, and life was sweet for J. S. Symkin, former poet/professor, recently turned entrepreneur. Just the day before, I'd closed on a real estate coup I'd been sweating over for six months, and now it was break time. Thanks to last night's heavy snowfall that forecasters had been predicting all week, the slopes were in top form, and this morning the skies were clear and sunny: I was heading for Aspen. I anchored the skis to the overhead carrier, tossed snow-play paraphernalia in the back seat of the Porsche, and pulled out of Albuquerque well before ten o'clock—plenty of time to make the six-hour Aspen drive before dark. This wasn't my first trip to the Colorado peaks; I'd made the drive often enough to pack a hefty selection of CDs because in that long, dismal stretch of two-lane asphalt between Santa Fe and the Colorado Rockies, you have a choice of radio stations that play Hank Williams, Jr., the evangelist hit parade, or ear-thumping Indian tom-tom favorites. When the NPR station started to fade a few miles north of Ojo, I shoved some vintage Stones in the player, revved the volume up to critical mass, flipped on the radar detector, and stood on the accelerator to the beat of "Sympathy for the Devil." It was that kind of day.

But even Mick Jagger and warp speed can't help much in the San Luis Valley—no matter how fast you drive, what you get is more of the same: long, flat, barren miles of high desert with sub-zero winters and tepid summers and high-velocity spring winds that blast sand straight through the continent's longest valley like a high-balling locomotive. It hits the west side of the Sangre de

Cristos and piles up the biggest, tallest sand dune collection in the nation. By the time I entered the foothills and left the Valley falling away behind, I had Etheridge on the stereo, pretty certain that if I never saw sand again, it would be too soon.

The road began to climb steeply and Melissa's voice came smoldering out of the speakers: I saw her ahead, standing in a patch of sunlight that slanted across the asphalt, her long gold hair falling across her shoulders, eyes squeezed shut to the sky as she gripped the guitar and we sang together: "I sold my soul for freedom, it's lonely but it's sweet." She took the high notes just like Joplin, her voice gritty and rubbing me in all the right places as the Porsche shot straight up into the ice-cold mountain air whipping in through the louver in the sunroof, air so rare and pure and heady, it tasted like freedom. I inhaled it, pressed it deep into my lungs, and held it there until I began to feel lightheaded with the sheer joy of being alive.

By the time I'd fed another CD into the player and Melissa and I were belting out "Skin Deep," the flat lands were far below, which was something of a mixed blessing. Highway 82 to Aspen is a narrow, dicey affair that curls into the peaks with corkscrew turns and hair-raising switchbacks, edging along spectacular cliffs where the world is spread out far below and keeps its distance. The sun turned the snow along the roadside into a galaxy of sparkling diamonds, but the asphalt was clear and dry. I leaned on the accelerator, sliding into hairpin curves on two wheels, skirting sheer-drop cliffs on one side with several tons of yesterday's snow hanging on the other. My mind was selling tickets on all four screens: hatching innovative schemes to put myself in Etheridge's path; remembering yesterday's coup at the bank, which had floated me a quarter million for my purchase of a crumbling historic ruin and another million to renovate it into a chic boutique mall; thinking about Tony Sandoval, my general contractor, who would need constant riding to keep the renovation running on schedule because a million looks like a fat figure but it was a slim, near-impossible budget for the work ahead. The trick was to make it possible. My thoughts turned to the shambling old ruin itself, a former governor's mansion from the last century, imagining its balconies rebuilt, the ceiling-high pile of pigeon shit on the third story removed and the shattered glass canopy above it replaced, the collapsed circular staircase restored....

Which is probably why one minute I was homing in on Aspen; the next I was somehow on the wrong road, a narrower asphalt two-lane with patches of unmelted snow. I watched for a place to turn around, but both sides of the road were piled waist-deep with embankments of snow left behind by the plow. After several miles, I hung a left on a well-graded, narrow road with a line of mailboxes, though a nearby curve made a turnaround dangerous. I had no choice but to follow the hard-packed snowy road, made several more left turns on several more immaculately graded roads, which nevertheless did not add up to a square nor take me back to the highway. Increasingly desperate, I cruised one road after another until my head was spinning. The blinding sun-dazzled day was now blotted out by immense, towering pines as I eased the car into first gear and crept through shadowy tunnels of looping, snowy, unmarked back roads, feeling the day slip away and anxiety start to gnaw at the back of my head.

But I have an excellent sense of direction, never been lost in my life. I drove stubbornly on, circling, turning right, turning left, mile after weary mile, deeper into the labyrinth, looking for a house, a vehicle, a set of tire tracks, a glimpse of the state highway ahead. The occasional cabins I spotted through the trees showed no signs of habitation—no vehicles, tracks, smoke from the chimneys. I calmed myself by taking deep breaths and reasoning that someone recently graded these miles and miles of roads; therefore, someone must live here. I began running this logic through my mind like a mantra while the minutes ticked away toward dark and the miles rolled off the odometer.

"Shit!" I banged the steering wheel and stopped the car. In pure frustration and near tears, glaring out the window at the deserted, frozen terrain where a glimmer of sunlight dappled the snow here and there, I had to admit I was lost. I pulled a map out of the glove compartment, spread it across the steering wheel, and finding no side road verging off Highway 82, estimated my position. Near as I could figure, I was about twenty miles west of a small town called

Crystal Springs, about thirty-five miles east of Aspen. I stared at the map until the lines ran together, then stared out at the shadowy, desolate road. No good dwelling too much on the consequences of getting stranded in an isolated wilderness, or how much crow pie I was going to eat after telling Tillie, my secretary, that I'd never be tied to her by a car phone. I didn't want them to be famous last words, but the fact was, I knew that death by freezing was an all-too-common occurrence in these spheres.

The console clock read 3:23; the gas gauge registered less than a quarter tank. Still plenty of time and gas to make Aspen before dark. I drove on. At 3:45, I began compiling a mental list of ways to survive an arctic night until, in the morning, I could strap on my downhill skis and attempt a cross-country search to find the highway or a warm human body, whichever came first. I had my parka, ski boots, the down sleeping bag I always kept tucked away in the hatchback, a coffee can with candles and matches that made an effective heater for the emergency I felt gaining on me. As I cruised one road after another, I began to see signs of life: plenty of deer tracks, jackrabbits poised in motionless profile, aiming one black, unblinking eye on me and close enough that I could see the veins in their translucent ears as they watched me pass. I went by a deserted-looking log cabin set back off the road, but its windows were boarded over, no sign of a vehicle, no smoke from the chimney.

Then I spotted a narrow side road, and although it was unplowed, a set of fresh tire tracks was gouged deeply into the snow. I felt a flood of relief as I inspected the tracks: wide tires, clearly imprinted with an aggressive snow tread pattern, and steady-moving enough that the vehicle had to be a four-wheel drive. I weighed the odds of guiding my own car along the same tracks, but the mound of snow between them was high enough to stall the low-slung Porsche in the first few yards. The road itself was very narrow, little more than a path through the dense trees, most likely someone's driveway, but there was no way to tell how far away their house might be, and I didn't want to add to my plight by getting stuck in the snow.

I switched off the engine, and opening the door, was hit by a blast of icy, stinging air that left me breathless. I grabbed my parka, zipped up, pulled on my boots, and walked over to inspect the road where the grooves that had cut into the snow disappeared into the pines. Then I looked around me, looked up and down the deserted snowy road where I stood.

It was the silence that struck me first.

I had been driving for hours, the music blasting with the turbo bass accelerator switched on. Now I stood alone in the center of an empty road in an eerie hush, the landscape blanketed in white, self-absorbed and still as a grave. The giant ponderosas were not green but towering black steeples, laid with mounds of white that weighed down their branches. Above the trees, the sky was flat and white as the ground, the air so cold and raw and virgin that just breathing it burned my throat. My skin began prickling with goose-flesh at the isolation of it all.

"Jesus, Sym, get a grip, old girl."

I set off down the road, stepping in the tire tracks where my boots crunched loudly in the snow. Then I began to hear the other sounds as I walked, first one and then another rising like circles on the surface of a still pond—a Steller's jay screeched and shrugged its feathers as it peered down at me with a shiny black eye, a wood-pecker hammered away worlds above. Along the left side of the road, a mountain stream murmured beneath a frosted canapé of ice, widening in spots where, evidenced by recent tracks, wildlife came to drink. The tiny cleft prints of deer and the larger ones of elk had trampled down the snow, and at one spot a singularly impressive set of huge cat tracks led to the stream and continued across it, disappearing into the dark, tangled underbrush.

I hurried along, reminding myself that mountain lions are inor-dinately shy creatures, not much interested in humans given the option of deer and elk, their natural prey. Still, I scanned the dense brush uneasily. Soon the road zagged sharply and began a steep climb, the tire marks punctuated with skids and deep cuts where rocks and bare earth had been overturned as the tires sought for a hold. The stream broadened; the water rushed loud and fast over large rocks and cascaded down sharp embankments. The terrain grew wild and increasingly dense along the far side of the stream, then dropped off into deep ravines and canyons. But to my right, the trees thinned to mostly small, gnarled piñon. On that side, the ground was rocky and sprinkled with low-growing prickly cactus in wide open areas where the sun had melted patches of snow.

I must have been in alpha mode or rubbernecking like a country cousin in Manhattan to have turned a bend and walked straight into a battered school-bus-yellow Jeep flatbed that was probably a collector's item even with the rust and dents. A green Colorado license plate with the white mountain logo dangled by one screw below a bumper pasted with faded decals: "Honk If You're Horny," "Cowboys Do It Better," and "Love It or Leave It." A black trash bag, twisted and tied at the top with rope, sat on the flatbed behind the driver's seat, but the cab was empty. I peered through the half-open window, filmed with a build-up of cigarette smoke from the smell of it. The passenger seat and floorboard was a tangle of blankets, articles of winter clothing in surplus camouflage, several generic beer cans, a rusty hydraulic jack, a bright yellow polyurethane tow strap, and assorted trash and crumpled brown bags. On top of the pile, an open box of Winchester .22 rifle shells leaned against the passenger window.

A set of very recent footprints the size of Bigfoot's led from the Jeep, made deep holes in the snow on the stream side, and disappeared into a thick tangle of brush. From the looks of it, I had been following the tire tracks of a hunter, one who was operating out of season. Stumbling on a poacher in the Colorado wilderness is a lot more dangerous than stumbling across a mountain lion—the age-old animosity between liberals and conservatives had revved up to Civil-War dimensions in the Highest State as yuppies moved in and locals fought to keep the status quo. Take the revered practice of toting guns and killing animals, no matter the season: fanatic militiamen or local hunters in the backwoods like this one didn't need much encouragement to "accidentally" shoot a smart-mouthed, six-foot female driving a red Porsche with a "Celebrate Diversity" bumper sticker.

I followed Bigfoot's tracks to where they disappeared into the thicket, noticing that after a short distance the terrain fell away sharply into a deep canyon where the stream ran far below. I strained to hear the sounds of footsteps crunching the snow, any indication that the hunter might be nearby. Nothing—no birds, no planes soughing overhead. Just that eerie silence that sent chills up my spine. I didn't want to be around when the guy showed up. And I most decidedly did not want to spend the night anywhere near here.

I turned to beat a hasty retreat back down the road when I got yet another surprise. On the other side of the Jeep, the cactus-packed terrain had fallen away and left a precipice with boulders stacked downhill the size of houses, so that the road verged along the edge of a steep cliff looking down over the wilderness. I approached the edge of the promontory and had a panoramic bird's-eye view of the area where I had recently been driving in circles. I could see portions of the snowy roads winding through the trees like white ribbons, and just below where I stood was the unmistakable splash of red that could only be my new Porsche. But I was even more startled to see a web of telephone lines draped from poles sprinkled throughout what I had taken to be a relatively uninhabited wilderness area, and in the far distance—the stretch of asphalt highway I had been searching for.

Seen from this high, the world was no longer cast in shadows. The late afternoon sun was still bright, made golden by the last shooting rays of the sun just beginning to slip behind the San Juans where purple, snowcapped peaks were pasted against the sunset. I could still make Aspen before dark. I snapped a quick mental picture of the scene just below, memorized strategic points and a series of turns that would take me back to the highway, leaned my head back and massaged the bunched, tense muscles along my shoulders. While the muscles relaxed, I watched the sunset's refracted light burn amber on the pine trunks and edge the bark with gold. Further up the road, a jungle of large, square-cut rocks were stacked high, their faces bronzed in the evening glow.

Suddenly, I heard something behind the silence, what I had taken as silence—the omnipresent distant sound of the rushing stream but also, above that, a greater, louder, unmistakable sound that flooded through me like an electric current. It was the distant roar of a waterfall.

My heart raced, and I struggled for breath. Blood drummed in my ears. A weakness rose in my legs that sent me stumbling backwards against the Jeep. Darkness prickled behind my eyes. I turned and lowered my forehead to the achingly cold metal, bent to it as in prayer, and I imagined that I heard, above the water's roar, the monstrous crunching steps of the hunter's boots approaching.

I turned and fled down the mountain.

2

AUGUST 25, 1951

THERE WERE RAINBOWS OF RIBBONS and streamers and trails of clouds in the sky. At the front Daddy took out the smooth leather wallet he let me smell sometimes. He handed money to the lady with long hair like sunshine and then he put the wallet in his back pocket and took my hand again and Mommy had my other and we walked under the high arch where the flags were bright colors snapping in the wind. They sounded like the sheets that Mommy pinned on the line and the winds came flapping and I ran between them and they smelled like the sea. They smelled like Amy Brown's swimming pool.

People were walking everywhere and they made crowds of noise. The pink sugar was cotton candy Mommy said. Her voice had bees in it when she told daddy it would make me sick but he took out his wallet again and he handed the stick to me. The pink tickled my tongue and it was sticky on my nose and cheeks and wouldn't stop. Mommy took out her white hanky and stuck out her tongue to it and her face came down. The hanky smelled like sheets and it felt soft and wet on my nose and cheeks and mouth and I turned up my face to the sky where her face was and squeezed my eyes shut. The hanky tickled and a laugh came crawling up like an ant inside my throat and then outside. The pink melted on my tongue and the tickle crawled up again laughing and it kept coming.

"How big, how big you are," Daddy said. He was laughing too and he put his hands under my arms and swung me up on his shoulders and I dangled my feet on his shirt. I rode up high and looked down at the people walking at us. The people were everywhere but now the air was open and the pink was in Daddy's hair too. "Big. Five years big," he said with his hands holding my ankles.

Daddy talks funny when he talks to me. He doesn't talk funny to Mommy or Uncle Roger.

"Harry, she is getting it all over you. Put her down. Put her down now." Bees were in Mommy's voice and she was looking up at me. Her forehead had lines on it.

"She's all right. She's fine," Daddy said. We walked in front of Mommy where all the people were everywhere with their faces coming at us and the ground was faraway and when I turned my head back Mommy wasn't there.

We were on a ride that went fast and made us spin in the air and when it stopped Daddy held me so I didn't fall over because my head had not stopped. My head was spinning in the air and the ground went sideways.

"Mommy's still not here," I said. Daddy lifted me on to his neck again. "Where's Mommy at?" The bright had gone out of the sky and lights sparkled against the black where the sky had been.

"She's lost, sweety, but she'll turn up. We'll just keep walking around. You are such a big five, such a tall five, that she will see you way up high. You are a high five," he said laughing and drinking from the cup with the white fuzzy on top. "We'll just keep on walking, high five, and you look for Mommy way up there." And we went into where the faces were walking at us and the lights made their skin green and blue and red. Their faces did not look like Mommy's face. Their voices were crowded and big. Their voices were too big to sing and I wanted to sleep while Mommy sang. I laid down my head on top of Daddy's and his hair smelled like home.

Then there were more lights. There were red lights and the faces did not look like Mommy's. The faces were red and red. Red. The noise hurt my ears. I put my hands over my ears and Daddy brought me down and my head was over his shoulder. Daddy put his hand on my head but I turned it and saw the water falling down loud from up high and people walking through the water carrying something. Daddy turned my head on his shoulder and put his hand on it again and I cried and shook my head. I saw the face. Its mouth was open and its eyes looked at the sky and the blood came out of the throat and made everything red all over.

"My god. Oh my god oh my god." Daddy was running with his hand on my head. His hand was hard and I couldn't turn.

JUNE 6, 1989

"And so you thought the waterfall did it?"

I considered that for a minute. "I didn't see it in those terms," I said, "not as cause and effect. I was only five years old, it was my birthday. Hell, I didn't even remember this until a few years ago when Sandy and I were vacationing in Tennessee."

Margot had some kind of New Age harpsichord music playing very low, and if it was supposed to have a calming effect, it was failing miserably because even mentioning Sandy's name still made my blood seethe. My cheeks burned; I gripped the arm of the loveseat where I sat facing Margot's desk, its surface clear and gleaming except for the ever-present yellow pad, an arrangement of silk flowers, and a pitcher of water. I took a couple of deep breaths and released them slowly, as I'd learned in biofeedback. Margot waited with her neutral expression. Psychiatrist Beige, I called it.

"It's not like I'd never seen a waterfall, you know? But Ruby Falls is not your average, everyday waterfall, either. It's located about half a mile down inside a cave. Takes an hour to walk it—a damp, cold hour, winding around stalactites and stalagmites, which didn't help my claustrophobia any. We finally get to the bottom, and here's this deafening torrent of water pouring from the top of the cave. Then the guide starts to get creative, right? He's talking about true darkness, how you can only experience it in certain rare situations, like being inside the earth. Then he flips the lights off so we're all standing there in pitch black, like a bad dream. Guide's getting a kick out of this. Says something about bats, chuckles, hits the lights again. But this time, they're red. *Ruby Falls*, get it?"

Margot's face maintained Psycho Beige, plaster perfect. I wondered if shrinks had to take a class in Face Fixation 1A—maybe practice in front of a mirror. Like I was doing at home, now that I had plenty of time. Margot tipped her head slightly to one side as she caught me gazing at her, a quizzical look in her eye. One eyebrow lifted.

"You think it was the red lights that..." she prompted.

"Right. Plus the waterfall. The sight of that long cascade of water down the rock, the sound of it, the darkness. And I'm standing there next to Sandy, teeth chattering with cold, that bloody light turning the waterfall red. Turning everything red. I looked around. Sandy's face was red, everyone's face was red, and then I looked back at the waterfall and saw them—the men in white jackets carrying the stretcher, coming through the water at the amusement park. I..." I stopped, my mouth moving but no words coming out.

"Sym? You okay, Sym?" Margot dropped her pencil and pushed herself up from her chair. I was looking at her, clinging to her image so clean and wholesome that she might have walked out of an ad for Tide or been standing beside the blue-ribbon rum cake at the state fair. She had on a green angora sweater that made her turquoise eyes blue and made her look soft as a close-up in an old Doris Day movie.

"I'm okay." I held up my hand and motioned her back down. "It's just remembering it now brings it back again."

Her office was insulated—the only sounds were the harpsichord music that trilled and drifted around the room, and somewhere an air conditioner kept up a low, steady hum. But it was 4:30, and I knew that outside, just a few yards away from where we sat, the commuter traffic had begun: horns were honking, tempers flaring, and drivers tried to keep their cool.

"Anyway, when I saw Ruby Falls, I suddenly remembered. My mother and father and I had gone to a local amusement park for my birthday, and the entrance to this particular attraction was a manmade waterfall, a thin wall of water spilling over a concrete entryway that you rode through in an automated canoe. We had been through this ride before, on a previous visit, and I had been terrified and cried a lot. It was called 'The Labyrinth,' and the canoe took you inside through this dark, narrow water canal with life-sized horror scenes that lit up along the way. They were based on real life. You know, Lizzie Borden, Jack the Ripper, stuff like that." I shuddered, wondering who thought up such ghoulish things and called them "attractions."

"And inside was where your mother was discovered?"

"Right," I said, feeling my father's hand pressing roughly against the back of my head, pushing through the crowd, running after the men carrying the woman on the stretcher to the ambulance, the sirens screaming, the driver refusing to allow him in the ambulance with a small child. But I had forced my head around and glimpsed her—my mother's face with her eyes open, staring up at the black sky, the blood. Not dead yet, not quite.

The harpsichord trilled, followed by the sound of ocean waves hitting the sand, and Margot leaned slightly forward with one forearm on the desk as she held a pencil poised over her yellow pad. We had held this pose, facing one another across her desk, twice a week for the last six months, and I was no closer to dealing with my anger and confusion and the devastation of my life than I had been my first visit. Nothing had changed—not me, not Margot, not this office with its soothing music and silk flowers and mauve carpet and crystal pitchers of ice water with thinly sliced lemon floating on top. It was a sham, a beautiful sham: perfectly controlled, perfectly safe, every detail finely tuned to convey stability, order, to argue the presence of a sane universe for clients like me who would not be here if, in fact, such a fiction existed. I felt as though I were suffocating, the lie of the room pressing in from all four walls. I wanted to smash the pitcher, break—

"Forty years is a long time to repress a memory," Margot said. "Your father never spoke to you about that night?"

I hauled my attention back to her. How to explain something I didn't understand myself, could barely remember?

"Our family didn't talk much about anything after that," I said. I tried to dredge up a memory of my father speaking to me, but as always, I came up blank. "He left, just disappeared a year or so later, and my uncle, my mother's brother, stayed on. I must have asked lots of things, like, 'What happened to Mom?' or 'Where's Dad?' but mostly what I remember is my uncle sitting in a chair in front of the television. He'd say things like, 'Not now, honey,' or 'These things happen.' "

The harpsichord did a long trill, followed by a chorus of seabirds and a wave kissing down on some mythical beach.

"And what was that like for you?" Margot said.

What was it like? I tried to locate a feeling to describe, but there was nothing there except an empty space pumping blood. It was like nothing at all. It was like putting a tape in the player and finding someone had erased it. It was like listening anyway. That's what it was like.

I shrugged: "I got older, they got older. I left home, my uncle died. After the incident at Ruby Falls, I found out the details of how my mother died by ordering microfilms of the old newspapers though the university interlibrary loan department." Margot made some notes; that was a sham, too. She always taped each session, gave me the tape and asked me to listen, make notes, bring them to the next session. I watched her pencil move across the page as I spoke: "She'd been raped, stabbed, her throat sliced open, then propped naked in one of the scenes. Jack the Ripper. Police never caught the killer."

Margot stopped writing. She wore her reading glasses on the end of her nose, and she watched the yellow pad for a few beats before looking at me over the tops of them.

"And your dad, you never saw him again?"

"Nope, never did."

We stared at each other while the seconds slid by. Her face had returned to plaster, and she seemed to be waiting for something. I felt the familiar anger hit my body, heat my face. My heart raced and my cheeks began the slow burn. Inside the darkness behind my eyes, white-hot explosions shot up and bloomed like fireworks on a July night, yet at the very center of the volcano lay that chill, untouchable center from which issued the smallest sound in the universe—a puppy whimpering at a winter's door, a small embryo of sound curled tight and listening to itself. I got up and paced the floor to stem the rage, but it didn't help. I stopped in front of her desk and stared down at her.

"What? You think I should have gone after him, hired a detective? I was six fucking years old when he left!"

"That's right, Sym. You were just a little girl." She leaned back in her chair and looked up at me. "Have you tried to find him since? Do you want to?"

"No, I don't want to!" I hadn't meant to scream. "I don't fucking want to find him! He walked out! Fuck him!"

The air had stilled, the music played out. I stood trembling in front of Margot's desk, her crystal pitcher raised high in my hands. It was empty, the ice cubes and lemon slices and water beaded across the mauve carpet in the June sunlight. Margot had recoiled into her chair, her turquoise eyes filled with fear as I lowered the pitcher and placed it gently back on her desk. My hands were shaking and dripping with lemon water. I stared at them as though they belonged to a stranger and then placed them against my burning cheeks as I eased myself back down to the sofa, the pitiful whimper inside filling my ears like sirens.

"It's all right, Sym. Take it easy, okay?"

"Sorry," I said. But I wasn't. Not really. "Shit." I crossed my arms over my chest and stared at the far corner where a silver mobile of slender moons moved gently beneath a ceiling vent.

Margot resumed her position over her yellow pad, but out of the corner of my eye, I saw the pencil quiver slightly. The moments stretched into a long silence as she stared at the pitcher and I watched the moons. Finally:

"Sym, we've spent six months trying to work through your anger at the situation at the university. When you think of Sandy's betrayal of your friendship, of being fired and losing your career, does that seem like the kind of anger you felt just now when I asked you about your father?"

Bingo. Margot had a way of nailing it down. I sighed, leaned back, closed my eyes. She was right. Of course she was right. I wanted to kill them all, all the people who had hurt me, had abandoned me simply because it satisfied some purpose of their own. One day I had a father and a mother; the next, they were gone. One day I had married a man I loved; the next, he had begun a pattern of self-destruction so consuming that his death was a relief. One day I had a career I believed in and friends I trusted; the next, my so-called friend had orchestrated the charge of theft and my subsequent expulsion from the university while my colleagues who knew better sat back and watched. I opened one eye a crack and considered Margot. She sat peering at me over her glasses, waiting.

"It's a pattern, isn't it? You feel yourself abandoned by those you care for. Each time you lose something important, even crucial, to your well-being. You're treated unfairly, and there's nothing you can do about it. You feel powerless on the one hand, an all-consuming rage on the other. Am I right?"

I felt my father's bony shoulders as I had sat on them, the smell of his hair, the impulse to lay my head down on his and sleep. I had the nearly overpowering impulse to sleep.

"Sym?"

Margot was sitting beside me, her arm around my shoulders. She smelled like roses and basil. She had been my psychiatrist since the hiatus last year at the university, a psychiatrist no longer covered by the insurance I no longer had. A career I no longer had. A life in shambles. I was living on the money I'd withdrawn from my retirement fund after I left the university, and it was dwindling quickly. Margot had started off as my shrink, but I felt she was more than that now. I considered her a friend at a time when I had fewer of those than I had money or options. Now I lay curled on the sofa, fighting tears, feeling her hand on my shoulder.

"Sym. Listen to me. It's not just the situation at the university you're dealing with. Do you understand that? It's abandonment starting way back when your mother died and your dad walked out. And it's continued. Your mind on its dark side feels every subsequent abandonment just as when you were a helpless child alone with an unresponsive uncle. You felt that way when Daniel left you by retreating into his poetry and alcohol and drugs. And you're feeling it now after Sandy set you up so you'd lose your job at the university, along with your colleagues and friends. It's exactly that same feeling, isn't it?" Margot kept stroking my back, lowering her voice into a croon. "These things are hard to get through, but they happen to people and we must learn to deal with them. People don't always get what they deserve." She paused, started again slightly louder. "This is not something that's going to pass overnight, Sym. We need to explore the pattern in order to break it, to create a new response by integrating the anger and the pain. Neither of these is a productive or mature way to respond to others. And they're both dangerous, very dangerous."

She paused again, still stroking the sharp angles of my back, and I knew she was wondering if I was listening and how she should phrase the things she wanted to say next. I could have helped her, I knew where she was headed.

"It's like the stuff your poetry is about," she said. "It's self-knowledge, come by the hard way. It's having to go through the rotten meat to find the good stuff."

I sighed and sat up while she went on. She was on a roll, so I watched the moons hanging and dancing, their silver curves twinkling in the corner where afternoon shadows were gathering.

"One part of you is Little Orphan Annie, a small child, helpless, unable to deal with the meanness that happens. She wants to curl up and cry, remove herself from the world because it hurts too much to live there. But there's another part, the shadow side, Medusa—she's angry and raging and she wants to hurt back. She wants to turn every single one of those bastards to stone, and good riddance. Her way of dealing with the world is...well, it could be dangerous, Sym. Unmediated, this rage can flare up in an instant, and it's very possible you might actually hurt someone." She paused. I ignored her and watched the moons do a tango. "Sym." She put her two cool hands to each side of my face and turned me to her. "Just now—"

I stared hard at her.

"Your anger...you really might hurt someone, Sym, but at least they can fight back."

I jerked my head back out of her hands. "I hate to be dense, Margot, but just where are you headed with this?"

She was right about the rage, but it felt a whole lot better than self-pity. Sometimes it felt like the only friend I had. The only fuel that kept me moving, kept me alive and set in a direction with the force and mindlessness of a locomotive. Without it, there was nothing but the unbearable whining in that cold interior room I could neither locate nor touch, that pathetic puppy scratching at a door I couldn't find. I scooted away from her.

"The flip side is this," Margot said. She stood, a diminutive woman nearly a foot shorter than I. She pulled at her skirt to straighten it and went back behind her desk. She sat down, massaged the bridge of her nose before slipping her glasses back on. "That little girl? She's still there, sad and lonely and abandoned, and if things really get rough and the lights go out, Sym," Margot said, her eyes boring into mine, "she'll take you out with her."

I stared back at this woman whom I considered more friend than shrink, someone I'd decided just a few moments ago not to see again. She was warning me about suicide, and how could I not think of my dead husband whose private demons had finally overtaken him? But it was a risk I had to take because anything less would cost me my freedom.

"Look, Margot," I said, struggling against her compassion, "I know your business is taking a human psyche, isolating those pieces that don't fit in. I know you mean to help, but sometimes those pieces, hurtful as they are, are the most precious part of us. It's like you've got this preconceived idea of a nice pastoral scene. You've got a red barn, a blue pond, emerald pastures, you've got plenty of white fences, a few horses and chickens running around. But damn, right out there in the middle of the foreground, right out there in front where you can't ignore it, there's this neon purple cow. Damn, you say. That cow's going to make you crazy, ruin the picture till you get it painted brown so it goes with the rest of the picture."

I stood up, walked over to her desk, placed both hands face down on its mirror surface, leaned across it toward her.

"Hear me on this, Margot," I said, measuring each word. "I. Am. Not. Fucking. Interested." She opened her mouth to speak, but I cut her off. "I understand you want to subdue the purple so it quits exasperating everybody that strolls by it. It's making everybody damned uncomfortable. But I'm here to tell you, that cow's at least as uncomfortable as everybody looking at it. But that doesn't matter either, because it's not about being comfortable. It's not even about choice, Margot, it's about..." I searched for a word, caught the twinkle of the dancing moons. "It's about integrity, it's about uncompromising honesty that will make you remember that picture and will change you a little from having seen it, that will refuse to reshape itself to keep the status quo. It's..." I went over to the window beside where Margot had been sitting for six months. Just a few feet away, behind the thermal glass, a border of daffodils and narcissus and iris surrounded a patch of new grass where a small fountain bubbled at the center. "Hell, Margot, it's all we've got left that's worth living for."

"And dying for?"

"Could be," I said, because that was the rest of the story, wasn't it? So I told her. "The other possibility is that if you can't change the cow, you can change the picture. Make the pond an ocean, the barn a lighthouse. Open the gate and let that purple cow run. That's the thing, Margot, the really exciting thing." I turned and looked down into the heart of her turquoise eyes that her sweater had turned blue. I spoke so low that I could barely hear myself. "I believe you can create an entirely different painting, Margot. An entirely new human being."

The thick silence fell across the room and lasted too long. Finally, Margot broke it.

"Sym, stop it." Her face had turned ashen, her translucent skin fragile as a child's. "You've got genetics, childhood behavioral patterns, social conditioning, cultural influences, environment. There are some elements you simply can't change. If you don't at least begin with that premise, there really is no hope. Be serious."

"I've never been more serious."

"I want to be clear on this." Her voice was edgy, unraveling. "Are you actually saying you think you can *become* another person?"

"Absolutely."

I leaned against the window frame and gave her my happy-face smile. In fact, I'd already chosen my model. Because for all the imagination one brings to bear on such projects, there must first be a model. I thought of Garbo, her voice, her walk, the videos of her old movies that I had begun collecting. I changed the happy face into another smile, the one I'd been practicing from *Anna Karenina*.

"Why are you smirking?" she said, finally angry. "Are you out of your mind?"

I laughed. "Hey, you tell me. You're the doc."

She shook her head, slapped her pencil across the yellow pad, leaned back in her chair, folded her arms across her chest. She looked over her glasses at me.

"You know, this intractable purple streak of yours is just the kind of thing that puts a lot of people off, Sym, just in case you didn't know that. It's probably an asset if you happen to be training as a fighter pilot, but down here with us ordinary folks, it's just damned irritating and exhausting."

"Why thank you, Doctor Trevelyn," I said, lowering my head bull-style, wishing I had glasses to look over the top of. "I just reckon I missed my calling."

Margot gave me a long, level look. She removed her wire-rimmed glasses and placed them carefully on the polished surface of her desk. She stuck out her lower jaw, clasped her hands together, and rested her chin on them, her eyes roaming across the room until they at last came back to mine. "Okay, Sym, maybe you're right," she said, tipping her head to one side, "maybe psychology *is* just trying to wear down all those sharp edges you're so proud of, thrashing around and cutting people to pieces so you can test them, see how long they can stand the glare of all that purple sneering at their shabby beige lives. So, okay, keep your purple, but you can't have it both ways—purple and beige don't mix."

"No problem, Margot," I said evenly, "I've given up beige. Fuck'em."

"That's not true, and you know it. There's a war inside of you, between the rage and the pain. And the anger is so overwhelming that you…"

"We've been there before, Margot." I glanced at my watch. She was way past the fifty-minute hour.

"A few minutes ago, that pitcher? What were you going to do with it?"

The empty crystal pitcher sat in a long arm of afternoon sunlight, the water now absorbed into the carpet in dark patches. I had not remembered grabbing it, spilling it. What I remembered was the blinding rage, standing poised to hurl it at Margot.

"And there's the other side, too," she went on. "All that pain you've been carrying around since you were five years old. That poor child is still huddled inside, desperate for a little beige, a little ordinary security and human community, approval from all those Ozzie-and-Harriet types you profess to despise. In the end, she may be your worst enemy."

The thing about Margot was that she left you nowhere to hide. She was working fast and hard now, trying to cover ground that would have taken months of time and lots of dollars. She knew I was pulling out. I stared at her and she seemed very far away, on the wrong end of a telescope. Even if she were right, what possible difference could it make now? I was headed down the only road I could find that didn't have a locked gate across it, and if my real estate scheme worked out like I was going to try to convince the bankers it would, in a few short years I'd have a mountain of money that would last a lifetime. I'd be richer than God, ready to climb the highest peak and leave the world behind. Which is just what I told Margot before I turned to leave.

"By the way," she said, as I was opening the door, "why in heaven's name would you want to go to a peak? Whatever would you do there?"

I couldn't resist. Like an actor on cue I stopped with my hand still gripping the knob and looked back at where she sat with her manicured face above her manicured desk in her manicured office. I used the new smile and the deep new voice I had been practicing in the mirror and testing on the tape recorder.

"I vant," I said, "to be alone."

And closed the door behind me.

3

APRIL 13, 1997
EASTER SUNDAY

I FOUND IT SIX YEARS AGO without even trying. That was before I knew it had a name, before I knew that between my first visit and this one, it had been put on the map by some enterprising developers and a few low-budget advertising campaigns.

I had come back because I couldn't get the place out of my mind. Pushing through a new real estate deal each year, sitting in conference rooms with bankers and investors and contractors, visiting sites for possible purchase, running cash flow charts and piecing together business plans in my office, my attention wandered. I thought about cashing out, thought about where I'd live: on a cliff above the ocean with waves crashing below, an historic winery in the Napa Valley, a lighthouse on the Maine coast.

But I always came back to that day in December when I'd made a wrong turn off Highway 82. Time had faded the image of the yellow Jeep and whatever threat it held, but the memory of the waterfall, the sound of it that had filled me with terror, didn't diminish as I became successful, and then more successful, and then extravagantly wealthy. But the sound changed over the years, from the thundering sound of my own fear, to a faint, interior murmur as though that great racket, crashing down from the peaks and canyons, had been picked up and carried by the winds across the valleys and mesas, through towns and city streets and at last into the hermetic offices where I worked, so that it reached me not as the howling demon of my childhood memories or even the muted trickle of the steams it fed, but as some strange and intimate lullaby as might be sung by a mother to her child, a gentle beckon that I heard more and more frequently.

I could see the place clearly in my mind's eye, knew exactly where to veer off 285, exactly how far to drive down the blacktop till I reached that left-hand turn, and the next left-hand turn, and the next.

It didn't happen that way, of course. Of course.

Because snow will do that. It will change distances and mute sounds and bandage the earth's deepest wounds. Spring, on the other hand, has no compassion. As I drove the roads again, the white had given way to a burgeoning greenness so profuse that I felt the hedonism at nature's core, the lush and seductive abundance of it all. Where, in my recollection, one ponderosa had towered under snow, fifty unruly ones seemed to have sprung up in its place; where a tangle of bushes followed the streams, now acres of wild roses surged through the forests. Where I had turned on that solitary road to the left after several miles on the county asphalt, now there seemed to be a side road every fifty yards.

Irony's a bitch.

I was doing a repeat of that day six years ago, except today, on a religious holiday that made any serious work at home impossible, I was losing daylight trying to get into the labyrinth instead of out of it. I took every back road, every piddling path, every rabbit run for a ten-mile stretch. At last, in utter frustration, I pulled over to the edge of the road and stared at the stretch of deserted pavement, trying to decide what to do. It was closing in on 4:00, the time of day when, all those years ago, I'd followed the Jeep's tracks through the snow and up the mountain, only this afternoon I wasn't lost and, what the hell, a drive into Aspen, a nice dinner and a little night life wasn't all that bad a prospect, was it? I heaved a deep sigh and pulled back on the asphalt when I felt the old familiar streak of determination kick in, hard and implacable and bull-headed as ever.

A few yards ahead, a deeply rutted driveway cut through a dirt yard littered with beer cans and an impressive collection of trash. It led to a decrepit A-frame made of unpainted plywood that had rotted and turned black at the seams from water damage, its upper windows patched with what looked to be pieces of buckled cardboard. What the hell.

I turned in and carefully edged the low-slung Porsche, a newer model but still red, alongside the deep ruts, noticing that one side of the yard was cleared off and contained a large circle, apparently made by children riding the brightly colored Big Wheel and a smaller tricycle parked in the center. I pulled up a few yards from the house where a shadow hovered behind a screen door. I got out, waded through crushed cereal boxes, smashed McDonald's Styrofoam, scraps of clothing, a staggering number of aluminum beer cans, and other assorted trash that had spilled out over the rims of two rusted barrels beside the house. By the time I reached the porch, a young woman had shoved open the screen and leaned with one shoulder against the door frame, holding an Old Milwaukee and a cigarette, wearing a skimpy pair of turquoise shorts with white polka dots and a matching bikini halter with strings that tied around her neck. Her auburn hair was pulled back in a ponytail, away from a heart-shaped face made up to look a lot like the ones on the covers of magazines at grocery store checkout counters. I put her in her early twenties, tall, maybe 5' 8". But I was taller still, so she squinted up at me against a shaft of afternoon sun that shot through a gaping hole in the porch roof. I could hear the sound of a sitcom laugh track coming from inside the house.

"Excuse me, I'm trying to find a residential community out around here," I said. I introduced myself and described the place I was looking for, including the waterfall.

"Hmm." She tipped her head and sipped from the can, looked past me to where my car was parked. "Well," she said, squinting against the sun, "I don't know of nothing like that around here. I think maybe you got on the wrong road. Only place what's a community is on down that way." She pointed with her chin in the direction I'd come from. "El Gato, it's called. But it sure ain't like the one you're talking about. It's a real fancy place, lots of millionaires and stuff." She had an accent thick enough to slice. Georgia, maybe. She took a drag off the cigarette, rested her head against the door frame, and stared wistfully at the car. "That's real nice," she said, drawing out the words in a sultry tone as the smoke drifted up into the shaft of sun. "What kind is it?"

"Porsche." I remembered the El Gato entrance sign beside a wide asphalt road with a private gate across it. It was the one road I hadn't taken because of the obvious upscale facade. "How long has it been there, the sign I mean?"

"Oh, that. Well, they just put that up a little while back when they paved the road. Used to be just a few folks lived out there. I mean, can you believe anybody spending all that money to live out in nowhere? You ought to see some of them houses." She glanced up at the sky and shook her head as though she were conspiring with a buddy, then let her gaze drift slowly back down and settle on the Porsche again. She had large, deep-set indigo eyes framed with heavily mascaraed lashes. Raising a slender, tanned leg, she pointed a bare foot at the car: "How fast's that thang go?" Her toenails were enameled dark purple.

I watched the leg settle back to the porch, poised on tiptoe like a dancer's. I gave her a long look, but her eyes were fastened on the car. "Fast as you want it to, I guess."

She nodded her head slowly, reminding me of the plastic dogs people used to stick on the insides of their rear car windows. I figured the place she called El Gato had to be the one I was looking for. That being the case, I had made this drive for nothing. Developers, by the sound of it, had gotten to it, and I figured the property looked like several thousand other exclusive gated communities that were cropping up across the country. It was the bucolic model of standardization, one more version of urban housing tracts and ocean-side condos. But what the hell, I was here, and the place had toyed with my imagination too long to let it go without a look. I figured the gate was going to take a combination or a card to operate.

"I don't suppose you'd know anyone who lives there, would you? I was hoping to drive through, looking for property."

"Oh, hey. I know ole Harv. Ever'body knows Ha-a-arv." She stretched out the name like a rubber band, tipped her head back to drain the last of the beer, and gave the can a hard squeeze in the middle. "C'mon in," she said, tossing the can across my shoulder to a pile beside the porch, "I'll give him a call. He'd be tickled pink to take a little spin with you in that car." She rolled her eyes, pronouncing the word "car" to rhyme with "whore."

Inside, the house looked pretty much like the yard. Decorated courtesy of Old Milwaukee—cans littered every flat surface, their tops sprinkled with cigarette stubs and ashes, spilling over onto the floor to mix with toys, dirty dishes, cardboard boxes overflowing with clothes and magazines, and more empty cereal boxes— "Booberry Loops" seemed to be the odds-on favorite. A rocking horse leaning sideways on its springs was parked facing the television where the sitcom was playing itself out.

"Oh hey. My name's Wendy. Kids is off visiting the old man for Easter." She fell back on the couch, grabbed the phone, tapped a generic cigarette out of a crumpled pack, and punched in a number. "He lives on down the road, got him a new girlfriend and a trailer all the same time," she said, lighting the fresh cigarette off the butt of the other and squinting against the smoke. "Living in a trailer, when we had that house— Hey, Harv. What you up to right now?"

No small talk for this girl. I removed a couple of headless Barbies and perched on the edge of an ancient platform rocker that had stains from the last century. She gave Ole Harv a quick rundown and hung up.

"Him and Edna's just finished their dinner. He's on his way. Said he'd give you the deluxe tour. They not supposed to let strangers in, but ole Harvey likes to do stuff to set'em off when he can." She did some head-shaking and rolled her eyes at the ceiling. "You move in there, you want to bring you a big gun along."

"Do they have problems with theft or what?" I prodded, suddenly remembering the box of shells in the ancient Jeep.

She gave a startling sharp bark. "Nah. Nothing like that. It's just them people is always fighting over stuff. I mean, they got into a big fight last week trying to make Harv take down his clothesline, for

Pete's sake. Said their 'covnants' say you can't have one. City folks."
More head-shaking, eye-rolling. She bounced up off the couch and
headed for the kitchen, waving me in. "Want a beer or something?"

I followed along. The kitchen looked as bad as I expected. The
odor of rancid meat was new, though, and something in the direction of the sink was ripe. "Nope. Not much of a drinker."

"Hell, you move out here and you'll turn into one." She opened
the refrigerator and grabbed a can. I sat at a table littered with several days' worth of dishes, open jars, stacks of unopened mail, and
lots of aluminum. "Not much 'recreational activities' out here, you
know what I mean." She put a spin on "recreational activities" as
though it had some special significance and eyed me to see if I
understood. I shrugged, mystified.

"You know." She tilted her head. "Guys. I mean, like, ever one
of 'em's married or…you know." She threw a hip out, made her
eyes big and raised her shoulder and a limp wrist. Universal bigot
body language for "gay." Yeah, I knew. I cleared a place on the table
and propped my chin on my hands.

"You don't sound like this is the place you want to be. Why
don't you move?"

"Don't I just wish." She sat down across from me and crossed
her legs. "This place is Gerald's daddy's. Let me use it after the sep-
aration, and what with the child support, I can make ends meet.
Only just. I took off with them kids, you think he's going to pay me
one dime? Uh-uh. Not Gerald. Outa sight, outa mind, is how
Gerald operates." Nevertheless, Wendy launched off on a discussion of her husband's fine qualities and his girlfriend's faults,
punctuated heavily with hits of tobacco and alcohol. Soon, I heard
the sound of a motor approaching.

"Hey, bet that's ole Harv. He acts like he's god's gift, but it's just
his way. He don't mean nothing by it. Lots of folks can't take him,
but Harv's okay. He's a straight-shooter, that's for sure. Just don't
pay him no attention. He's all talk, you know?"

We heard the engine shut down, a door slam. Wendy threw
back her head and let out an ear-shattering, *"We're in here!"*

The screen door squeaked and banged, and then Ole Harv filled
the kitchen door. He had a wide barrel chest, short bowed legs, and

hard blue eyes that penetrated like a drill bit. He stood with his feet planted apart and his hands on his hips, a wide, toothy smile lighting the bottom half of his face. He lowered his head like he was going for a tackle, then charged toward Wendy.

"Hey hey, girly." He gave her a man-sized hug, pulling her chest against him. She was ready: she planted a forearm against his shoulder, forced a little distance. He didn't seem to notice. He let her go and turned to me. "You must be the one wants to bust through our gate?" He headed in my direction—a bull making for a heifer, head down and arms wide. He had on a red plaid flannel shirt and threadbare blue jeans that drooped below a healthy paunch. His voice was startlingly melodious, deep and rich as an opera baritone.

I stood up and pushed my hand out so that he had to shake instead of squeeze. But his left hand grabbed my upper arm and held it longer than it should have. Introductions performed, I followed him and Wendy outside, and even before I laid eyes on it, I suddenly knew what he'd be driving: parked next to my car was the yellow Jeep that looked exactly like it had six years ago. He'd added a new bumper sticker, I noticed, as we circled behind it— "YES on Prop 2," referring to Colorado's anti-gay legislation of a few years back that had been ruled unconstitutional in the federal courts. Figured. Harv and Wendy stood side by side, bent at the waist, staring through the window of my car on the passenger side.

"Hey, never had a ride in one of these hot dogs before. Okay if we take it?" He opened the door and stuck his head inside.

"Well…" I looked at Wendy who straightened up and shrugged. She grinned, rolled her eyes, took a drag off her cigarette and a pull at her beer. I ran through my options: at the bottom of the list was riding with him in his Jeep. Mark that one off. I wanted to follow him through in my car, but I didn't figure he'd go for that and I couldn't come up with any reason to insist on it. I could simply forget the whole thing, go on to Aspen, but I wanted to see the place again, and this was my chance. Besides, the guy was a little free with his hands, but he would have to be retarded as well to pull anything with Wendy a witness to where I'd gone. What the hell.

"Okay," I said, getting in and revving the engine, "you navigate, I'll drive." I gunned it a little for effect while he adjusted himself into the seat, delighted as a child at Christmas. He snapped the seat belt, sat up straight with a broad smile across his face. It was hard not to catch his excitement. So I did.

I laughed as I backed out the driveway, and by the time I took the short distance to the El Gato security gate, I was hitting a hundred. Harv's grin stretched ear to ear as I braked and cruised up smoothly to the slot for the plastic card to open the gate. It had a punch pad next to it, but Harv fished out a battered card from his pants pocket and passed it to me—a white card with the scrolling El Gato letters and the snarling cougar logo. I stuck it in, and as the crossbar flew up and I drove through, I thought about how most people in gated communities fail to realize that in truly remote areas, a locked gate attracts more attention than an open road; the gate keeps out tourists, but I've never known one to keep out a thief. I cruised down the asphalt entry road, which soon turned to smoothly manicured gravel, with Harv chattering nonstop while we followed the road around an elegant lake that had not been there my first visit. The water was so still that it reflected the four-teen-thousand-foot snow-capped peak towering in the distance and held it like a mirror image on the lake's perfect surface. On the other side of the lake, we came to a wide dirt road, graded smooth as tarmac and stretching out before us, lined on each side with tow-ering pines sprinkled with juniper and flourishing underbrush. It looked like it might be the same road I'd taken that day, but now it was much wider.

"Just follow this road right smack-dab up the middle of the place," Harv said, taking out a crumpled pack of cigarettes from his shirt pocket and rolling his window down. I glanced over at him and shook my head, and he sighed and stuffed the pack back in his pocket. "Graded this baby myself just last week. Right pretty job, hey? I'm kind of the resident caretaker," he said, pride swelling his voice as I drove slowly up the road with the chilly afternoon air drifting in through his window. We passed several expensive, showcase homes set back among the trees while Harv pointed and chattered, rattling off names and thumbnail backgrounds, mostly people who spent the summers in residence. The houses thinned, and Harv leaned back into his seat, occasionally pointing out a lot he thought might be for sale.

"Used to be just seven of us out here for years," he said. "I been here over twenty myself, but all them rich folks is moving in and everything's changing now. Water probably won't hold out for many more wells, but they still moving in and building. We got ten new houses right now, makes seventeen of us out here." His voice had grown an edge as he talked.

My mouth fell open, and I glanced around at him. Was he kidding? Apparently not. Seventeen? "And that's on how many acres?"

"Oh, not much. A thousand, but it's divided into one-acre parcels, mostly, so you see the problem."

Yep. I saw the problem. Saw it every day. It was called greed, and it had made me rich.

"Course, most folks buy more than one. One fella, he's got over four hundred," he said, frowning as we rounded a bend and passed a particularly ostentatious house set back off the road.

It was monstrously huge and looked like a log castle, designed in three stories that poked up over the pines, and it was hung with enough balconies and porches to please a British king and enough acreage of plate glass to satisfy Frank Lloyd Wright.

"Dean Brandenberg." Harv's baritone sounded hard and mean. "Him and another fellow together, they got a majority vote in the Homeowners' association, just elected himself head of it." He scooted down in the seat and crossed his arms. An uncomfortable silence descended over us, thick as black smoke. It didn't lift until we came to an attractive cedar A-frame surrounded by several levels of rock garden terraces. Trellises bordered wide greenhouse windows, thick with curling vines. Sitting on the top rails of its balconies, potted plants flowered in a rainbow of colors, and several bird feeders hung below the eaves where flocks of junkos and sparrows fed.

"Wolf and Andrew," Harv said, sitting up and pointing. I slowed the car, admiring the house as Harv talked. "Moved in from San Francisco, year ago last spring. One decorates inside, the other outside. Queer as three-dollar bills." In spite of his bumper stickers, Harv's voice was light, and he chuckled. He cut his eyes around at me. "Hey, it ain't *my* thing," he said, holding his hands up, his blue eyes twinkling and feigning innocence, "but I'd take fags any day over some of these folks. Now the Gillmans there," he said, nodding at the next house, a box of a place that distinguished itself by virtue of its nondescript appearance, "they ain't so bad. Kind of silly, but you can get along with them. Retired couple that come out here on their summer vacations from Michigan, put up that house there out of a kit." He went into an hysterical cackle as we drove past. He wiped his eyes. "Can you beat that? A damn kit! Now, their favorite thing is to have a 'Bar-B-Q.' They'll invite the whole damn bunch of us and wonder why it ends bad. Some folks get drunk and mean, 'fore it's over, somebody'll get punched ever time. That Joe Gillman, he's something, all right. Says we need 'Community Spirit.'" Suddenly Harv's mood plunged again as we left the tidy frame house behind, and he hunched back down under his black cloud.

It was not until we left the main road that Harv's spirits returned. He directed me up and down a maze of spiraling side roads, pointing out various streams, calling them by name: Moon Springs, Cat Man's Creek, Elk Meadow Brook. The homes were sparse and less ostentatious than on the wide main road, although one was a tasteful chalet-style cedar house with a sharply pitched roof and several dormers, set like a jewel in a thicket of high pines. Behind it was a small barn with a corral on one side.

"New folks just moved in there last month. Now I'm here to say that Eva Blake is one fine-looking woman, but if she thinks that high-f'lootin' Hollywood husband of hers is coming to roost with her here in the boonies, it's my opinion that she's got a shock in store. Ain't nobody here even laid eyes on him yet and don't figure we never will."

As we passed, a tall, slender woman dressed in black led an unruly black horse from the barn to the corral. A late-model four-wheel drive truck, also black, sat parked in front of a detached double-car garage.

"Man must be out of his friggin' skull, you ask me. Like my wife says, just one more case of trading down young. Buy the old lady a house in the sticks and tell 'er you be along later." He paused and squinted over at me. "Why that Miz Blake, she might even be taller'n you," he said with a grin. But she wasn't.

As we snaked back into the far corner of the development, the roads became narrow and the forest grew thicker and darker, like the place I remembered. "Most of the old-timers live on back off the main drag. On down that road's Ole Myra Jones's place," he said, pointing vaguely with his shoulder. "Watches birds. See her all over with them binoculars hanging on her neck. She can call 'em all by name, even sound like some of 'em. Minds her own business, which is more'n I can say for most of them new folks. Right up here's Professor Moss's place," Harv said, waving at a man who sat reading on the porch of a small log cabin set in a clearing back off the road. I recognized it as the deserted one I'd passed during my first visit. "Don't see him much. College professor, comes here to write couple times a year. On up here's the road that follows the main stream. Only one to run year round, 'Camilla Creek,' it's called. We'll take it on up. It's a real pretty drive."

Harv motioned me up a side road that was no more than two overgrown ruts. Soon we were climbing steeply as the road tunneled into the dense wilderness. I had lost my bearings a good while back, so I gave up trying to remember the tangled route we'd taken and concentrated on guiding the car around rocky switchbacks and across deep gullies made by spring runoff while Harv kept up his tour guide's monologue.

"...used to keep most of the roads graded year-round, 'cept for some of these don't go nowhere. But the Homeowners' Board's got them new folks on it, been acting up about the cost. You'd think with all that money they collecting in dues, they could afford to keep their roads up. Even when they was just the seven of us, I was out here first thing after a good snow, grading them roads. Even them ones nobody lives on. I kept them clear so we could drive through and do some deer watching, bird watching." And maybe get in a little out-of-season hunting, I thought, remembering his Jeep parked on the snowy road that day. Soon Harv grunted and grew silent as he gazed out the passenger window. His black mood had inexplicably taken him over again.

Which was just fine with me, because at last we had left civilization behind, and now, as I drove along, I gazed out the window without the distraction of his words. The trunks of the immense pines were wider than my car, the ground beneath them an immaculate carpet of pine needles with pockets of dense shrubbery. As the road climbed higher, the spell of the ancient forest settled in the shadows and my pulse raced. I felt as though a gate were opening to the mysterious, reclusive world that I had come here to find, and I imagined I heard the faint voice calling to me from up higher in the distance. I felt the mountain's spell grow with every number that rolled off the odometer, felt it bloom in the darkening shadows as the stream plunged wildly alongside the road, and in the sudden shafts of mote-filled sunlight that slipped down in golden blades through the branches. It stirred in the miniature-leafed rose bush that edged one side of the road, and the rampant glossy-leafed shrubbery with its red berries on which the bears feasted following their winter's hibernation. Each of these combined to create a singular effect, in the way of flowers arranged in a particular bouquet, and I savored it as I drove and hungered for more—tasting the solitude that charged this air, a composition of earth smells and forest sounds and the smallest movements of its private creatures who lived in both the shadows and the light.

But the low-slung Porsche was floundering badly among the large rocks and deep crevices. When I could go no farther, I stopped the car and glanced over at Harv, whose dark mood apparently rendered him oblivious to our position on the planet. The panel clock read 6:35, but the towering trees blotted out the afternoon light. A chill crept up my spine as I recalled my first visit, the large footprints that left the yellow Jeep and disappeared into the wilderness. I glanced at Harv out of the corner of my eye and realized I would have to back down the narrow road until it widened enough to turn around and descend the mountain. I struggled with the transmission on the steep incline, jammed it into reverse to a loud grinding of gears. Harv roused with the startled expression.

"Hey, all right," he said, looking around. "This'll do. You up for a little hike?"

He popped open the door, leapt out, and was taking the road ahead in long strides as I watched in amazement. I switched off the engine and set the emergency brake.

"Them developers," he said, glancing around and slowing as I trotted up beside him, "they bought up all them back-tax lots, didn't have a whole lot of luck selling them, then moved on. Told me if I was to sell any, they'd give me a cut, but if I'm hearing you right, you ain't interested in that showcase property. You wanting way out back, am I right?"

I muttered that he was right, and as he slowed, I steamed past him, jumping over a deep gully in the road, wondering where the hell we were hiking. As much as I loved the wild beauty of this place, the shadows had grown too dark too quickly. I was tired, anxious, hungry, and growing crankier by the second. And then all the sound seemed to be sucked out of the air, and I heard the odd tone in Harv's voice booming behind me.

"Well, little lady," he said, "I believe I got something you might want to look at."

When I turned around, Ole Harv had disappeared.

4

I STOOD IN THE ROAD, looking first at the empty spot where Harv had been and then farther down at where the Porsche was telling me to get in and get the hell out of there. I debated whether to stay or go, figuring if Harv meant me harm, he'd had plenty of chances before now. But I knew there was more to it than that. A lot more. Start with the mere fact that I was standing here at all, thinking of buying property in an area where I had once nearly fainted from sheer terror. It was just the kind of situation Margot would get off on. She materialized in my mind's eye, standing where Harv should have been and twisting a strand of her copper-colored hair. Peeping over her reading glasses, she gave a bitter-lemon smile: *Tsk tsk, Sym. So self-destructive.*

Maybe, but I didn't want to think about it. I was frazzled and tired and out of patience. *And scared?* I leapt back over the gully and headed Margot off down the road. She disappeared, re-materialized on the hood of the Porsche, leaned back on one hand and crossed one knee over the other in a fifties cheesecake pose. I ignored her and looked around for Harv. On the north side of the road, the stream was much too wide and turbulent to cross easily. On the south side, a few yards away, I spied a faint path leading through a barricade of dense shrubbery. Harv must have gone in there, but why? On the hood of my Porsche, Margot's forty-watt image kicked up to a hundred.

I turned to her. "Look, you want to call it self-destructive, fine. I call it curiosity. You shrinks, always shooting cannons at gnats."

I knew how to handle Margot, could have pulled out an impromptu on confronting-your-fears, made a pitch for the

Bradshaw ten-step program for the Perfectly Beige Life. I could even have made it interesting and upped the stakes a little, told her I'd been hearing the waterfall while I was wrangling multi-million-dollar real estate deals, and that it sounded a lot like my mother's voice calling to me. She would really have a field day with that one. On the other hand, let's be fair; she had a point. I admitted to a certain fascination with—okay okay, a certain addiction to—situations loaded with risk. That's when Margot would drag out her "contradictory impulse" lecture. Old stuff. Even the truth's boring if you sprinkle too much corn on it.

So I stood there between the path and the car, trying to decide whether to stay or go: if my boredom theory were right and I simply enjoyed taking risks, I'd take the path; if Margot's self-destruction hypothesis were right, I'd still take the path. I grinned at the empty air where Margot had been sitting. I've always suspected free choice is eighty percent delusion and twenty percent bullshit, grounded in desire and tempered with retrospect. I followed Harv. What the hell.

I put my head down to protect my face, pushed through the branches as quietly as I could manage. Just as the underbrush became impossibly dense, I fell through it head first and butted right into Harv's red plaid back.

"Hey, kiddo," he said, turning and grabbing my arm, "what took you so long? Have to make a pit stop?" He gave a raunchy laugh, and I jerked my arm out of his grip.

"Where the hell—"

And then I saw it. Spread out like a blanket just below us was a spectacular sunlit clearing surrounded by aspen, their tiny lime-green leaves shimmering in the late afternoon sun. Through the center, a stream meandered a crooked path, sending up a gentle murmur.

"Oh, Harv," I said, wading down the incline through knee-high grass, "it's beautiful."

"That it is," he said, his voice filled with pride as though he'd created the place himself. He pulled out a crumpled cigarette and lit it as we walked. "I just thought you might be the right person to show it to. Not too many even been up here, and them that have think it's too much trouble to get to. Damn fools, I say."

We reached the clearing and walked along the stream until we entered the light-filled grove of aspen, their smooth trunks straight as pillars with the leaves twinkling high above. Walking among them, I understood how Alice must have felt after leaving the dark closet, walking through the looking glass into a bright and magic land. I was so mesmerized that when I turned to speak to Harv, I discovered he'd disappeared again. I found him standing at the edge of the aspen grove, looking off in the distance toward a pine forest. As we set off in that direction, angling through a patchwork of rocky terrain and scattered piñon before entering the pines, Harv talked, his words resonating through the green shadows.

"This is kind of the heart of El Gato you're looking at. Used to be a fella, weird duck, last name of Barlow, but folks just called him the Cat Man. Lived out here way back in the twenties, back when right-minded folks didn't live off alone if they didn't have to. But the Cat Man did. Right at first, he had his wife and baby, built a little cabin, all of 'em lived out here awhile. But womenfolks don't take to this kind of living." He glanced at me quickly. "No offense, but most of 'em don't, you know."

I nodded. I knew.

"Well, I've thought some about it." Harv took a deep pull on his cigarette and watched the ground as we walked below the high pines with their thick carpet of needles. "I believe that Cat Man loved three things in this world. I believe he loved his wife and he loved his kid, but I believe mostly he loved this land better than either one of them. Because the wife left, took the baby. But the Cat Man, he stayed on. Even when the Killer Snow in '41 come and folks from town traveled out here to talk the Cat Man into town for winter, he wouldn't budge. They say it was the cats, had them cats running wild and thick as rabbits and wouldn't leave them. Well, the snows come and gone, and in the spring folks come again and carried him out. Been dead most of the winter, body still froze. But there wasn't much for 'em to carry out no way. Seems them cats of his made it through the winter just fine, made a meal of him, they did."

I glanced around to see if he was putting me on, but he kept talking with his eyes on the ground. I tried to piece together the chronology as he narrated, and by the time we had come to the faint ruts of an overgrown road, I learned that years after the Cat Man died, his only child had finally turned up in the late sixties to look over her inheritance. She had been married and divorced a couple of times by then, and her name was no longer Claire Barlow but Claire James, and she arrived in the Colorado Rockies drawn not from a love of the wilderness nor sentimental curiosity about her father's land, but for the more common and expedient purpose of making a buck. She sheared off a hundred acres for her own use, sliced up the remaining thousand into one-acre plots, put in the requisite electric lines and roads according to county guidelines, and christened the new development "El Gato" in honor of the mythical cougar of local legend rumored to guard these peaks. She stuck a "For Sale" sign by the road, some ads in the papers, and waited. It was a good idea, as far as it went, which was thirty years past where it should have, because in the 1960s people were still reeling from their migration to the suburbs, which was about as far in the sticks as they ever wanted to imagine themselves living. So with more foresight than buyers, Claire James did what she could to keep herself out of bankruptcy court. In fact, Harv explained, his own acre was Claire's payment to him in return for working around the development. But it was a lost cause. When the place finally bottomed out, she jumped off the sinking ship, left the unsold plots to the county, and went back east. And the unsold lots took up ninety percent of the whole.

When we came to the faint ruts still visible beneath the weeds, I stopped and looked around. Nearby, among a scattering of huge old-growth pines, were several whose enormous trunks were carved with odd burn marks where a cameo of bark had been carved away to bare wood. Just as I began to ask Harv about them, I saw it. In the distance, partially visible through the trees, stood a huge, sprawling house.

"What in the world...?" Someone actually lived out here. Or *had*, I thought, as I began walking toward it, because even at this distance I sensed that unmistakable air of desolation that hovers around an abandoned structure.

I stopped at the edge of its weed-choked yard and surveyed an extraordinary, shambling ruin. Unlike most houses, this one seemed not to have a center. It began traditionally enough with a staircase high and wide enough for Greek columns, led to an old-fashioned wraparound porch like those I recalled from houses in the South, and had an entryway where California-style, double-wide doors would have been if they hadn't lain rotting on the porch. The first story was small and round with lots of windows boarded over with weathered plywood, a kind of pedestal on which the upper story grew and expanded and wandered like wooden tentacles in several directions, sprouting countless decks and balconies in a multitude of sizes, and made even more bizarre by the fact that each of the wandering additions was supported from below on huge tree trunks. A third level capped the second, a modified octagonal structure inset with long vertical windows on each of its sides, with three dormers worked in for good measure. This was just possibly, I thought, the strangest house I'd ever seen, and I'd seen plenty in the last seven years.

As I approached it, I realized it was not an old ruin at all, but a house recently built. Without either paint or weatherproofing to protect the exterior, the wood had bleached nearly white where the sun struck it and rotted dark with moisture damage where it hadn't. The balconies and sundecks and staircases were collapsing, their joints splayed like broken bones, and the roof was a shambles of decomposing shingles and leaning chimneys. The upper windows that had not been boarded over were gaping holes, open to the wind and rain and snow.

Yet for all that, I stood riveted by the place, its grandiose and squalid splendor, while Harv climbed the stairs, gingerly testing each decrepit plank before he placed his weight on it.

"Miz James, she lost the development, but she kept this back part for herself somehow. Still owns it and might, I hear, not think too long about selling. She'll be up in her seventies now, maybe figuring to leave something besides this mess to Wendy."

"Wendy?" And then, as I pulled my attention away from the house, I saw the bleached aluminum cans, the scraps of trash and discarded toys that nested in the weeds and around the porch thick as autumn leaves.

"Yep. Little Wendy, that's Miz James's grandbaby." Harv faced me from his height at the top of the stairs, looking as though he'd scaled Olympus, his arms folded across his barrel chest and an "I dare you" smirk plastered across his face.

Hadn't I just admitted to being attracted to danger? I looked at the cracked and rotting wood and started climbing. The steps creaked, the banisters shuddered, the newel posts shook, even the balcony overhead swayed. Harv was working his way across the porch toward the front entry.

"Oh yeah, little Wendy and Gerald and them kids, they all used to live out here while Gerald was building on the house, up till he wandered off with Willa Hanks last winter. That Wendy was one sad case—stranded out here with no money, no car, them two kids hanging on her like mice. It was real pitiful, I'm here to say. Well, finally, Gerald's daddy come got her, let her live in his A-frame."

Harv made it to the front door and stood leaning in, his hands braced on each side of the frame, his neck extended. I was approaching when he sprang back, his face squeezed tight as a fist. I edged past him and looked into a murky darkness. All I could make out at first was a large room lit uncertainly by the light of the missing entry doors and a hole in the ceiling. As my eyes adjusted, I saw that on the far side a kitchen was separated from the larger room by a built-in island, bordered on the two back walls by ply-wood over windows that would look out on the western moun-tains. The front portion of the ceiling was high and open, crisscrossed with supporting beams. In the center of the floor, a rusted potbellied wood stove crouched on concrete blocks with a trashed-out sofa facing it. A chimney was attached to the rear of the stove and rose high in crooked segments to the ceiling, just beneath the hole. From the weak afternoon light that seeped in, I could see that the floor was covered with something I couldn't make out. It was then that the odor rose up and struck me with the force of a springing beast.

"Ugh!" I stepped back, my hand over my nose. "Jesus, what the hell...?"

"Them cats!" Harv was already picking his way down the porch steps. "They been shitting in there. Wheeeuw-wee!"

I joined him in the yard, the two of us appraising the ruined shambles of a home. I wanted badly to see the rest of it, but all the stairs to the upper stories looked dangerously rotted, and I tried not to imagine the condition of the inner staircase with its combination of decay by natural elements and the layers of animal excrement. I gave it up.

I followed Harv through the pines along the north side of the house to another clearing with a structure in the center of it—a large, elegant building with simple lines caught by the shadows of the setting sun. It appeared to be a barn topped with a clerestory.

"That's as far as Miz James got with her horse farm," Harv said. "Cared more about that damn barn than having a house. Had the loft fixed up where she could live while she put the development together." I wanted a peek inside, but night was coming fast. Besides, I'd seen enough. I was in love. No doubt about it.

"…so Miz James, she lives back in Tennessee, still owns the place," Harv continued, as we walked along the edge of the clearing toward the aspen grove. "Guess she figures since Gerald run off and Wendy's never much liked it out here to start with, might as well get rid of it. What I've heard anyway. Especially after…"

We had reached the top of a gentle knoll with the aspens and stream just ahead when Harv paused. He turned back to gaze at the black shape of the barn in the distance with its clerestory windows facing west. He took the crumpled pack from his pocket, lit up, and let the smoke drift slowly from his nostrils. Somewhere an owl hooted. Bats slipped through the darkening air. The sun hung motionless, suspended like an orange ball on the highest peak of the San Juans. As it descended behind the mountains, its last rays shot across the clearing and struck the clerestory windows, setting the glass ablaze. A gypsy wind wandered down from the eastern peaks and played briefly through the trees, churning the air into the sound of ocean waves. Faintly, below the wind, came a keening howl that turned my skin to gooseflesh.

"Coyotes," Harv said.

His face was screwed into a fierce frown, his eyes riveted on the open doors of the barn as though waiting for someone to step out of the darkness inside. The owl gave a piercing shriek, and in the purple evening it glided on silent wings across the clearing. I saw a rush of rapid movement on the ground, streaking shapes headed for cover. Cats, lots of cats, I suddenly realized, and running for their lives. Harv turned away toward the aspen grove. By the time we'd fought through the dense bushes and arrived at the car, darkness had come.

I started up the engine, switched on the headlights, guided the low-slung car backward inch-by-painstaking-inch down the steep, rocky incline. At a widening in the road, I maneuvered the car around to head it forward. The headlights swept across a wide swatch of the impenetrable black wilderness, and for an instant, through a tangle of brush, two enormous, unblinking eyes glowed in the beams. A cougar's eyes.

I turned to Harv, but he was peering out through the side window, his cloud of gloom wrapped firmly around him. I waited till we were leaving El Gato through the security gate before asking him for Claire James's phone number. I'd anticipated his reluctance, his suspicions, his intent to negotiate the sale himself, with Claire James cast as his generous benefactor. Maybe, but I had my doubts. Harv would fare better with me, as he was quick to see when I promised him a six percent finder's fee.

"Not to worry," I said, as he wrote down the number in the dim glow of the map light, "I'll pay you the same commission a real estate agent gets, but if you think Claire James will pay you more, you go ahead. Sounds like she might be a tough bird, though." I looked around at him, and he nodded. "And, hey," I said with a grin, as I turned into Wendy's driveway and pulled up in front of the porch where a bare yellow bulb was burning, "if I don't keep my word, you can just blackball me with that Homeowner's association you have over there."

"You'll keep your word," he said. His voice was cold and hard as granite as he passed me the slip of paper with the phone number. "And I'd take it right kindly if you didn't let it around it was me told you of Miz James's place." I reached for the paper in the yellow glow of Wendy's porch, but Harv held on to it, his cold blue gaze sending a chill through my blood.

5

APRIL 13, 1997

EASTER SUNDAY

Morgan

It was Pasonombre's first lesson: Know thy surroundings.

"Ah, *figlia*. We begin now," he says, driving out of the airport and through the streets of Milan where he points out the landmarks, explains his system of mnemonic devices, methods to commit the most complex information to memory. When we come to an alley running alongside an innocuous gray building with the word SCHOOL lettered above the door, he says, "If you do not know first the alley, how can you know your assignment has disappeared into it and waits in the darkness for you to pass? How can you know first that it is a blind alley, and that your assignment is now trapped?"

From the window of my workroom in El Gato, I watch the black horse below, and near his corral, the stream, and behind that: the endless profusion stretching up the mountains, the green needles and tendrils and narrow-leaved tree branches that whisper when there is no breeze, the leaves nodding softly among themselves like cloistered nuns. These last three weeks since I have come here, I have ridden the land, committed her paths, her knolls and canyons and secret caves, to memory. I can ride them in the full moon or dead of night. Proportion permitting, I could draw my finger over this terrain, probe it as easily, as familiarly as the contours of my own body.

I turn away from the window and face the cluttered walls of my work-room where I have thumbtacked the pertinent information. It is not a difficult assignment, not comparable to those during my years with Paso's Company. Easy enough to piece together Camilla's life and death for Claire. I would once have considered such work child's play, a bonehead project for a dull-witted amateur.

And yet...

I sense some mystery here, some malevolence as familiar to me as my own reflection. Is it possible that I, that any one of us, might be pulled to evil as a magnet to iron? Or is it the other way: it is we who lead and evil which follows?

I do not mean that biblical Evil with its capital letter. A mishmash of overheated rhetoric: penned by a sequestered monk with hyperactive genitals, delivered to a congregation in a thundering baritone. That old, obscure amalgamation of words, piled high and useless as cinderblocks. It is a danger, such abstractions. To wit: define "good" as the "absence of evil," as St. Augustine did, and you will wander helpless, blind and deaf, doomed to camp naked among psychopaths and rapists and call them good fellows, as content to nurture villains as murder friends. One must be specific.

Evil is like the luxury automobile, the filter-tipped cigarette, the lace brassiere: a man-made device. It rises not from some celestial hieroglyph, but from this bone cave of the mind. Herein.

"And your next lesson," Paso says, pulling into the parking lot, "know Thyself and thy weaknesses before thine enemy can use them against you."

The year is 1982. I have just left Cruz in New Mexico, arrived in Italy. I follow Paso into the School, along corridors and classrooms where I meet the instructors, enter the dormitory room on the fourth story that will be mine for the next two years while I train to join Paso's Company.

The thing about self-knowledge is that you can never go home again. After you have ferreted out the latent, nasty memories, you understand that your past is built on sands that shift and reconfigure and scour your eyes time and again. The price of wisdom is to watch your innocence tied to the stake and burnt, to discover that the screams you hear behind the flames are your own.

Before I took The Company's required entry-level psychology course, I would have told you of my idyllic childhood with storybook parents and a Kentucky home that looked like Scarlett's Tara, racehorses grazing the pastures inside miles of white fences. I would have told you that when I was fourteen, my mother took me and ran away to live in an Indiana commune with a woman named Claire James. And when the commune burned down with my mother inside it and I returned home to my father, I would have described to you our weekend diversions at the racetracks; the enormous, white-suited man from Italy, Psichari Pasonombre, who sometimes joined us there; his attractive colleague, Simon Cruz, who owned a laboratory outside of Santa Fe, and with whom I lived for two years before flying to Milan that summer of '82.

It was a good story, a truthful one so far as I knew, though I wondered after The Company's psychology class whether Paso had known the deeper truth of my parents all along, before I recalled it during the hypnosis sessions. Before the instructor extracted those memories with the unambivalent workmanship of a dentist removing a tooth. The sultry Kentucky nights were still there, filled now with more than the orchestra of crickets and the nicker of Thoroughbreds. Filled now with screams that I can never repress again, and between them, my father's voice raised and slurred by bourbon, the vibrations down the hallway and into my room of a sound I now understood to be that of a woman's body thrown against the walls.

1985. A restaurant in Milan. Paso sits across from me, the candlelight flickering over his broad features, his expansive bald dome shining. I am twenty-nine years old this day, have been graduated several months from The Company's school, received a few niggling assignments, but I am impatient, hungry for danger. Tonight, Paso has brought with him a folder of background materials, discussed the details of my first important assignment, the surveillance of a political figure in Brazil. I do not know then that I will soon become The Company's ace Specialist, but as Paso hands me the folder across the table, I believe now that he knew. The waiter has removed our plates, brought wine for the prodigious man in his linen suit, vodka over ice for me.

"So you are not merely my *figlia*, now, you are a woman of the world."

I tell him I am still his *figlia*, his daughter, and he is still my father. He has no other, and I want no less. I prepare myself to ask the question that has nagged me for these years since the psychology class. I take a long drink of the vodka, letting the cubes rest for a moment on my tongue, and then ask it.

He stares into his wine. A sadness descends.

"It is a difficult thing, this knowing. This looking back at the father, the mother, is it not? You have recovered a memory from your childhood, your mother's screams, yes? You believe now that you know this man, this John Krevlin, your father: a drunkard, a man of violence to have so beaten your mother that she fled for her life? And now you wish to know if I knew of it then." He drinks in the preoccupied way of one who does not taste, sets down the glass. In the expanding silence I look around to see that we are the last people left in the dining room. When Paso shrugs, his vast white suit seems to convulse with movement. "Let it go with your mind, *figlia*. What does it matter? Your parents, they do not belong to you, they belong only to themselves, as I, as you, each of us our own exile. The life inside, you cannot know. It is one of our most arrogant fictions, to suppose that we can by such means know another, that we can even, my poor lost *figlia*, know one's self."

The waiters busy themselves about the perimeters of the room. Pasonombre ignores them. He is a well-known man, respected. Feared. They would have busied themselves without complaint till daybreak if need be. He turns in his chair, looks out the window where the lights of Milan sprinkle the darkness below. Or perhaps he muses at his own ephemeral reflection on the black glass.

"Remember this, my daughter," he says, turning to me, his eyes enormous and dark and glistening as he places his hand huge as a plate over my own, "to be shielded from the full knowledge of one's inner self, that is the human animal's greatest blessing."

It is unspeakable, perhaps incomprehensible as well, that thing Pasonombre sensed hidden behind the mind's perception of itself. As though one could look into a mirror, but not through it. I see now that he was right, and while I have not looked directly on evil, I have lived with it and slept with it and can recognize its coming by the stench and rhythm of its breath before it arrives. I have tracked it, touched its sleeve in dark

theaters, held it in my sights and known a hundred times that its single-
most effective defense is not modern weaponry nor a brilliant mind. I will
disappoint you when I say: evil's most potent weapon is merely the vacu-
ous plainness of its face, unremarkable as a sock and common as a nail.
Anonymity is the only priceless commodity whose worth is not measured
by its deficit.

I pace the walls, the scraps of paper and clippings and pictures infor-
mation about the residents of El Gato, about Camilla, Claire, myself. I
pause before the portion on El Gato.

What is this mystery that lives here? That stinks the barn, hangs like
kudzu from the tree branches and coils like a drop of india ink in the
waters. When I ride in this wilderness, it lurks in places with the force of
iron pressing at my center, pounding against the bone, and if I were
winged, I would fly shrieking and circling above this ground until the air
was scoured of every sound but one. The sound of retribution. You may
wonder if I am mad, but I tell you that evil is no ethereal villain manifest
only to the saintly eye. It is real and tangible as the air inside a room of
perpetual atrocities, when opening its door you are hit by the stench of old
blood coagulating and putrid below the fresh hot metallic odor of the new.
It is that real.

I look at the wall where I have tacked every scrap of information about
this place. I hear Paso's voice from those years ago: Know thy surroundings, *he said.* If you do not know first the alley, how can you
know someone waits in the darkness for you to pass? How can you
know it is a blind alley, and that your quarry's hiding place is now
become his deathtrap?

I sense that the missing piece, the answer to this lurking presence in
El Gato, is among the ragtag collection here: A clipping about the
Smithsonian officials who, at the request of Myra Jones, plan to visit the
area to inspect the burned markings on the trees. A Denver Post *story*
about the archeological dig near the mouth of Cougar Canyon, where the
same Smithsonian visitors stumbled on artifacts of prehistoric mammoth
hunters. The newspaper story two weeks ago citing the dig's bizarre dis-
covery of a human hand that had been buried approximately six years. A
thick packet of sheets stapled together: on top, my notes listing the results
of the subsequent bone analysis—young adult female, Caucasian, identity
unknown, bone severed at wrist by means of circular saw, presence of

organophosphates; beneath the top sheet is an NCIC computer printout, the National Crime Information Center's extensive list of missing persons in Colorado from 1991 to present. Another sheet of paper listing the results of my database search, inputting specifics of gender, age spectrum, and race—twenty-seven unexplained disappearances of young women. Looking for similarities among them in the time frame noted in the article, I have isolated seven females cited as problem children by their parents, "probable runaways" as cause of disappearance, and living within a thirty-mile radius of Denver. I have highlighted with yellow one name, Christine Bowdell, a young woman employed by an animal-grooming service called Faux Paws. When I phoned the establishment under the guise of the missing woman's high-school friend, the owner said that Chris Bowdell's hands were often rough and painful from her habit of bathing the animals without the prescribed rubber gloves. It is true, as one of the news articles mentioned, that organophosphates are used in biochemical warfare, but they are also commonly found in insecticide dips used by veterinarians and grooming shops. I know that the unidentified hand is Chris Bowdell's, but not how or why it came to be buried in Cougar Canyon, or most importantly, by whom.

The afternoon grows late. I turn away, eager for my afternoon ride. On the worktable beside my computer is Camilla's spiral-bound sketchbook. It lies open to the drawing Claire referred to dryly as "the family portrait." The book, she said, had arrived in the mail the day after Camilla's death, opened to this page. It is a black-and-white pencil sketch with Gerald on the far left, Wendy beside him, the two children in front of them, posed in a parody of an Olan Mills family pastoral. Their likenesses are photographically precise, realistic and vapid in the way of such productions. In the lower right foreground near Wendy is a wispy, roughed-in sketch of Claire. The background, however, has been darkly shaded, and hovering just behind Gerald's left shoulder is another figure—a woman who seems to have stepped for a moment out of the darkness and into the light that touches her cheekbones, forehead, chin. She is a dark-haired, spellbinding, seductive woman looking boldly from the page. No Olan Mills photographer would have posed her so.

Claire had handed the sketchbook to me, running her fingertips across the dark woman. "Gerald's mother," she says. "We were once friends."

Before leaving the room, I scan the several small monitors which show black-and-white shots of El Gato's front security gate, the main road, the *turnoff to my house, my driveway, my backyard. Downstairs, I set the audio alarm system. I am restless, irritable. I dislike holidays, the traffic on the roads, and particularly this holiday with its archaic mythology: it is Easter Sunday, a day of rebirth, though no one hangs there to save us any longer, perhaps ever did. I slam the door behind me.*

As I halter the horse and lead him across the corral for saddling, a red Porsche drives slowly by. The man called Harv sits in the passenger seat, and behind the wheel is a wild-haired woman. I stand watching the car travel slowly down the road. She is younger, of course, much younger. But she has the features of my mother.

Part II

Home

6

FRIDAY
OCTOBER 17, 1997
6:15 A.M.

O CTOBER, MORNING BREAKS LATE in the Rockies. By the time the sky began to gray in the east, I'd finished the Denver *Post* before a crackling fire, poured the last cup of coffee, and headed out to the deck Tony had added on the kitchen-side of the house. I stood in the chill air, leaning against the railing and staring into the fading darkness, so dark yet that the birds still slept. In the slow metamorphosis of a mountain morning, a looming shadow through the trees became a barn, dense patches of ground fog rose up through the high meadow grasses and disappeared. The stream whispered; a bird called out a brief note, and after a measured silence, another answered. Before long, juncos and sparrows were dancing along the railings, shrill and contentious, competing for seed I'd sprinkled there. As the sun topped the Sandias, it lit the barn that Tony's crew just yesterday had finished painting. I walked around the deck to the stairs, scattering birds as I climbed.

From the height of a second-story balcony, I looked down across the pines to the brilliant orange circle of aspens, their tiny sunlit leaves shimmering around the clearing. Built at the center, the barn was a large structure with simple, elegant lines, freshly painted a pale olive gray to match the house. The large sliding double doors had been shoved open so that the wild cats, rendered homeless after Tony began construction on the house in April, were enticed to new quarters. I'd had a cattle feeder installed inside and stocked with cat chow, and although the barn was several hundred yards down a mild incline from the house, I could make out cats milling through the low grass.

Quite a large number of them, I realized as the minutes passed. They were such eccentric animals, had always intrigued me—their arrogant autonomy perhaps; add to that their grace, beauty, inscrutable intelligence. I watched the orange and gray and black and multicolored shapes, seeing more with each passing moment—hundreds of cats winding their way across the meadow. Making a mental note to check the food levels in the feeder bins later today, I was about to turn away when my eye caught a flick of movement in a nearby pine. I scanned the shadows, saw a snake-like shape dangling from a branch. Above it: a pair of glowing eyes staring straight into my own. I stepped back with a yelp of surprise, but as I continued looking into the trees, I saw another, then another—countless pairs of golden, unblinking eyes. The trees were thick with cats, crouching behind the foliage with their tails whipping and their eyes burning. All watching me.

I faced them, my back against my new home that had been theirs only a few short months ago. I had a pretty good idea what they might be feeling, because nine years is not enough time to forget the prospect of homelessness. Not even close. I had gambled on my real estate plans while trembling on the brink of disaster before the business took hold and flew, and for a time I'd looked into the abyss, fired with blind rage at the loss of my life's work on the one hand and a debilitating helplessness on the other. Margot had thought she could integrate those two, but anyone who's had them both shrilling full-throttle through her veins can tell you they mix about as well as Penzoil and Perrier. They square off and fight like evil twins; they poison your blood and shred your cells and stake out your brain as their personal battlefield. They might call a truce now and then, but I can tell you one thing the shrinks can't—truce or war, you will never be the same again.

I pulled in a big drag of mountain oxygen, held it deep inside my lungs, leaned my head back to the sun, exhaled and thanked whatever spirits held court up past the blue air for every splinter of the place where I now stood. I made a silent promise to give every single one of those homeless cats permanent refuge, then opened my eyes and faced them.

"So how about it, guys? I take the house, you get the barn. Deal?"

The eyes kept staring. And then a voice from above:

"Cabin fever already?"

I jumped into the next county. Coffee splashed down my robe. Birds shot from the railing in a wave of terror. The cats' eyes disappeared. Leaning from a third-story balcony just to the right and above me, Tony squinted down through a mess of tangled bangs.

"Jesus," I said, my hand over my pounding heart and dripping robe. "Don't do that!"

"My, my. Aren't we nervy?" he said. "Isn't this the Great American Outdoors? Don't lock your doors, don't even own a house key, right?" He turned to the great sprawl of forest and sky and mountains, threw his arms wide, leaned back his head, squeezed shut his eyes, let out a long, loping coyote howl. The birds that had begun to return to the railing took flight again.

Maybe Tony got his kinks out early in the morning, before he went out to meet the crew, because—coyote impersonation and this morning's silk paisley robe aside—he bore scant resemblance to my partner and contractor extraordinaire who hauled ass during the day. He was a good-looking, narrow-hipped fellow, all the earmarks of a model conservative to watch him with his construction crew: clean-shaven, judicious, Ford 250, IRA, GOP, same uniform day after day—faded jeans and white shirt, short-sleeved in summer, long in winter. About the last person you'd guess as the son of Miguel Sandoval de Domingos, a glowering Native American painter known across the Southwest for his surreal portraits of the New Mexican desert, strewn with eerily realistic figures from local legend—the wraithlike shape of La Llorona, the dancing Kokopelli bent over his flute. Tony had leaned on his mother's gene pool and tapped it dry—that gorgeous, blond Colorado mountain woman de Domingos had disappeared with into the Colorado Rockies for several years before bringing her back to run his art gallery at the center of Albuquerque's Old Town. Tony hadn't inherited his dad's passionate originality either—while he loved construction, had even given UNM's architectural school a whirl at the prompting of his father, he'd dropped out after a few months. The prospect of creating original structures left him stone-cold, he'd said that serendipitous day I bumped into him in the architectural section of the UNM library. I'd been researching the basics of purchasing and restoring historic buildings at the beginning of my real estate career; he'd pointed out the best texts, talked about Albuquerque's turn-of-the-century buildings with a gleam in his eyes like some people get when they talk about their children or their lovers. Standing there in the empty aisle of the university stacks in the dull, vaguely sinister light, Tony and I could not have been more star-crossed if our names had been Juliet and Romeo. I smiled, watching his chortling coyote aria subside into a yawn before he turned and grinned down at me.

"Hey, got a minute? C'mon up. Best view in the place."

Damn. Tony looked more serious than he should have. I knew he wanted to talk more about what I'd said last night. I was dreading it as I entered the second story through the sliding glass doors, thinking about sitting with him last night in front of the fire after the crew had left. We'd chowed down on leftover pizza, chatted in the merciful quiet of the evening, after long hours of buzzing saws and deafening hammers and randy men shouting lewd jokes above the racket of construction. The major work was done, Tony said, only a couple, three more weeks of finish-up. I stared into the flames, told him I wanted the crew to leave, him too; that I needed to be alone here. But Tony wasn't about to be pulled off an unfinished job without a fight. I sighed, walked heavily across the empty bedroom that reeked of paint and sawdust and men's sweat. The oak boards of the new floor were still raw, unsanded. Several one-gallon cans of stain and polyurethane were stacked in one corner; strips of eight-foot quarter-rounds lay in a neat pile along one wall, waiting to be cut and installed.

This was the last bedroom at the end of a long hallway, one of three leading off the second story's central room built directly over the ground-floor living room. As I left it and walked down the hall, I realized more clearly that Tony was right about the house's odd structure—this floor was uniquely designed, all right, each of the three wings constructed separately, on three different occasions and without any apparent overall design or plan, in Tony's opinion.

I entered the central room, a large, airy affair with its triad of hallways and a door standing open with a set of steep, roughly cut stairs leading to the third story. With my heart surging, thrilled as a kid ascending to a secret treehouse, I climbed straight up, steadying myself with the banister Tony had installed on the interior wall, looking down on the driveway far below through a series of narrow, vertical windows inset into the exterior wall. I climbed, pulling myself up, finally reaching the large third-story room with eight walls of beveled glass. It was flooded with morning sunlight dancing around the room, shimmering on the white-tiled floor, dipping into the enormous shell-shaped marble bathtub carved into the floor's center. I stood inside the light, inside this room that glowed, feeling suspended inside some rare jewel where I could see across treetops to the distant mountains, jagged horizons where moons rose and suns set. Between several of the windows were doors, three in all. Each opened into a dormer bedroom. I entered the largest room where my oak desk and computer sat on an intricately woven Native American carpet. A rocking chair and small table were placed near the balcony door, new bookcases lined the walls, boxes of books were stacked on top of one another, several paintings leaned against the wall waiting to be hung.

Through the opposite sliding door, I could see Tony standing at the edge of the balcony, facing the eastern peaks with his hands clasped behind him. I stopped for a moment beside my desk. In spite of his misgivings about the house, and this floor in particular, I savored this lofty height, its delicious solitude. This room, unlike the others, had been totally finished off—the oak floor stained and glistening under several coats of sealant, the windows caulked and the trim carefully painted. I stood for a moment with my eyes clothed, straining to sense the venomous presence Tony had told me about three days ago after I'd arrived and he'd given me a tour. I had been utterly delighted by the entire house, but especially with the third floor. Tony had frowned, leaned a shoulder against a window frame as I explored.

"I don't know. This house, something weird about it, especially up this high." He shoved his hands in his jeans pockets and tipped his head to one side, looking down where the men worked in the yard. "You can shrug it off down there, tell yourself it's all these windows and balconies and decks and stairs getting to you. But up this high, the feeling's stronger, you can't lay it off on your imagination. You just don't build a house this size, this high, without some plan. It's crazy, like taking off in an airplane before you know where you're headed."

I was opening doors, discovering the toilet and basin tucked out of sight in a small compartment, checking out the bedrooms. Tony voice came from a distance, words without sense. When I walked up to join him, he was still looking down through the window, talking in that way he has of going through the back door to get to the front, so I started listening, but I wasn't happy about it. I was restless, irritated at this sour note.

"See, the design of a building's a reflection of the designer's mind, like a painting or a novel. Place is lovely, don't get me wrong. Very unusual, I can see why you were drawn to it." He reached out and traced the bevel near the window's edge, letting his fingertip slip slowly down the glass. "You saw the beauty of this place, even under all the cat shit. Didn't need to come inside to know it was here. You've an instinct about buildings. That's why it surprises me, I guess."

I sighed loud enough for him to hear. "Yeah?"

"Yeah. Surprised you didn't pick up the vibes."

I looked at him hard. "*Vibes*? Did I hear you right? Did I actually say *vibes*? Are you losing your fucking mind? This is a home in the goddamn mountains, not some spaced-out crystal shop in Sedona. Jesus, Tony, what's got into you?"

"I knew you weren't going to like this."

"No shit?"

"Yeah, well." He shoved out his chin, hunched his shoulders, jammed his hands farther in his pockets. "You know, I been out here for, what, six months now with the crew? All that time, putting in extra support beams, reinforcing the place so it doesn't collapse when you're sleeping some night. Because I can tell you one thing, that guy who built this? Gerald, you say his name was? He didn't know beans from Shinola about holding a place like this up. It's just pretty amazing it stayed standing till we got here." He pulled his eyes away from the crew and looked around at me. "You didn't know it, but the cat shit was the least of your worries."

"You were making a point? Or did I make that up?"

"Okay. So I get here, me and the guys. Take a couple days scoping the place, the supports. Got to thinking about what kind of nutzo would build a place like this to start with. Thinking all the time, something's familiar about this place, trying to nail down what it was."

"Tony."

"Okay. So one day it just hit me. Can't get it out of my mind. It's the structure, the way it goes off all directions, resting on ground-supports kind of haphazard. Made out of tree trunks, for Christ's sake."

I narrowed my eyes at him. He looked away, out the window toward the east, then began pacing from window to window, frowning at the sky like he was looking for witches or something, talking in a low, thoughtful tone.

"You know the black widow spider?" he said, pausing at one window, walking to the next. "She's a different brand of arachnid, not like the ones turning out perfectly symmetrical webs. The black widow, she spins first one direction, then another, no sense of pattern, no strategy, proportion, whatever. No balance or logic, maybe that's it. Like her intuition or instinct, that radar the others have, like she's missing that part. You can tell her web a mile away, all jumbled and skewed sideways with scribbles like she's trying to write something but it's scrambled, crazy." He stopped beside me, looking out the window and speaking low, to himself. "People who study spiders, entomologists? They say it's because the black widow is born psychotic."

If he hadn't lost his mind, he'd certainly misplaced it. I wrote it off to his aversion for being any place without dial-up pizza delivery, maybe poisoned by the Colorado mountain air that his mother had despised as much as he did. I headed on toward the balcony, stepped over a rumpled sleeping bag where Tony had spent the last three nights since he'd stopped driving into the Crystal Springs motel with the crew. He glanced around as I walked up beside him.

"Jesus, Sym. Doesn't it give you the willies, all this space? I mean, what in *hell* would anyone do out here?"

"Not your most original question." My bankers and investment brokers, even the teller who'd closed out my personal checking account last week had already asked it. Problem was, the only people who would understand the answer were the people who knew and didn't have to ask the question. Like Daniel, like Tony's dad. It was the kind of question that, when your friend asks it, you want to cry.

"Yeah? So?"

"Well, like you said, there's plenty to do just working on the place, sanding the floors, painting, right? Hell, just caulking all these windows will take me into next spring."

"You better get cracking," Tony said, squinting at the sky. "Another week, maybe two, this place'll be buried under a foot of snow, and that's just the first layer. You won't see ground again for months." An awkward silence descended as we stared up at the sky where a hawk was circling. "I can't figure why you won't let me finish this job. Give me and the crew two more weeks, tops, it's done. Why are you pushing us out?" He was angry, not real anger but the surface stuff that keeps your voice from whining and your feelings from showing.

I had to give him something, so I gave him the easy words, the credible explanation. But it wasn't just the noise and the boom boxes jacked up to full volume with Willie and Hank, Junior. It wasn't even breathing the sawdust and making the sandwiches for the crew, sweeping floors behind them. It wasn't their crude jokes, the soft-porn ones they culled out as "inoffensive in mixed company," as one of them had put it. Call it impatience, then. Not being able to wait one more day to take possession of the hermetic existence I'd set out seven years ago to buy for myself. The hawk circled higher, not much more than a brief shadow leaning against the sky, and I thought of the way the air inexplicably changes when you're the only one breathing it, how the rhythm of feet walking across a wood floor sounds different when the feet are yours and you're the only one listening. "I'm just, you know, tired of the noise. Call it selfish," I said, wanting a piece of the truth.

"Call it pure lunacy."

"Maybe." But it didn't matter what we called it, not now. "So what's the big deal? I can always give you a call if it turns out the north wind's coming in faster than the central heat can handle. You're hot on sticking around here or what? Developing a taste for the Great Outdoors?"

"Shee-ee-it! Maybe you like the company of elk and mule deer, not to mention those cats you been feeding, but just wait till the snow comes. You'll be chewing bark off the trees with the rest of the herd, gaping at the full moon like all those cats in heat. Didn't I just hear you talking to yourself?"

"Well, I'll be damned! If that isn't just like a man, thinking if a woman wants to live alone, she's got to be crazy. Like she'll go stark raving mad without injections from the Great American Dick."

"Hey!" He heaved the word, gave it a redneck spin. "Watch your mouth. This ain't Stanley Kowalski you talking to—"

Suddenly, a high-pitched caterwaul filled the air. Cats shot from the barn, a yellow tom in hot pursuit. He was big and fast. Gaining ground, he pounced, and ear-piercing shrieks tore through the air as cats screamed and fought.

"Sweet Jesus," Tony said, after the air cleared and the yellow tom had trotted back into the barn with his tail straight up. "Listen, you can't keep feeding those cats like you're doing. I'm telling you, come spring, the bears are going to come out of hibernation, show up here in droves and tear that barn to pieces getting to that cat food. Come on," he said, turning toward the house. "Let's get dressed, take a hike over and see what we can figure out."

Half an hour later, we entered the barn to the sounds of frenzied movement as the cats scurried for cover and streaked in terror past us, fast as bullets. Tony and I stood together, looking around at the enormous building, large enough to accommodate an inside riding ring with a long line of stalls on each side. Glistening in the shadows at the far end was an aluminum cattle feeder piled high with cat chow. Tons more of the stuff was stored in a couple of large Dumpsters in the corner.

"You know, considering the state of the house," Tony said, walking along the line of stalls and peering through the iron bars on the upper half of the doors, "it's amazing those cats didn't do their business here as well. I mean, here's a structure with dirt galore, a veritable mansion of a litter box, but no cat shit."

It was true, the place was immaculate. I glanced at Tony and laughed. "For being born a Colorado country boy, you sure don't know beans about cats," I said. I stretched my arms out and turned in a circle, loving the earthy smell and the high freedom of the place. "They're the cleanest species of animal you'll ever find. But you let your housekeeping slide a bit, it won't be any time before a cat will follow suit, kind of like they think it's not fit for living quarters anymore, it's a shit house instead. Take Wendy's place, that A-frame. If she had any cats, which she doesn't far as I could smell, they'd be doing their business from one end of the place to the other. That's what happened over there," I said, nodding toward the house. "She lived in filth, so the cats took her lead. She moved out and they moved in, used that house like they figured it was meant to be used."

"You might be a crack domestic feline psychologist, but those times when I was a kid and dad drug us back to living on the res, I learned a lot more than I ever wanted to about feral cats," Tony said, walking over to the cattle feeder and Dumpsters. He was dressed in his standard working uniform—jeans and white shirt, long-sleeved in the October morning. He leaned back against the Dumpster and crossed his arms over his chest and stared past me, out through the barn door where cats were milling through the grass. "Let me give you a little update on wildlife, maybe cause you to reconsider your feeding plans. Because nature's got a pretty good handle on population control. You're not dealing with neutered, spayed pets here, you're sticking your nose into Mama Nature's system with its checks and balances built right in. Long as you let wildlife alone, let them live unimpeded in the wild, the amount of their food supply—in this case, mice, birds, rabbits, chipmunks—will limit their population. You got more cats than food, their numbers fall back without you doing a thing but minding your own business. But you feed wild animals like you're doing with these cats, you'll play hell with the natural balance. Especially cats." Tony pushed himself away from the Dumpster and walked toward the barn door, a bright square of sunlight. "Female cats, they're regular baby machines. Most people don't know it, but a female cat stays in perpetual heat except when bred. Gestation period of sixty-three days, say six litters a year. Basic math: theoretically, one female cat can spawn over 400,000 cats in seven years." He stopped and leaned against the doorway, looking out over the meadow. "Now I don't have a clue how many cats you had back in April when I got here, but there were plenty. Let's take a conservative estimate, let's say you had thirty females. Say six kittens a litter, half female. End of six months, you got three thousand cats. Give or take." I stared past him, watching the creatures slithering through the grass, climbing the trees, crouched in the branches. Tony shook his head and turned to me. "You've got to let this go, Sym."

Tony's mathematical abilities were a constant amazement and an asset when it came to a quick take on square footage and building costs, but I didn't want to think about the cats. I turned on my heel and walked away from him, toward the far end of the building where a long, diagonal set of wooden stairs led to a midlevel platform, and then up higher to the clerestory loft. I'd taken a brief peek into the loft room when I'd arrived. I knew someone had lived there, but not who.

"I know it wasn't Wendy, though." I pulled a cord to release a lock from the inside and pushed open the heavy door. "No trash, no beer cans."

"No cat shit," Tony said, following me in. The room ran nearly the entire length of the barn, a room larger than most houses—closing in on two thousand square feet was my guess. It had a small kitchen area at the far end, a door leading to a bathroom in the corner, and a black potbellied stove at one side. Light from the clerestory windows lay across the oak floor with its layer of dust and an elaborate, threadbare Oriental rug at the center. High above, open beams made an intricate pattern of diagonal lines in the shadows. I imagined the place furnished, imagined watching an electrical storm flashing through the night sky, visualized a Sunday morning with a slow drift of snowflakes turning the meadow white. Tony strolled toward the bathroom where an old trunk sat beside the door with several boxes beside it.

He opened the trunk, fished inside, and came up with a black lace teddy dangling on one finger. "Female, anyway."

"Oh yeah?" I said. "Since when are you into stereotypes?"

"Since I saw these are all size threes," he said, pulling out a small pair of faded jeans and a turtleneck sweater that wouldn't have fit around my thigh. "I can't think of a single one of my friends who can wiggle into anything under a size twelve." He gave me a droll look and dropped the clothes back into the trunk.

"So you don't know who lived here?" Tony asked, as we closed the door and headed back down the stairs.

"Not a clue."

As we left the barn and walked across the meadow, he stopped to glance back. "It's weird, the house being so shaky and the barn built so well. Oak doors on the stalls, the loft floor. First-class job." He turned and we walked on. "Mrs. James, she didn't mention somebody living in that clerestory? Maybe it was her?"

"She hadn't been here since she left in the sixties, according to Harv. Planned to raise horses, apparently. Got as far as the barn, lived there while the development was in process, but then took off when things went to hell."

"But those clothes, they're fairly recent, not sixties."

"And Claire James is no size three," I said, remembering the woman I'd flown to Tennessee to meet back in April. I knew her age, must have expected Miss Havisham, decked out in decaying lace and quivering with Parkinson's Disease. Claire James hadn't read Dickens. She had a choke hold on the past even Dick Clark would have envied. I'd sat across from her at an upscale Nashville restaurant where the carpeting was plush and the lights muted enough to do some airbrush tricks with wrinkles. I suspected a little help from a cosmetic surgeon, as well, because her skin was taut over prominent cheekbones that even old age couldn't ruin. She'd been a pretty woman, Wendy's prototype, with the same blue eyes and sensual mouth. But there was nothing falling down around the ears of this woman—I'd made my offer, she'd turned it down, I'd made another, she countered, I countered back, she accepted. A done deal. In one smooth gesture, she bent down, drew a set of papers from a leather briefcase beside her chair, filled in a few blanks while I wrote her out a check. I'd worked a long time to do a business deal like that. I think she had too.

"Hope you'll be happy there, Ms. Symkin," she said, pushing back her chair and rising. She stood leaning over the table, briefcase in one hand, the other extended toward me across the table. "I had big plans for that place once," she said, looking not quite at me. She paused as if she were going to add something, shrugged instead, her razor-sharp eyes framed by a network of fine wrinkles. She locked her eyes to mine, gave my hand a hard squeeze, a flash of smile that never reached her eyes. Not even close. "Things happen sometimes, best plans turn to dust. The trick is to know when to let go." Then she turned and walked away, her high heels silent on the carpet. I guessed her to be a size ten. A very trim size ten.

"But I'll tell you what," I said. "I got the distinct feeling she was glad to be done with the place. When she walked away from me that day in the restaurant, I could nearly hear the doors slamming. It was like she was walking away from more than the title to the property, and was damned glad of it."

"She didn't mention Wendy, her husband leaving her for another woman, deserting her and the kids out here? Didn't you tell me that guy, that Harv fellow, didn't he say she promised it to Gerald and Wendy if they built here?"

"It wasn't a gossip session, Tony." I felt a sudden flash of heat and irritability. "She never mentioned Wendy, and I think she didn't want me to either." We were nearing the house when three trucks with Tony's crew came flying up the driveway.

"I thought we agreed they were going home. What the fuck..."

"Hey, hey," he said. "Take a breath, Sym. I forgot to call them this morning before we walked over and, frankly, now that they're here, we might as well finish the damned caulking."

The trucks stopped, and the men were jumping out, slamming doors, laughing, turning on the ghetto blasters.

"Shit!" I left him standing there and stomped into the house. It was just past eight o'clock. Upstairs, I pulled on a set of warmups, laced myself into cross-trainers, and went back to the kitchen to fill a water bottle. I was about as interested in taking up walking as I was in parachute jumping, but it had been Garbo's favorite pastime and I was determined not only to do it, but like it.

That was the secret to Becoming someone else, I thought, clipping the bottle to my waistband and heading for the door as the crew revved up their saws and drills and jokes. You had to move into a personality like you moved in to a house—because it felt exactly right to be there. I slammed the door behind me.

7

I'VE KNOWN PEOPLE who walk, and I can put every single one of them into two groups. There are the ones who go outside to do it—these are the people who won't eat anything with eyes, people who are laid-back and process-oriented and keep the health food stores in business. These people watch a lot of television after dinner, too, and will go to their graves denying it. The ones like me, we're definitely Type A's, and the only walking we consistently do is on a treadmill while reading the morning paper or talking with a client on the phone or taking notes on whatever project is at hand, and sometimes all these at once. So while I were walking beside the meadow stream, I pulled out the map the secretary of the El Gato Homeowner's association had sent when I called the number listed in the local phone book. I figured if I was going to spend the next few hours walking, I might as well get something accomplished while I was doing it.

Someone had penciled in little boxes for houses on the map and labeled them with names. I looked for Harv's box, thinking that it was a good time to confirm his commission, but there was none with his name on it. Then I saw the waterfall drawn in and labeled "El Gato Falls." With my finger, I followed the road leading to it backward down the mountain, matched it up with the position of my house, discovered that the road Harv and I had taken was, in fact, the same road I had climbed in the snow seven years ago. It was also the property line separating Claire James's hundred acres, now mine, from the development she'd created and named El Gato. Anticipating such walks as I was now taking, I had also bought one lot at random in the development in order to be a bona fide property owner and have legal access to explore the grounds. I stuffed the map back in my pocket, and when I came to the rocky road where Harv and I had parked, I took a right and began hiking up the steep incline.

The sound of cascading water grew louder as I climbed, and when the enormous square-faced rocks came into view, I recognized at once the spot where Harv's yellow Jeep had been parked. To the right was the steep cliff where I'd looked down over the tangle of gravel roads and the tips of electric poles, and discovered the county highway. On the left, where I'd seen the footprints disappear in the snow, was a faint path leading through underbrush to the edge of a steep precipice and a stream running through a canyon far below. This time, I thought, returning to the road and facing the sound that seven years ago had driven me away in terror, I was ready. Excitement rushed over me as I climbed toward the sound of the falls.

I wound through towering boulders as the blast of cascading water increased with each step. By the time I entered into a dark clearing where immense, old-growth pines shut out the sky, the noise was deafening. To one side, a reservoir of water pooled and spilled over the lip of a rock and into the canyon below. It was fed by a broad sheet of water flowing, I saw with a start, from a crack formed by the fusion of two monolithic boulders that shot straight up, high as New York skyscrapers.

If I'd come here believing I'd laid my childhood fears to rest, I could kiss that good-bye. And if I were perfectly honest, I'd admit to harboring a half-baked superstition that the waterfall had some magic about it, that just being in its presence was going to somehow, though I couldn't have explained how, put me in tune with my mother's spirit. Okay, so it was crazy, but there it was. The explosion of sound and the abrupt darkness had unnerved me, though, and I felt the terror of that day in December flooding back. I brought out my big gun: rationality. I reasoned that this was, after all, only a clearing in the mountains—a few trees, some big rocks, not the scene of a Third World massacre. Jesus, get a grip, Symkin.

"Get hold of yourself!" I yelled into the clearing where the noise was so loud I could no longer distinguish it from the blood pounding in my ears. My words bounced and echoed: "...hold... your... self," they said, just before the falls swallowed them.

I stood alone in the clearing, terrified but refusing to turn back, staring straight up at those twin granite shapes that leaned together, waiting. They were not mere slabs of monolithic stone, as I'd first thought, but sinuously shaped granite, their surfaces worn smooth by centuries of wind and rain, sculpted with curves and swells in such voluptuous proportion that I imagined them as twin bodies, rising from foot to leg to thigh, from waist to long-ribbed torsos, breast-to-breast and lip-to-lip against a single patch of dazzling blue.

And so I steeled myself and went toward them, leaping from stone to stone that poked above the sheet of running water until I reached the other side, climbed an embankment to a narrow ledge, crept along it until at last I came to the dark split between the rocks. My heart hammered, my chest ached, and I repeated, *nothing but big rocks, nothing but big rocks,* like a mantra. But behind the beating and the words and the water rose another sound—the high keening of sirens as the clearing darkened, and then began pulsing with flashes of red shooting down from the patch of sky above, shooting shards of red light that struck the water and made it boil like blood. I clung to the stone and shut my eyes, because finally when there is nothing but terror, the world stops mattering. I turned to the fissure, left thought behind, and stepped through the crack where the falls shrieked and thundered, shattering the air and splitting the ear and echoing like a chorus of demons.

I felt myself standing blind and alone in that dark center. And then I lifted my face and opened my eyes.

I stood in a stone room, not dark at all, but silvered with light filtering down from a tiny point of sky, bathing the cave in a kind of ethereal glow. Directly in front of me and several yards overhead, a narrow ledge ran along a wall behind where silver water slid and splashed from the sky for what seemed a mile, into an unseen chasm below, where a fine silver mist rose up and filled the cave.

Where my heart had raced with terror, now it beat wildly in what seemed to be a sacred place. Gazing up at that silver spill with the mist drenching my face, I imagined I heard the voice then, the one that had called out to me in conference rooms and the abyss of my dreams—though whether it was the voice of angels or demons, I couldn't say. And something else: a pair of eyes slowly opening, some creature rousing itself as it watched me in this ancient place. This private place, I understood, not for humankind. So I withdrew, easing backward through the fissure and into the clearing. Here, after the cave's thundering blast, the world seemed oddly hushed. High above in a shaft of sun, a blue jay darted through the branches, the odor of pine needles hung in the air, and the two fused women towering over me returned to stone.

I made my way back down the path, shaken but feeling somehow oddly rejuvenated. I debated about whether to return home or finish my walk, and chose the latter. I took the side trail to the precipice and looked down into the canyon below. The descent was formidably steep, not for the faint-hearted or acrophobic, but by following a latticework of narrow ledges, a descent into the canyon was possible. My adrenaline stash was gone; this was small potatoes. I started lowering myself down the cliff, clinging to rocks and small saplings as I went. At the bottom, I tunneled through an animal path beside the fiercely rushing stream. The vegetation was dense, almost impassable in spots with tangles of wild roses. At last, the stream widened into a small, sandy clearing. A watering hole, I realized. Scratched and bleeding, I hopped across a bridgework of rocks to the far bank where I knelt beside the stream and splashed the icy water across my face, washing away the blood and soothing the scratches. Then I drew out the map, found a rock in the sun, and sat down to study my position. The stream descended the mountain more or less parallel to the route Harv and I had traveled, but by cutting across a swatch of land just ahead, I could intersect El Gato's main road. I was more than ready for a little flat-footed walking. I folded the map, stuck it in my back pocket, took a long pull from the water bottle.

I was turning to leave the clearing when I saw them. Huge and recent—cat tracks the size of plates. Then I remembered other things: the print I'd seen that day in the snow, the set of unblinking eyes reflected in the headlights of my Porsche during my visit with Harv. I practiced some serious deep breathing and tried to recollect everything I knew about big cats. Mostly I focused on their shyness and their dietary preference for deer and elk, and then I made a fast beeline through the clearing, heading for a stand of trees and the road I hoped was somewhere on the other side of it. Bingo! A road had never looked so good as El Gato's main drag just ahead, just down a brief grassy slope.

Halfway down, I saw a road grader, its blade raised, chuffing down the mountain under a black cloud of diesel smoke with Harv perched in the cab. I figured news of his fifteen-thousand-dollar commission was a good enough reason to flag him, so I quickened my pace and waved both arms for him to stop.

But Harv was busy. He was going full-throttle, gripping the steering wheel and yelling something I couldn't make out as he barreled past me. I stood on the slope and watched as the grader kept gathering speed, and when the road curved, Harv and his grader kept going straight ahead. Right into the side of Dean Brandenberg's log castle.

I was a good half mile from the crash, which seemed to shake the ground I stood on. By the time I arrived panting and with searing pains stabbing at my sides, a crowd had collected around the grader whose front blade was deeply imbedded into logs below the shattered front window. The main attraction, however, was not Harv, who was being lifted out of the cab by one man and caught on the ground by two others, but a big-bosomed woman screeching at him from the front porch of the house, her hands balled into fists and beating the air.

"...goddamn nutcase heathen, who the motherfuck you think you are anyway, you scumfucking lowlife..." The expletives flowed, unrelenting and apparently inexhaustible—a veritable Mississippi of obscenities. I stood behind the crowd, awed. "...shitfucking goddamn sonofabitching fuckface, think you can fucking run into my house, you shitassed slimeball..." The woman was wide and imposing as an opera diva, with a voice to match. Her steel-colored hair was heavily lacquered into a scrolling twist, and she wore an ankle-length heavy sweater rolled at the cuffs. She had phenomenal lung capacity, never stopped for breath, and the fact that Harv was unconscious didn't faze her. Her face had turned purple, and just as I thought she'd topple, a square-cut woman with a wide leather strap across one shoulder and straw-colored hair that looked like someone had used wire cutters and a bowl to cut it trudged up the Brandenberg stairs. She placed herself between the screaming diva and the crowd below, planted both her hands on the diva's shoulders, shoved her out at arm's length, then jerked her forward in what seemed to be a hug. The diva closed her mouth, and the two women stood there chest-to-chest, the square woman crooning something low.

As they disappeared inside the house, the crowd's attention turned to where Harv was being positioned flat on the ground by the three men who had retrieved him from the cab. In a sudden rush, the crowd surrounded them. Somewhere inside the huddle of people issued a high-pitched scream, and a short, round man pulling a short, round woman extricated themselves from the group. The woman had flyaway gray hair pinned in a series of rolls on top of her head, and she hung limply on the shoulder of the man who led her toward the porch steps where they sat together. The woman lay her forehead on the man's chest and sobbed.

By the time a Bronco pulled up with a sheriff's star on the side of it, the milling group had thinned and left two men kneeling next to Harv, who stared up at the sky, a thin rivulet of blood seeping from his hairline down his cheek. The blue eyes that I had last seen under Wendy's yellow porch light were neither cold nor threatening now; they were filmed over in the gaze of the dead. The man who got out of the Bronco was leather-faced, tall and lean-boned, wearing a denim jacket, faded Levi's, and scuffed boots. His hair was dark, graying at the sides, and combed back to curl above his shirt collar. He walked over to where Harv lay with the slow, heavy gait of a man dogged by exhaustion or sorrow or both, and after kneeling briefly over the body, he began working his way through the crowd, talking to first one spectator and then another. By the time he got to me and I was describing my single contact with Harv back in April, the coroner's station wagon was pulling away down the road and the sun was heading toward the western ridge.

"So you actually saw the whole thing?" the sheriff asked, in a voice carefully scraped of all emotion. He was a good-looking man, somewhere in his mid-fifties was my guess, with penetrating gray eyes that set something fluttering inside me like the wings of a butterfly pinned live to a wall.

I looked away from the eyes, to the plume of dust left hanging in the air by the coroner's wagon, and nodded. "But I was a long way off," I said, indicating the grassy slope. "I tried to wave him down, but he flew by, yelling something. When he got to this curve, he just kept going straight instead of following the road."

The sheriff had a few inches on me, stood about six-foot-three was my guess. His denim shirt was open at the top, and that's how I knew his chest hair was graying, too. The butterfly trembled.

"You hear what he was yelling?"

"I can fucking tell you what he was yelling!" a voice squealed above us.

We looked up at a beefy fellow leaning over the porch railing. He had a red face and tiny eyes deeply buried in layers of flesh. His yellow leather jacket was buttoned so tightly at the neck that a roll of fat bulged out over the sheepskin collar. Just behind him stood a slender young man in his early twenties wearing a white silk shirt with voluminous sleeves, tight black riding jodhpurs, and English riding boots. His sun-streaked blond hair fell in waves to his shoulders, and his face was so perfectly sculpted that it was stunning as a model's. He stood absolutely still, lips faintly curved, as he watched the sheriff with odd, pale eyes tilted slightly at the corners.

"Crazy sonofabitch was probably yelling 'Geronimo!' Drove right fucking into my house, nearly gave my wife a heart attack, the dumb sonofabitch!"

"You saying he did this on purpose, Dean?" The sheriff's words were low, controlled, the iron voice of reason and totally without inflection.

"Now, Marle," the man said, his tone wheedling. "I don't want to say anything against the dead, but I can tell you that Harv Benton was a dangerous man." His voice began to squeal out of control again. "And he was goddamn crazy as they come! He'd been threatening me, and make no mistake, he came right down that road meaning to go through my living room and take everybody in there out with him!"

"You're saying he was so mad at you, Dean, he wanted to kill himself?" the sheriff asked. His thumbs were hooked in his jeans pockets, and he looked down at his boot toes with his lips tightly set. I thought I saw a bare twitch of a smile, but I might have been mistaken.

"Goddammit, Winslow! I'm telling you he did this on purpose! Any fool can see that! He came down that road, and he drove right into my house! What more do you need?" Behind the beefy man's shoulder, the blond fellow watched still as a statue, his eyes riveted on the sheriff, with lips that could have been smiling or could have been sneering.

Marle Winslow nodded in his abstracted way, glanced down the road where the coroner had disappeared. He cocked his head sideways, squinted one eye, looked back up at the porch. "You pressing charges?" Someone behind me snickered.

Brandenberg's face, which had been the color of raw meat, turned purple, shining with sweat. I wondered if he was on the verge of a stroke. The tiny eyes glittered. "You go on and joke, but when that wife of his starts yelling about that grader being unfit, you can just bet she's got a lawsuit on her mind. And you would do well to remind her that her husband has spent the greater part of his days threatening to kill me! And that's just what he's tried to do here!"

So that was it—Brandenberg was expecting Harv's wife to sue the development for every penny. I looked over to where the grader sat, an ancient rusted-out machine with bald tires and mismatched fenders.

"You report these threats, Dean?" the sheriff asked. He used the tone of someone talking about the weather. I thought I saw a smile flicker around his lips, but I couldn't be sure. It had been a long day.

"No, I didn't goddamn report it! If I reported every time that crazy sonofabitch threatened me, I wouldn't be doing anything but making reports! He was a nutcase, and everybody here knows it!" He looked around for confirmation, but the crowd had disbanded. "And I just want to know who's going to get that goddamn thing out of my wall," he said, glaring at the decrepit grader.

"Well, if I were you, Dean," the sheriff drawled, "I'd call me a tow truck. That grader belongs to the Association, right? I expect they're the ones will have to deal with it. I hear you're head of that group now."

After Dean Brandenberg had huffed back into his house, followed by the young man, the sheriff drifted toward a large tree beside the grader, motioning me to follow. He crossed his arms over his chest and propped a shoulder against the tree and looked out across the yard to where a group of four people stood talking. I leaned against the other side of the tree. I wanted to be home, back where even the hammers and saws were an improvement over this, but it was a two-hour walk.

A black truck cruised by, slowed, then parked on the road across from Brandenberg's house. A tall, slim woman dressed in black got out and surveyed the group before walking toward where the sheriff and I stood. I recognized the woman with the horse that Harv had pointed out the day of the tour. She had unusually long legs and a feline walk. Her black hair was clipped very short, swept back from a face with dazzling bone structure. Large dark glasses covered the top part of it, and she kept them on even when the sheriff introduced her to me as Eva Blake, nor did she remove the black glove from the hand she offered. She nodded but didn't smile, and I sensed her scrutinizing me from behind the glasses.

"Hear you bought the James place," she said. Her voice was unusually deep, the kind women used in old movies where they drank lots of whiskey and smoked lots of cigarettes and had honky-tonk music playing in the background. The kind of woman Daniel sang about when he sat on the porch at night with his guitar and bourbon and the ashtray overflowing. "Looks like you got the worst end of it."

"Pardon?" I stared at her. The dark lenses hid her eyes, but I had the uneasy sense that she was staring hard at me.

"Looks like you been in a fight." She lifted her hand and brushed her gloved fingertips like a black wing near my cheek with an odd, sideways smile, then turned abruptly to the sheriff.

"I passed an ambulance on the highway," she said, glancing at the grader. The sheriff told her about Harv while the people still lingered in the yard, speaking in low tones beside the porch. "Any idea what happened?" she said. "He was pretty good at driving that contraption."

The sheriff shrugged. The curtain behind the Brandenbergs' broken window fluttered, and a couple of people by the porch glanced quickly over their shoulders at us. I recognized the short, round fellow and the woman who had cried on his shoulder. The other two were men in their late thirties or early forties, standing shoulder-to-shoulder. One was slender with olive skin, a wide forehead, and high cheekbones, his black hair slicked back in a terse ponytail; the other was shorter, sandy-haired, with broad, muscular shoulders. Eva Blake left us, strolled over to join the two men.

"She's right, you know." He touched his face to indicate the scratches on my own. "You ought to get something on those."

I nodded, mumbled something about the walk I'd taken, and felt irritation gnawing at me. I remembered the tiny cut along Harv's hairline, such a small wound.

"So you only met Harv just the once?" the sheriff said. His gray eyes were penetrating as drill bits. "You weren't what you'd call a 'friend'?"

"Right," I said, "Just that once when I came here to look at property."

"And he showed you Miz James's place?"

My memory flashed back to the night in front of Wendy's house, the threat in Harv's eyes as he'd asked me not to reveal his role in the sale. I glanced uneasily at the group of people beside the Brandenberg porch. The round man and woman had strolled nearer and stood within earshot; the two men and Eva Blake were walking off toward the road. Harv hadn't wanted someone to know his role in showing me Claire James's property. But why? And who? I couldn't see any way to duck the sheriff's question, and besides Harv was dead. What difference could it possibly make now? I stuck my hands in my pockets and nodded as I watched the two men walk together down the dirt road while Eva Blake climbed in her truck and started the engine. But instead of pulling away, she sat for a long moment perfectly still, looking directly at where I stood talking with the sheriff. Maybe she knew him. Maybe she was merely waiting to get his attention. And maybe it was just my imagination that felt her eyes weren't on the sheriff at all, but burning into me from behind the dark glasses.

The sheriff shifted his weight to one hip and scuffed a boot in the dirt as Eva Blake drove off in her truck. "You gone to one of the homeowners' meetings yet?"

I jumped slightly and turned my attention back to him. "I'm not a resident," I said. "As I understand it, Claire James's property isn't technically part of the development." For reasons I couldn't explain even to myself, I wasn't ready to admit owning a lot here quite yet, although apparently news about my purchase of the James place had gotten around.

"Ah." He didn't seem particularly surprised. "Well, I expect you'll get invited anyway."

I expected I would, too. And I expected I'd take a pass. I had not moved here to thrash around in local squabbles and petty feuds.

"You know if anybody called Harv's wife?" he asked.

The short, round couple strolled over. "Hey, Marle." The two men grabbed hands and did a little male chit-chat for a moment, and then the sheriff introduced me. Joe and Janie Gillman.

"We live right down the road," Janie said, red-eyed but smiling. She pointed toward the kit house as she and her husband nodded and beamed together. They looked enough alike to be siblings, with blue eyes and the open, anxious faces of people eager to please. Joe's bald head was topped with a baseball cap and a visor that extended out past his forehead, and both of them wore blue thermal warmup suits. Janie smiled in that perpetual, unconscious way of women who have spent their lives over a stove or sewing machine and profess to have enjoyed it.

"I can't believe it," she said, shaking her head at the grader. "I guess it'll be me and Joe that will go over and give the news to Edna. I wish the doctor could have stayed for a while. It's her heart—"

"—her heart, you know," Joe said. "That's why nobody's called her. We have to figure out how to break it to her. I think we ought maybe to have somebody that can do CPR, I'm afraid—"

"—she's liable to have a heart attack. You know she's already..."

"I understand, Mrs. Gillman," the sheriff said. "I think maybe I'll just go over with you, just in case."

"Oh no!" Janie said. "If she sees that sheriff's vehicle drive up, it will be all over for her, don't you know?" Janie Gillman's eyes were round as eggs as she gripped the sheriff's arm with both hands. "You don't understand about Edna, Sheriff. You have never met her, have you?"

The sheriff patted the woman's hands. "Tell you what," he said, "we'll just take your car if you want to do it that way. That sound okay to you?" He had let the leash off his voice, and it was full of chrysanthemums and sonorous notes and the hush of a funeral parlor.

Janie released his arm, an expression of beatific satisfaction on her face. I looked closely at the sheriff. Was it his voice, the way he had touched Janie Gillman's flesh, the closeness of his body to hers? Something in the eye? Whatever it was, I realized this man was more potent than Prozac.

"But let me go in to her first," Janie said, regaining her composure. "Prepare her, you know. And then if we need you—"

"—you'll be right there close at hand," Joe finished, nodding happily as the sheriff sent them off home with a promise to join them directly.

As we stood watching Joe and Janie Gillman waddle off toward their kit house, I remembered Harv's fifteen-thousand-dollar commission. I suddenly wanted to tag along. I wanted to meet his wife, let her know the money was there if she needed it. When I told the sheriff about the commission and asked to go along, he became silent, gazing off to the west where the sun was edging down toward the horizon.

"Guess you know you're not under any legal obligation to pay that money," he said.

"I know, but I consider it Harv's money, and I'm guessing his wife is his beneficiary." I glanced sideways at him, wondering if he was discouraging me from turning the money over to her. And if so, why?

But he only shrugged and strolled over to where the old grader sat. He squatted down and peered around under it, climbed into the cab, climbed back down and crawled under the machine. In a few minutes, he emerged covered with oil. As I watched, he entered the cab again, stuffed some papers into a wrinkled bag, and when he came walking back, he was wiping his hands with a red cloth, carrying the bag of papers clamped under one arm. The Brandenberg curtain shifted slightly.

After the sheriff set the bag behind the driver's seat of his Bronco and locked the doors, the two of us walked down the road toward the Gillmans', finding the tiny, round couple waiting in the front seat of a GMC the size of a tank.

8

IT TOOK ABOUT FIVE MINUTES riding in the back seat of the Gillman GMC before I was lost again. El Gato was a labyrinth. My last familiar signpost was the one-acre corner lot I'd bought that gave me a gate card, access to the community, a two-inch-thick dot-matrix printout of the covenants, and one vote out of the total one thousand "for use in deciding issues of self-governance." Yeah, right.

I gave up trying to keep track of how to get to Harv's and relaxed in the back seat beside the sheriff, mulling over the place as we wound through the tangle of roads. Beneath all the hype about "majority vote" and "self-governance," it didn't take a genius to do a little basic arithmetic: anyone with enough money to buy 501 of the total one thousand lots was going to be laying down the law for everyone else, take it or leave it. The one-lot-one-vote policy made El Gato about as democratic as Richard II's England. Hadn't Harv said that Brandenberg owned over four hundred lots? That put him on the fast track for King Dick. You can read Machiavelli's *Prince* till your eyes cross, you can argue the case of the beneficent monarch till your nose falls off, but you will always come back to Square One: human greed. As much as absolute power makes for a snappy, page-turning read, it's still a formula plot with an ending as predictable as a Louis L'Amour western, because sooner or later all those subjugated, pissed-off masses—whether they're Russian peasants or stay-at-home moms—are going to turn around and do some serious ass-kicking. The only amazing part of this bloody old epic was not that it had been replayed so often, but that there was anyone alive who would still fall for it. I'd been living next door to El Gato for three days, and already I felt the classical, subterranean rumblings provoked by the abuse of power. Subterranean rumbling and one dead body. And counting.

I pulled my attention back to the front seat where Joe Gillman was chattering about his next scheduled barbeque.

"...figured we would make a little social event out of our monthly homeowners' meeting. I'll just fire up my grill while Dean runs through the agenda, and we'll eat and have a real good time for a change. I'm calling this one our El Gato Oktoberfest, and it just so happens that the last Friday of this month is Halloween. What about we all come dressed up? What do you think about that?" He twisted his head and gave me a look, his eyebrows raised.

"Um." I glanced over at Marle who was working on his neutral expression, with a smile trying to bloom. "Guess it's not really up to me," I ventured, "seeing as I'm not a resident. But it sounds like it might be some fun for your group." It was true, I insisted, stifling the scrappy little voice nagging at me, I'm not actually a *resident*.

Janie twisted around quickly, her eyes wide enough to show white all around. "Why Ms. Simpson," she said, "don't you know, me and Joe's the secretary/treasurer of the Association? I just saw your name the other day on Lot 143 when I was doing the monthly update of our ownership records, and it was me sent you that map you asked for." Her look nailed me as a serial killer—tried and ready for sentencing.

"Symkin," I said. A silence descended in the car. Marle cocked his head to one side and raised a brow, clearly amused. I realized that all along the residents of this small community had known that I "belonged." I wondered what else they knew.

"Well," I shrugged. "I thought you meant an actual 'resident.' You know I've renovated the place I bought from Claire James, and—"

"Oh yes," Janie said, apparently mollified. "Wendy and Gerald's place." She pursed her mouth into a tight rosebud and twisted back around in the seat, facing forward. "I don't think Wendy minded much, but Gerald was right—"

"Janie, goddammit!" Joe snapped at his wife. "We've all had enough gossip, and I'm not having any more of it! Now, what's done is done, and that's the end of it."

Apparently the folks at El Gato had been following my purchase of Claire James's place while I'd been busy cashing out in Albuquerque. Even more reason, I thought, to steer clear. Joe made a sharp turn onto a road so narrow that the pine branches scraped both sides of the wide-bodied GMC.

"Well, I hope your barbeque works out," I said, hoping to ease the tension between Joe and Janie. "I guess it'll be a little strange without Harv there, won't it?" The silence fairly roared across the front seat, and I looked uneasily at Marle who was staring out his side window.

At last, Joe said, "Harv had quit coming to the meetings a couple months ago, I guess it was. Him and Dean just wasn't seeing eye-to-eye on some things."

"'Some things'?"

Silence again. Then Joe said, "Well, when Dean bought his acreage and..." he slipped a look at his wife, "well, I guess you could say he elected himself president, he reminded all of us, Harv included, of our covenants. Nobody'd much paid attention to them before that, not that many people live out here and go to the meetings, but Dean said our property would lose value if we didn't start enforcing them."

"What covenants, exactly?" I asked.

"Well, now, there were several—"

"More than several!" Janie interrupted. "It was just about every one Harv was breaking, you name it. He was—"

"Well, now," Joe said, giving his wife a warning look. "Mostly just little things. He wasn't supposed to have a clothesline, and Dean told him to take it down. And his fence is higher than what it's supposed to be, and it's too close to the road, and..."

Clothesline? A fence too close to the road? What road? I looked at the narrow path where we were crashing through tree limbs.

"...and you're not supposed to live in trailers here. That was the biggest thing," Janie said.

I wanted to be sure I had this right. "So Dean wanted Harv, who'd been living out here for twenty years or so, to take down his clothesline, move his fence, and get rid of his home?" Harv's anger the day we'd driven through the development was starting to make sense.

"Well, now," Joe said, defensiveness creeping into his voice, "it wasn't just Dean wanting him to move it, it was the whole Association. Dean's just the president."

"With the controlling vote?"

"There's that," Joe said, frowning. "Him and John Crawford, Gerald's daddy."

Gerald's daddy? "So what happened?"

"That's when Dean got to looking at the records," Janie said, suddenly excited, twisting around to the back seat again with the fire of the gossip-monger in her eyes. She shot a nervous glance at Marle, who looked out the window with his neutral mask in place. "He found out that Claire James had just give Harv that lot, a-way back in 1970 or so, in exchange for doing some work for her, and when she went bankrupt, Harv hadn't went down to the county and recorded his title yet, and that made the lot technically a part of the bankruptcy proceeds, and them's the ones Dean had been buying up, all them back-tax lots that was lost a-way back then, so he was claiming title—"

"Janie!!" Joe glared at his wife as we broke through to a clearing and pulled up beside Harv's yellow Jeep.

The dwelling in front of us was a makeshift building composed of rough, unpainted plywood spliced onto a battered trailer. A stream ran along a bluff above where someone had arranged several small boulders together in such a way as to divert a rivulet of the water, creating a miniature waterfall and a subsidiary stream that collected into a small pond near the house.

"Tsk, tsk," clucked Janie Gillman, who was looking out her window into the surface of the pond where several water lilies floated. It was a lovely, sequestered surprise of a place. The splash of the tiny waterfall was as musical as flutes, and in spite of the rough dwelling nearby, the place felt as though fairies and water nymphs might dance beside the pond and among the rocks positioned around it. Janie opened her door, speaking to no one in particular: "...such a pretty place, but you know, it's just not fair to the rest of us, damming up this stream that belongs to all of us and—"

"Janie!" Joe Gillman banged his door shut and rounded to the passenger side where his wife stood mumbling over the water lilies. He had his hands on his hips, glowering at her as the sheriff and I joined them. Facing her husband, Janie opened her mouth, and then her face crumbled. "That water," he continued, "all gets to where it's going, and I want you to hush up about it." Janie wrung her hands and tears gathered in her eyes.

A sound turned us around. A woman, much younger than I expected Harv's wife to be, stood in the open doorway of the trailer. She was thin to the point of emaciation, the bones of her face sharply prominent beneath drawn, parchment-colored skin. She had burning dark eyes and straight dark hair that curved in at the chin, and she wore gathered khaki slacks and a long-sleeved khaki work shirt knotted at the waist. One hand lay across her breast holding several red, long-stemmed paper flowers.

"Edna," Janie said, moving around her husband and toward the trailer, her voice trembling, "could I come in for just a minute, dear?"

The woman closed the door firmly behind her and stepped toward us. The hand with the roses fell to her side, and she stood looking down from the height of her shabby, crooked porch. She studied each one of us separately while the water trickled across the late October air, and when her dark, sad eyes reached mine, I could tell that somehow she already knew.

Her eyes came at last to rest on Marle, and something seemed to flicker behind them for a moment. "Ah, you've come. Sheriff Winslow." She spoke in a slow, musical voice, almost a whisper. Laying the flowers on the porch, she stepped down the three wooden stairs with the studied grace of an actress. Whether she was a natural or whether she'd been rehearsing, I couldn't tell. She walked to the little pond, and although several wooden benches sat nearby, she lowered herself to the ground next to the water.

"He's dead," she said, her eyes on the lilies. "I've been waiting for you to come. I've been waiting, seems like years, but maybe it's just months or weeks. You lose track of time out here." She picked up a stick and pulled it through the water, watching the ridges fan across the surface, and then she looked up at the sheriff. "I guess you've come to make me move now."

Marle walked over and squatted down next to her. "You all," he said in a low voice with his back to us, "you can go on back to the car, and I'll be there directly."

The sheriff had exactly the right voice for his job, the kind that made people follow directions even when they didn't want to. From inside the car, the three of us sat wordlessly, leaning toward the windshield and watching the backs of Edna Benton and Marle Winslow. When Marle finally slipped into the back seat beside me and Joe Gillman had backed out the driveway, Edna Benton was still sitting beside the stream with her stick.

By the time the Gillmans dropped us out at Marle's Bronco, the sun had set and the sky had turned a dark turquoise in the east. I wasn't an enthusiastic walker during the best of times, and this wasn't even close: I was tired, hungry, and the thought of hoofing it across miles of rough terrain in the dark, even with a full moon, was about as appealing as the Gillman barbeque. I was just on the verge of asking the sheriff for a ride when he read my mind.

"Like to run you home, if you don't mind." He unlocked his door and stood with one foot on the frame. He looked at me across the top of the Bronco, his long fingers dancing on the edge of the door. "Want to talk to you a little more about a few things." He got inside and leaned over to unlock the passenger side.

"You think maybe the mountain lions might get me?" I asked, sliding in. I needed some levity. I figured a little black humor was better than none.

"Wasn't mountain lions I was thinking of." He slammed his door and started up the engine. I looked across the seat at him. In profile, the man was a hawk—the angled forehead, the beak of a nose, the strong chin. "There's some things you need to know about this place, you going to live here." He tipped his head forward toward the window, where the sun had left a bright fire above the peaks. He danced his fingers on the steering wheel.

"Okay, sure," I said, catching the ominous tone. I directed him out of the development and down the asphalt road toward my driveway. Harv's left-handed approach through the rear of El Gato was more picturesque for a prospective real estate sale, but the actual driveway to the place intersected with the county blacktop. It also had the virtue of placing me at a remove from El Gato and its happy clan.

"By the way," he said, fishing with his right hand back behind the seat. "You say you couldn't make out what Harv was yelling when he drove past you today?" He brought the sack from the grader into the front seat and set it between us.

"No." I looked at the bag. "What's that?"

"Did he sound like he was yelling because he was mad? Or could the grader have been out of control and he was yelling for help?"

I thought for a minute, running my last glimpse of Harv back through my mind. But I had been too far away. He could have been ranting and yelling "Geronimo," as Brandenberg said, or he could have been screaming for help.

"No way to tell, but if the grader was out of control, are you thinking that Edna Benton might have a case against the development?" I pointed out my driveway just ahead, and he turned into it. We snaked around through rocky juniper terrain in the gathering twilight.

"Not thinking about Miz Benton at all," he said evenly. He fished in the paper bag and held up a handful of papers. "Receipts, odds and ends." He stuffed them back in the bag. "On one of them, shows Harv bought some parts to do some brake work just last month. If he lost his brakes, could be he didn't know much about fixing them to start with."

We had left the junipers behind and begun to climb up into the pine forest where the shadows were deep and the evening had fallen. I waited for him to continue his line of thought, but he didn't.

"So …?" I prodded.

But at that moment we pulled up in front of my new home, and I was probably as impressed as Marle at the sight of it. He switched off the engine, and we stared at the refurbished house in the dusky evening light. He whistled.

"Hey," he said, getting out. He shut his door and stood in front of the Bronco with his hands on his hips. "Never would have believed it could look this good."

It was a spectacular sight—the huge windows, the restored balconies and decks and dormers, the scrolling steps and wraparound porch. The fresh aspen-colored paint with the darker trim, the contrasting accents of magenta and lavender. I came to stand beside him, and I inhaled the night air, smelling pine and earth and the high freedom of the mountains. Along the eastern ridge, the sky was a deep indigo. Suddenly I heard what he had said. "You've been here before?"

He pulled his eyes away from the house where lights shone dimly inside and looked out toward the meadow for a long moment, as though he were searching for something among the trees and shadows. "Yes, ma'am," he said, an edge to his voice. "I been here before. You didn't know that?" He turned to me in the evening light, probing with his intense gray eyes. The butterfly slowly brought its wings up to prayer position.

"Well, no." I moved away, down the walk and toward the porch, which had been recently stained and varnished. It gleamed softly in the yellow light beside the door. I climbed the porch stairs, paused before the glass entry doors. The sheriff walked up beside me, and I turned to him. "Are you a friend of Gerald's? Or Wendy's?" I could see Wendy hanging all over this guy, even if he were old enough to be her father.

"I know Wendy and Gerald," he said. Carefully. The iron control was back. "And what I was getting at in the car, about the brakes, was that Harv might have been pretty good at fixing brakes." He reached for the doorknob, turned it. "In which case," he said, pushing the door open and standing aside in the way gentlemen must have done in the generation before mine, "could be somebody messed with the lines."

I stood in the open door, not seeing the floor of the room that had been raw and rough this morning. Not seeing the room at all, but looking instead at the sheriff, and then out at the darkness descending around the house. I shivered and went inside.

Tony and the crew had gone, but not without a thoughtful farewell gesture—the entire lower floor of the house glowed with newly polished oak floors surrounding the freestanding, circular fireplace in the center of the room where the old potbellied stove had once been. The flames of a low fire crackled, and propped against a dim reading lamp was a note.

"Dinner's in the oven. 425 for 1 hr, 15 min. For two—just in case. Tony." I smiled and looked up to where Marle waited beside the door.

"My contractor," I said, holding up the note and then dropping it back on the table. "And a prophet, too," I added under my breath. I waved the sheriff toward the kitchen where I checked the oven: two Cornish hens and several side dishes. I set the time and temperature, and surveyed the refrigerator.

"Drink?" I asked.

Marle sat on a stool at the wraparound bar that separated the kitchen from the rest of the room. He crossed his arms on the counter, raised a shoulder. "Sure. Whatever you're having."

I put the kettle on for tea, trying to shut out what Marle had said at the front door, filling in the empty air with anything but that, with talk of Tony, of my need to have the house to myself, my plans to do the remaining work. I chattered and poured the tea and wiped at the counter and arranged napkins and spoons and honey and finally I stopped and took a deep breath. Marle hadn't said a word, merely sat with the tea between his hands, watching me over the rim of the cup.

What the hell. I switched off the glaring overhead kitchen light and the lamp in the living room so that the house was dark, lit only by the moon's face beaming through the tall windows. I took the stool beside the sheriff and leaned back against the counter, watching the night grow light.

"About the brakes," he said, turning on his stool to face the moonrise, "I'm just speculating. Only mention it to you because if there's any chance at all it wasn't an accident, or malicious suicide if you believe Brandenberg, I want you to know it. Anybody who was after Harv..." He paused, stared into the tea.

"What?" I asked.

"Well, there's some hard feelings about you buying this property. Brandenberg's had his eye set on it for a long time. I guess he thought hooking up with the Crawfords would give him an inside on it, might even have thought to pick it up himself one day."

I waited.

He shook his head. "Long story. Brandenberg and Gerald, they're pretty thick. Don't think I want to know much more than that about it. When Dean found out you bought this place, especially after Gerald told him Claire James as much as promised it to him, he was right upset. I suspect he figured it was Harv that turned you on to it, just to spite him." The sheriff paused and took a sip of the tea, then grimaced as though he'd drunk lye. "Jesus Christ! What the hell is this?"

"Goldenseal," I said. "Want something else?"

"Anything else."

I went to the refrigerator and pulled out a bottle of cabernet that Tony had left behind. I poured a glass and handed it to him. The moonlight came in through the living room windows and into the kitchen where I stood.

"So there's a lot of strong feelings circulating over next door," he said, sipping the wine. "I don't know just why anybody might want Harv out of the picture. I don't see that Brandenberg, no matter how mad he was, had anything to gain by it. He wanted that piece of land Harv had, but it was just one lot. Not enough to kill somebody over when you already got the majority vote sewed up. Not knowing why somebody might have done Harv in, and some folks over there kind of pair you and Harv up together, thinking he set you on to this place, it's my thought that you ought to be careful, that's all. Lock your doors; folks out here don't do much of that. I don't mean to scare you, just take ordinary precautions. That's all I'm saying."

I stared at him. "I don't think it is."

He took another sip of wine and set the glass back on the bar. He seemed to be watching me, but I couldn't tell for sure, because the moonlight from the window behind him slanted into the room and cast him in black silhouette. "There's a few more things, now you mention it. You asked me if I been here before, Miss Symkin?"

"Sym. Just call me Sym."

I didn't like the ominous tone in the sheriff's voice. I thought of a hundred ways to keep him from saying whatever it was he was going to say next. I could ask him about Edna Benton, or why

Harv's house wasn't on the El Gato map, or why Dean Brandenberg thought Gerald would have sold him this hundred acres of property.

"I kind of figured you might not have got the whole story from Harv or Claire James before you bought the place."

"It's haunted, right? The Cat Man?" Levity. I needed pounds, tons of levity.

"Well, I wouldn't rule it out." He grinned, and I relaxed a little. "But that's not what I'm here to tell you." He stared out the kitchen window to the west where the moonlight filtered through the trees in bright shapes.

"September '95." The sheriff stood up and walked around the bar, around where I stood leaning against it. He went to the kitchen window, his back to me and his thumbs hooked in his Levi pockets. From the window, the far end of the meadow could be seen, where the moon lit the silhouette of the barn. "You know Wendy and Gerald lived here, that Wendy is Claire James's granddaughter?"

"Yes," I said. The fire popped behind us. In the lower branch of a pine tree outside the window, I saw the hunched figure of a cat, the triangles of its ears caught in the moonlight, its eyes glowing. Then I saw another on a branch above. And another.

"And Wendy's mother, Camilla?" Marle said. Countless pairs of eyes glowed through the window.

"Camilla? No, I..." He turned to me, his gray eyes on mine, touching something that set the wings beating wildly against the wall of my chest.

"September, two years ago. In the loft of your barn there. That's where she was found hanging."

9

OCTOBER 17, 1997

Morgan

October is the moon's brightest month. The faintest glow begins to burn the eastern darkness, backlighting the mountains.

I should have resisted all this silver moon pull. Those who are truly alone, we can resist anything; it is the price of freedom. I could have drawn the curtains and bolted the door and stood with my shoulders pressed back against it. I could have listened to the crash of Wagner through the house, forgotten that the moon was mounting the sky. Or I could have acquiesced another way, so many ways: lain naked across my bed, opening myself to her. But some weakness stabs me, this damnable all-pervading inexhaustible bone-crushing boredom more lethal than any blade. It will be the end of me one day.

I lead the horse from the paddock. He is eager: tossing his head, rolling his eyes toward the east. I fasten his lead rope to the post, lay my head against his neck, breathe him in. He becomes still, so like the great stillness of the forest tonight. Its infinitesimal variations of black on black. Excepting now the glow that is still little more than mere intention.

I position the saddle across the horse's back. I fasten the girth, eye the brightening sky. I fit the bridle over the horse's head just as the great curve of moon, orange and full and huge as a continent, swells above the peaks. I place my boot in the stirrup, ease myself onto the horse's back.

At the moon's coming, any scientist will tell you that the oceans rise up. Blood pounds and crashes against its vessels. Wolves howl and docile secretaries and submissive wives sharpen their nails and watch the hands of the clock grow erect; red-eyed men leave home to hide in the streets and alleyways.

The horse plunges sideways as we enter the road and turn east, toward the moon's immense face, gold and obese as she slips clear of the mountains and waits at the road's end. The horse surges beneath me, fighting the bit and eager for speed. His hooves strike the road, a volley of noise, ricocheting among the trees.

The moon shatters the night with her silver, lies across the road ahead. The overhanging pine branches appear serrated, crystal glazed. Their shadows fall like shrapnel across the road. The horse and I begin to move through quick blades of silver and darkness, a strobe light quickening as the horse gathers speed.

I lean forward in the saddle, moving with the rhythm of the horse's neck. Ahead, the moon pales, climbs higher, grins above the trees as we move toward her, toward the clearing and the barn. Toward the house and the Symkin woman: even this afternoon as I drove past the Brandenberg house where the sheriff's vehicle sat parked along the road, even then I could feel the pull of her leaning against the tree. The pull of the moon. Some familiar unnameable presence. I would know it anywhere.

It is best to avoid these lunar types if you are in hiding.

I relax the reins, and the horse surges. His hooves pound the earth, perhaps remembering in his blood some ancient track, some foreign drum. It is the moon that churns him, the moon that charms him, reminds him. Reminds me, as well, of racetracks and my youth and the foreign soil which followed. Of another life. He is an animal, a slave to his blood memories.

As I am not.

The moon has taken to the higher sky, out of reach. We slow, turn north, and follow a steep rocky road and then a narrow path to the meadow. A familiar route. A light glimmers through the trees—the Symkin woman's house. I have come here many times in the darkness, visiting the barn. It is a pulling place, this land.

I stop the horse in the clearing. The aspen leaves quake with silver. The barn is the color of ash. It looms huge and pale, a haven for lost souls. If I entered, climbed to the loft, I would see her there. Swinging.

The barn doors are spread wide. Cat shapes slip into the moonlight and then dissolve inside the shadows. There are so many they weave like ribbons through the night, in the branches of the trees, across the meadow and through the grasses and among the tangle of undergrowth, emerging and dissolving.

I ride the horse along the stream, its surface moon-rippled. We wind through trees until the house comes fully into view.

Parked in the driveway is the sheriff's Bronco.

The tingling begins in my toes as I dismount, tie the horse to a branch; it creeps up my legs, my spine and neck, as I approach the lit windows.

I am no longer bored.

10

"...WHERE SHE WAS FOUND HANGING."

The sheriff's words circled around the high, open room. He stood leaning back against the kitchen cabinets, his features muted in the dim light. In the windows behind him, the moonlight streaked through the trees where I imagined menacing figures skulking outside, hiding in the shadows. But, as I stared into the night, I noticed with surprise that the countless sets of glowing eyes watching from the tree branches minutes earlier had vanished. I shook my head, trying to dispel the ominous feeling that the sheriff's words had triggered. No luck.

I slipped off my stool and switched on the overhead lights in the kitchen, but the fluorescent glare turned the windows into black, opaque mirrors where I confronted my own image—a tall woman with wild, waist-length hair and large, frightened eyes. I switched off the lights, took the wine from the refrigerator, and filled a glass for myself. When I glanced at Marle, a sharp stab of inexplicable anger hit me, and I banged the wine bottle on the counter in front of him. In the living room, I sank into a chair before the fireplace and stared at the dying coals.

"So she didn't tell you," Marle said. He had refilled his glass and followed me into the room where he knelt before the fire, poking at the ashes. From a box of kindling, he arranged a pyramid of sticks over the embers, added pieces of freshly split piñon, and squatting on his heels, blew till small flames began to lick the wood. He twisted around toward me as the fire crackled behind him. "Well," he said finally, his voice soft, as though he were speaking to a frightened child, "I don't reckon there's any particular reason why she needed to."

I hugged myself, shivering, and leaned toward the flames. Toward him. His face was so close to mine I could see the network of fine lines around his eyes. The faint odor of a man's sweat and freshly cut wood.

"No, I suppose not. But you felt like *you* needed to tell me. Why?"

His arms were balanced on his knees, his hands hanging between them. Large hands, long-boned and tan. I remembered the way they'd touched Janie Gillman. He turned back to the fire and patted the space on the floor beside him. I slipped from my chair, and we sat with our shoulders touching, watching the flames as they sent shadows flickering through the room. I thought he'd forgotten my question, but finally he spoke.

"One reason, I'd want to know if something like that happened in a place I was living. Especially a new place. Seems like you got a right to know that as much as you got a right to know where your property lines are. Thing is, there's no law requiring that kind of information."

I had suspected that Claire James was relieved to be rid of her property. Of course she was—her daughter had died here, and her granddaughter's husband had abandoned her here for another woman. Yet there was more to it than this, and Marle was working up to it. One part of me wanted to stop him, show him the door, lock it against all the sinister spirits I felt collecting in the darkness surrounding the house. Do exactly what Garbo would have done, which was get in my new truck and head for the next continent. Yet it was that other irrepressibly curious part of me who asked the questions before I could stop them:

"I don't get it. Why was Camilla living here to start with? What was she doing in the barn when this house is as big as a hotel?" I gestured toward the ceiling, the rooms above us. Eleven bedrooms, not counting the third story. "And why...why did she kill herself?"

"That's part of what I wanted to talk to you about," he said. He peeled a long splinter from a piece of wood and held it in the fire. When he drew it out, a tiny flame burned at the end. He watched it with such intense concentration as the fire ate slowly toward his hand, leaving behind a glowing skeleton. It was just the kind of thing Daniel would have done, but Daniel would not have tossed the end of it back into the fire as Marle Winslow did. Daniel would have held it and felt the fire eat into his flesh.

A buzzer sounded in the kitchen, and I jumped. I pushed myself up, switched on the reading lamp, looked down at where the man sat staring into the fire.

"I haven't had a bite all day," I said, "and I vote that we eat while we talk. Think you can stand it?"

While I filled our plates, Marle carried wine, tea, and silverware to our chairs by the fire. We settled in over the food, and he began to describe Camilla. He told a good story. I could picture his office door flying open that April day two years ago as a distraught, green-eyed woman burst through it. Were her eyes really green enough to "direct the flow of traffic"? Did her wavy black hair really "shine like sun on silk"? Well, as I watched Marle relive the past, I knew that for him they did. Camilla might be dead to the rest of the world, but this man was still carrying her around with him, living and breathing and still running through that door.

She had rushed into the office where Marle was working the Denver *Post* crossword puzzle while his young deputy read the sports section. Even on the high side of forty, he said, she seemed much younger, not because of cosmetic surgery or makeup or clothes, or any deliberation on her part, but because, as he explained it, she had a "congenital case of naïveté in the face of all experience and evidence to the contrary." At which phrase I nearly choked on a mouthful of wild rice, wondering if the sheriff were practicing for the kind of professorial job I used to have. I could have told him he'd find barroom brawls and dodging bullets more pleasant work, but I listened instead as he followed Camilla out to her old beat-up '53 Plymouth. On its front seat was a box of kittens, apparently orphaned as a result of Gerald's fondness for using the feral cats for target practice.

"Old car didn't look much like it was going to get her back home, much less fifty miles to Aspen and the nearest animal shelter, so it being a slow day, I drove her and the kittens on up there myself. She petted them, chattered at them and me like a teenager geared up for the prom. That was the thing about Camilla, like a kid, always excited about one thing or another." He stood up, took our empty plates to the kitchen, came back with two cups of coffee. He settled into his chair and stretched his long legs toward the fire, leaned back watching the flames. From the expression in his eyes, I didn't think it was the fire he saw, though.

"She'd believe just about anything anybody told her, that's the way she was. The guys selling all that Arizona oceanfront property, they love to run across someone like Camilla. I guess you could say that made her an easy victim, but she didn't seem to have suffered much from of it. Just the other way around. Didn't seem to be anything could stop her when she got a notion in her head. Like coming out here in the middle of nowhere—she talked like she'd just arrived in Paradise, fixing that barn loft up, dragging old furniture from the dump and refinishing it. Found that old Oriental rug and liked to have made it new again." Marle smiled as he talked.

"You must have known her pretty well."

Marle was not a man to be rushed: he studied the flames for awhile. "If I hadn't known her as well as I did, I wouldn't have the questions I do about how she died."

"I thought you said …are you saying you don't believe she committed suicide? That someone …?" My ears were ringing, and my thoughts scattered in all directions. The doors to the house were unlocked, downstairs and up. *Weren't they?* Harv had been alive this morning, and the sheriff had looked under the grader and found something to suggest that the wreck was no accident. Tony and the crew were gone, and when the sheriff left tonight, I'd be in this house alone. For the first time. I put down my coffee and sat on the edge of my chair.

"Are you telling me you think Camilla was murdered?"

He got up and stood with his back to the fire, his hands clasped behind him and his gray eyes looking out across the room. His Levi jacket hung over the back of the chair, and the blue work shirt with the top two buttons open was not as crisp as it had been a few hours ago.

"I'm telling you suicide doesn't quite add up for me, and I'm trying to tell you why." His eyes went from abstracted to laser-beam, and he turned them on me. "I don't have one single shred of physical evidence to officially call it anything but suicide. I want you to remember that. Could be I'm too involved here to be as objective about it as I ought to be. But whether that's the case or not, I haven't been able to convince myself there wasn't more to it. That being so, I believe it's my duty, as a fellow human being if not as a sheriff, to let you know this because you're living here."

"Okay, but I'm still not following. What is it that makes you think she didn't kill herself?"

"This. September third, it was a Sunday night that Wendy had noticed no lights over at the barn, went over to check on her mother and found her dead. The day before, Saturday afternoon, I'd been there to see Camilla. She'd decided to move back to Nashville a week or so before that, and I'd come by to ask her again to stay. When I left that night, she was still planning to leave the next day, Sunday. Turned out she hadn't told anybody else about leaving, just me. Gerald or Wendy didn't know. Called Claire in Nashville, she didn't know either."

"Why would she tell you and no one else?"

Marle was silent for a while, back to the abstracted gaze across the room. "I was leaving my wife for her, trying to. Guess it wasn't happening fast enough for Camilla. Said she'd be in Nashville when I was ready, nothing I could say would change her mind about leaving that next day."

"I still don't get it. Why did she want to leave? I thought you said she loved it here."

Marle shoved his hands in his pockets, looked down at where I sat. He shook his head and shrugged. "Same questions I asked her. All I could get out of her was that she needed to get back to the city for a while, said being so far out in the sticks was getting to her."

"But you didn't believe her?"

"I'd never heard her say a good word about any city, Nashville in particular, before that. Never struck me just right, I guess, but that's all the answer I ever got."

"Maybe she missed her mother, or maybe her friends in Nashville?"

"Not likely," he said, shaking his head. "Never mentioned Claire all the time she was here, or anybody else in Nashville, either."

I paused, then asked it: "Maybe she had some health problem? Maybe...could she have been pregnant?"

A sad smile flitted across his lips. "Pregnant? I can say for a fact that she wasn't. She'd been having some female trouble, made making love painful so we didn't. Asked me once for the name of a woman doctor, wanted to get hormone supplements for menopause."

I bristled. "People, especially men, seem to think menopause is a joke, but I can tell you that many women, and this is no exaggeration, experience deep, even suicidal depressions, Sheriff."

"I hear what you're saying, and she'd seemed a little down for a few weeks, kind of quiet when I'd come by. Could be, she really did need to go to the city for a while, or somewhere. But I think I'd have known if she'd been so far into a depression that she was suicidal."

"Maybe, but I wouldn't rule out the possibility," I said, crossing my arms. "And I still don't understand why she had come to visit her daughter and grandchildren in a house this size and was living in the *barn*? Isn't that a little strange?"

Marle chuckled. "You say you stopped by Wendy's place that day you saw Harv? Well, Camilla and Wendy, they weren't a whole lot alike. I mean, beside the fact that she was dark and didn't look much like Wendy or Claire, Camilla was so neat she couldn't walk across the road without stopping to wipe the dust off her shoes. 'Compulsive' wouldn't be too far off, I reckon. She probably liked the barn a whole lot better than trying to navigate through Wendy's house."

I sat for a moment trying to assess the information. "So you have a...'feeling' that Camilla might not have committed suicide, is that right? No evidence of a struggle, nothing unusual when you found her?"

"Nope. Even went over the place for fingerprints, off the record. Without something to go on, it wouldn't have done any good to tell everybody in the county about me and Camilla, about her plans to leave. All I could do was ask questions unofficially, but I didn't come up with anything."

"Nobody over at El Gato she was having trouble with? Those people seem pretty intense."

The sheriff's gray eyes were the kind that lit up and got crinkly lines around the outside when he was amused. I recalled his inspection of the grader Harv had been riding, and I felt myself blushing. "I'm a pretty thorough man. I talked to all the folks around here about her without letting on why I was doing it. She liked to stay pretty much to herself, wasn't involved in all that feuding they do next door. What folks she knew over there liked her well enough. Was Harv fixed up his old Plymouth for her to get around in. And while she was Claire James' daughter, it was Gerald and Wendy in line to get this property before you stepped in."

"You said she loved it here, she didn't feel any resentment at being passed over?"

"Never mentioned it to me if she did. Didn't have much interest in owning things, and I figure Claire had more real estate than just this place to pass on to her. Claire James is not the kind of woman going to let anybody change her mind once she makes it up. Had some deal with Gerald and Wendy when they came out here—if Gerald would build and make their home here, it's be his and Wendy's."

"And then she sold it to me?"

"It's no secret, Gerald wasn't happy about it when he found out. I guess he figured even with Wendy and him separated, Claire wouldn't just turn around and sell it. The way Gerald sees it, he was just taking a little detour, don't think he ever meant to stay with Willa any length of time. Might just have needed a little rest from Wendy and the kids, you know?" Marle grinned and raised his eyebrows. "But when his daddy heard about it, told Wendy and the kids they could live in that A-frame, Gerald hadn't figured on that. I believe he thought Harv'd probably come on out here and check on them, make sure they had enough wood, groceries, like he used to do with Camilla, that's if Gerald thought about it at all."

"Sounds like a real nice guy, this Gerald," I said. "He shoots cats for sport, takes off with another woman and expects his wife to stick around till he comes back. Sounds like he ought to be locked up, or at least run off."

"Lots of folks wouldn't give you an argument about that. But Gerald's right persuasive when he wants to be. Not as easy to write off as you might think."

"So he's still around here? Wendy said he was living in a trailer with some woman...Willa?"

"Yep, more or less. Been hanging out with Brandenberg and that bunch lately. You saw him today at the scene."

I thought back over all the men I'd seen there, and none of them seemed to fit. I looked at the sheriff and shook my head.

"He was up there on the porch standing by Dean, thin fellow, blond hair?"

That was *Gerald?* I'd taken him for Brandenberg's son in his expensive leather riding boots and flowing silk shirt. I remembered his eerie, almost angelic good looks, how absolutely still he had been, the faint smile as he watched the sheriff. Well, what had I expected, Stanley Kowalski, belching and popping beer cans in a torn T-shirt and ragged jeans? In fact, I realized, that *was* what I had expected. I tried to imagine that immaculate figure sitting on the soiled couch in Wendy's living room and drew a blank.

"But I thought he was a friend of Harv's," I said. "He didn't seem too interested that the man was lying dead in the yard right in front of him."

"Well, like I said, Gerald was none too happy about you buying what he thought of as *his* property. My guess is Brandenberg had convinced him it was Harv contacted Claire James about selling you that place, Harv knowing Dean had some kind of dibs on it, and it would be Harv's way of getting back at Dean for trying to take his home. Dean wouldn't even let Janie Gillman draw in Harv's house on the El Gato map, said it would weaken his lawsuit claiming ownership of Harv's piece of land. It's not been a real peaceful place to live out here lately."

That explained why I couldn't find Harv's house on the map this morning, but all that seemed very far away now. Suddenly a loud shrieking cut through the air, another cat fight.

"Sounds like you got a granddaddy of a cat problem out there," Marle said.

I closed my eyes and waited till it passed, hating the sound of it. The sound of conflict, and it went beyond the confines of my property lines.

"This Gerald, do you think he could be involved in Harv's death?" I asked, realizing that if the sheriff were right, if someone had deliberately killed Camilla and made it look like suicide, her death and Harv's might be connected.

"He's a little weird around the edges, I'll grant you, but a killer? I don't see anything in him shows he could work himself up to kill much besides a few cats, some deer and elk maybe, things that can't shoot back or get him put in jail." He rummaged through the wood box, lifted out a large unsplit log, knelt and arranged it carefully on top of the burning logs, talking as he worked. "Him and Camilla, I think they just stayed out of each other's way. Maybe he was worried she might try to talk Claire into giving her a piece of the land out here, but I doubt it. She sure didn't like him shooting those cats, though. But, much of a rascal as Gerald can be, I can't see him hanging anybody. No, Gerald's more the type had rather have something alive to aggravate than dead where he can't get to it," he said, brushing his hands together and sitting back on his heels.

I remembered Gerald standing on the Brandenberg porch, watching the sheriff with the strange smile playing around his lips, and I felt a chill and leaned toward the fire, just as Marle was turning to me.

We were so close I could feel the warmth of his face from the fire, the smell of wood smoke, and beneath that the other, the male scent. His eyes, which had been gray before, were dilated, and I wondered if he had set off that same fluttering in Camilla's breast that he was setting off in mine. And his wife, had she felt it, too, maybe still felt it? His wife...I looked away, leaned back in my chair.

The sheriff watched me for a moment, then put his hands on his knees and pushed himself up.

"I didn't come out here to scare you. I just wanted to give you some facts about your property, ask you to take ordinary precautions. Lock your doors and windows, no sense inviting trouble." He lifted his coat from the back of the chair, began putting it on and walking toward the door. I got up and followed. "I'm having somebody come out and look at that grader, run some tests, and soon as I hear, I'll let you know if there's anything more here than an accident."

He opened the door and stood on the porch beneath the entry light, which shone dimly. His eyes had gone abstracted again, looking out across the interplay of moonlight and shadows toward the barn. He seemed to be considering something, debating with himself.

"If I was to be a hundred percent honest with you, I guess I'd have to admit to another reason for coming out here. Outside of my wife, who's gone now anyway and it's just as well, you're the only one knows about me and Camilla." He turned under the yellow light, his eyes in laser mode with enough force behind them that I nearly stepped back. "I'm going to ask, if you come across anything that might explain her death, to let me know. Even if it's something you think I won't want to hear. Would you be willing to do that?"

"I don't expect to have much contact with the people over at El Gato," I said, looking up at him, "but if I come across anything, I'll get in touch." I paused and nodded. "Even if it's something you don't want to hear."

In the distance, an owl called out, and then there was silence. The silver along his temples picked up the yellow light, and he seemed to lean closer, his lips moving slightly as though he were on the verge of saying something, but then the same look that I had seen as he watched the flame eating toward his hand returned to his eyes. He fastened the bottom button of his jacket, turned up the collar, nodded.

"I'd appreciate your keeping what I told you tonight just between us," he said.

The words struck a familiar note, a moment of *déjà vu*, until I located where I'd heard similar ones: Harv, sitting in my Porsche under Wendy's yellow porch light, asking me not to mention that he'd shown me Claire James's property. But someone had found out, and now Harv was dead.

Before I had a chance to mention this to Marle, he was trotting down the stairs, backing down my driveway, his headlights cutting across the black shadows beneath the trees.

11

A S THE SHERIFF'S HEADLIGHTS swept through the trees, for
a split second, I imagined I saw a figure on a horse.

It had been a long, grueling day; I'm no stranger to the tricks
tired eyes can play. Who hasn't walked across a room and seen an
enormous spider hunched on a table, looked again to find an ashtray or hairbrush or smattering of writing pens. Or passed a window, gray with falling rain, and seen a hunched old woman peeping
in, looked back to see the thorny tangle of a dormant rosebush. I
stared at the dark trees where the figure had been, waiting for my
eyes to adjust after the Bronco's glare, waiting for the darkness to
resolve itself into the familiar slouch of a juniper or gnarled piñon
wedged among the pines.

A horse stepped out of the shadows. It was jet black with a profuse mane, tossing its head and jangling its bit. As it trotted toward
me, I understood how in another time the myth of the centaur
must have evolved—like the horse, the rider too was black:
dressed, gloved, and booted, with dark hair and eyes. As she
neared, I saw that it was the same woman who had stopped this
afternoon at the accident. Without the concealing glasses, and
mounted on the horse as it stopped at the porch beneath the yellow light, I saw that she was perhaps the most beautiful woman I
had ever seen.

She sat very straight, her shoulders back and her long neck
wrapped in a black turtleneck. Same full pale lips and wide jawline, but without the glasses, her cheekbones lent an exotic, Asian
cast to her eyes. Above them, her brows were dark wings across a

wide forehead. She sat very still, though a shadow of movement played at the corners of her lips.

"Sorry to barge in," she said. "Eva Blake. I met you this afternoon?"

The husky voice seemed more at home under the moon than it had in the Brandenberg yard. She held the reins low, one in each hand, and pointed at the house with her chin. "I'm afraid I totally forgot someone lives here now. I was riding by and saw the lights, saw you standing on the porch. Thought I'd better come over and say hello, even at this hour, rather than ride off and let you think the woods were filled with spooks or something." She stared at me intensely, as though I had two heads or a third eye. "I'm terribly sorry if I've frightened you."

I realized I was gripping the column beside the stairs with one hand, holding the other over my heart. I shoved my hands in my pockets. The anger I'd felt earlier with the sheriff had surfaced again.

"You always ride around in the middle of the night?"

"I do when the moon's full," she said, "but if I'd been thinking, I'd have asked you first before I rode across your property. Thoughtless of me. I'm terribly sorry."

I didn't know much about horses, but this one seemed to have a problem. It was dancing around in one place like the ground was too hot to stand on, shaking its head, chewing on its bit and tossing flecks of foam in the air.

"I don't really mind," I said, feeling exhaustion wash over me, "it's just been a long day. The accident and all."

"It's too bad, I liked Harv."

"Did you know him very well?"

I remembered Harv had been riveted by her as we'd passed her house the day of my visit, had called Eva Blake a "looker," and he had been right about that. I wondered if her husband had wound up his business in Hollywood and joined her yet. According to Harv, no way.

She grinned sideways and cocked her head. "I knew him well enough," she answered, with the odd flicker of movement around the mouth, the intense look. "Could I bother you for a glass of water? I'm afraid I came off without the canteen I usually bring."

The horse snorted and suddenly plunged sideways. She was riding in an English saddle, no pommel to hang on to, but she sat the horse as though she were a part of him. She angled the animal back in front of the porch where she stood up in the high, iron stirrups and rolled her head first to one side and then the other. She wore skin-tight black pants and knee-high black riding boots, but she carried no crop.

"Would you like to come in?" The words sprang out of my mouth like Hitchcock birds. Shit! I was beat, desperate for a hot shower and bed. But there it was, and she was dismounting. She bounced to the ground and wrapped the reins around the banister. I watched her, then switched to watching the horse and the banister.

"Not to worry," she said, climbing the stairs. "He's eager to be off back home, this is the point where we usually turn back, but once he's tied, he's a lamb."

Sure enough, the horse was standing quietly, his head lowered and his eyes half-closed. "What's his name?" I asked.

She raised a shoulder, looked down the long veranda where the entry light glowed softly on the new planks. "Hard to believe this is the same place."

Inside, she downed a full glass of water, then accepted my offer of tea, removing her gloves and warming herself by the fire as I set the kettle on.

"Nice place," she said, looking around. "I've never been inside here, always looked interesting when I rode by. I stuck my head in once, but it smelled to high heaven. Cats, wasn't it?"

"Big time. Using it for a dumping ground," I said. "My contractor scraped for days on this place. The whole crew had to work in masks, at least that was the report I got. I just arrived a few days ago, my first night alone here, in fact."

When I came in with the tea, she was sitting in Marle's chair with her long legs stretched like his toward the fire, elbows propped on the chair arms.

"Thanks," she said, taking the cup in both hands. "Thought I saw somebody pulling out as I rode up."

"Sheriff Winslow," I said. I sat down and leaned my head back against the chair. "Wanted to talk to me about the accident. I was watching when Harv crashed into that house."

"You saw it?" Her voice was sharp, her dark brows pulled together.

"I think the grader might have been out of control, though Mr. Brandenberg has the idea that Harv did it out of personal spite," I said, unable to keep the sarcasm from seeping in.

She laughed, a deep, earthy sound. "Those people need something to keep them busy," she said, and I noticed for the first time a slight southern accent. "All that spare time they have, they use it to see how mad they can make one another. I don't know when I've seen so much meanness to so little end." She scooted further down in the chair, nearly horizontal, her head leaning back at the ceiling.

"That's saying a lot from someone who's been living in Hollywood," I said.

"Word does get around, doesn't it? Probably Harv. He was always going on about how Jack was crazy leaving me out here by myself. Thing is, in L.A. you expect everybody to be meaner than snakes. Out here, it kind of a catches you off guard. I mean, all that Brandenberg racket over an acre of Harv's land? Lawsuits, all that screaming and fighting. You ought to go to the next meeting just for entertainment, though without Harv, I guess they'll have to get somebody else in the crosshairs. Probably Edna." She talked at the ceiling with her eyes closed, but she looked very relaxed with her arms stretched along the chair arms, the cup held loosely in one hand. "I thought Harv took it pretty well, considering that acre's all he had in the world. If I'd been him, I'd have shot the fat sonofabitch." She said it in the same tone she'd used to thank me for the tea.

I know people say such things in semi-serious jest, like doctors relieving tension with their black humor over a bloody, pulsing heart. But there was something sinister about this woman who spoke of murder as she lay in my living room in an alpha state, the steel-hard edge to the words still humming in my ears. I thought of Sandy, my own nemesis, who had in one petty, arrogant gesture annihilated my career, and I wondered what Eva Blake would have done in my place.

But how do you fit a punishment to a crime? Countless nights I'd stared into the darkness above my bed, spinning out one demonic fantasy after another—harvesting deadly nightshade, grinding it, placing it in the shaker of basil she kept beside her stove; collecting black widow spiders, plucking them from their skewed webs with my hand gloved in leather, dropping them into a glass container and tumbling the spindle-legged creatures between the pillows of her bed; tracing the crook of her neck for just the right place to sink a long, needle-sharp canine tooth, feeling the throb of jugular and the prick of the tooth entering it. But at last I'd enter sleep with the more homely, more tactile, and immensely more satisfying feel of her neck bones between my fingers, squeezing tight and hard until I felt them splinter.

I came out of my reverie to find Eva Blake propped on one elbow, her large brown eyes fastened on me with such a penetrating look that she might have been watching my fantasies. And then she smiled, if that's what it was—a slow, sustained, sensual movement of the lips that climbed up one side of her face, climbed impossibly high, until there was no doubt about it: between the devil in her eyes and the in-your-face defiance of that smile, this woman had the kind of Attitude that could get you arrested for just walking down the street.

If I'd been him, I'd have shot the fat sonofabitch.

"You're serious? You'd have killed him?" I asked.

She laughed. "Shot, not killed."

"You're kidding?"

"Probably," she said. "Justice is a tough call. I've got enough money he wouldn't have tried that on me. But Harv? He was taking just about everything Harv had. Not even because he needed it, but because he could and no one was stopping him, even though everybody over there knew it was wrong." She eyed me for a minute, weighing something. "Just for the sake of argument, let's say Harv was still alive, say Brandenberg took his home and left him with nothing, no home, no money to buy another, no pot to piss in. Say he did it legally, so you can mark off the judicial system as far as Harv getting justice. Now if you could mete it out, what would be the appropriate punishment for Brandenberg?"

I stared at her. How many times had I asked this question about Sandy? How many times had I come up blank? I shrugged it off. "You can't fabricate justice for someone, like you'd measure a suit."

"Says who? If the perpetrator can devise all manner of crimes and commit them, why can't we be just as inventive in devising the punishments?"

"That's why we have courts." I was tired, abysmally tired, wanting all those old, angry feelings rising to the surface to settle back down again. Silt at the bottom of a crystal lake.

She laughed. "You're kidding, right? Sure, if all you're after is punishment—and that's not only if you're lucky, but if you can also afford it—we have the judicial system. But even in the best-case scenarios, conviction for a crime and the application of punishment is a standardized process. Like going into Penney's and buying a size ten. What I'm talking about is a custom-fit kind of justice, justice with a brain." She paused and nailed me with her eyes. "True justice is a very intimate affair, exquisitely conceived to fit not only the crime, but the criminal. You want punishment, go to court. You want justice," she said, with the slow, sideways smile, "let's talk."

"So what are you," I said, feeling spooked, "an avenger?"

"Not lately," she said. She stood up and stretched. "Okay. Back to Harv, let's do a little one-on-one. Brandenberg didn't take Harv's life, not physically at least. He didn't inflict any physical pain, didn't shoot him or knife him or rape him. Therefore, imprisoning Brandenberg would be punishment, but it wouldn't be justice. Neither would shooting him, though many people use that method out of frustration or lack of imagination, feeling it's the only means available to them." She put her back to the fire and faced me. "It's not."

"All right." I sat up in my chair. "You're saying measure the punishment exactly to fit the crime, right? So you find some means to work financial ruin on Brandenberg, even to the point of taking his home—"

"Exactly, and diminish his capability of financial recovery. Toss in humiliation before his wife and the community, as well as various and sundry elements to keep him in a constant state of helpless outrage and fury for a couple of years, which will pretty much kick his health in the teeth."

"Sounds fair to me," I said.

"That's right, fair. Thinking of just the right method is where creative thought comes in. But justice can always be had if you're interested enough in having it. And if you've got a brain larger than a pea, you can get away with it."

"So how is it you've given this so much thought?" This wasn't a glib question, I really wanted to know. And I realized that my exhaustion had completely vanished.

Which was a good thing because for the next two hours we traded stories. I walked around in her life, which was a backstage perspective of the Hollywood scene. She'd started off as an ambitious actress, had several years of bit parts and melodramatic relationships, finally ended up marrying a fellow named Jack Blake, a behind-the-scenes mogul who pulled strings sometimes just to watch people jerk. She said he told people he was in the entertainment industry because he liked being entertained.

When my turn came, I took a deep breath and rolled out my own story because she had done it first, done it without hesitation or reservation or apology, and to have responded with any less than equal candor would have set a tone at the beginning of our friendship, if that's what it was, that would infect whatever might follow in the coming months. And so for only the second time in my life, I told the story of my mother's death and my father's disappearance. I told of my husband, Daniel, whom I had met during graduate school, his death by motorcycle accident, if you believed the newspapers and the coroner's report, and the tall shadow cast by a writer of manic genius in the tragic grip of his own self-destructive impulses. His death, more than anything, had been a release from the prison his poems had built around us both—I passed his manuscripts with relief to a long line of scholars and found a patch of light by which to write my own work. And I told Eva Blake about Sandy—a woman whose sad, ruined face was beautiful to me, made so by the grace of our friendship, but which finally could not incite the passion that she herself felt. A woman to whom betrayal came easy, given the naïve trust I placed in her. And finally I described the loss of my career, my disillusionment with my colleagues in particular, and with the human race in general. As my department chair had said, "It doesn't matter if you did it or not, Sym, you are perceived as having done it." And lastly, I told her of my subsequent venture into the realm of high finance, the mountain of money I'd made, not for the satisfaction of physical possession, or security, or whatever other motive impels the accumulation of fortune, but for the simple expedient of escape.

And there I paused. How to confess the bizarre experiment that lay before me? How explain the extinction of one psyche for another? Eva had been listening with her expression of rapt attention, one leg crossed over the other, one elbow on a knee with her chin cupped in her palm.

"So here we are," she said, taking my pause for the end of the story, "the thug's wife and the poet's widow, both in exile, both in high piss." She stood up, walked over to the black windows, looked out with her back to me. "You, still in your rage at that dimbulb, fake friend. Me, knowing that Jack is fucking every skirt in sight, has not an intention in the world of ever coming here."

So Harv had been right, and Eva had known it. "Well, as you said, we could shoot the sonsabitches."

Eva's laugh was deep and throaty and full of Attitude. She stretched again, catlike, leaned with one shoulder against the window frame, speaking to the darkness. "Could, I guess. For my part, they both seem like your ordinary, mundane, minor-league jerks. That kind of hate you're carrying around, you want to save that for something that deserves it—racism, bigotry, atrocities of premeditated cruelty. For Hitler or Attila or maybe Richard Nixon, but Sandy of the pocked face? Jack of the heated gonads?" She gave the laugh again. "Think of all the great poems you could write with that furnace of energy you're lavishing on this cretin who gets off on slipping a knife when you're not looking. Small potatoes, Symkin. Get over it. An expanse of energy for such bovine fare." She strolled to the bookcase in the corner where I kept the videos, television, VCR.

"Garbo fan?" Eva asked.

"She's okay," I said. The hour was late, but that wasn't why I wanted to curl up and sleep.

"Must be more than 'okay.'" She bent toward the shelves, her head sideways, reading the titles on the video boxes. "*Anna Karenina. Ninotchka. Anna Christie. Grand Hotel*...looks like you've got them all." She scanned another shelf. "Biographies, too," she said, looking at me closely as she returned to the fire holding a large-format book. "What, you're a film critic now? Biographer? I don't mean to be nosy, just curious. You mind?" she asked, sitting down and leaning toward me, opening the book.

"Well, I…" I started to push myself out of my chair, the polite hostess's gesture that the evening was over.

"Because Garbo walked around breathing, but she never was alive."

Half-standing, I looked at her in utter stupefaction. "You can't be serious," I said, sitting back down. Eva Blake waited: legs crossed, gorgeous, thin as a spike, sizzling with some kind of electric vitality. I caught drifts of a leathery horse scent, saw some animation like sparks in the depths of her eyes. "Garbo was the most fascinating human being who ever lived."

She opened the book, revealing glossy portraits of the eternal Garbo, drawing her finger across one photo after another—all different, all beautiful. Each with the signature thin-chiseled lips, the slightly oversized nose, the eloquent eyes. "Fascinating. Mysterious. Enigmatic," she read.

"So?" I crossed my arms over my chest.

She looked up from the book, her spine perfectly straight, the book splayed open on her knee. "The thing about such mystery as Garbo generates—it relies on absence," she said. Her voice had changed, not the timbre of it, but the articulation. It had lost the soft curves of the South, replaced by the precise English spoken by those for whom it is not a first language: "The mystery is present in direct proportion to the absence of a self within. It is only in this environment that we can project that which we most need, or perhaps most desire, within our selves. It is illusion, a thing seen, created, and completed within the mind of the beholder. Garbo was a great genius—the consummate Nothing." She snapped shut the book, tossed it on the floor where it landed with a heavy thud. "The human mind cannot, by the nature of its composition, tolerate an absence. It must fill in the emptiness. The way a person perceives Garbo will tell you more of the perceiver than the perceived. And that is why she is so fascinating," Eva said. "An absence always is."

In the dim glow of the lamp between us, the woman's face was a miracle of light and dark, elegant planes so flawlessly arranged that she might have been sculpted. I went over to stand by the window where the moonlight drifted down through the pines and made bright patterns on the porch. Far away, the protracted shriek of an animal was followed by a chorus of laughing coyotes. The branches of trees nearby, where I had expected to find cats, were empty.

"What makes you say she never lived?" I asked.

Eva switched off the lamp, and the moonlight brightened. Her boots made a hollow sound as she walked up behind where I stood looking out the window. I felt the heat of her at my shoulder, the perfume of leather and horse.

"What exactly do you admire about her?"

Her voice was a very deep, throaty whisper, her breath warm on my neck. Before us, on the black window, our reflections stared back, superimposed across the moonlit night. In her boots, she stood exactly my height—two tall, dark-haired, dark-eyed women, one with hair long and flaring, the other precision-cut. She was younger than I, of course, and beautiful, but I noticed with a start a certain resemblance.

"I admire her stillness, her..." Garbo was like an exquisite porcelain vase, meticulously hand-painted, requiring no flowers, no water, nothing at all to fill the absence inside; she was a container complete unto itself. "...autonomy."

"Ah," Eva whispered. "You'd like that? No attachments. No desires or connections to anything or anyone? The world fucks itself or it doesn't. Is that what you want?" Her reflection stared at me, eyes glittering with that strange intensity that seemed to penetrate my thoughts. At my back, at the protruding angle of my shoulder blade, I felt the very slightest touch of her breast. A thought of Sandy flew by, that old distant time when passion seemed an impossible thing. A slight smile began to form at the corner of Eva Blake's lips.

And so I told her then. I turned on the light, went to the corner and pulled the videos off the shelf one by one, explained and demonstrated the nuances of Garbo: the way she moved her head, closed her eyes; the way she held her words and tilted her chin and turned her wrists and pivoted her hips when she walked. Every movement that could be studied, I had studied, practiced, preparing for tomorrow or the day after or the day after, just the right day, to use those gestures so that my own self was gone, annihilated.

When I had finished, I saw by her expression that Eva Blake understood, not just understood, but acknowledged that such a thing could happen. This, more than anything, astonished me: of the two people I'd told, Tony and Margot, the former was utterly mystified, the latter blinded by academic theory. Eva had been leaning with one shoulder against the door frame, her arms folded. We gazed across the room at each other. She stood-stone still, her eyes probing, staring at me for a long time.

Then without speaking, she turned, opened the door, and walked out. By the time I'd followed her outside, she had mounted the horse, and it resumed its mad thrashing and plunging and gnashing of teeth. The night, too, came alive. From the direction of the barn, a piercing scream exploded into the embattled, unmistakable shrieks of a cat fight. And then another wail, another explosion, another fight ensued until I covered my ears to shut out the animal screams that made the night a war zone of squalls and shrieks and blurred shapes racing through the shadows, cats pursuing cats.

Eva bent to the neck of her horse, her lips moving while she stroked its neck. When the horse stood quietly, she sat upright in the saddle and waited till the sounds faded. She looked over to where I stood on the porch.

"You got a problem here, Symkin."

"Sym," I said. "Just call me Sym."

I explained about my bargain with the cats, the barn in exchange for the house, my feeding regimen. "And I know all about the balance I'm upsetting, and I don't want to hear it. I'm not letting those cats starve, and I'm not going to let anyone shoot them, either. So that's the end of it."

She sat looking in the direction of the barn for a moment before speaking: "At this moment, there are injured animals lying out there among the trees, bleeding to death, dying slowly from their wounds—the fittest do survive, and so they should. But the wide-spread notion that the natural order is somehow sacred has its flaws. Not least of all, the inconsistency of the philosophy when applied to the human animal." She turned in the saddle and gave me a long look. "Male cats fight other male cats over available females. The winners, the more aggressive males, will impregnate the females, often violently and without permission. That's nature." She turned back to the barn. "Consider: the human animal, while prizing this approach in other life forms, ironically rejects the application of it to our own species, citing the rational mind as cause for exception. Given the model we promote in other animals, is it surprising that our own culture has become increasingly violent, overrun with murder and rape in epidemic proportions?"

She was talking in that weird, precise way again, but I stopped listening early on. I was back at the beginning, imagining the wounded animals, bleeding and dying in the forest. Eva's words hit me with an impact that Tony's argument hadn't. And it was only going to get worse. I knew that. What I didn't know was what to do about it.

"Lots of things you can do," she continued. "Gerald's method of population control was simple, effective, made for those who find pleasure in killing. It's the logic behind hunting seasons and issuing hunting permits, after all, and if you have the stomach for it, the law allows it. Or you can remove the animals' food; they'll eventually find their own balance again, though quite a few will have to starve to do it. Or you can trap them all, keep the ones you want, and take the others to the SPCA to deal with. Hitler's approach. Or there are feral cat societies who will help you trap them, neuter them, give you advice on care-taking them. A good approach, though excessive."

In the nearby trees, I began to make out their shapes again, hunched into the elbows of branches, lurking among the pine fronds. I saw the points of their ears; their flourescent, unblinking eyes; their tails drooping here and there, flicking mildly as though waiting for some decision to be made. I felt the tingle behind my eyes as tears crept up. Eva glanced around at me. Whatever it was behind her own eyes, it wasn't tears that caused them to glisten as though fires burned there. And then the slow, sideways smile spread up her cheek.

"This is an easy one, Symkin," she said, in the dark velvet voice. "No problem is more difficult than you allow it to be: you can keep all your cats, provide them a home, stop the population growth, and end the violence. All with a minimal amount of effort on your part."

I stared at her as she explained the method of capturing only the males in cages, the simple materials required to perform a simple operation that she would teach me, one that would not only solve the reproduction problem, but the aggression one as well. "After all, it's a kind of justice, isn't it? Why penalize the female for the transgressions of the male? I once had a friend, a veterinarian," she said, turning her horse toward the path home, "could do this operation in three minutes flat."

I watched as she rode off. When she reached the place I'd seen her in the sheriff's headlights, she paused and glanced back over her shoulder. Her smile was slow and high, and it carried enough Attitude to change the planet.

"My friend, the vet? She called it the Final Solution."

And then she was gone.

PART III

El Gato

12

I WOKE HOT, lying in a blanket of sun and a tangle of sheets, a few piranhas of anxiety munching around the base of my skull. I lay listening to the birds nattering on the railing. I'd wasted four days of my new life, and the seconds were ticking by fast on this one. I knew Garbo wouldn't have looked more than a couple of seconds at those swearing, sweating dudes with their saws and their boom boxes blasting last Tuesday before turning on her heel and splitting, catching the first flight to Switzerland.

Then I sat up, stock still for a moment, listened hard: silence. No saws, no hammers, not a single anguished twang from Willie or Hank. So I anointed this Day One. I tossed back the covers, leapt out of bed already prioritizing a list of things to do. I pulled on a T-shirt: the crew had finished the caulking, completed the downstairs floor. I grabbed a pair of jeans: I'd start with sanding... I stared at the Levi's I was stepping into. Habit, pure blind habit. I tossed first the jeans, then the T-shirt across the bed. I'd have to do better than this.

I rummaged in the dresser for the new clothes I'd bought before leaving Albuquerque, my Garbo Wardrobe. She liked dowdy stuff, muddy colors. The kind of clothes people I knew dumped at second-hand stores. I'd come as close as I could stand. I dragged a wool plaid shirt and a pair of mustard-colored baggy pants out of the bottom drawer, still with their Land's End tags attached. Jesus. Me, I went for skin-tight denims, boots with a little height to them.

What the hell: you make a habit, you break a habit.

I buttoned the shirt, pulled on the pants, zipped up. Laced on the trainers, grabbed my walking gear and the El Gato map from the kitchen, and wrote out Harv's finder's fee, a check for fifteen thousand dollars that now belonged to Edna. I slipped it in my shirt pocket and slammed the door shut behind me.

It was a brilliant morning. I didn't know much about Colorado weather, only that it snowed in Aspen, but if the last four days were any indication, mornings were bright and the sky turquoise. I followed the path down past the barn, scattering cats as I went, looking at the map and finding the shortest distance to where I estimated Harv's house to be. I stuffed the map back in my pocket and walked along the stream, thinking about how the future looks when you're standing right in it. Just a few months ago, this place had been no more than a dream with that soap-bubble sheen of the insubstantial about it. But I was in the dream now, looking back. From this angle, the march of past events appeared so obvious, so familiar and mundane, that it was easy to believe you could not possibly have arrived anywhere but exactly in the place you're standing. But something was happening to those events as I walked. I didn't see the rocky road Harv and I had taken that day, didn't notice I'd veered off the path to Edna's, because the past had shut out the sky and morning, had slipped on that soap-bubble sheen of the impossible like it belonged to a stranger, not mine at all. I walked along the earth softly carpeted in pine needles, wound among the soaring pines seeing Daniel's brooding face as it had looked the day I'd walked into a graduate course on the British Romantic Poets, felt the weight of our marriage years descend like gray, dark-bellied clouds. Saw not so much the great golden shafts of sun drifting down through the branches overhead, but the faded images caught inside them: my mother's eyes staring at the night sky; Daniel hearing that his book of poetry, *Lazing down the Blade*, had been awarded the Pulitzer, throwing his leg over his motorcycle, disappearing down the highway. Knowing now that if he had not died on the road, he would have died by his own hand…or mine. Saw Sandy's colorless eyes floating behind a blade of light. Suddenly, without warning, I was standing in a bright clearing, thoroughly lost. El Gato had worked its magic again.

"Shit!"

I walked over to a dead tree lying near the stream, sat down, pulled out the map, and gauged the distance between the stream and my house as best I could. I wasn't sure where Harv's place lay, but by continuing due north, I'd eventually come to the main road. I folded the map, shoved it back in my pocket, stood up to leave.

The clearing had fallen oddly silent. I glanced around the grassy meadow, stared up at where the treetops made black spikes against the sky. I felt slightly dizzy with an eerie sense of dislocation and estrangement that seemed to seep from the earth and the vegetation and the very air of El Gato. The birds that had been darting and trilling through the branches, the two squirrels that had been nattering around the dead tree where I sat, even the breeze that soughed through the pines had stilled. The sun hung precisely overhead, its rays too bright. I felt someone, or some thing: a pair of invisible eyes watching me from the shadows. An image of Eva Blake flew across my mind, and I turned slowly, scanning the shadows.

"Lost?"

I jumped, whirled around. No one. And then, on the other side of the stream, standing in a recess of tangled undergrowth, stood a shape dressed in a baggy brown jacket and pants. It was the woman with the unsightly haircut who had hugged Mrs. Brandenburg yesterday at the scene of the accident. She stood watching me, motionless. Today she had on a beige hunter's cap with flaps dangling like beagle ears over her straw-colored hair, and she watched me from gray eyes framed in the same straw-colored lashes. She had a lumpy nose, splotchy skin, thin straight lips pressed hard together. A pair of black field glasses hung from a leather shoulder strap.

I walked toward her, stopped at the stream across from where she stood. I pulled the map out of my pocket and held it up, looking for a way to cross the water. "I'm not quite sure. I'm trying to find the Benton residence?"

"How come?" Her voice ground like tires on gravel.

I talked myself out of a snappy comeback. The way she looked, she already had enough problems. "I'm, um, just wondering if it's near here, which direction?"

"She don't want company."

The stream made happy sounds, strumming over the small rocks of its bed. The woman and I stood staring at each other through the noise. She neither blinked nor smiled. I did a quick survey of all the things Dale Carnegie said I should do at times like this. I took great interest in the puckered skin around her lips, under her eyes. I thought about the rotten childhood she must have had. I clenched my teeth, took a breath.

"That may be." I gave her a bright smile that blew hell out of my Garbo persona for the rest of the day. "But she'll have to tell me that herself. By the way, my name's—"

"I know your name. Judith Samantha Symkin. J. S. Symkin. I've read you."

"I, uh...." I felt my hand drop to my side, still holding the map as I gaped at her. The birds returned to the air, the squirrels resumed their quarrel, the sun headed west. The brown woman with the beagle ears did not move a whisker, might have been carved from stone. I wondered how long the human eye could go without blinking. "You've read—"

"Your book, *Night Mother, Night Father*." They were a robot's words, some kid reading lines in a high school play.

I searched for a response, didn't find much. "I hope you liked it."

She stared.

"The poems, I hope you liked them."

Silence.

"Um...Mrs. Benton's place? Is it—"

"Saw you in Cougar Canyon yesterday. Ought not to go in there. Big cats. Bone was found there, from the dig."

Yesterday? Cougar Canyon? That dense canyon I'd tunneled through after leaving the waterfall, where I'd seen the large paw prints? But I'd not seen this woman. We stared across the stream at each other some more, and I thought back to yesterday, her running up the Brandenberg steps just minutes after I'd arrived. Following me, then? But why? Was she following me today? Before I could speak, she raised an arm as though it were a stick of wood, without bending the elbow, and pointed it north.

"Benton's. Walk that way. Come to a road, cross the stream. Follow it east."

She turned and disappeared into the trees. I stood staring at the empty spot where she'd been, figuring she must be Myra Jones, the woman Harv said prowled the woods with her binoculars. If she was still lurking around, watching me, there was no way to tell, so I headed north as she'd indicated, wondering how Myra Jones had come across my first book, a chapbook printed by a small university press over twenty years ago, one thousand copies and half those remaindered. How many people outside academic circles even knew I published poetry under the name J. S. Symkin? Hardly any. Who in hell was Myra Jones, anyway, and what was she doing living out here in the remote mountains reading obscure poetry? Why was her attitude toward me—if not rude, certainly antisocial? I wasn't having any luck coming up with answers when I stumbled into the Benton yard and stood looking in astonishment: yesterday's lily pond lay devastated, a heap of mud and broken rocks and dismembered plants.

I'd lived in academia the lion's share of my life, didn't know much about mutilated bodies or grisly crime scenes, but the devastation of the lily pond hit me in my stomach and took my breath away, like looking at the butchered corpse of something that just yesterday had been exquisitely alive and beautiful. The diverted trickle from the stream was dammed. The place where the lilies had floated was a mire of torn lily pads whose stems wound like shredded veins through the mud, tangled around shards of splintered wood and protruding rock. An immense sledgehammer lay to one side.

But the battered trailer hadn't changed, if you didn't count the curtains pulled across the windows, and Harv's yellow Jeep was gone, so that now I could see past it, into the tree shadows where an old car sat parked, its color nearly obliterated under a thick coat of dust. I ran up the stairs to the trailer, knocked on the door just to be safe, then made a beeline to the car that, sure enough, was a dark red Plymouth, the one Harv had given Camilla.

The door opened with a grinding creak. The inside was dim, the trapped air smelling of motor oil and the kind of neglect that takes you back to a time when women crossed their legs at the knee and wore silk stockings that gleamed in the near-dark of black-and-white movies. In spite of the dust on the outside, the interior was tidy, just as the barn loft had been—no discarded cans, wastepaper, matchbooks, not even a gum wrapper. I peeked under the seat. Nothing. Crawled in, leaned over the backrest, poked my hand along the crack of the back seat. Nothing. Pressed the silver button on the glove compartment. The old metal door fell open. A pencil stub, safety pins clipped together, spool of brown thread with a needle stuck in it, United States road map. I pulled the map out, unfolded it. The logo in the corner read 1995, the year Camilla had died. A yellow marker line extended from Denver to St. Louis using Interstate 70, zigzagged southeast to Nashville. Kansas City was circled, probably the halfway point, an overnight stop. I folded the map, put it back. I sat there in the odor of the old car, a machine from an era as dead as Camilla James. The sheriff was a thorough man; I had no doubt he'd already seen the map. Whatever it did for him, for me it relieved some gnawing doubts about his story, told me he wasn't a man whose grief had overwhelmed his good sense. Camilla had meant to go back to Nashville. Okay, so why kill herself the night before she'd planned to leave? I felt a growing unrest, then heard a vehicle approaching. I leapt from the old car, slammed the door shut and was standing in the driveway when the snub nose of Harv's yellow Jeep appeared through the trees.

Edna pulled up fast. She hit the brakes, killed the engine, slid out. She banged the door shut with significantly more force than she needed to and jammed her hands on her hips. She had on a pair of yellow cotton slacks tied with a drawstring and a long-sleeved yellow shirt tucked in at the waist. Her hair was tied back with a yellow ribbon, and if she'd been grief-stricken yesterday, she looked ready for bear today, her eyes shining like someone just itching to wield a sledgehammer.

"What do you want?" This was a new, hard voice, not the one from yesterday when she'd been taking lessons from Blanche DuBois. This one was from a woman who'd been talking burial costs at the local mortuary. "If Harv owed you money, it's too bad. I don't have any." She marched past me toward the stairs.

"Hey, wait!" I followed, afraid that once she entered the trailer, she wouldn't come out again. "Harv didn't owe me a penny," I said, talking fast as she mounted the stairs with her door key aimed. "It's the other way around. I owed him some."

She froze in mid-step, and I rammed into her back. She wheeled around.

"How much?" Her eyes narrowed. "What'd he do, you owe him money for?"

I edged down a step so we were the same height and plucked the check out of my pocket. Held it up to her.

"Finder's fee. For showing me Ms. James's place. Six percent of the purchase price."

Edna squinted at the check, tipping her head sideways.

"Fifteen thousand dollars?" Her voice was low, like yesterday. She took it, looked closer. "Hey, it's not signed. What is this? You're in it with Brandenberg and that rat pack, aren't you?" Her voice shot up, way too shrill. Nudging hysteria.

"Hey, hey. It's all right. Get me a pen, I'll sign it. I just wanted to wait till I actually found you." She looked mean. I edged another step down. "Look, I've only seen Brandenberg once in my life, yesterday at the scene. That check is good. Let's go inside, I'll sign it, you call the bank and verify it."

"No phone." She turned and climbed the stairs, key ready, still looking at the check. "Come on in, but I'm telling you right now if this is some kind of trick, you'll be sorry." She jammed in the key, banged open the door with her knee.

While Edna yanked back the curtains, I stood in the doorway, staring into a long narrow space with a kitchen on one side, a living room with tattered furniture on the other. The kind of furniture college students dicker for at thrift stores and leave behind at Dumpsters—a couch threadbare at the arms, cushions sprung; a recliner covered in black plastic with a ripped seat. A couple of sawed-off tree stumps flanked each end of the couch. But one piece didn't belong with the rest. The heavily lacquered surface of a spectacular free-form coffee table in front of the sofa caught the sun streaming through a window and shot light back across the room. The top was made of a thick wood slab, its edges still trimmed in bark, balanced on a base of intricate tree roots. I walked over and stared down at it. The wood was a rich amber burl with a surface of spiraling, concentric circles lying deep below the shellacked surface.

"Harv," she said. "He makes...made them."

"It's very beautiful." And it was, though its brilliance cast an even deeper pall over the room.

Edna was in the kitchen, staring into the open door of the refrigerator. A red Formica table edged with a wide band of aluminum was pushed next to a window with two plastic-backed chairs on opposite sides. "Have a seat. Something to drink? Coke? Beer, Harv left some...." Her voice cracked, and her shoulders began shaking silently.

I walked over and closed the refrigerator, gently pulled her toward one of the chairs. I sat down across from her. Beside a stack of papers piled on the table, I found a pen, and while Edna sat holding her head in her hands, I slipped the check from her grasp and signed it.

"This is Harv's money. *Your* money. I'm just sorry I didn't get it to you, to him, sooner. If I'd known..."

She raised her head and stared at the check. She touched it with one long index finger, and then she looked up at me with her sad, wet face. "It wouldn't have changed anything, you know. He'd still have been on that damned grader, no matter what." She picked up the check, folded it in half, slipped it under the stack of papers. "Sure, he did it for the money, when the Association got around to paying him, but it was more than that. He just loved riding that old thing, grading the roads. Liked to see how smooth he could make them, no bumps or rocks, middle a little higher so the rain'd run off to the ditches on each side. He took a lot of pride in it." She smiled out the window, like she could see Harv sitting out there on his machine. "Sometimes he just went out and graded roads like other people go off sailing their boats, didn't even charge for it. When he'd ask the Association for gas money or for a part he'd had to buy to fix the damn thing, that Brandenberg'd raise a fuss. Harv'd come home so mad he could hardly talk, go right to the fridge and pop a beer and sit down in his chair, stare out the window for hours with murder in his eyes.

"Everything was fine till that Brandenburg showed up. Seemed like everything Harv did, he had some complaint about it. I went to one of the meetings, gave that whole damn bunch a piece of my mind, letting Harv ride around on that grader, held together with a prayer and some baling wire. After Brandenberg got on the board, the Association wouldn't pay to have anything done on it, not even parts."

"You threatened to sue if anything happened to Harv?" I already knew the answer to this one.

"You're damned right I...How'd you know that?" She blinked a couple of times, fast.

"Brandenberg yesterday, seemed to think that might be on your agenda."

"Somebody ought to sue this whole damned place. There's nothing but fighting goes on here. You can't just live here in peace, you got to listen to that windbag get on everyone's case about anything he personally doesn't like."

"Such as?"

"Such as our trailer. He says nobody's supposed to have a trailer on their land unless they're just living in it while they're building their house. But we've lived here over twenty years." She gave me a hard look as though I were an enemy spy. "Who's he to walk in and tell us we can't?"

Edna had fire in her eyes, but I'd take fire over water any day. I let the question slide, it was a no-win.

"He starts going in to the county treasurer's office, looking up properties he can get for back taxes. Happens to see the date on those old records when Claire James started the development, then lost it. Some technical thing—Harv hadn't recorded his deed on the lot Claire gave him before the unsold lots were lost in the bankruptcy, so technically..." She heaved a sigh so deep her body shuddered. "There's nothing to be done, looks like this place is going to be his. But I don't have to like it."

"So you destroyed the pond?"

"What, I should leave it for that scumbag? Me and Harv and Camilla, we worked so hard on it, and Harv carried..." Her shoulders were shaking again, tears rolling down her cheeks. She pressed her lips together and looked away.

"Hey, it's okay," I said, leaning toward her, squeezing her shoulder. I looked around for a box of tissues. Nothing. "So when are you supposed to be out of here?"

"I don't know, don't think it's definite yet." She swiped at her face with her sleeve.

We sat there without talking. I thought about real estate, ways to get it and ways to lose it. Finally: "You and Harv moved here when?"

"Back before Claire left. Be 1970, give or take."

Twenty-seven years. I didn't know what the statutes of limitations were in Colorado, but I could find out easy enough. And what was it Janie Gillman had said? That Brandenberg told her to leave Harv's house off the map because it weakened his claim to the property? If it was as cut-and-dried as Edna seemed to think, why was he worried? It never ceased to amaze me how in real estate even smart people would believe just about anything anyone told them without taking the time to check it out.

"Listen, whatever it is you're thinking of doing, suing, moving, premeditated murder, can you hold off? I want to check out a few things."

She kept looking through the window, her lips set hard.

I thought about her husband's death, the petty politics and ill will among El Gato residents, the beat-up trailer we were sitting in. "Tell me, if you could stay here, would you want to?"

She gave me an odd look. "Sure. It's my home. But Brandenberg's not making it up about trailers being illegal, it's written right in the covenants. No offense, but fifteen thousand's not going to build a house, even if I got to keep this lot."

It wasn't until later, as Edna watched from the porch while I headed down her driveway toward home, walking past the muddy remains of the pond, that I remembered what she'd said, that Camilla had helped build it.

"She sure did," Edna said, a smile spreading across her face. She stood with her arms crossed, her spine rigidly straight on the shabby, crooked porch, the angular bones of her shoulders poking against the thin fabric of her shirt. The air had turned chill, clouds moving in from the west. "Camilla, she…she was my best friend. My only friend, really…It was Camilla had the idea to build it to start with. She was sitting there one day, right about where you're standing, took out her sketch pad and started drawing while we talked. She sketched a picture of it, then mailed off for water garden stuff that showed us how to build it. Got Harv hauling around those big rocks for us." She was looking into the middle distance, her smile a lot like Marle's last night. "She was something, she really was."

"I guess she loved it, living here. Helping you with the pond, living close to her daughter and grandchildren."

Edna's eyes fastened on mine. A cloud edged over the sun, passed on. "You're wondering why she did it. Why she hung herself."

"I've been here for four days, seems like every direction I turn, I run into Camilla. I don't mean to be morbid, but I can't help wonder—"

"I've wondered, too," she said, "I think we all have. She wasn't easy to figure, never talked much about herself. She was kind of moody, happy like a kid one minute, down in the dumps the next. I wouldn't have called her 'suicidal,' though. Wouldn't even have called her depressed particularly, but she'd seemed kind of quiet those last few weeks…."

I glanced at the red car in the shadows. "She mention anything about a trip, going back to Nashville?"

She gave me a long, level look, that flare of movement behind her eyes like yesterday when she'd looked at the sheriff. That's when I knew she knew about Camille and Marle; that's the kind of things women who are best friends will tell each other. Count on it.

"Funny, sheriff wondered the same thing right after it happened." She stared hard, waited, but I said nothing. "Well, like I told him, look at that car. Harv kept it going for her, just barely. Got her to town and back, but that's about it. Tires're bald, muffler's shot, you name it. If that's what she was thinking of taking, I don't think she'd got very far."

Maybe. But what I knew of Camilla told me she wouldn't have thought about bald tires or a muffler. She'd have jumped in and driven, waited tables for gas money. She was the type who didn't draw lines between what's possible and what's not. People like that, they can do anything.

"What about Wendy?" I said, "or Gerald? She talk much about them?"

Edna gave a sharp, dry laugh. "Wendy? Well now, what're you going to say about Wendy? Her and the kids, they're like wild animals. Camilla'd make a wisecrack about them once in a while, but if you've met Wendy, you know she wouldn't be much help." She frowned at the clouds drifting in overhead. "Gerald? They kind of kept out of each other's way was my take on it. She hated him shooting the cats. She never said it straight out, but I think Camilla believed he waited till she was around to see him do it. Like he took pleasure not so much in killing them as in her seeing him. It was all a little weird, gave me the willies when she talked about him." She hugged herself. The air had turned cold as the clouds blocked out the sun, but I didn't think that was why she shuddered.

"Do you know Gerald?" I said.

"I guess so, much as you can know a guy like that. Him and Harv, they were pretty thick till Brandenberg moved in. Gerald started hanging out over there, didn't come around after Harv and Brandenberg got into it."

I remembered Tony's remarks about the house, the person who built it. "This Gerald," I said, "you think he's got all his marbles?"

She laughed. "Depends how you look at it. Gerald's side of the cat-killing is that cats're like deer or any other wild animal. Need to be kept thinned out, keep the population down. Like getting a hunting permit for deer or elk, but there's not any hunters to clear out the cats, right? I can see his point. I mean, what are you going to do with all those cats out there running wild and having litter after litter? But I wouldn't have wanted to see them shot. I'd probably have felt just like Camilla." Edna paused, her face absorbed in thought. "No, I don't think Gerald's much of a psycho. He's just a kid needs to grow up. He does whatever strikes his fancy at the moment, not thinking any more about tomorrow than a dog in heat. He run off with Willa Hanks, but you know, I don't believe he never dreamed Wendy would leave him. Probably wouldn't have if Gerald's daddy hadn't come out and took over."

I turned back down the drive for home, then remembered what I'd meant to ask Edna. She was leaning against the porch railing, gazing at the bog.

"You said that the lily pond was Camilla's idea? That she sketched it for you? Did she draw a lot?"

"All the time," Edna said, pulling her attention away from the heap of mud and vines. "She was an artist, lived in Paris, the whole bit. Took that sketchbook of hers everywhere she went, stuck down in that shoulder bag with all her pencils and drawing equipment. We'd be sitting, talking, she'd pull out her pad and start in, kind of like some women knit. Like she never could just sit in one spot without being busy at something." Edna smiled. "It was a real pretty thing, that sketchbook."

"You wouldn't happen to know where it is?"

"Now you mention it, I don't. Funny, I never thought about it before, but it must be up there in her loft. Nobody ever claimed anything that was up there, far as I heard." She hugged herself again, rubbing her arms briskly. This time she was responding to the elements, a good sign. "You happen on it, I can't think of a thing I'd like more than to sit down with you and go through it."

Hiking back to the main road, I wondered what kind of artist Camilla had been, how long she'd lived in Paris, why she'd moved to these mountains, to this place. I was seized by an overwhelming desire to see her sketch pad. I knew it wasn't in the barn loft, so Wendy had probably packed it away somewhere. I'd have to brave the A-frame again, ask to see her mother's artwork.

At the wide gravel road that ran through the center of El Gato, I stopped and took out my map. I was cold, the afternoon was fading fast, and I meant to head home the quickest route possible. I traced the shortest distance from the main road to my house. It took me right across Eva Blake's backyard.

13

Morgan

I know about Camilla, that she fell in lust with a painter of local fame during her art school years in New York, that he was not much interested in marriage, and that Camilla was not much interested in child rearing. In spite of the suspicious circumstances, I know she committed suicide, and I have a working suspicion of why.

It is the most common cause of death, suicide—though little studied, seldom acknowledged, grossly misunderstood. Few people, particularly the slow feeders, are going to admit to practicing it, mostly because they are only subliminally aware that the ghostwriter, hacking out the script by candlelight and sending it up to the mind's CEO, has a hidden agenda made to order for the potential addict—which is to say, for us all. This century has seen more than its fair share of death-dabbling clichés, ready-made for the unimaginative and the fainthearted who would do the puppet's fandango with nicotine or alcohol or whatever designer concoction has hit the bestseller list. One might forgive the predictable plot and celluloid characters were it not for the one unpardonable sin: it goes on too long. Me, I've always respected a sharp blade.

The Symkin woman is a different matter. She has written her own script: original, challenging, sporadically incoherent. A James Joyce of the soul. Who could resist?

Consider: Victim takes vengeance on her own body, the working subtext of all suicides. Give Symkin a read—a relatively entertaining use of videocassettes and biographies, a scholarly attention to detail, a twist ending: just as the Old Man of the Scythe appears to reap his harvest, she whips out the new consciousness. *Casts herself in a dual role—both victim (the body sacrificed) and perpetrator (the body snatcher with the new resident consciousness). Nifty, I like. One problem: her chosen resident consciousness is brain-dead. Garbo, for Christ's sake. It is a final ironic twist, the stroke of gloomy genius.*

Exactly the kind of thing that would have appealed to Cruz's perverse sense of humor. He once said that the real miracle of the Resurrection was not that Christ could be brought back from the dead, but that after being dead for three days, He would not come back a zombie.

"Now that's a book to catch your interest, call it *The Revised New Bible: The Wanderings of the Divine Retard.*

"Oh, stop. If the press gets hold of that one, you're in deep shit, Simon." Conrad Vogel sits across the table, his jowls shaking with laughter. "They wouldn't blink at the blasphemy, but they'll swear you're developing some new, exotic chemical in that laboratory of yours. God knows there's enough talk already, building that place back into the mesa like you did. People love to think the worst, you know."

"They're generally on the right track, they just don't go far enough. Lack of intelligence, greatly exacerbated by lack of imagination." Cruz gives a thin smile around the group, his glasses catching the light.

I watch him from my end of the long table. He is the color of pewter—highly polished, immaculate. The gray suit, the silvered hair, eyes the color of ice behind the glass. A study in lethal monochrome.

"Morgan, tell us the man's joking. Tell us he has a heart."

Ry Vogel glances at me, turns back to Cruz. She has long, sorrel-colored hair like the mane of my father's horse who won the stakes race at the Downs this afternoon. From our third-story dining room solarium, I have been watching the diminishing band of orange above the mesas, that last bright aura of refracted sun along the horizon as the deep indigo of night presses down. I turn away from the sky, look at Cruz for a long moment. Then:

"I haven't cut him open yet to do any on-site cardiac inspections, Ry, but I'll give you even odds that if you told Conrad where you really were last night, he might be willing to perform that operation."

After the guests have left, Cruz enters the bedroom where I have been staring up into the darkness, waiting for Paso's call, waiting for the Italian man's response to my phone message asking for a job with The Company.

"That was an entertaining stink you made, Cordelia," Cruz says after he has lain beside me in the darkness for some time. "It's going to cost me a government contract, you know. That fool Conrad, leave it to Washington to appoint an idiot."

"It was an expensive fuck, wasn't it?"

A half hour of silence later, he says, "If I didn't know you better, I'd think you gave a damn."

Several seconds before I know the phone will ring, I say, "I do give a damn, Cruz, about payback."

Just for good measure, as Cruz stood beside the window and watched the cab idling in front of the building the next morning, I lifted his keys and drove out the back way in his vintage MG. It had been British racing green for the seventeen years since its manufacture, and for the twenty minutes or so it took to drive it to Jim's Auto and Body and have it sprayed pewter. It was the least I could do. But just in case Cruz had issued the alert for an MG of any color, I kept to the back roads, all the way to the Tucson airport.

The alarm begins to ring, the horse outside neighs in his corral. I check the video monitors and watch the black-and-white image of the Symkin woman crossing the creek and entering my backyard.

I like.

14

I PUSHED THROUGH Eva Blake's backyard, which was a waist-high tangle of weeds and brambles, making my way toward the front of the house. Behind me, the horse tore around its corral, whinnying and setting up enough fuss to wake the dead.

Suddenly the doors to the upper deck flew open. A black figure stood in the open doorway. Maybe my nerves were shot from the recent events, maybe the spooky forests of El Gato were gaining on me, maybe I should have eaten breakfast and lunch, but for whatever reason, a flood of adrenaline hit me with such force that for a moment I stood dazed and wobbling in Eva Blake's backyard. Brief as the click of a camera's shutter, the sun disappeared and the birds stopped singing and the freshening chill of autumn air turned bone-cold. It left my flesh creeping and my imagination as bewildered as if it had glimpsed an unlit region and the presence of something unnameable.

"Lost?" Eva Blake stepped into the long brilliant rays of afternoon sun. She wore faded Levi's, a white cotton shirt, and Western boots, and I felt myself blush at my foolishness.

"Actually, for the first time in a good while, I'm not," I said, blinking away the last bit of dizziness and walking toward the deck. "I was out for a walk and your place was on the way home. I hope I'm not intruding."

"Come around to the front," she said. She disappeared inside, shutting the doors softly behind her.

I plowed through the rest of the weeds to the front yard, which had been professionally landscaped. Bordering each side of a wide, curving flagstone walkway were elaborate cactus and rock gardens, studded with indigenous flowering shrubs and plants. Beyond them, plateaus formed by railroad ties and rocks extended to a recently added screen of trees and shrubs shielding the house from the road.

I followed Eva Blake inside, where the interior of the house had the same professional veneer as the front yard. The entry room was a large square space along the front portion of the house, with plentiful windows and miles of pale diaphanous drapes giving the impression of an elegant country showplace—polished oak floors, a stone fireplace large enough to hold a dining room table, a scattering of tapestry rugs, furniture in mauves and bleached yellows with accents of a flowery green print and lots of open space in between. On several small tables lay trendy magazines; oil paintings and watercolors of nature scenes in expensive frames were color-coordinated to the decor. It was expensive, immaculate—and absolutely anonymous.

As Eva Blake ushered me in, she explained that Andrew Jacobs and Wolf Condidos down the road had been interior and exterior designers from San Francisco in their past lives before El Gato. "They wanted to do the place," she said, shrugging and motioning me to follow her down a long hallway to the back of the house, "so I gave them two weeks, unlimited funds, and voilà."

"Looks like they missed the backyard," I said, as we entered a huge open kitchen and dining area where the weed-strangled back yard was the view through patio glass doors. I pulled out one of eight stainless steel chairs arranged around a long oval table and sat down while Eva went to the kitchen, reciting a menu of drinks. I turned down the vodka over ice at the end of the list in favor of herbal tea.

The kitchen was a glass and steel affair with an oak block in the center and pans hanging above it. Their pristine brass bottoms gleamed in the late afternoon light. I watched Eva examine the contents of three cabinets before she found the tea.

"Some people like the frills," she said, pulling out one of the boxes and stripping off the cellophane wrapper, "some take it straight. Truth is, I could live in a room over a dive with an orange crate for a table and a mattress on the floor. Just the bones, nothing hidden." She took two cups from a shelf, filled them with tap water, dropped a tea bag in each, and set the cups in a microwave. Bending at the waist, she studied its buttons, pushed several, and the machine began to hum. Eva leaned on the island and looked out at the weeds. "That," she said, nodding toward the brown, grizzled yard, "I'd take that any day over the stuff out front."

"Why have the guys decorate, then?"

I followed her gaze to the horse that stood in its corral, looking off toward the wooden bridge. Finally, she said, "Jack likes it that way. Thought he was coming when I moved here." She kept staring out at the yard. The microwave beeped several times, but she watched the yard a little longer. Then she grinned as she pushed herself from the island. "Besides, there's probably a covenant against orange crates, you think?"

I wasn't hot on orange crates and floor mattresses, dives either, but I let it slide. Instead, I told her about my visit to Edna's, my odd exchange with Myra Jones.

"Far as I can tell," she said, putting the steaming cups on the table, "she's garden-variety weird, not an authentic space cadet." She pulled out the chair opposite the glass doors and sat down. "Nature addict, mostly. According to Wolf down the road, she used to work as a librarian down in the village. But there was some kind of trouble, she lost her job, wanders around out in the wilderness now. Kind of self-appointed Nature Police ever since the Smithsonian crew came through and found the Indian relics. You might want to be careful with those big trees up around your place, the ones with the burn marks on the trunks?"

I nodded, recalling the odd, hieroglyphic-type markings.

"Turns out those are ancient Indian markings," she said, blowing at her tea. "Anasazi, Ute, something. Myra contacted the Division of Wildlife about them, then the Smithsonian got involved. Now those trees are protected, even if they are on your private property. I think if you lay a finger on them, somehow old Myra knows it by osmosis." She paused as though she were thinking and then continued, holding her cup between both hands and staring out across the weeds. "And that's when they turned up the famous bones." She narrowed her eyes against the steam and sipped.

"Bones?" Myra had mentioned something about bones, but I'd forgotten until now.

"It all happened right after I moved here. The archaeologists had hit the jackpot, digging up one relic after another—pottery, tools, stones, cutlery, weapons, you name it. One day they came up with a surprise, a human hand to be specific, only it wasn't two thousand years old, turns out this one had only been buried a few years. They were doing more tests to determine age, more specific time of death, but I haven't heard anymore about it. Nobody has a clue who the hand belongs to or how it got there."

"Where?" I asked. But I already knew. Myra Jones had already told me, hadn't she? Cougar Canyon.

"That canyon, just north of your place," Eva said. "Down at the far end of a ravine, upstream from where the relics were discovered. Cougar Canyon, they call it—it's pretty hard to get to, but I guess cougar paw prints have been seen there. It's all part of El Gato, protected from hunters."

Maybe not. I remembered Harv's Jeep the first day I'd wandered lost through the snow. The rifle shells on the seat, the camouflage clothing. Harv had been tight for money; I wondered how much dead cougar were bringing. I told Eva about walking through the canyon yesterday, about my suspicions that Myra had been following me.

"Wouldn't surprise me." She put her cup down and propped her chin in her palm. "So how was it, your first night alone? Do you dream like Garbo, too?"

I can ignore sarcasm when I want to.

"So," I said, "you say your husband's not coming. Are you staying here, going back to L.A.? Any plans?"

"Oh, you know. The usual," she said, "Pace the floor. Cry. Curse the sky. Slit my wrists." She gave that peculiar shrug of one shoulder that I recalled from last night and heaved a deep sigh as she looked back to the yard where the horse was trotting around the corral, whinnying.

"No scars," I said, looking at her hard, narrow wrists, the network of blue veins.

"Heal fast." She raised both her hands in the prayer position over her tea and rested her chin lightly on her fingertips. She tipped her head back a little and gave me a smile that did not reach her eyes. The angular planes of her face glowed in the afternoon light. "What would you do if it were your husband?"

I didn't think Jack Blake and Daniel had much in common, but I tried to imagine my husband pursuing other women. The only image I could dredge up was the one that endured as all the others had faded: Daniel sitting in the back bedroom, squinting over the old Woodstock typewriter with an ashtray overflowing with butts and ashes beside his right hand, a gallon of cheap wine and half-filled glass at his left. Screwed into the top of a battered oak desk was a praying-mantis-type lamp. A cone of light fanned across the desk. Smoke hung suspended in heavy gray layers across the room. Daniel pecked at the keyboard with one hand, cursing, ripping sheets from the carriage of the machine and crushing them into balls that littered the carpet like funeral chrysanthemums. The room was thick with the raw male odor of Daniel and his habits, the clatter of the typewriter into the night and the darkness where I lay sleepless across the hall. The marvel was not that he had died so young or lived so long. The marvel was that the next morning the poem that was still gripped tightly in the jaws of the old Woodstock was as clean and pure and exquisitely shaped as the sound of a silver spoon kissing a crystal bell.

I looked into Eva Blake's beautiful eyes.

"I would not have left him there."

She studied me for a moment, then picked up her cup, tilted it slightly, sipped. When she lifted her eyes to mine, they carried the amalgamated force of an oncoming train.

"*You* might not have left him there, but *Garbo* would have."

Too late to curse myself for confiding my grand scheme, but I did it anyway. Silently. When that didn't help, I tried something more difficult and risky—talk, the bread and wine of friendship.

"I suppose you're right, she'd have left him sitting in the smoke and alcohol fumes years before," I said, "but how can we ever imagine when we're young how we'll change through the years?" I felt as though I were groping in the dark, touching first one thing and then another to find my way. Outside, the horse was stretching its neck over the corral again, its black coat glistening in the late afternoon sun, letting out yodel after yodel. "I'm not the woman I used to be anymore, and the person I am is not the person I want to be. Can you understand?"

"I understand that you see yourself as someone who needs other people, and that you wish to destroy that self for one who feels nothing." She got up and walked around the table to lean against the patio doors and watch the animal through the glass as we talked. "I understand that you risk your soul to become someone who had none."

"Look, can we skip Garbo? You talk about a soul as though it's something you can pour into a cup and measure. Who the hell are you to judge how much soul someone has? A soul isn't something you can even *see*."

I had a moment of hilarity, hearing the girlish petulance in the words as though Eva Blake and I were sisters in a rivalry over a pimply-faced boy. She must have caught my mood because suddenly, simultaneously, we laughed—the high, effervescent kind of laughter that bubbles up from the inside with the force of a geyser and doubles you over during the small hours of slumber and cocktail parties alike, the kind of irrepressible laughter that only girls and women can share. I realized that my body had been hard and tense as an over-stressed muscle, and with a combination of relief and utter abandonment I laid my arms and head on the glass table and let the laughter flow over me as though they would never end.

Eva Blake was laughing too, braced against the patio door. When the horse stepped up his nickering campaign, we both wiped our eyes and watched him tearing around in a cloud of dust. Eva pushed the patio door open, and still laughing, we waded through the weeds to the corral.

We sat side by side on the top rail, two long, thin women, having some old-fashioned girl talk about nothing in particular. I'd had precious little of such friendship over the past few years, hadn't realized I missed it until this moment. After awhile, the horse settled down and wandered over beside Eva, shoving his forehead against her shoulder, his musky smell drifting toward me in a sharp gust of wind from the north. The trees shook, and the air filled with ocean waves. Above us, up the mountain, the wind combed across the treetops. I zipped my jacket and turned up the collar as we sat in silence—me, thinking of the long climb home, and Eva staring out through the forest.

Finally, she said: "They never found the person who killed your mother?"

The trees around us were still again, so I knew that the crashing sound I heard, more like water falling than ocean waves, must have been for my ears alone. When the noise subsided, I shook my head.

"No, they never did," I said.

"And your dad?"

"Nope. Never saw him again."

"And Sandy? Still teaching?"

"Mm-hm." I nodded at the mountain peaks with their chaste white caps that were turning a russet color as the sun set. The Sangre de Cristo mountains. Blood of Christ.

If I'd been him, I'd have shot the fat sonofabitch.

The horse extended its black muzzle toward me, its velvet nose sprouted with several long, bristling whiskers. I dug in my pocket for some granola mix, and he fumbled his lips in my palms till it was gone. His breath was warm, and he snuffled softly against my jacket, searching for more. But I was out of snacks, and as the sun dropped behind the western ridge, I knew it was time to head back.

We pushed through the tall weeds, followed a path that ran along the side of the house, and entered the front yard. Eva walked me out to the road, where she pointed out a trail ahead that would shorten my walk home. From the other direction, the main road, a hint of dust rose above the trees, and as I thanked Eva for the tea and turned to leave, a vehicle came into sight. The sheriff's Bronco. He slowed, stopped, rolled down his window.

"Two finer, taller ladies it would be hard to find," he said, playing with a Texas accent. His tone was jocular, but his gray eyes were not. "No sense putting off telling you, both of you, since you're here. I was going to stop by your place, Ms. Symkin, on my way back into town, let you know about Harv. The brakes."

"The brakes?" Eva looked from me to the sheriff, and Marle briefly explained.

"Had Jim Sykes put the lines under his scope. No doubt about it now. Not much, to my mind, before. Lines were cut. Those receipts?" he said, addressing me. "Some for new brakes, nothing to do with the lines, though. He didn't touch those lines, not unless Brandenberg is right and Harv was getting creative about his suicide plans. According to Edna, Harv drove the grader Thursday, parked it Thursday night by the house. Sometime between then and Friday when he got on it again, somebody crawled in under it, did some cutting. I've already talked to a few of the folks out here this afternoon. Few more stops to make. I'd appreciate it if the two of you would let me know if you hear anything." He paused with his fingers dancing on top of the steering wheel. "Guess I don't need to tell you both to keep your doors and windows locked, you hear me?"

I nodded, but Eva was staring off past my shoulder, down the road to where a dark figure in the distance had emerged from the trees beyond her house and was crossing the road to enter the forest on the other side. The figure was moving fast, and if it hadn't been for Eva, I would never have seen it. But the sheriff probably would have.

"Who's that?" he asked.

"Mm. My guess is Myra Jones," Eva said, turning to me. "You saw her earlier, right?"

I nodded, watching the spot in the forest where the figure had disappeared. With the sun behind the mountains, darkness would come quickly now. I wasn't particularly afraid of Myra Jones, but was that who the figure was? I thought about the discovery of a woman's hand, Myra's own warning about cougars, the unsatisfactorily explained death of Camilla James, and now Harv's murder. I looked in the direction of my home with about the same enthusiasm as I'd look on a wilderness filled with starving wolves.

"I'll be finished here in a half hour or so," the sheriff said, following my look. "I'll drive back by, give you a ride to your place if—"

"No problem," Eva interrupted. "It's not that far, and I'm not busy. I'd be glad to drive her over." The sheriff and Eva exchanged looks, her odd smile creeping up on one side. "Save you making that drive again tonight, Sheriff."

Marle Winslow's gray eyes hit laser mode. He studied Eva with a long, thoughtful look. It was my turn to read minds—he'd be wondering how she knew he'd given me a ride last night, and then he'd think I'd told her. After that, he'd wonder why I was here this afternoon. If I'd been the sheriff, that's what I'd have been wondering. He was toying with something else, too. He was thinking how you never could tell about women these days.

After he'd headed back down the road in a cloud of dust, she burst into laughter. "I guess we gave him something to think about, didn't we?" she said, turning toward her house.

"We?" I said, following along behind her to the front door where she set about fiddling with a digital computer pad with rows of tiny lights on the inside wall beside the entryway. She seemed much more accomplished with it than with the microwave. Finally, she closed the front door firmly and turned toward where her black truck was parked beside a double garage with a padlocked door.

Eva unlocked the passenger side door, held it open for me, and said: "Our earlier discussion concerning the soul, which you cannot see?"

"Yes?" I said, climbing in, but thinking I might really rather walk through the wilderness with the starving wolves.

"I think you're absolutely right." She smiled broadly, and I relaxed. I should have known better. "*You* can't see it," she said, "but maybe *I* can."

And slammed the door.

15

I WAS IN NO MOOD TO TALK ABOUT SOULS, visible or other-wise. I had spent the last few years living in New Mexico, not far from Santa Fe, which had pretty much been voted in as the New Age capital of the continent, and people who believed in seeing souls and auras and their dead ex-husbands and channeling two-thousand-year-old Japanese warlords were a dime a dozen. Fruitcakes are big business in the Southwest. I stifled a yawn, adjusted my seat belt, hoped Eva Blake was not going to take advantage of the situation to preach white-light politics.

I was in luck—she started up the truck without a word. She buckled herself in and let the engine idle a moment as she sat with one hand draped over the wheel, the other over the back of the seat, scanning the grounds in the gathering evening. Zipped into a black jacket, her face framed by the black cap of hair, she looked very much like the midnight visitor I remembered from last night. This evening, however, the horse stood watching mildly as Eva drove into view of its paddock, following the driveway that circled around the garage.

The road from Eva's house to the main El Gato road was bumpier than I remembered. Recent rains had left behind several rib-shaking washboard stretches that sent the truck into convulsions. With my right hand, I grabbed the armrest on the door to brace myself in the seat, and with my left, I cradled my breasts, suddenly struck by a dim memory that floated just at the edge of consciousness, another truck on another gravel road, but invariably, just as I was about to grab the image from the past, it burst like a soap bubble.

Added to that frustration was the mere fact of being here at twilight for the second night running—in this strange place where death and sinister events and menacing people seemed to lurk in the shadows. Here I was, like yesterday afternoon, being trolleyed down the road yet again to a home that had turned cold and empty and whose doors and windows I was under instruction to lock against some nameless but pressing danger. And now the kicker: riding shotgun in a pickup truck, which is a special kind of grief. Not only are you powerless, swept along by the whim of whoever is driving, but without the bolster of a steering wheel or the cushioned ride of a passenger car, you're exposed to the further indignities of being knocked and bounced and lurched about like a discarded rag doll. I recognized the beginning slide into self-pity. I gritted my teeth and sat up straighter, tightened my grip on the armrest, and braced my feet hard against the floorboard.

I looked around the truck and remembered Eva Blake's preference for orange crates. In spite of being a shiny new Dodge Ram, this model was stripped down and basic inside. A "real pickup" by those who leaned toward No Frills: a four-wheel-drive, full-sized, Detroit-made machine with a black plastic floor liner, thinly upholstered and possibly unpadded bench seat, no CD player or tape deck or even a radio. Besides the standard steering wheel and heater and dual gear box, the only extravagance was the large black roll bar over the truck bed. It couldn't be that this woman was short of cash, I thought, picturing her elegant home and the expensive landscaping. And then I got it: what Eva Blake had told me was true—she simply didn't care. She had probably walked onto a car lot somewhere, pointed at the first truck she came across, kicked the tires a time or two, and said, "It'll do." I could see the salesperson, standing where the truck had been on the back lot, looking after her with the check in his hand. It was the kind of truck that in a few more hard-driving years would be about right if you lived in that room over the sleazy bar, especially if they played lots of country music on the jukebox and the truck had picked up a catchy assortment of dents and rust under a seasoned patina of dust.

I said as much to Eva as we bumped along and turned onto the smooth gravel of the main road.

"Close, very close." She glanced at Dean Brandenberg's log castle where the lights were already twinkling in the windows of all three floors, and the grader, wrapped with yellow crime-site tape, was still stuck in the wall. "Actually," she said, "I phoned the car lot down in the village, asked if they had any four-wheel-drive trucks in stock, had them drive this one up to me." She gave a deep-throated laugh, following the exit road to the lake. "Hey, it was the only one they had. What could I do?"

"Maybe have them install a radio?"

"Nah. Then you couldn't hear the music of the spheres."

Radiating from all those visible souls, I thought sourly, as we rounded the lake that shone with the darkening sky and entered the blacktopped state highway. Entered it pretty fast, it seemed to me, without much interest in the stop sign beside it.

Eva was jabbing at the brake pedal, gripping the steering wheel with both hands, but the truck was gaining speed, heading downhill into a treacherous strip of curving, mountainous road with a spectacular cliff, a sheer drop on one side and a solid bank of trees along the other. The headlights were on, and they swept crazily across the tree trunks as we slid around a curve and the tires screamed and the truck tipped and I was looking straight down over a drop of several hundred feet.

I glanced at Eva. She was leaning forward over the wheel, intent on a short, straight corridor of steeply plummeting highway ahead, and for an instant, in the uncertain twilight, I could have sworn she was smiling. The truck was picking up speed rapidly as it flew down the incline. Eva hit the clutch, downshifted to third. She yanked the emergency brake out, but nothing happened. When she downshifted into second, the tires screeched and the truck's rear end skidded sideways, fishtailing toward the edge of pavement and the cliff. She steered into the fishtail, straightened the truck, and then we were approaching a blind curve where the road made a ninety-degree angle to the left. Straight ahead, the cliff loomed. Eva shut the headlights off, then snapped them on again. She downshifted to first, and the truck skidded sideways into the turn and across to the left side of the road. The wheels squealed, the rear end swung wide, and I did the only thing I could possibly do. I cursed myself for being in the passenger seat with an incompetent driver at the wheel, closed my eyes, and prayed that no car was headed our way on the other side. When I opened my eyes, we had cleared the turn, and Eva was laying on the horn to alert a vehicle headed toward us a few hundred yards away. It veered sharply off the road, which now had a margin of shoulder on the tree side, and Eva began easing the truck to the left, toward the soft border of earth between the asphalt and the trees.

"Hang on," she said, her voice easy and cool. "Try to relax. We're going to roll."

I could feel the front driver's-side wheel leave the pavement and lurch down into the soft earth. The truck tipped forward, then sideways, as the rear tire left the pavement, seemed to hang suspended in the air for a long, sickening moment, and then the air was black and spinning. When I opened my eyes, we were sitting upright in the truck, a few inches from the trunk of a large pine. The headlights were still on, and a wild swirl of dust was caught in the beams.

I sat frozen in the seat, still clutching the armrest and my breasts. Eva was slumped across the steering wheel—her back and shoulders jerking sporadically.

"Eva?" I reached across to her, but I was held back by the seat belt. My hands were trembling uncontrollably. I tore at the clasp, and finally it opened. I leaned toward her. "Eva. Oh my god. Eva."

When I touched her, she sat up. Her mouth was open and moving, her eyes clenched tightly shut. She had one hand at her chest, one at her temple, and a tiny, crooked stream of blood was trickling down her forehead, along the inner eye, wandering down her cheek, to the edge of her mouth. Her chest was convulsing, her mouth opening and closing like a beached fish.

"Eva, for Christ's sake, talk to me!" The blood seemed to be coming from behind her hairline, and I thought of Harv, his seemingly innocuous wound. An odd sound bubbled up from her throat, and suddenly I realized with a shock that she was not choking, but laughing. Soundlessly. Ghoulishly.

"Are you out of your fucking mind! Talk to me!"

I could hear the hysteria in my voice, and so, apparently, did Eva. She forced open her eyes to a bare squint, seemed to look me over, satisfied herself that I was unhurt, and collapsed again across the wheel in great heaving guffaws of laughter.

"Jesus." I sank back against the seat as a car pulled up in front of us, the same one that had veered off the road as we were headed toward it.

A man in overalls and a broad, florid face got out and approached Eva's side, then came around to stand beside where I sat. I tried to roll down the window, but it wouldn't budge. The man and I stared at each other through the window, and then he said, "Hey, you girls awright in there?"

He stepped back and looked up and down the truck. "It's too bad, good-looking truck." He stepped back to my window again where we looked through the glass some more. I pulled on the handle, but the door wouldn't open. The man made gestures, pointing toward Eva, shouting as though we were behind soundproof glass. "She okay? Been drinkin', huh." He nodded his head at Eva who was still hanging over the wheel. Finally, he said, "Well, why don't you see if you can start her up, see if you need me to give you a ride." Eva's convulsions increased. The man and I looked at each other a while longer. "Um, well," he said, looking down at the ground and then up at the sky. It had turned a deep navy blue, with Venus getting top billing. The man began chewing on something in his mouth, coughed, spit something on the ground. He shifted his weight from one foot to the other several times. Finally, Eva sat up and looked at him.

She was wiping her face, the blood smeared grotesquely across her forehead and cheeks, running into the tears so that her entire face was a travesty of watery, dripping gore. Her hands, too, were dripping with blood, which she had smeared across the white blouse beneath her jacket. She was still gulping air, her mouth wide, fighting the laughter, trying to speak, gesturing through the window at the man. He stood watching her for a moment with large bulging eyes, looked back at me, then turned around and got into his car and drove away.

Eva collapsed over the wheel again. I sighed and waited and looked out the window at the navy blue sky and talked to it: "I've never been in a car wreck," I said. I waited for a moment, then tried again: "I once fell out of a tree as a child. One time I tripped over my bike and had a fractured pelvis bone." Venus winked, and just above the eastern ridge, the coming of the moon began brightening the sky orange above the peaks. "I've always wondered, you know, what it would be like to be in a car accident." I said each word separately, listened to the sounds as though they could transform the sky, the blue air, the woman beside me in the truck, into something familiar. The words rolled slowly out, one by one, separate and meaningless as marbles. I might as well have been on the moon, sitting on her bright upper curve as she rose above the mountains.

When Eva sat up and asked me to open the glove compartment for a box of tissues, I opened it and stared at a gun whose edges looked soft and lovely in the tiny light from the compartment's bulb. I glanced at Eva, then burrowed under cold metal, beneath several envelopes with handwriting that seemed vaguely familiar even if nothing else did, and extracted a battered plastic packet of Kleenex. I handed it to her.

After she'd cleaned herself off, she said, "You have no idea. Someday maybe I'll have a chance to tell you..." She paused, searching for words, "...well, just tell you more about my life. You'd understand why being killed on a mountain road out in the sticks would be...well, ironic." She squeezed the last wet, red tissue into a tight ball and tossed it on the floor. Blood still dribbled down her forehead, and the moon made a huge golden face that leered through the window over her shoulder.

"I fail to see anything 'ironic' about dying any way at all."

"You wouldn't. It's the life you've led."

She unbuckled her seat belt, leaned across me, and lifted the gun out of the glove compartment.

"And just what kind of life is that?"

She slid the weapon into an inner pocket of her jacket. The part of my mind that cared about such things wondered whether a jacket must be custom-ordered with instructions on the size and placement of the pocket, or did one sew in the pocket to fit the weapon?

"Sheltered."

She jerked the door handle, and when it didn't open, rammed her shoulder hard against the door, and it flew open. After circling the truck and shrugging, she faced the road in the direction we'd come as a set of headlights appeared in the distance. When the vehicle neared, Eva walked over to the highway and performed a series of semaphores, then stood back as the car slowed, cruised past, made a U-turn, and approached with the two of us caught in the blinding glare of its headlights.

The light was agonizingly bright. I squinted as bolts of pain shot through my head and raised my hand as a shield. Somewhere in the distance, against the exploding brilliance, I saw figures moving, voices.

The last thing I remembered was the black shape of Eva Blake, walking toward me from the blaze.

16

THE PROBLEM WITH SATURDAY NIGHTS is Sunday mornings. Like the movie said, payback's a bitch.

I was having trouble remembering exactly what it was I'd done,
but it must have been spectacular to still be seeing double this late
in the morning. I lifted my head up a little more and squinted
through the drums and daggers doing a jazz number in my skull:
two windows covered with yellow roses on a yellow background;
two single beds, same yellow roses; two golden oak night stands
with yellow lamps and fuzzy yellow rugs by each bed. I shut my
eyes. Eased my head back carefully on the pillow. A yellow pillow.

I sank into the darkness behind my eyelids. I'd seen double
before, lots of times, but I quit drinking when Daniel did, the day
his Harley hit the guardrail and he'd kept going, right on over the
cliff. Then I remembered: the truck speeding out of control down
the mountain road, the wheels dropping off the pavement, the
truck tipping sideways, rolling. I squinted, pulled my head down
between my shoulders as far as it would go, inched myself upright
in the bed. This wasn't a hospital room—too many roses, no gown
split up the back. I had on my bra and underpants; my Garbo duds
were folded in a neat stack on top of my suitcase, sitting on a yellow chair in the corner. I positioned my feet flat on the fuzzy rug,

stood slowly till I got my balance, tiptoed to the window. When I peeked through the roses, sun scalded my eyeballs. I squinted deeper, tried again. I was on the second floor of a house; below, a black horse stood eating in a corral.

By the time I dressed and found the bathroom, a clock on the vanity read 8:45. I wandered down a deserted hall where all the doors were closed. Behind one, I heard familiar humming and beeping noises. I pressed my ear against the wood. A computer modem made faint squeals. I knocked, tried the knob. Locked.

"Hey, you up?" Eva's voice.

"No, I'm in bed." I was feeling surly. Seeing double through a splitting headache will do that.

"Coffee's made. Down in a sec."

I was on my third cup half an hour later when Eva pounded down the wooden stairs in her boots, black jeans, black turtleneck sweater, and black hair wet and slicked back with the comb marks still in it. She tossed a sheet of paper in front of me, sailed on into the kitchen.

"How you feeling?"

I stared at the sheet without taking too much of it in, long words, some figures. Behind me, doors opened and closed, kitchen gadgets whirred. Eva filled me in about last night, the sheriff saying I needed to be under observation a day or so, possible concussion; he'd packed a suitcase for me, had his deputy follow him over in my truck so we wouldn't be stranded. Thoughtful guy.

I wasn't paying much attention. I was reading: Texazol, Ketamine, Xylazine, Atropine, mosquito hemostats, lamb gut, scalpel blades. It went on. At the bottom was the name of a vet supply in Denver, a UPS tracking number, delivery date. Monday, October 20. Eva sat a brandy snifter the size of an aquarium in front of me, filled to the brim with reddish slush.

"What's this?" I asked, indicating the list as she sat across from me and took a long pull from her own fish bowl. She set it down, licked a rosy mustache off her upper lip.

"Breakfast."

"Lamb gut?"

She stared at me; I held up the paper.

"Vet supplies. Feline castration." She looked down at the pink goblet. "Drink."

I picked it up and sniffed. "You ordered vet supplies, *drugs*, off the *net*? You can't do that."

"No kidding?" She raised her glass and chugged more of the stuff. Licked. "Ten to one, it'll be here tomorrow. Bet?"

"But how—"

"Friend of mine's a vet, used his DEA number." She grinned, nodded at the snifter I was still holding. "That headache you've got? Give you twenty to one, you drink that, it's gone."

"Let me put it to you this way," I said, spacing the words, squinting at her through the drums and daggers, "I don't want any fucking breakfast."

She quit grinning and gave me a long look. It reminded me of that scene in *The Black Stallion*, the close-up shot of the cobra. "Give it a shot, Symkin. Nothing to lose but the pain."

Ten minutes later, we were headed out the door, and I was glad that gambling wasn't one of my addictions. Eva was fiddling with the security system beside the entryway, talking.

"...any kind of disagreement between Harv and some of the folks around here, Andrew and Wolf will have the scuttlebutt. Nice guys, decorated my house. Not homophobic, are you?"

"Depends on who you ask." I stood in the shadow of the doorway and thought about Sandy; then what the hell, I quit thinking about Sandy. "So we're going to see these guys to...what, help the sheriff come up with suspects for Harv's..."

Suddenly I got it. My headache had disappeared, but I was behind a synapse or two. Eva finished with the security controls and closed the door. We stood facing each other in the doorway: someone had cut Harv's brake lines, then someone had cut Eva's. The difference was, Eva Blake wasn't dead. In her boots, she stood my height. The air had gone dead still, like it does before a tornado touches down. I felt energy coming off her black clothes, a little sizzle of lightning dancing somewhere just out of sight. I heard her words coming back, the night she'd visited me and talked about Brandenberg taking away Harv's place: *If it'd been me, I'd have shot the sonofabitch.*

When I stepped back a little, the smile worked its way up one side of her cheek. She turned, and I followed her down the path. She'd been an actress, after all. Been living in L.A., all those people a little crazy, like they're living some kind of nonstop melodrama. She was just some rich mogul's wife, bored, stuck out in the country, having a little fun playing cops and robbers—

"Hey." She was standing by the passenger door of my truck, her arm resting along the top of the cab. "Want to see something?"

My truck was parked beside her garage with its double door pulled shut, padlocked. So was the entry door at one side where Eva took out her keys again and unlocked a large silver bolt lock. She shoved open the door and stepped back, waiting for me to go in. I stood at the threshold and stared into the darkness.

"Just a few dead bodies, nothing of import." Her voice was smoke and lye. She reached across where I stood and flipped a switch inside the door.

Overhead fluorescent lights flooded the interior—unfinished Sheetrock walls, concrete floor, a square of plywood nailed across a rear window. On the far side, an object was hidden beneath a fitted cover. A car of some sort, about the size of the Porsche I'd sold a couple of weeks ago. Eva Blake strode over and whipped off the cover. There, pristine under the harsh light, was a vintage MG. Black, newly painted by the gloss of it.

I gave a low whistle and circled around. Mag spinners over wire wheels, original insignia on the trunk, a cloth top with the back plastic window in crystal-clear, mint condition. New Mexico license plates, 1993. When I tried the handle, the passenger door glided open. The interior smelled of saddle soap and leather. On the other side, Eva slipped into the driver's seat and started the engine. The car sprang to life with a sound that made me itch for wind in my hair and landscape blurred by speed.

"I guess this means you're not grounded."

"Not really." She switched off the engine and pushed herself out of the low-slung seat. "Needs tags."

"Guess you don't drive it much," I said, indicating the plates as she tossed the cover back over the car. "How come?"

"Kind of a souvenir." She closed up the garage, replaced the padlock, gave it a tug. We headed toward my truck. "Anyway, be snowing soon, salt on the road. Might drive it next spring."

"Sure, but it's not snowing yet. Probably lots of times this winter you could drive it between snows." For that matter, how much snow was there on the freeways of L.A.? Why hadn't she driven the car the last four years?

"Mm. I'll think about it, maybe pick up some plates in town when I have time, but around here I need a truck. Figure I'll stop in tomorrow, lease one when we go for the cat stuff, drive it till my insurance kicks in. Sheriff thinks my truck's totaled."

We got in my Nissan, and I backed out the driveway, set off toward El Gato's main road. "By the way, probably wouldn't hurt to check your brakes."

I hit them hard, throwing us both forward and killing the engine. Eva laughed as I stared out the windshield, wondering whether this meant the brakes were all right, whether I still had to check them. I didn't have a clue what to look for, or even where to look, for that matter.

"Sit tight," she said. "Put it in first gear, set the hand brake."

She watched while I did it, then slid out, slipped under the truck, popped back in the passenger seat in a flash. She slammed her door shut. "All clear. Hit it, hot-rod."

It always amazes me, the kind of eclectic knowledge women outside of academia acquire. I once knew a woman who could roof her own house, another who cut out leather and made her own shoes. This one knew a lot about vehicles. I imagined actresses came by odd bits of knowledge researching their roles…then a scene from after the accident last night began to return, a memory of the sheriff talking to Eva, saying *That's a real miracle, rolling that truck where you did. Chance in a thousand anybody could navigate that road without brakes, then to just happen to roll it at the one place where there's enough room. 'Cause if you hadn't rolled it here, no way you'd have made it on down the road without going over the side.*

The sheriff and Eva Blake had been standing in front of the truck. I had been sitting in the passenger seat, feeling sleepy and disoriented, staring into the Bronco's headlights that shone between the two black silhouettes, talking.

Sheriff: *Either you're just about the luckiest driver I've ever seen or else you're a world-class demolition expert.*

Eva Blake: *Your call, Sheriff.*

"There," she said, pointing at a driveway made of white crushed shells. It was the cedar house Harv had pointed out last April—sharply pitched Alpine roof, lots of glass, flowering plants dangling from the eaves. I parked and followed Eva along a flag-stone path beside the house, through a stretch of dead weeds that served for the backyard. Or so I thought. What I'd taken for a high, weather-beaten privacy wall at the back of the property proved an illusion. We walked behind it, into a zigzagging labyrinth of juniper trees and fence, until Eva pushed open a wrought-iron gate.

An oasis lay before us: flourishing plants and deciduous shrub-bery and skillfully laid flagstone spiraled around a freeform swim-ming pool whose blue surface twinkled in the morning sun, all of it surrounded by an immaculate carpet of emerald grass.

A man lay beside the pool on an intricately carved redwood chaise lounge. He was darkly tanned and naked except for a skimpy elastic brief. One hand dangled over the armrest holding a glass, his chin pointed up to the sky. He rolled his head in our direction, looked at us from behind dark glasses. It was the man from the Brandenberg yard whose jet-black hair two days ago had been tightly caught in a brief ponytail. Today it was damp and gleaming, slicked back behind his ears.

"My God, a turtleneck. You must be roasting." In one unbro-ken motion, he lifted both legs, tilted himself sideways, sat upright.

Eva introduced us and dropped into one of several redwood chairs, also elaborately carved, placed back under a lattice bower. I took a chair beside hers while Wolf Candidos kept his dark glasses trained on me.

"Symkin? I thought so," he said. "Bought the James place, right?" He had small, perfect teeth, brilliantly white against his tan.

"News travels."

"It can. That's a problem sometimes." He looked at Eva. "You warn her?"

"Don't worry." She glanced at me, talking as though she'd memorized her lines and was bored with them. "Not to tell a soul about the backyard pool, the grass. Scout's honor?" She raised her eyebrows at Wolf.

"Eva finds a lot of humor in El Gato. Black, mostly." He stood up and walked over to a glossy azalea in a redwood container beside the pool. The brief he wore didn't cover much—he was essentially naked, an elegant body with long bones and muscles rippling under the tan and oil. He ran his fingers through the plant's leaves, an oddly erotic gesture. "The Association knew about this, they'd force us to tear the whole thing out. Not funny."

An image of Edna's devastated pond flashed across my mind. No, not funny at all.

"It's a beautiful place, I won't say a word. But what's the problem? You can't have a backyard?" The book-length El Gato bylaws I'd received after purchasing my lot, printed out in faint dot-matrix typeface, was still in its mailing envelope at home.

"Sure you can, long as there's nothing in it to water—no grass, deciduous plants…"

I watched spoons of sunlight dimpling across the swimming pool and imagined Brandenberg firing up over it.

"I told him not to do it." A voice from the labyrinth. A pleasant-looking man of medium height, wearing oversized khaki slacks and a white knit polo shirt, pushed through the wrought-iron gate carrying a tray of drinks. Every mother in America hoped her son-in-law would look like this guy. I expected to see Lassie come bounding up behind him any minute.

He smiled. "Andrew Jacobs," he said, setting the tray on the table and sticking out his hand, "you must be Sym."

"You read fortunes, too?" Why was it everyone around here seemed to know my name?

"Our newsletter came out yesterday, mailed to all the property owners. I guess you haven't checked your mail. You're the cover girl this month, complete with a welcome note from the Association secretary, Janie Gillman."

Shit. "I don't get it, what's the big deal? I own one measly lot, no intention of ever building on it. I'm not even, never will be, a resident."

"It's not so much you're a part of El Gato, as you've bought Claire James's place," Andrew said, handing me one of the drinks and taking a chair. "Everybody knows about that. I suspect some people here even had their eye on it to buy, probably waiting for Gerald to get himself in a bind and sell out."

Eva reached over to the tray and took a glass with a thin slice of lime floating on top. She sipped as she spoke. "That's just what I wanted to talk to you and Wolf about. All this conflict going on around here. Harv's been at the center of it, then gets himself killed."

"Killed? But that was—" Andrew began.

"Probably not an accident. Cut brake lines, according to the sheriff," Eva said. "You'll hear soon enough, I rolled my truck taking Sym home last night. Brake lines again. Sheriff thinks somebody's deliberately cutting them." She told them about my visit yesterday, the accident.

We were all silent for a moment. Wolf came over and took the chair beside Andrew. The four of us sat in a circle, facing each other. Wolf removed his dark glasses. He had shockingly pale, ice-colored eyes between jet black lashes. I felt a chill creep up my spine as he turned them on me, then Eva.

"Who—"

"Don't know," Eva said, "but I'm going to find out." She slipped down in her chair, nearly horizontal, with her long legs reaching out across the flagstones and the silver tips of her boots glinting in the sun. She took a long pull on her drink, shook the ice cubes, looked around the circle at each of us. "Wolf, talk to me about Harv. I can't figure how Brandenberg had much to gain by his death, maybe some peace and quiet. Any idea who else wanted him gone?"

Wolf and Andrew exchanged a quick look.

Andrew said, "Just about everybody, Harv wasn't winning any popularity contests. He took tact lessons from Attila the Hun. He spoke his mind straight out, rubbed most people the wrong way."

Wolf made a steeple of his fingers and rested his chin lightly on the tips. "You want more than our impressions and opinions here, am I right?"

Eva held his eyes, two reptilian creatures fusing. She nodded faintly.

"Wait. I think you're jumping off the deep end here," Andrew said. "You're talking murder. Maybe someone just cut the brake lines meaning to scare Harv, not kill him."

"Doesn't wash," I said. "After it backfired and Harv was dead, the mechanic wouldn't have tried it again."

"You're assuming it's the same person." Wolf said. He frowned at the flagstone in front of him as though he were deciphering something written there. "Okay, let's play it through, Andrew's way. Say someone set out to scare Harv, figured he'd be working the road grader in a confined area, figured he'd probably lose the brakes, drift a few yards, maybe bump his head at worst. But it doesn't happen like that. Harv gets a jones to grade the roads, machine runs away, gets himself killed." Wolf looked up, his pale eyes resting on each of us before stopping on Eva. "Now, let's suppose someone's watching all this. Harv's dead, and this someone guesses the brakes were cut, sees an opportunity to use the same method on your truck. Figures whoever did the first one is going to get caught, get blamed for your truck as well."

It was sounding more and more farfetched to me. "You're saying there are two mechanics, two motives? One sets out to get Harv, the second to get Eva?"

"Wait," Andrew said again. He sprang up and paced the edge of the pool, clearly in the spirit of the thing. He stopped and looked at Wolf. "What about this? That black truck parked in our driveway? What if the mechanic saw Sym at Eva's place yesterday, saw Eva's black truck in the driveway, assumed it was Sym's. Maybe it wasn't Eva they were after." He looked at me. "Maybe it was you, Sym."

I didn't want to hear this. I felt my headache starting to do a riff along the back forty of my skull. "You're telling me that someone with enough mechanical skills to cut brake lines couldn't tell my four-cylinder Nissan from Eva's Dodge Ram Charger? Come on."

Andrew grinned sheepishly and said he didn't think he was cut out for detection. Eva drained her glass, and he took it, gathered the other empties on the tray, and disappeared through the wrought-iron gate. Wolf watched Andrew leave, a preoccupied look on his face. He stood up and pulled on a pair of tight-fitting jeans from a pile of clothes beside the pool. He zipped his fly with no hint of self-consciousness, slipped on a gauzy white shirt without buttoning it. He picked up a damp towel at the pool's edge and fiddled with it as he took the chair across from Eva where Andrew had been sitting.

"Listen, you two." Wolf used his thumb and index finger to worry the corner of the towel into a point a few times before he went on. "You need to let this alone, let the sheriff do what he's paid for. Whoever it is cutting brake lines, he finds out you're nosing around, that'll turn the volume way up. Whether it's one person or two, there's no doubt about one thing—whoever did the number on your brakes?" He looked up from the towel, caught Eva, then me, in his icy gaze. "He wasn't expecting you to walk away."

Eva remained horizontal, her forearms stretched along the redwood armrests, hands dangling off the ends. She watched Wolf with her eyelids at half mast, not moving a hair. I felt the air go still, tornado weather.

Wolf sighed, tossed the damp towel on the table. "All right, so let's talk Harv. I think you're right, Eva, about Brandenberg not having all that much to gain. All the people didn't like Harv, I'd give Gerald top marks. What I understand, Harv had helped Gerald out a lot over the years, pitched in every summer to build his house, used the Association grader to level the land, make his driveway, kind of thing people did back before us newbies moved in. Before the Brandenberg era."

"So what was the bad blood between Gerald and Harv?" I said, pulling him back to the subject.

"What do you think? After all Harv had done for Gerald, then to see him start hanging out with Brandenberg, his archenemy? Harv was mad as hell over it. Skinny has it, Harv called his old buddy Claire James, asked her if she'd be interested in selling that property if he could come up with a buyer. It was still technically Claire's place, she hadn't signed it over to Gerald and Wendy yet. And little Wendy, she didn't mind helping Harv do it after Gerald took off and left her for another woman."

That fit. The day I'd wandered into Wendy's house, asking about property at El Gato, of course she had called Harv. Of course he had practically flown over—and a commission hadn't been his primary motive.

Eva spoke, her words tight as a fist: "Property belonged to Claire James, didn't it? Why shouldn't she sell it if she wanted to? Maybe she needed the money. Maybe she was pissed about her daughter dying there, wanted to be rid of the place. Why should she feel obligated to hand it over to some bastard who'd left her granddaughter and the two kids stranded out there to freeze to death?"

"All that may be true," Wolf said as Andrew came back through the gate with fresh drinks. He set the tray on the table and took the chair next to Eva. "But that wouldn't make Gerald like it any better, would it? No, in his mind, Claire James promised him that property if he built on it. And why is it you're always defending Claire James—she didn't even care enough about her own daughter to come back and claim her belongings from what Gerald said. Speaking of which, I've not come up with much on Camilla. Kind of a loner, had some contact with Harv and Edna, not much with anybody else, far as I've heard."

I glanced at Eva, wondering at her interest in Camilla. But for the moment, I was more interested in Gerald and his architectural skills.

"He certainly did build, no argument there," I said, thinking of the eleven bedrooms. "But why such a huge house?"

"He's a strange guy," Andrew said. "His dad's a builder back in Nashville, friend of Claire James. Maybe it's genetic, got building in the blood. I heard him talking at one of the homeowners' meetings about this house he'd heard of in California, some woman thinking as long as she kept building on it she wouldn't die. Gerald got this glazed look on his face like he does sometimes, said he knew just how the she felt."

"Serious nutcase," Wolf said.

"Nutcase enough to actually kill someone over a house?" I said.

Wolf's pale eyes rested on mine. "Who of us, under certain conditions, wouldn't kill?" The sun was straight up, laying shadows along the edges of his facial bones, a sinister touch.

"Sure," I said, "defending your children, yourself, that kind of thing. But premeditated murder? Even so, why would Gerald want to kill Eva? Or me?"

Eva spoke. "People who kill out of revenge or passion, they're not reading any textbooks, Symkin. You want rational criminals, get into politics, white-collar crime. Could be this guy Gerald sees you living in a house he built, was very possessive of apparently, sends him right around the bend. First he takes his revenge on Harv, then on you because you have something that belongs to him, in his mind anyway."

"Right. And mistakes your Dodge for my Nissan?" I tried to keep the sarcasm out of my voice, but it bubbled up like acid. Eva's eyes narrowed. I picked up a frosty glass from Andrew's tray and felt the bite of cold against my palm. I turned to Andrew. "Okay, so anybody else have it in for Harv?"

He glanced at Wolf. "Um, well, he kind of had it in for us a few weeks back. Guy that was supposed to buy a burl table from Harv changed his mind after he bought one of Wolf's redwood chairs, said it didn't match."

While Andrew described Harv launching into a tantrum, furious at the loss of a sale, I admired the intricate carving on the chairs where we sat, remembered the high-gloss burl table in front of Edna's threadbare sofa. No, they were definitely not a match.

Eva was staring off in the distance, the wheels turning behind her eyes. I sipped my drink. And then I nearly choked, showering liquid across the flagstones.

"What the hell...?" I said.

Eva leaned quietly toward me, smiled thinly, took my glass and handed me another from the tray. She sat back in her chair, crossed her legs, sipped. What I had tasted was one hundred percent vodka, maybe a drop of lime. Andrew reached for the towel on the table, dabbed at his polo shirt, then dabbed at Wolf.

"Jesus. I think I just fell off the wagon," I said to no one in particular, sipping some sparkling water to chase away the taste in my mouth. The boys looked at me, smiling like two foxes. Eva sipped and contemplated the sky.

17

EVA BLAKE AND I LEFT Andrew lounging in his redwood chair, watching Wolf swim laps in the pool. The sun was straight up, and I was tinkering with the notion of reclaiming what was left of my Sunday and heading home as I climbed into the truck and reached for the ignition key. But Eva stopped me. She stood with her passenger door open, her hand raised with the index finger pointing to the sky, ear cocked to the clouds. It was a gesture so utterly familiar that I laughed.

It was the signature greeting of my mechanic in Albuquerque. His happiest moments, for all I could tell, revolved around the appearance of me and my Porsche at his bootleg backyard auto garage down the street from where I lived. He would be leaning over an engine with the concentration of a heart surgeon, but when I pulled up, he'd set his wrench aside and come trotting toward me, wiping his hands on an oily mechanic's cloth. Before I could shut off the engine, he'd raise his hand, cock his ear toward the motor, and nod as though Mozart were in live concert. I'd set the parking brake, get out, and he'd slide behind the wheel, revving the engine several times with that ear still aimed at the motor.

I took my car to this man for years, and this scenario played every time. It was not until one day when I showed up to have a sunroof latch replaced that I realized he performed this routine not with the purpose of identifying the nuances of engine dysfunction, but with a hedonist's sheer pleasure in the process itself—sitting in the deep leather seat, gripping the custom walnut steering wheel in both fists, savoring the symphonic music of the engine that played its pistons and plugs for him alone.

I watched Eva Blake disappear. She dived beneath the truck, and in about the time it took me to dredge up the image of my mechanic sitting in the driver's seat with his head leaned back and his eyes closed, a sappy grin spread over his face, she reappeared and hopped inside. "Full speed ahead." She slammed her door.

And that's how I knew.

I started up the engine and let it idle while I twisted in the seat to consider Eva Blake. Even with her husband pigging out on star-let salad, even with the chilling accident yesterday which must cer-tainly have been an attempt on her life, maybe mine, too, this woman stayed cool as yesterday's news.

"What?" she said, as I continued staring at her.

"You like this stuff, don't you?"

"Stuff?" Her chocolate eyes were lustrous and round as a deer's, the picture of innocence. Or maybe it was the vodka.

"All this hide-and-seek, killer-on-the-loose, checking-the-brakes stuff. Like yesterday. You were actually smiling as we were heading toward that cliff." I began backing out the driveway, pausing, undecided about what direction to take. Maybe it was the indecision that made the frustration pour over me, or maybe it was just estrogen depletion—a hot flash. "I mean, shit, people are getting killed, and I suppose I'm glad we're trying to figure this out, but my life's a muddle, I don't feel nearly as cute or as confident as Nancy Drew says I should, and this is not Disneyland, you know?" I headed toward the entrance of the development, suddenly intent on making that visit to Wendy I'd been thinking about. She had helped Harv sell her grandmother's property out from under her husband, and I wanted to ask her some specific questions about how Gerald had received that news.

Eva leaned back into her seat as I drove down the main gravel corridor of El Gato between towering pines and orange-leaved trees in the distance along the stream. The temperature was still mild for this late in the year, but today a high wind swayed the pine tops overhead.

"Well," she said, finally, "there's truth to what you say. I'm an adrenaline junkie, I admit it. I once had a bit part in a movie, driving a Corvette down the coast on Highway 1. The director wanted to have a stunt man do the roll, but I talked them into giving me a shot at it. I spent a couple of weeks at a driving school, demolition training. It's really not all that hard to do, or dangerous either, especially in a truck with a roll bar." We were rounding the lake where the reflection of the peaks in the distance lay still as a photograph across the water. "Yesterday, it was a little tricky finding a place wide enough, but once I did, the odds of us being seriously injured were relatively small. Actually, rolling a vehicle is a lot like an amusement park ride, maybe not Disneyland, but—"

"Okay, okay!" I said irritably. I did not want to think about amusement parks; few people were more aware than I of how dangerous they could be. I went through the crossbar gate and eased up to the stop sign at the edge of the asphalt road, suddenly gripped by a vivid recollection of yesterday's hair-raising ride. I sat looking at the road and saw Eva and I plunging out of control toward the sharp curve and the cliff ahead. This was something new, and I didn't like it. I'd always loved to drive—fast and even recklessly; now I was a bundle of frayed nerves, paralyzed by fear. I glanced uncertainly down the highway both ways—deserted except for a hitchhiker in the distance.

Eva's hand floated across the cab and landed on my own, which gripped the wheel. It was cool and smooth as marble. She spoke slowly, mother to daughter in spite of our ages.

"It's okay, Sym. It's natural to feel nervous," she said in her husky voice. "I was insensitive a minute ago, and I'm sorry. I'd be glad to take the wheel, but sooner or later you'll have to do it. Sooner is usually better."

I whirled on her, snatching my hand away. "What are you, some kind of fucking expert on everything?" My fear had grown teeth and turned bitchy, but knowing that didn't slow me down. I began ticking off her virtues, finger by finger. "You're an expert on Garbo, you see souls, you're a performance driver, you even know how to crawl under a fucking car and look at a brake line. And now you're a psychiatrist? Is there anything you don't know about?"

Eva and I sat in the truck beside the stop sign and stared at each other across the seat: me, flushed with anger; she, with an expression that had settled into cool amusement. One side of her mouth rose in a grim half smile.

"I know everything I need to," she said, "and a lot more than I ever wanted to."

Well, that cleared every fucking thing right up. I snorted, pumped the brakes a little to make sure they were still working, and edged out onto the pavement, turning right, toward Wendy's place. I gave it a little gas, working up to ten miles an hour, reasoning that going this direction on the uphill mountain side of the road, rather than downhill along the cliff's edge, the vehicle wouldn't gather speed even if there were no brakes, simply go slower and slower until it stopped. All I needed to do was open the door and step out before it started rolling backwards.

I was mulling this over, closing in on thirty, when Eva suddenly yelled, "Stop!" She was looking behind us, at the hitchhiker we'd just passed. "I think that's the professor, Doc Moss, the guy who lives down the road from me. Back up." She glanced around at me, an eyebrow raised. "Please."

I backed up, gingerly, until we were looking out Eva's window at a man in his mid-forties: medium build, medium height, quick blue eyes behind wire-rimmed glasses. He had a pale, clean-shaven face and even, pleasantly bland features. If owners resembled their pets, this guy probably kept a blond Labrador retriever that slept a lot in front of the fire. Perched on his medium-brown hair was a wool tam with a visor that matched his tweed jacket and brown pants. Except for the layer of dust over his loafers, the man had been spit-polished and detailed right down to the gold Cross pen peeking out of his breast pocket. I'd spent most of my adult life with colleagues who could have borrowed this guy's wardrobe, and probably his car and family and home as well, without missing a beat. Stereotypes needed this kind of soil to grow in; I could have picked him out of a faculty line up of apple-polishers trying to make the president's short list for dean. Me, I signed up in the other army, generally hung out with the misfits who had their own kind of uniform—frazzled-looking, long-haired types wearing blue jeans and a big Attitude. We weren't much interested in the Dean's List. Still, I knew a teamster that dressed like this guy, so I fed myself the canned quickie lecture on the pratfalls of pre-judging, categorizing, type-casting. I waited for the scales to fall from my eyes. Nothing much was happening, though.

"Excuse me?" Eva said. I stared at her, startled at her new voice, that sounded like a Type-A yuppie working a room. "My name's Eva Blake? I live just down the road from you? Professor Moss, right?"

She'd also climbed the tonal scale a few octaves, somewhere around Valley Girl level. But neither her manner nor the bare fact that Eva Blake was an eye-popper of the first order seemed to have reached this fellow—he could have been deaf and blind for all her effect on him. He did a flatliner smile, the kind busy professors use on irritating students who nevertheless cast their popularity votes at the end of the semester. He covered his bases and ducked his head to extend a hello-nod in my direction, dipping the visor of his tam and mumbling something about a flat, no jack.

"Could we give you a ride?" Eva said. "I live just down the road from you, the cedar house with the new trees?"

The professor widened his smile by flattening his lips. He looked up at the sky and picked up Eva's sing-song, cocktail-lounge tone: "Actually, I'm enjoying my little walk. Just on the way in to my cabin, staying for fall break? They say exercise is good for the soul as well as the body? I'm afraid I get precious little of it in my line of work." He let his gaze drift back to us and lifted his eyebrows. He bobbed his head loosely as he spoke, Howdy-Doody style, and stretched his lips a little more. He glanced down the road first one way and then the other, then back to us. "But thanks, I appreciate the offer. I'll just give Triple-A a whistle when I get to the cabin." The head bobbed loosely on the neck, the blue eyes twinkled. "Nice meeting you." He dropped the visor at me and then at Eva before turning to walk on.

Eva Blake sat with her spine rigid at a post, staring down the road as though she were in a trance. In a voice void of inflection and hard as steel, she said: "Back up, park across his path," and shot a no-nonsense, do-it-now look. I did it. I backed quickly, angling the truck diagonally in front of the walking man. Eva bounced out and stood a couple of yards in front of him.

"I hate to be a pest, Professor Moss, but I just can't, you know, pass up this chance to talk to you. I was thinking…"

The man had stopped in mid-stride, startled, the sunlight hitting his glasses.

"…of taking a few courses next semester, hoping you could help me out."

Professor Moss squinted up at her, this long, lean woman in black, and jammed his hands into his jacket pockets. This was probably just the kind of incident he'd bought his mountain retreat to avoid. His eyes shifted from Eva to the truck and to the path on the other side of it as though he were calculating the most expedient route. He pulled his attention back to where Eva stood, boots planted on each side of his immediate route.

"…English major, and maybe you could tell me which classes I'll need to sign up for. I always meant to finish my B.A., but—"

"I'd really like to help you out, Miss, um…"

"Eva," she said.

"Yes, of course, Eva," he said, stepping around her, "but, actually, the registrar's office is who you need to talk to. You call them the Monday after break, hmm?" He rattled off a phone number, then waded through the weeds and jumped over a shallow ditch to detour around the truck. He aimed a smile at the ground as he trudged past where I sat.

"I've been meaning to do just that," Eva said, stepping over the ditch after him, "but if I could just get your opinion on which teachers are the best ones? Like insider information, you know? Hey, tell you what, I'll just walk along with you and you can still, like, get your exercise, and I can get my information," she said brightly, wiggling her fingertips at me as she passed. "Catch you later, Sym." She drew alongside the professor, a head taller, shortening her stride to his and talking fast and nonstop.

I sat in the truck feeling irritated, abandoned, and more than a little embarrassed at Eva's behavior. I watched them in my rearview mirror: they strolled for a few yards, and then the man came to a dead stop, his shoulders drooping slightly. I saw him spin around on his heel, and the two of them came walking back toward the truck. Eva beamed, opened the passenger door, and held the seat back for him while the man struggled into the limited passenger space behind. His lips had disappeared into a white, hard line, and his jaw muscles were clenched in knots.

"So," Eva said, twisting around in her seat as I made a careful U-turn and headed the truck back to El Gato. "What do you teach, Mr. Moss?" Her smile was bright, her eyes empty. I was enjoying this. The cinema had lost a real talent when Eva dropped out.

The professor cleared his throat and stretched his neck a bit. He wore a pale yellow shirt under the suit jacket, buttoned to the top. "*Doctor* Moss, F. Scott Moss," he said, and I rolled my eyes as I drove through the entry gate again, "but just call me Scott. I teach literature. British Romantics."

"Oooooh," Eva squealed, bouncing in her seat. "I just love that stuff. Could you recite some?"

"Some?" In the rearview mirror, I could see him squint and study Eva from behind his glasses as though she were a beetle.

"Like, you know, a poem? Like, um, 'Tiger, tiger, burning bright, in the forests of the night.' Um, how does the rest go?"

The doc's glasses flashed below his visor. "Now, Miss um…"

"Gabor," Eva said.

"Yes, of course. Miss Gabor, just what classes have you had so far, and where did you have them?" he said, staring out the windshield ahead as we cruised around the lake. I'd heard this tone a thousand times: professors wear the hat of advisor to a circle of students each year. Few like it, but most pretend. Doc Moss wasn't going to make the Dean's List if he didn't sign up for some acting lessons.

During our ride back through El Gato, Eva received advice in a professorial monotone on which of her classes would be accepted, and the insider's scoop on the most popular teachers. By the time we passed her house and I had followed directions to Doctor F. Scott Moss's cabin, Eva had the skinny on the small state college where the professor was serving as interim department chair. I turned into his drive and recognized the modest log cabin I'd passed the day I had first wandered into the development in the wake of the snowstorm. Then, the landscape lay under a fresh blanket of snow, and the place had been deserted—no tracks in or out, no telltale smoke from the chimney. I remembered how desperate I'd been to find a living soul, how disappointed I'd been at finding no one home.

Today, even without the snow, the place appeared no less deserted. The log cabin was a small, square building with a steeply pitched roof and a tiny deck extending over the front door, forming an overhang for the porch beneath. A clearing of dead calf-high weeds covered the front yard, bordered along the back with gnarled piñon and leafless bushes that formed a dense tangle. Heavy wooden shutters with padlocks covered the windows. As I pulled into the driveway beside the cabin, I noticed a small garage behind the house and another structure attached to it.

I had barely come to a full stop when Eva bounced out, then collapsed on the dirt driveway, clutching her foot and yelping. She sat rocking back and forth with her boot in both hands, moaning in pain as I jumped out and rushed around to her. I helped her carefully pull off her boot while the professor pawed at the seat catch, trying unsuccessfully to force the back of the seat forward so that he could climb out. Finally, he gave up and began pushing himself between the seats. His upper torso wriggled through, and then he gripped the top of the door frame with both hands, trying to extract his legs which were still caught between the seats. Suddenly, he lost his hold on the frame and plunged head-first into the driveway, where he landed on his forearms. Steadying himself on them, he began to creep forward, one forearm after another until his legs slid from the cab and his body lay in its entirety, like an aquatic creature, beached in the dirt.

Eva had stopped moaning while we watched the man's exit. "A truly unique methodology," she quipped under her breath, as he was pushing himself upright.

"Probably a deconstructionist," I whispered, as he regained his feet.

The professor stomped each foot several times in his driveway, dislodging the dirt and brushing vigorously at his clothing while Eva resumed moaning and asked for ice to numb the pain of her ankle. We had worked off her boot, and suddenly she pushed herself up from the dirt, hopped on one foot toward the cabin, tossing the boot in the truck as she passed. The professor had stopped batting at his clothes, and I ran to overtake Eva. Shoulder to shoulder, arms around each other, we hobbled together and, joined at the side like Siamese twins, lowered ourselves to his front porch. Doctor Moss's mouth had uncompressed and fallen open. He had his tam in his hand, and I noticed that the top of his head was balding.

"Even a towel and some cold water would help, Scotty," Eva yelled out, "if you don't have any ice."

The professor smashed the tam back on, yanking it solidly down with a tweak of the visor, and then he simply stood facing us with his elbows slightly out.

The eerie silence that I had begun to recognize as peculiar to El Gato descended across the yard as though we were being cast in a frieze, carved into this position forever: the professor facing us, sun striking his glasses, shoulders hunched and arms rigid, one dusty loafer raised and poised in our direction. From his view, we must have appeared as twin women, arm in arm, blocking his entry—I with my electric cape of wild hair shot through with streaks of gray, the woman beside me bent in pain, her hand inched inside her only boot just below that exotic face he seemed not even to have noticed.

Till now.

The man's skin had faded pale as a corpse. I glanced around to see what he had seen—a stranger's eyes in Eva's face, their surface black and cold and empty as caves.

18

Morgan

I slide my hand into my boot, cradle the Smith and Wesson Airweight and keep my eyes locked on the professor's. He is poised, skewered on his own indecision. If he chooses to draw the weapon which has been weighing down the right lower pocket of his tweed jacket, I will have a world of time and more to draw my own weapon from its concealed holster. I wait: I have no particular preference one way or another.

The Symkin woman sits on the porch beside me, her arm still around my shoulders. She is not quite aware of how the danger of living in the world can be a connection to it, but she has been relishing the melodrama, the new dynamic operating around her, pulling her back into life. She is a woman who has spent too little time outside the mind, so that now, her body revels in the adrenaline, the stimulation of the external world. As she turns and stares at me, I feel the tightening of her arm along my shoulders, the quickening of her blood, though I do not take my eyes from the professor who remains paralyzed in his front yard. An interminably slow man.

I wait. It is a small thing, an easy thing. I can slow the seconds as effortlessly as feign a sprained ankle. If need be, I can outrun the moment, anticipate my adversary's next move before he is even conscious of having made a decision to move. These are not vestiges of a psychic power, some eerie sixth sense, but, as Paso pointed out to me, merely the development of a latent prescient faculty common to us all.

"We, each of us, have the magic, figlia," he said, after I'd complained of Cruz's latest obsession to understand how I anticipate a phone's ring,

call the winning horse before the race is done, open a door before the visitor knocks. "It is not a matter for the supernatural, it is a matter of trust. You have heard your spirit whisper these things, and you have listened. That is the difference between you, between us, and the others. They do not heed the whisper."

The sun rains down on the burnt yard, the dead weeds, the man caught there. I am told he is a professor of literature, and I think of the thousands of books that line Pasonombre's library. I wonder why it is that this man in tweed who has spent a lifetime studying such books for his profession and his livelihood and the instruction of his students has no more faculty for wisdom and compassion than a barnacle stuck to a ship, and why it is that my surrogate father, my lost Pasonombre who has dedicated his life to developing such a business as The Company, can read the inscrutable universe and its life forms as though they were sacred texts.

"Too much you ask for, *figlia*."

His library is dim this night. I have returned from an assignment in Berlin. A diffuse cone of yellow light above his shoulder falls onto an open book. The massive stone house sleeps around us, above us. Outside the patio door: the pale outline of a pool, the scatter of sky reflected on the water's surface.

"He's a friend of mine, Paso. He's young, a little rebellious." I lean against the open doorway, looking from the dark pool to this man with his high bald dome, dressed not in a white suit now but in a burgundy robe. I shrug, thinking of my colleague who waits in the car. Who, having bolted from his first assignment, has been in hiding from The Company. "He's a good kid, not made for the field."

The bald dome dips slightly in the muted light. He places the book in his lap, his hands over it. The dome lifts again; his eyes are glimmers in the shadow sockets. "You are perhaps right about him. Yet it is not a matter of this one man, this good young rebellious friend you have come here to champion. It is a situation of larger dimension, *figlia*. You must think again of it, strip away the personal, understand that for an Employee to behave so, there are many endangered. For me to shield the one, to break my own code as others watch, this is a very bad thing. As with a father who in forgiving one child a rude word, teaches blasphemy to the rest.

There are some laws, my daughter, that none of us can be allowed to break."

It is an irony not lost I am sure on Paso from his side of the planet: that several years later, in 1993, as the August sun dawned on a New Mexico mesa, I completed my last assignment by myself defecting. Because I have not given him the documentation, he cannot know of Cruz's deception, the unscrupulous corruption that endangered not only The Company, but compromised the lives of untold numbers of people, perhaps of the planet itself. Only by retaining these documents could I protect the woman I was sent to observe, Anna Lee Stone, from Cruz's retaliation—though by doing so I have become the prize fox in a blood sport, hunted by both The Company and Cruz.

The professor's eyes shift from mine to his cabin, to the garage attached to it. The angle of his right elbow narrows infinitesimally. My index finger slips into the stainless steel ring, lies against the surface of the Airweight's trigger.

19

EVA WAS IN THE PASSENGER SEAT pulling on her boot as I backed out the professor's drive. Moss didn't look our way, I didn't wave, and in spite of my protests, Eva Blake didn't seem inclined to fill me in on what kind of weirdness had just happened back there.

"Hey," she said, "you think it's weird now, anything I could tell you isn't going to ease your mind. Trust me on this one." She pulled her pants leg neatly over her boot, crossed her arms, and scowled out the window as I navigated back down the mountain.

"If you say so. But we can at least mark Doc Moss off our list of suspects. He wasn't even here till today."

Eva gave a dry laugh. "You'd make a hell of a cop. You always believe your suspects without checking them out?"

I thought about that for a minute. We had met the professor hiking in to El Gato, his car apparently was on the highway up ahead with a flat, and he had said that he was just arriving here from home. It had not occurred to me that he might be lying, and I realized that I believed him without question for no other reason than that he and I shared the same academic background. Professors were not liars or thieves or murderers, after all.

"What's so funny?" Eva asked.

I stopped the truck and waited until the hysteria had passed. I shook my head and wiped the tears from my eyes, still breathless from laughter. "You don't believe him then?" I asked, driving on.

"I'm just saying I wouldn't mark anybody off the list without making a few calls. Whoa, stop. There." She held up her hand like a traffic cop and pointed to a road up ahead almost concealed by a heavy overgrowth of junipers on each side. "I've been meaning to have a chat with the resident weirdo. How about it, you up for an interview with Myra-the-Odd?"

I stopped the truck at the edge of the turnoff. "Don't you think we ought to call first? We can't just drop in."

"No phone, but I suppose if you feel that way about it, you could always send her an engraved invitation with your card enclosed, ask her to drop by your house, mention you'd like to chat with her about murder and her alibi. Or maybe the next time you run into her in the woods, you—"

"Okay, okay!" I nosed the truck into the trees, the dense branches scraping against the sides. The afternoon light disappeared, and as we tunneled deeper into the interior forest, I began to make out the sound of the stream. Finally, after a great many crooks and turns, we broke into a small clearing where sunlight fell in golden shafts through towering pines. I parked the truck at a row of rocks marking the end of the road. There were no other vehicles, no tire prints to show that one had recently been here. Eva and I opened our doors to the crashing sound of rushing water. In the distance, on the opposite side of the clearing, a small, odd structure sat next to a stream, encircled with a wooden deck extending over the water at one side.

"It's not Hansel and Gretel," I said, slamming my door.

"Ain't Kansas, either."

What it was, I realized as we walked toward the structure, was a revamped boxcar. It was painted a dark brick red and large windows had been added, as well as a wooden entry door and probably a wood stove from the looks of the chimney visible on the roof. Eva raised her fingers to her lips and gave one of those ear-splitting whistles like macho women love to do.

"Yoo-hoo! Anybody home?" Eva yelled loudly, walking on up the pathway toward the front door. I tagged behind and scoured the surrounding foliage for the camouflaged figure I'd run across yesterday near Edna's place.

"I really think we ought to go," I yelled over the sound of the water as I climbed the set of wooden stairs behind Eva. "Can you imagine living in this racket day in and day out?"

We were standing on the front porch, and while Eva banged on the door, I strolled to where the deck extended over the stream and touched down on the opposite bank. In the rushing stream just below my feet, the water boiled around rocks and carried sticks and leaves spinning along down the mountain.

I turned around just as Eva was trying the doorknob. Locked. She reached into her pants pockets, withdrew something, and in a few seconds the door glided open.

"Eva!" I said. "I don't think..."

But she was already inside. Anxiously, I looked around the clearing. I paced the length of the front deck a couple of times, then darted in the door after Eva. She'd disappeared yet again. On the far wall, a sliding patio glass to the rear deck stood partially open. The boxcar was divided into four sections—a kitchen, a living area situated around an iron stove, a bed covered with a colorful quilt and placed on concrete blocks in one corner, and a large wood desk beside the front window where I stood. A floor-to-ceiling bookcase held an eclectic selection of hardbacks—mostly nature books, particularly ones on birds, but also others on architecture, carpentry, dendrology, firearms, photography, sewing, solar energy, weaving, and wicca. Most of the books had jackets in clear plastic covers, and I noticed as I pulled out several that they were stamped DISCARD in red letters along the top. The inner cover of each book was affixed with an empty manila library card holder inscribed with "Property of Crystal Springs Community Library." On the shiny surface of the desk, two stacks of plastic file holders were filled with papers. On the top of one stack lay a stapled packet, the top sheet a photocopy of the title page of a book: *Blood Kin* by J. S. Symkin. The lower half of the sheet had been stamped INTERLIBRARY LOAN in large blue print. I smiled; it must have taken her a while to dig that one up. I glanced out the window, saw no one, and thumbed through the materials underneath. Apparently she'd not been interested in reading my next three volumes.

The farthest corner of the room was blocked off with a diagonally placed room divider, probably the toilet area although no trace of unpleasant odor hung in the air. In fact, the boxcar was showcase-tidy, the wooden floors recently waxed and the windows sparkling. I glanced around uneasily.

"Eva?" I called toward the open sliding door, just loud enough to be heard over the stream.

"Here." Her voice boomed through the small room, and her head popped around the divider. "Had to make a pit stop. Interesting concept," she said, emerging from behind the divider, zipping her fly and buckling her belt. "Compost hole in the floor."

I sniffed. Still no odors. She grinned at me. "City folks," she said, shaking her head.

"Right," I said, stage-whispering. "This from an L.A. woman?"

"I've been around." She walked out on the back deck through the sliding door.

I wandered into the kitchen area. A wooden shelf installed above a narrow table that ran along the wall held books on vegetarian cooking, herbal remedies, and homeopathic medicine with a couple of bricks for bookends. The kitchen had no running water, though several plastic gallon jugs of it were lined up against the wall beneath the table. No electricity either, I realized, recalling that I'd seen no electric poles as we drove in. But a small light fixture was installed on the bottom side of the shelf, and when I flipped the switch, it illuminated the work area where two large bowls comprised a makeshift double sink. Next to the table, a small gas stove was piped to a five-gallon propane tank stored on the far side of a dorm-sized refrigerator. When I peeked in the fridge, which was stocked with small plastic containers, several jars of condiments, and a couple of unopened wet packs of tofu, a light twinkled on.

"Water-generated electrical system," Eva said, returning from the deck. She jerked her chin toward the edge of the deck where a large wooden storage cabinet was secured with a padlock. "Nifty little setup. Water runs the generator, which charges the battery pack." She walked to the front door.

"Yeah, well," I said, following her on tiptoe, "I'd really like to get out of here before…"

In front of us, at the bottom of the steps, stood Myra Jones. She still wore the brown Snoopy cap, the camouflage clothing, but her colorless eyes had turned to steel.

"Hey, Myra," said Eva, using her Type-AAA personality networking voice. "How ya doin'? Thought maybe ya didn't hear us up there in your bear blind. This is a really nice place ya got here. Eva Blake, glad to meet ya." Eva bent double at the waist and extended her long arm down to where Myra stood on the first step glowering up at us.

Bear blind?

Myra stared at Eva's hand for several days, then pulled off a raveling purple knit glove. She took Eva's hand and held it without changing her expression.

"Ya know," Eva said, covering Myra's hand with her free one as she descended the stairs to the ground, "I been thinking about getting one of those lots way on up the mountain, have kind of like a little hideaway, ya know, and this is exactly what I was thinking of doing." Eva released Myra's hand and made a sweeping gesture at the boxcar. "Now if you're interested in, like, working with me on this, kind of an advisor, I'd sure be happy to pay for your time and your expertise."

Myra's expression softened. The puckers around her eyes relaxed. She darted a black look at me, then returned her attention to Eva.

"Ya don't have to decide right this minute," Eva said, patting the air in front of her. "Just be thinking about this, maybe if ya know of somebody wants to sell a lot up here, maybe that lot right on the other side of Doc Moss's? Ya know Professor Moss?"

Myra bent her head several times, nodding. Her features had smoothed out, a little color drifted across her cheeks. "Not his lot though," she said in a rusty monotone. "He only has the one, where his cabin sits."

"Well, that's all right," Eva said. "Any of these high-up lots would do. Anyone ya know might want to sell, ya could just stop by, let me know..." Eva stepped back toward the truck, gave a salute of her index finger, pivoted around on one heel and walked off as Myra and I watched.

When she turned back, I stood trapped at the top of her stairs. The skin around her eyes had gathered up again, and black lines were spreading around her mouth and across her forehead. I took a deep breath and started down the stairs, stepping over a shiny black beetle half the size of my foot as it trudged along gripping the edge of the top step. I sidled down the stairs, my lips pressed into a smile that felt like stone, and muttered something about hoping she would visit me. As I reached the bottom stair opposite her, Myra took her eyes from the beetle and faced me as some great eruption of inner turmoil started to boil across her features. I stared at her face, which appeared to be seething with movement just below the surface, and I was reminded of dragons breathing smoke from their nostrils as Myra's began to broaden and tremble. I stopped cold and braced myself, expecting her to leap at me. Her lips stretched back, forming a rictus of bared yellow teeth. For a moment I was stunned, and then I realized that Myra Jones was smiling.

She shot a straight, stiff arm toward me, narrowly missing my stomach, and I took her hand and pumped it vigorously.

"You can come back," she said. "Her, too." She swung around and dipped her head in Eva's direction, dropping it down like a lowing cow.

I held the woman's hand which lay heavy as a rock in my own. "Um, I really *really* love your place," I said to her. I had been struggling for words when I discovered these, but I suddenly realized that they were true—Myra Jones had created a unique home in the wilderness. She swung back to face me, and I let go her hand. Standing less than three inches from her, I saw the gullies and the small pits that disfigured her entire face where some childhood disease must have eaten away her skin. I took another deep breath. "We should have waited till you were here to go in," I said, avoiding her eyes, "and I'm sorry."

She jerked her head forward several times, and the ears of the Snoopy hat flapped against her cheeks. I turned to walk away, then turned back.

"Thanks for warning me about Cougar Canyon, too," I said. "I didn't realize that there were mountain lions that came down this far."

"They do," she said. Her eyes lit; her face became almost mobile and her words embroidered with emotion. "It's a blind canyon. They trap their catch there, but only deer and elk, never human."

"And eat them there? That's where the people on the archeology dig found the bones, the woman's hand?"

Myra Jones stared at me, the light draining from her odd colorless eyes in her ravaged face. She shook her head sadly and studied the ground. "They don't eat them there. They just catch them there. Not people though." Then she turned and walked up the stairs and closed the door.

There was no room to turn around in the narrow road to Myra's house. As I navigated the truck back the way we had come, I wondered if she had maneuvered her vehicle like this through dense thickets of trees every day she had gone to work at the library. I couldn't picture her doing it. And what had she driven? I hadn't seen a car or any evidence of one.

"Well?" said Eva, as I backed through the scraping tree limbs.

"Well, what?"

"You engaged Ms. Odd in probably the longest conversation she's had this century. What's up?"

I shook my head. "She's a strange bird, all right. Is she…well, does she have all her marbles, you think?" I plowed into a low-hanging juniper and pulled forward to get a better position. I navigated the sharp turn and backed more carefully into the next.

Eva shrugged. "All I know is what Harv told me. She used to work at the community library, had some trouble there and left. Has an obsession about bird watching." She paused for a minute. "'All her marbles,' huh? Looks to me like she's got enough marbles to figure out one hell of a living arrangement without standard electricity or running water. I figure there are folks with Ph.D.'s that might not be able to do that." She grinned at me. "What do ya think?"

I was concentrating on negotiating the dense overhangs on each side of the road. "I think I'd like to know why she left her job at the library. And she's got a photocopy of my first volume of poetry. It's pretty hard to come by. I wonder where she got it."

"She *is*, or *was* anyway, a librarian, after all," Eva said.

I finally reached the larger road, backed into it, and headed down the mountain. "Shit!" I blanched and hit the brakes, remembering that we had been out of sight of the vehicle for a while. They seemed fine.

"Already checked," Eva said.

Of course. "But anyway," I said, still thinking of Myra Jones reading my poetry, "why bother to track it down? Of all the books I saw there, poetry wasn't one of her interests. How did she even know I write poetry, and once she did, why did she want to read it?"

"Don't know. What's it about, the poetry?"

I thought about Eva's question as we bounced down the potholed road that had apparently not been on Harv's list of roads to grade.

"Well, it was my first book. I wrote those poems not long after Daniel had died. Most of them are…angry, bitter. The world is savage, so are the people, the animals. They're surrealistic, very unpleasant, really." I thought about Myra Jones's colorless eyes and how they would perceive the depraved beasts and the torn flesh and the mindless violence where I had hacked away at my anger. "I don't like that book very much, and frankly I wish there were no copies at all of it. But I think I had to write it before I could write the next three. The others, the books that came later, they're much different. Gentler, easier." I smiled over at her. "Better."

Eva had that odd look on her face, the intense one as though she were looking through a face instead of at it, reading the thoughts scrolling behind the forehead. The hairs along the back of my neck rose. I looked back to the road ahead.

"And by the way," I said, "what the hell was that about a 'bear blind'?"

"Tree to the right as you walk up? Couple of steps fixed to the back of it. Platform built up there. The kind of place a hunter will use when he's looking for bear, big cats, large game. Puts the bait out under it, animals get in the habit of coming by, hunter goes up there one day at his leisure, dead bear."

"Legal?"

"Depends on the state, time of year." She pursed her lips. "Legal or not, it's not quite the gentleman's way, is it?"

I had never been able to see much in the way of a fair match between guns and animals, no matter how it happened. "You're saying Myra Jones is killing bear, or whatever wild animals she's baiting?"

Eva laughed. "Not hardly. I think she's using it just as she did today. To make herself scarce while she keeps an eye on anybody who drives up. Call it 'people baiting.' "

"So she heard us coming and went up to the platform to watch?"

"That's my guess. She's lived by that stream long enough, she could hear over it. Probably doesn't take much to visitors, uninvited ones anyway, so when someone drops in without warning, she screens them. Kind of like the way we use an answering machine, see if we want to talk to the caller first before we pick up. She hears a vehicle approaching, goes up to the platform, decides if she wants to make an appearance or not."

"But why not just hide in the corner, behind the room divider? Why go outside and climb a tree?"

"Good question. Don't know the answer to that one." Eva leaned her head sideways and grinned. "Could be, she's a little worried about a locked door stopping some people."

"And you knew she was up there watching all the time, even when you broke in?"

"Yep. Only two things she could do. She could stay up there, in which case, no problem. Or she could come down. From where she was, it would have looked like I turned the knob, walked in. She came down thinking she must have been mistaken about locking the door. And, sure, I shouldn't have gone in, but after all, she knows who I am, seen me at the homeowners' meetings, and I didn't steal anything, did I? I was only checking out her setup, right? She was pissed for a minute or two, but then she was flattered that I admired her place. So," she lifted a shoulder, "what's the harm?"

"Maybe none, but what's the point? How does she fit in with our brake specialist?"

"Or how does the professor, for that matter, right? Well, they both live in the development. Let's start there. Most likely Myra Jones was somewhere on the grounds between when Harv last drove the grader and Friday afternoon when he was killed on it. The professor says he wasn't around during that time, but I'm not marking him off my list till I do some checking. And—"

"Checking? How are you—"

"Hey, there's not a wife in Hollywood who doesn't know how to check out an alibi," she laughed. "Leave it to me."

I remembered how quickly and smoothly Eva had opened Myra's locked door, her performance for the professor, the chilling look that passed between them in his front yard. The more I was around Eva Blake, the more she unnerved me. The truck bumped to the end of the ungraded road where it met the smooth gravel one that led past Eva's house. I hit the brakes again, relieved when they held, and decided that El Gato and all that had happened during the short five days since I'd moved here was more than even my creative logic could explain.

"Okay," I said, turning right, toward Eva's house, "but we still don't know where Myra was during the period in question, although she was definitely in the area when you and I were talking and someone was apparently tampering with your brakes. I'd just seen her a couple hours or so before that, and I thought she might have been following me. But stopping by there today didn't tell us anymore than we already knew about her."

"Sure it did," Eva said. There was a smile in her voice. "Looking around someone's living space can tell you almost anything you want to know about a person."

"Like what?" I pictured Eva Blake's home—the showroom decor, the lack of personal items, the vacuous gloss of it all. I'd felt more at home at a Holiday Inn.

"We know that Myra Jones, for all her obtuse mannerisms, is actually quite accomplished mechanically. Of course, she could have had the solar setup done by someone else, but I doubt it judging from the books she has on the subject and by her obvious lack of monetary resources."

"So you think she might know something about brake lines?"

Eva smiled. "Could be. For sure she knows something about Doc Moss."

"How do you know that?"

"That blush at the mention of his name was a dead giveaway, don't you think?"

Blush? "I missed that, but even so—"

"Plus, she knows exactly how many lots he has. I think she knows Doc Moss, and I think it's more than a lonely woman's fantasy."

"Pretty hypothetical and, even if you're right, what difference does it make?" Up ahead the row of new privacy trees beside Eva's house came into view.

"You know," she said, "I really should be checking out some things from home while you go ahead and drop in on Wendy. I'll make some calls, find out for sure if the professor was where he said he was. We can cover more territory that way, and Wendy might think it's a bit odd, the two of us dropping in. Just one visitor would look more natural, less threatening. What do you think?"

As I dropped Eva off at her driveway, I realized I hadn't stopped to consider how Eva and I might have appeared to Wendy, two women closing in on six feet tall walking up to her screen door. For that matter, I thought, as I rounded the lake where the late afternoon sky lay flat as a plate across the water, I hadn't stopped to think what we must have looked like to F. Scott Moss, sitting there on his porch with our arms around each other and blocking the entryway to his cabin. It occurred to me for the first time that Doc Moss must have, from that stony look that settled into his eyes, been absolutely petrified.

20

I PARKED BESIDE A LATE-MODEL TOYOTA TRUCK, waded across Wendy's yard kicking cereal boxes and aluminum cans out of the way, wondering how long you could live in trash before you turned to trash. Or maybe I had it backward, I thought, climbing the stairs and knocking on the door, cupping my hands against the screen to look through when no one answered. Maybe the human trash came first, then entropy kicked in.

The living room looked about like six months ago—except now the television was upside down in the middle of the floor with a hole through its screen. I knocked again, stepped back, looked around. No one in sight, no tree for a bear blind: what the hell, I'd just had a lesson in illegal entry, hadn't I?

"Yoo-hoo! Anybody home?" I tried a macho whistle and blew air. Unlike Myra Jones' door, this one wasn't locked. I pulled it open, poked my head inside, tried another couple of loud yodels before entering. In the living room I stood uncertainly, surrounded by ankle-deep, wall-to-wall trash. To my left, a bare wood staircase cluttered with toys led up to an open loft. At the end of the dim hallway straight ahead, a triangle of light from the kitchen cut across the floor. The air reeked of spoiled food and neglect, spiked with the acrid electrical stench of the shattered television. I stood stock-still, listening. With each passing second, an unnatural silence filled the house, straining its walls, pushing against the windows. Every instinct I had was screaming at me to turn around and get the hell out of there.

I walked toward the triangle of light.

In the kitchen, Wendy sat facing me behind the Formica table. Her face was cut and bruised, her hair tangled and matted with blood. One eye was swollen nearly shut, and a red trickle made a crooked path from her nose, down her neck, and disappeared under a torn, bloody T-shirt. Behind her, two small children cowered in the corner space beside the stove. Mother and children rolled their uneasy blue eyes to me, then back to the figure sitting across the table from Wendy. Even with his back to me, I recognized the wavy silver-blond hair, the white silk shirt that Gerald Crawford had worn on Dean Brandenberg's front porch.

"My God, what—"

Wendy said, "It's okay, Miz Symkin, ma'am." A capillary in the swollen eye had burst, and the cornflower-blue iris sat on a field of red. "We was just getting some things worked out here, is all. It don't look too good, but it's all right now, ma'am. You can go on." She swiped at the squiggle of blood seeping from her nose and smeared it across her cheek.

I took several steps across the kitchen toward her, rummaging in my pocket for a tissue, before Gerald turned in his chair. His shirtfront and cuffs were smeared with blood, and the face I remembered as angelic wasn't angelic anymore—not unless you counted that renegade from the Old Testament. His lips were twisted and his pale eyes seethed with rage. I stopped in my tracks. And then, as though a curtain dropped, the angelic expression returned. He spoke in a whispery, musical voice with a heavy southern drawl:

"Why, yes *ma'am*, I bet you right happy to know we are just fine, *ma'am*." He put a hillbilly spin on *ma'am*, lifted his upper lip like I've seen drunks do when they say the word *fag*. "We just having us a little dispute resolution here. Now you broke in, you might as well pull you up a chair, give us your perspective on it."

"Actually, I—"

"Fact, I believe I'll insist on it." He pulled out the chair next to him with his foot, gave it a savage kick in my direction. I stared at his shirt, the mad, pale eyes, and sat down at the table.

Gerald might have done a little housecleaning. The table top was cleared off and piles of broken dishes and food containers covered the floor. Wendy sat rigidly with her hands in her lap, but

Gerald placed his elbows on the table. He folded his hands together, framed in bloody silk cuffs, as though he were beginning a prayer, then rested his chin on his interlaced fingers and glanced around the kitchen at each of us. I watched him in fascination—the elegant bone of his nose, the slanting eyes, the blond brows tipped up like wings. His voice was low, the room hushed.

"This here's my wife. Them my kids." He nodded toward the others, but his eyes held mine. "Just wont you to know, *ma'am*, we had us a real nice little family 'fore you come along, bought our home from under us. I feel like you ought to know where I stand on you taking my property. Now it was my mother-in-law's in name, I don't dispute it, but she had word-of-mouth promised it to me, to me and mine." He glanced at his children, let his gaze rest on the woman across from him.

"Now Wendy here, she got to share part of the blame, too. That right, girl?" Gerald's smile flickered. Wendy nodded her head mechanically, as though moved by invisible strings attached to the ceiling. "Her and Ole Harv," Gerald went on, returning his gaze to me, "I figure they the ones put you on to buying my home, and 'fore I even known it, the papers was signed. Can you believe now, *ma'am*," he said, biting the word, his eyes glinting in the fluorescent glare of the ceiling light, "that I did not even know my house I been building over these years was not mine no more? That I got up one day to go visit my home, drove up to see all them trucks and people out there messing with my place. To find out that it was not even mine. Now you wont to tell me how a man's to feel when that happens to him, *ma'am*?"

So it was Gerald that Tony had told me about, the strange guy who'd stopped his truck at the head of the driveway, who'd gotten out and watched the men work for a long time before Tony approached, explained he was doing renovations for the new owner. Tony said the man had never said a word, had gotten back in his truck and sat inside it for a long while, then backed up and drove away.

"...don't expect somebody like you to understand," Gerald went on, "somebody what never built a house with their own hands, who just puts out the money to—"

That was when the anger began. That was when I knew it was still buried down in the pit lying under the heart, hidden down there and doing nothing but waiting for exactly the wrong time. I felt it first like my blood had turned scalding hot, shooting hot wax through my flesh. I felt my face burn and my pulse fly.

"I worked hard for that money," I said. "And that house you're calling a home was not much more than a nightmare of cat shit and rotten wood when I first saw it. How could I know you thought it was yours? Mrs. James—"

He leaned forward like a shot, slamming both hands down loud on the table top. Half standing, he shoved his face so close to mine we nearly touched. I felt the force of his breath against my skin. "Fuck Miz James," he hissed. "And I wont you to shut your fucking face till I'm done talking, *ma'am*. You think you able to do that? 'Cause if it's going to cause you some trouble, I will give you a lesson in manners so you don't interrupt me no more. *Ma'am*."

My heart was beating so hard it hurt. I recoiled.

"Good, that's real good." Gerald Crawford nodded and sat back in his chair. Wendy hadn't moved except her mouth had fallen open in a perfect circle, and she watched me instead of her husband. He surveyed the kitchen with a distant, glazed look, turned to me. His pupils had shrunk to pinpoints, and his eyes were nearly transparent, bits of aquamarine. My pulse raced, and I felt faint. I wondered what Eva Blake would do if she were here. If she really could see souls, what would she make of Gerald Crawford's?

"I reckon you got your title all nice and signed and legal. That old cunt, she probably got twice what it was worth, but that don't matter 'cause it's yours now. That how you thinking?" He narrowed his eyes. "I'm here to tell you, *ma'am*, that house is more than can be put to paper. Everything you have that says it's yours is as sorry as a candle in rain. I built that house, *ma'am*, and it will always, it will always be mine no matter what piece of paper you got saying it ain't. You living there, in my house, for the time being, because I *allow* it. We having this talk so I can tell you how I appreciate you fixing it up like you have." He glanced at Wendy and his children. He placed his hands in prayer position, fingers to his lips, and smiled the sweet smile of young Gabriel himself. "And I sure do like the way you have turned that top story into a library. *Ma'am*."

I stared at him, dumbfounded. The top story was three flights up, the library accessible only from the inside. No one could see in; the only way to know what was in the room I'd chosen as the library was—to have been there. Gerald's eyes glittered. The smile flickered, made small convulsions around his lips.

And then it struck broadside, rage that slammed home like a hurricane, sweeping away every thought that might have stemmed it. In that blinding instant, I saw my mother's bloody throat, my father's indifferent gaze from the height of the tractor with his white house in the background. Saw Daniel walking out the door in his black leather jacket, swinging his leg over his motorcycle, and roaring down the driveway; saw Sandy's smug grin as she watched from her office door as I walked down the hall with a cardboard box containing the twelve years of my demolished professional career. In that one consuming moment, I stood naked with desire, driven by a force beyond my understanding or control. I leapt from my chair and faced Gerald Crawford.

"Let me tell you something, you rotten little maggot, people like you, you ought to be locked up. Your whole life doesn't amount to more than rain on shit. You beat up women, go off and leave your family to freeze to death in the woods. You lost that house because you deserted and neglected it, just like you did your wife and children." Gerald sat looking up at me, stunned. Wendy's mouth opened and closed, the blood still oozing down her face. I fished in my pocket again for the tissue, extracted it and leaned over the table toward her. "And if Wendy here has any sense at all, you won't have a chance to do it much longer. You'll be locked up—" Suddenly Gerald soared through the air, exhaling a long hissing syllable as he rocketed me backward against the kitchen wall. The children screamed. Wendy called out her husband's name, pronouncing it over and over like a mantra as he pinned me against the wall, his hands around my throat, his fingers pressing into my flesh like iron. He pulled my head forward and back, hammering it against the wall as I struggled to loosen his grip. I glimpsed Wendy's face hovering above his shoulder, repeating *Gerald Gerald*

Gerald like some mindless metronome while the children screamed behind her. I fought for breath, felt my head smashing against the wall over and over. Gerald's mad aquamarine eyes were close to mine, enlarged, turning red, his smile flickering and widening.

Somewhere in the distance, in the very far distance, I heard a crash. When my eyes opened again, I looked up into Wendy's battered face. A cold cloth lay across my forehead, and she was lifting my head with one hand, pressing a paper cup against my lips with the other. Water dribbled down my neck as I lay stretched on the kitchen floor, awash in trash and broken dishes, a pillow stuffed under my head and the two children peering round-eyed over their mother's shoulder like small owls. I guessed the boy to be five, his sister three.

"Hey, girl, you okay?" Wendy attempted a smile, but one side of her mouth had swollen and pulled her face grotesquely sideways. The damaged eye had completely disappeared behind purple flesh. "Try a sip of this," she said, offering the cup again. "Here's some aspirin."

The tablets felt like thumbtacks creeping down my throat. I squinted around the kitchen.

"He's done gone," she said, sounding a little sad. I sipped the last bit of water from the cup, handed it to Wendy, and she tossed it over her shoulder. "I'm real sorry about this, Miz Sym. Gerald's always had a right bad temper, but he's not never behaved like this, never attacked nobody but me that I know of." Her eyes skittered for a moment. I wondered who else Gerald had attacked.

When I tried to sit up, a light show exploded in my head. I squeezed my eyes shut, gingerly eased my head back to the pillow.

"You better just stay put till you feel better," Wendy said. She stood up, lit a cigarette from a crumpled pack in her jeans pocket, blew the smoke out of the undamaged side of her mouth. She limped over to the fridge, snagged a can of beer, righted an overturned chair, and sat down. Popping the beer, she nodded at the children to come to her: "You, Shawn, Tiffany," she said. She took a long drink from the can and set it on the table. She clamped the cigarette in the undamaged side of her mouth, squinted the already swollen eye against the smoke as she leaned forward quick as a striking snake and snatched the little girl to her. "He don't mean nothing by it. My fault, setting him off about hanging around that Brandenberg so much. He was already right tense, you moving into our...into that house and all. Gerald's a real tense kind of person."

She snatched a rag from the table, clasped her legs tightly around the little girl, holding her fast. The child retracted her head deep into her shoulders. She squeezed her grimy upturned face into a tight knot as Wendy balanced her cigarette on the table edge and began scrubbing with the concentration and persistence of a mother cat.

"And you've been married...how many years?" My words came out painfully, as a barely audible croak. I took the wet cloth from my forehead, pressed it to my throat, and eased myself upright inch-by-inch.

"Be six next June. Back in Tennessee. Our folks was close, known each other forever, went to the same school." Her voice smiled. "Ever girl there was in love with Gerald. I was just a freshman, he just graduated, fixing to go off to college when we decided to marry. Well, you know, we *had* to," she said, aiming a look over the child's head. She finished her grooming, opened her legs, released the girl while snagging the boy before he could dart away. She ignored his screeches as she snapped him tight between her legs and began scrubbing.

Fifteen. That put her at age twenty-one—no skills, two children, a psychotic husband, and a mother who...I already knew this story. It was an old one, and I knew the odds on how it was going to end, too. I suspected somewhere in the locked closets of her mind, she did, too.

She was eyeing me over her son's head, making some decision. Finally, in a plaintive voice, she said: "You planning on turning him in?" The boy tried to pry his face away from her grasp and look at me, too. The little girl stood round-eyed beside her brother, her thumb going to her mouth.

I thought about it. Wendy had set the forces in motion to be rid of the home she hated, would she now with a little encouragement go the distance and blow the whistle on Gerald?

"I think Gerald needs to be stopped before something more serious happens," I said. The words came painfully, hoarse and raw. I watched her closely for a response. She opened her legs, released her son.

"You two, y'all get on out and play," she said to the children. When they ignored her, she swatted at them with the filthy cloth. They howled and danced around the kitchen out of reach until Shawn shouted, "Indy Five Hunted" and dashed off with his sister close behind. We heard them stampeding down the hall, the screen door banging. Wendy contemplated the cloth in her hand a moment. She tossed it toward the sink, missed, picked up her beer, then helped me up from the floor.

"Well, Gerald, you know, he's right upset about this house business. Reckon me and Harv shouldn't of put you on to it," she said, guiding me toward the living room where we sat together on the couch, watching the children mount their tricycles in the front yard.

Wendy talked in her slow southern way about how Gerald had pursued other women, but had never left her for one of them. This last winter, instead of going to work as usual for Dean Brandenberg's construction crew in Florida, first stocking the wood pile, leaving the truck for her, sending money regularly, he'd taken up with Willa Hanks.

"Mr. Crawford, that's Gerald's daddy back in Tennessee, he offered us his cabin here when he heard, and I couldn't hardly say no." She touched the outer edge of her puffy lip and winced. I noticed that the long purple nails had been bitten down to the quick. "We been living here going on five months when you showed up that day. I already told Harv, joking like, how I wished I could find somebody to buy that ole place, gave him Gran's address."

Selling the place, as she saw it back then, was the golden ring—she hated the wilderness, hated Gerald running off each winter to earn money to keep building on the house, and she especially hated the way her husband kept tripping over women in the woods and "taking up with them." She was sure that in the city things would be different. They would have friends their own age,

Gerald would have a job he reported to each day, and she couldn't quite explain why, but she believed in the city he would no longer feel the need for other women.

"But I never thought Gran would sell the place and not give us a penny after Gerald spent all that time and money building that house."

It dawned on me for the first time that Wendy and the children were homeless, but for the grace of Gerald's father. But there was a piece missing here. I placed the damp cloth against my burning throat and whispered, "Are you saying your grandmother, Claire, sold the property to punish Gerald for deserting you, then left you homeless herself?"

Wendy examined the hole in the beer can very closely. "Well, she did offer to bring me and the kids back to Nashville, said she'd buy us a house of our own there if we wanted one. With part of that money you give her."

I waited.

"But Gran..." A tear glistened in the corner of her good eye, spilled over in a slow, crooked path down her cheek; she blinked hard and more followed. Silently, the sobs came. Her voice shook with grief: "...she said Gerald couldn't come with us, Miz Sym, ma'am. And I just couldn't never leave Gerald."

Piece found. Wendy wasn't the first woman I'd known to stand by her man—to the bloody end, in some cases. And I'd known enough addicts to understand no magic combination of words in the world can penetrate their particular brand of hearing disorder. I watched the children pedaling around the track outside, racing each other on their tricycles, and waited till Wendy's tears subsided.

"So Gerald goes off every winter and works for Brandenberg? Why not last winter?"

Wendy dug in her pocket and extracted another mangled cigarette from the pack and lit it, tossed the dead match to the floor. She stretched her legs out, leaned her head back on the couch, and blew a long, pale stream of smoke at the ceiling. "Well, I figured he was taking the winter off to stay home for a change, thought maybe business was slow for Dean Brandenberg. He manufactures them log houses, sends out crews to build them all over the country, lets Gerald work anytime he's a mind to. Dean and my Gran, they started off together back in Nashville when I was little. Gran selling people the land, Dean selling them log houses. But when Gerald run off to live with that Willa, I figured they must of been carrying on some time, reckon Gerald got obsessed or something." She rolled her eyes. "I got right tired of it," she said, using the language of the deep South where *tired* rhymed with *hard*.

"Sounds like most of Nashville has moved to El Gato." I tried to count up all the Tennesseans but kept losing track.

"Well, that's 'cause after Gran started the development back in the sixties, she sold off as many lots as she could to people she knowed. Gerald's daddy bought him a few, bought this little place a year or two back when it come up for sale for nearly nothing. Dean, he'd bought a couple back then, moved out here not long ago to retire, decided to buy up what lots them last bunch of developers left behind. Said he figured it's just a matter of time till folks would be retiring, Baby Boomers looking for country. Hop, skip, and jump from Aspen. Figured he'd make some right good money off them. It was his idea to put up that fancy sign out by the road, put in that gate. Said everbody these days was looking to live in a gated community."

"So you and Gerald had been living here some time before Dean Brandenberg moved in?"

"Yeah, we moved out here, um…be 1992, right after Shawn was born. Gerald had got in some trouble, and Gran said for us to go to Colorado, look over her property with the barn on it she'd kept out of the bankruptcy, said she'd give it to us if we wanted to build on it. We lived in that barn till Gerald made some money by working for Dean Brandenberg that first winter and started building that house."

I didn't expect an answer to this one, but I asked it anyway. "What kind of trouble was Gerald into?"

She took a deep drag off the cigarette. "Just kid stuff," she said, bending deeply at the waist, her elbows propped on her knees, her chin in her palms. She stared out the window where litter flew up in the wake of the two children on their trikes. "Fact, I don't rightly know what it was he done. Gran told me, let it be, and Gerald, he don't like to be 'interviewed,' as he calls it." She began chewing on a fingernail, tearing off pieces with her teeth. The sound of the children's squeals drifted through the screen door.

Wendy twisted around. "I heard the sheriff thinks somebody fixed them brakes on the grader, caused Harv to wreck that thang. You think it's Dean done it?"

"I don't know the man," I reminded her. "What do you think?"

She examined her mutilated fingertip where blood sprang up around the bitten nail. She sucked it a moment, shrugged. "Don't know. Harv and Dean, they was fighting from day one. Brandenberg wanted to change everything, Harv wanted to keep the old ways. Their latest go-round was about Dean planning to use Board money to pay for ads on late-night TV to sell them lots. Said they'd bring in piles of money in dues for the development. But what it'd really do was make Dean a pile of money selling them three-hundred-dollar lots for ten thousand apiece. And he wouldn't even have to pay the advertising costs."

I remembered Harv saying Brandenberg had more than four hundred lots. Math wasn't my strong suit, but I rounded off a quick estimate, came up with four mill and climbing. Sounded like a motive to me.

"But hasn't Brandenberg got voting control of the development, him and Gerald's dad? Sounds like Harv couldn't have done much about it."

"Might could of. Had a friend told him it wasn't legal to use nonprofit funds, like El Gato dues, for personal gain. Harv was planning on going to a lawyer with it."

I wondered what kind of shape Brandenberg's finances were in. If Harv prevented him from using El Gato money, could he afford to run the advertising himself? Did he need the money badly enough to want Harv silenced? Wendy knew nothing about Brandenberg's personal finances, but she thought Claire James might.

The afternoon was getting late. The aspirin hadn't touched the pain in my throat, and my head was thumping like a maxed-out bass in a Saturday-night low rider. I wanted to get out of here, check in with Eva, go home to bed. I thought about Marle and Edna Benton and pulled out my last topic.

"Do you mind talking about your mother? I'm a little curious about her since she was…found…"

Wendy didn't bat an eye, just kept leaning on her knees and staring out the window. "Well, I didn't hardly know her, don't remember ever seeing her till she showed up on our doorstep. Gran said I was just a couple months old when Camilla brought me to Nashville, saying she was married but nobody never come to prove it. She left me with Gran right soon after, said she'd be back but never come." Wendy shrugged, sipped her beer. "I liked her all right, she was real polite, kind of distant, just a nice lady. We talked some at first, but we was like strangers going on about the weather, them cats, housekeeping. We just run out of words, seemed like. I was real sorry she done what she did, though. Marle, he took care of shipping the body back. I packed up her stuff, took that old furniture she refinished into town and sold it."

"Why was she living out in the barn?"

"Just moved out without saying much, but it was her and Gerald, you know?" Wendy sighed and slouched back against the sofa. "I couldn't see she ever done nothing to set him off. She never talked back to him or nothing. But from the day she walked in the door, Gerald took a dislike. We put her in one of them rooms way up on the third floor, out of the way, and she stayed to herself, didn't hardly never come down. But it wasn't long before she moved in that barn loft. Didn't see her much after that."

"The boxes and trunk with your mother's things are still there, Wendy," I said softly.

"Yeah, I packed 'em up. That secondhand store in town said they couldn't use the clothes, so I just left that stuff up there."

"Do you want me to bring them over to you?"

She looked at me like I'd lost my mind, then glanced around the room. "Them clothes don't fit me. Where do you think I'd put them things here?" We surveyed the tiny room filled with trash and soiled furniture and the mangled remains of the television in the center of the floor. She started eating on another finger, tearing savagely at the flesh around the nail.

We watched young Shawn lose several yards to his sister who squealed with delight and pumped her trike wildly to keep her lead. The boy swerved diagonally across the infield so that when he turned back on the track, he was trailing far behind. He leaned his chest close to the handlebars, rear end in the air, and began pumping ferociously to narrow the distance.

When I asked Wendy if she'd kept her mother's sketch pad, she shook her head.

"Don't remember seeing it in her stuff. Course, I seen her drawing in it, used to drag that old satchel all over, walking off to the woods with it hanging on her shoulder. She was a right good artist, done a family picture of us all that I'd liked to of framed. Had me and Gerald and the kids, had Gran in it, too. She even sketched herself in, kind of shadowy-like, up in one corner." It was the first note of sorrow I'd heard in Wendy's voice since she'd begun speaking of her mother.

A silence descended over us as we sat in the dismal living room. The stench from the television still hung in the air. Outside, little Tiffany was squealing in triumph, pedaling madly with her blond hair streaming behind. Her brother was bearing down fast, rapidly closing the gap between them. As he slipped up behind her, instead of veering to pass, he kept the central path and rammed hard into the back of her smaller cycle. Tiffany's trike lurched, flew forward, tipped sideways as it hung suspended for a moment, throwing the little girl backward to the ground. By the time Wendy and I reached the child, she lay in the dirt, screaming and crying, the tears streaking across her face. Wendy picked her up and bounced her in the air a couple of times, checking for injuries, then lay the little girl snuffling and hiccuping across her shoulder. She patted her back rhythmically and glared down at the boy.

Shawn sat rigidly upright. He held the handlebars of his tricycle and smirked at his mother and sister with his father's blue stare and odd flickering smile. He shifted his gaze to me, his eyes empty as marbles.

"You going to tell on my daddy?" he said. His voice was a five-year-old's, but it was ferociously defiant, tinged with the melodic undertones of his father's. The little girl stopped crying and both she and her mother turned and waited for my answer.

I looked at them—the filthy yard, the tear-stained child, the battered woman with her ruined face, her discolored eye and swollen lips. Without their testimony, I'd have a tough time getting a conviction of Gerald Crawford, which didn't mean I might not try anyway. At the very least, I was going to stop in and have a talk with Marle.

"Tell you what," I said, "how about I bring my television out here for you folks tomorrow after I get back from town, maybe bring a few groceries if your mama'd be willing to cook us a meal. After dinner, we'll sit down, the four of us, and talk about your daddy and how he…" I paused, at a loss for words "… *behaves*. What do you say?"

Shawn kept his absorbed, worried eyes on me for a moment, but his sister began bouncing in her mother's arms.

"Yes, yes!" she squealed. "Television, mommy! Hamburgers! Mommy knows how to make hamburgers, don't you, Mommy?"

Wendy placed the little girl on the ground and opened her mouth to answer, but I cut in.

"And," I said, giving each of them a stern look, "the other half of this deal is that you have this place shipshape and ready to do some entertaining tomorrow at six o'clock sharp."

The three grew immediately silent. They exchanged looks, then glanced at the house.

I nodded. "Yep. Time to clean up," I said, turning to my truck. And then I saw it, the source of that loud, unidentified noise as I'd lost consciousness—the entire length of my truck had been sideswiped, a bright silver scar slashed deep into the black finish. Gerald's signature.

"Shit!"

I counted to ten, which never worked before, still didn't. I opened the door to get in. Or tried to. The space between the front side-panel and the hinged edge of the door was bent. I tugged and pounded and jerked until bolts of pain shot through my head, but at last the door sprang open with a loud crack. I started to get in, but remembered that a sore throat and scraped truck were not the worst things Gerald Crawford might have done. I sighed, squatted beside the truck, looked underneath. My head and side pulsed in great waves of pain as I knelt and lay on my back in the trash, inching my way beneath the vehicle. I didn't have a clue what I was looking for, merely stared at the underside for anything dripping, any sign of leakage below the engine. Nothing. I extracted myself, climbed in the truck, banged shut the damaged door, and glared through the open window at the woman and two children who now clung to her sides.

"I am going to be here tomorrow at six o'clock exactly," I said, squinting at them through the pain, "and I'll bring you a twenty-five-inch television and all the hamburger you can eat." I stared at each one of them hard. They looked stricken. Little Shawn had the glint of mutiny in his eyes. I said to him, "Of course, if you don't want to do this, I'll just stay in town and have my dinner there, maybe have it with the sheriff—"

"No! No!" Shawn leaped up and down, clutching at his mother's clothes. "You tell her, Mommy, tell her we going to do it! Tell her!"

Wendy nodded her head, as though strings were attached to it from the sky.

21

Morgan

I stand in my front yard watching the Sym woman's truck pull away. She believes we are searching for the person cutting the brake lines, but there is more at large in El Gato. More here to be riddled than the vagaries and mysteries of Garbo. Than the petty betrayals of people who have driven the Symkin woman to this time, this place.

For people are like water—the mainstream will always follow the path of least resistance. The trick is not to flow with them or against them; the trick is first to cherish, then ignore them. There is no direction without resistance, no mystery without inquisition. Beware, however, a trifling truth—the Holy Grail stinks of hemlock.

Thus I have come here for Claire who wishes to understand her daughter's death. (Consider the mind's prevarications and beguilements, its attempts to conceal through linguistic misdirection: it is not Camilla's death, but her life that Claire wishes to understand. This mystery of the mother line: women begetting women, those who once shared the same body dividing into strangers of the flesh.) And have watched my own mother's death a hundred times on the FBI's master tape, scoured the flames on the video, rewound the tape and played again and again that moment when the solitary woman runs screaming from the fire toward the camera with her flaming hair and flaming clothes—not her. Not Rachael. I have frozen that face on the screen, magnified it, watched her burning lips, her melting flesh. Not her. I have lain in the darkness, turned up the volume, closed my eyes so the images do not impede my concentration, but behind the roar of the flames and the volley of rifles, the eighty-three screams will not divide. There are worse things, I tell myself, than to live and die communally, and I shut off the video and let her last image swim to me as I lie in the darkness, her face caught in the frame of the bus's window, a waving hand against a summer sky. But my eyes are scarred by fire, stung with smoke. The image fades. The past shrieks away like a locomotive in the night, incomprehensible, for the language of screams has no consonants.

Only at certain moments, with the horse pounding between my legs and the moon's cheek nearly at my fingertips, does some answer—of recollected things reshaping themselves into the present—seem close at hand, poised to unfold as neatly as a bird's wing.

Almost.

The dust from the Symkin woman's truck rises into the air, disappears. I disarm the security system, enter the house, climb the stairs to my workroom. I check the surveillance tapes, then review the folders arranged on the table. I open the first, the gray one with the word HARV written across the front, sift through the contents, pull out a form with the heading Moss highlighted in yellow at the top. Most of the form is blank. I sit before the computer, log on to the Internet site of the college where the professor teaches, scroll the home page until I find the faculty directory. Make a note of the professor's home address, phone number, name of the English Department secretary, Lucille Grubar.

When Mrs. Moss answers, I introduce myself as Mrs. Grubar's work-study assistant, explain that she has asked me to work overtime preparing the stipend checks for faculty members attending this weekend's state conference on curriculum improvement. I have Dr. Moss listed as tentative for the Friday, October 17th session, but I cannot find the travel voucher request to tell whether he actually decided to attend or not. Mrs. Moss tells me her husband left for his campus office at 7:00 Friday morning to prepare the lecture for his 11:00 course, then planned to drive directly to his cabin in the mountains to write, and she doesn't recall him mentioning the conference. She recommends I ask him when he returns after break, October 27th. I thank her and hang up.

I check the professor's schedule—British Romantic Poets, 11:00-11:50 MWF. No course roster is available on the Web site, but I find a student phone directory that includes such data as major course of study, level, campus address, phone number, and e-mail address. I download the directory, perform an automated search for all students identifying themselves as English majors. The lit course is 400-level, directed to fourth-year majors. I target senior English majors and, on my second call, reach a student enrolled in the professor's course. I explain that I am a friend of another student enrolled in the course who was ill and could not make it to class Friday, but who needs the assignment; she tells me there is no homework, the class was canceled.

After I hang up, I know this about Dr. Moss: he has most likely not been on campus Friday and therefore could have been at El Gato as early as 9:30 Friday morning, but more importantly, I know that Dr. Moss is a liar. Wherever he went Friday morning, it was not to campus to prepare his lecture, as he told his wife. I write in the information on the form and insert it on top of the other pages in the gray folder. I stick a small, bright yellow square on its cover, noting information to pursue concerning Moss.

The next folder is red, fixed with a white rectangular label at the center bearing the word CAMILLA. I open it, scan the sheets of papers inside. I have collected all the information concerning Claire's daughter the first three days of my stay in El Gato. Although I am still searching for one piece of information, I know that it will not substantially change what is before me: the answer Claire has sought. I am in no hurry to discover the missing piece because, for Claire, speed will change nothing.

I review the remaining the folders, a daily habit. I pace the back wall where I have thumbtacked other information in sequence. I reorganize the materials at several points, pace again, letting the information drift through my mind like notes from an orchestral arrangement, taking first one shape and then another: Claire James in March, a prelude; my arrival in El Gato, purchase of the house, contact with the members of the community; recent appearance of the Symkin woman, the Benton man's death, my truck squealing down the mountain road yesterday, Moss's self-absorbed eyes. Somewhere in the sequence, a silence spoils the rhythm, a jolt of ill-timed silence. Not the premeditated sort that suspends and holds the sound that has come before, gathered in readiness, promising consummation—that most articulate silence. Not that, but the unauthorized sort, a missing note—the silence of discord.

I study the materials at the end of the wall.

I dress in my riding clothes, saddle the horse, ride through the central greenbelt, up the mountain, angling to the north of Cougar Canyon.

Above the tree line, the terrain changes to scrub brush, and the horse gallops along a path toward the crest of the mountain ridge where the eastern side of the mountain spreads out below: a fire road begins abruptly, zigzags into the forest for several miles and leads eventually to the outskirts of Crystal Springs. I can also look down across El Gato to the west, follow the bright thread of deciduous trees that begins near the highway and borders the central stream as it runs through the pine forest, all the way up to its source at the waterfall where the two monolithic boulders lean together. Directly below me is the site where the hand was discovered by the Smithsonian crew, and by following an imaginary line straight up, I can mark the exact point of the waterfall access road above the site.

I ride the horse down toward the canyon, and when the terrain becomes too difficult, I guide him into the stream. The horse blows his nostrils loudly against the water but refuses to drink from it. We follow the stream up, navigating farther into the canyon, toward its source. The horse snorts loudly, his eyes rolling even though the smell of cat is less pervasive in the water.

By the time we reach the clearing near the bones site, the horse is plunging furiously, resisting entry into the grassy opening where the late afternoon sun lights only the tree tops. I stroke the horse's neck. I croon softly and guide him across the clearing, toward a path that climbs through large rocks, up the opposite side. When we reach a large boulder overlooking the clearing, I dismount and speak softly to the animal whose black coat is white with foam around his mouth and chest. His eyes roll, his body trembles. I take the lead rope and halter from where I have fastened them behind the saddle, slip the halter over his head, and tie him securely to the trunk of a large pine.

I climb to the top of the boulder where I can see the stream and the clearing below. The air is crisp, the wind sporadically shaking the trees, the shadows. I know that the cougar comes here to drink at the stream beside the clearing, for I have seen tracks during previous rides. I stretch myself flat on the boulder, which is hard against my pelvis and still hot from the sun. As I lie waiting, watching through an outcropping of weeds, I consider the history of El Gato that I have thumbtacked to my wall: the Cat Man who was Claire's father, who introduced the domestic cats here and who loved them, ancestors of those proliferating on the Symkin woman's property but which will not proliferate much longer, after tomor-

row. Small cousins to the great cat of legend—an enormous golden beast, long as a horse and half as tall, a phantom cat, keeper of the mountain, without need of food or consort. Hidden in this canyon, which for centuries has been inaccessible and remote, the cougar has survived because it has left behind no nattering trail of bones to reveal its presence.

Like most of earth's creatures, the cat is an animal of habit. It is one of life's persistent ironies that, popular belief to the contrary, habit provides both danger and security in equal proportion: the sun drops behind the western range, and emerging from the canyon's deepening shadows, the creature materializes. Its heavy head bobs and its muscles ripple as it pads along the narrow path toward the watering place.

It stops beside the water, whipping its tail as it inspects the circle of trees, the rustling shadows. It lifts its head, looks up, and I feel the electric shock of its gaze, though I know I am too still and well-hidden to be seen. Yet the gaze is penetrating, exhilarating—the bronze eyes, their snowy border, the black-tipped ears. The cat wags its head, drinks, continues up the path toward the falls. The bursts of wind are too high and northward to carry my scent; the stream rushes downhill, concealing any sound I make tunneling through the brush. At the upper ridge of the trail, I climb the last yards into the dim clearing where the boulders tower above the shallow dam and the waterfall is almost deafening. Standing in the fissure between the two boulders, the cat waits—still as the two stones themselves, its sleek head looking back over its shoulder, its eyes luminescent, on mine.

It whips its tail once more, then disappears.

22

I BUCKED ALONG THE ASPHALT TO EL GATO, navigating the steep downhill grades and sharp turns with my head pounding and my throat burning and my hands shaking, hitting first the brakes, then the accelerator, as I fought off the vivid memory of yesterday's hair-raising ride down the mountain.

I've always believed that if you look closely enough at the choices people make, you can explain their present circumstances, so when I drove through the El Gato gate wondering how I'd gotten myself into the present pickle, I did a quickie retrospect. From this angle, it didn't take much to see that my bold new venture to become Garbo was really just old stuff, a snappier version of the withdrawal tactic learned in youth and practiced throughout my adult life—Garbo wasn't an annihilation of J. S. Symkin, she was her most austere incarnation, and the question was no longer whether I could *become* Garbo, but whether I could *avoid* becoming her. Which made me wonder whether the same might not be true of Harv: had he likewise followed an MO that resulted in someone killing him? And if so, what acts and what someone?

He'd been a brusque, outspoken man whose hardheaded opinions made him argumentative and abrasive. In locking horns with the powerful Brandenberg, he'd initiated a series of events that not only alienated him from his buddy Gerald, but set him at odds with almost everyone at El Gato. Was Harv's attempt to block Brandenberg's use of El Gato funds to launch the multimillion-dollar sales campaign serious enough for Brandenberg to want him not only out of El Gato, but dead as well? Was Gerald Crawford so

enraged at Harv's collaboration to sell Claire James's hundred
acres that he would have killed Harv for revenge? And what about
Harv's hands-on approach to women: was it as harmless as Wendy
thought, or had Harv provoked the hostility of some irate husband? Had Harv attempted to seduce Camilla, perhaps offering
her the old car as a perk, and if so, how had she responded? I
thought of the sheriff, the look in his eyes when he spoke of
Camilla, and I wondered what his reaction might have been if he
knew of Harv's ploy.

By the time I turned into Eva's driveway, the sun had set, and
evening was coming fast. My side where Gerald had kicked me
was aching badly, my head pounded with about the same fre-
quency and reverberation as a high school marching drum, and my
throat was swelling so that swallowing was painful. I desperately
wanted to lie down. Tough luck. Eva Blake's windows were dark,
and I knew the house was empty even before I read the note stuck
to her door: "Have dinner w/boys if you beat me back. Later." I
rounded the house to find the horse gone from its corral and felt a
rush of exhaustion at the thought of socializing with "the boys";
the mere thought of swallowing food made my throat throb. I
could go home, of course, but it seemed impossibly distant and
uninviting.

I spotted a couple of Wolf's carved chaise lounges up on the
deck, climbed the stairs, and found a blanket tucked neatly under
the floral cushions on each one. I tried the French doors just for
good measure, unsurprised to find them locked, with tightly closed
mini-blinds covering all the windows. I adjusted the back on the
chaise nearest the doors, lay down and zipped my jacket to the
chin, pulled the blanket around me, and curled into a fetal position
with my head screaming and side aching. In spite of all that, I must
have slept deeply, because when I woke, the sky was black and
thick with stars, and the windows along the deck were thin knives
of light that seeped between the blinds. A shadow moved behind
them, then Eva's voice:

"Claire? It's me. I didn't wake you?"

I lay still for a moment, feeling drugged and disoriented. I tried
to collect my thoughts: Eva must have returned, put away the

horse, entered from the front door in order to deactivate the alarm system, and was now talking to someone on the phone. I was about to call out to her when I heard it. *Claire?*

"...let you know I'll be sending you some things, what I've found out about Camilla, a few boxes of her clothes and personal items over at the barn if you want them. I guess I've done about all a hit man can do around here, under the circumstances...." Laughter. Pause. "A few more days will do it, I think, wrap up some loose ends...."

I began to ease myself up, and suddenly floodlights drenched the deck and yard with a million watts and counting. The voice inside the room stopped.

I sat frozen in the brilliance, knowing I should make a run for it down the stairs, go for my truck, get the hell out of there. But let me tell you: *frozen* in real life is a lot more incapacitating than the *frozen* you read about. Terror short-circuits the brain, throws a switch, turns your muscles to custard.

The doorknob turned, and the earth on its axis came to a grinding, ear-splitting halt. I knew without any doubt, with the absolute certainty that shoots out of the sky like the first bolt of summer lightning, that Eva Blake, whoever she might be, was lethal—the creature that yesterday afternoon, for one nerveless instant, I had glimpsed.

She opened the doors, switched off the floodlights, and stood there: a tall black figure in the doorway with the light behind her, standing motionless while inside my skull the words bounced around like .22 calibers: *Claire...Camilla...hit man.* It was then I caught the image that had been playing tag with my memory since the accident. The image that lay inside Eva's glove compartment, beneath the gun, scrawled on envelopes. Letters written with the uniquely triple-looped "E" that I'd disregarded in my panic to find the tissues. Letters that could only be from Claire James.

Suddenly time started again, this time going too fast, way too fast. Everything falling into place at once, a perfect kind of ruthless sense to it all: Claire James had sent this woman to El Gato, must have sent her to kill Harv for some reason I didn't know. Eva the expert driver, a driver who knew just how to roll a vehicle, who had not only cut Harv's brakes, but cut her own to throw off suspicion. And now, having killed one person, she must...

"Symkin. You'd better come inside." Her voice hadn't changed: it was still low and smoky, using the stripped-down language without inflection or softening curve. The voice of an automaton. I opened my mouth to speak, but nothing came out. She withdrew slightly into the room, holding open the door. I glanced at the stairs, estimated how fast I could negotiate them in the darkness, noticing with the crazy illogic of crisis situations, that the moon was just rising over the mountains, that I could round the house where my truck...

"Symkin."

She stepped onto the deck beside my chair, blocking the stairs. She reached into her pocket, withdrew something and held it toward me. My keys.

"I saw your truck when I came home, figured you'd walked down to the boys'. Just running the surveillance tapes when the motion detector set off the floodlights." She put the keys back in her pocket and nodded toward the door. In an unbearably low whisper, she said: "Inside."

I stood up, steadied myself on the arm of the chaise, walked ahead of her through the doors. And heard them shut behind me.

What had I expected? A bedroom done in Barbie-Sees-Double like the one down the hall? A sterile Designer-Duh showroom to match the ones downstairs? One thing was certain: no designer had ever set foot in here. This room had plenty of character, and it scared me to death.

It was long and rectangular, one end butting up against the bedroom where I had slept last night, the other bordered by the deck. It was a room for someone who meant business and didn't give a damn about color or furniture or comfort, someone who either had no sense of aesthetics or didn't care. Yes, someone who could live in a room over a dive and like it. Naked strips of fluorescent lighting crossed the ceiling from one end to the other, raining down a white glare that made me squint and sent pains shooting through my head. The floor was raw, pale planks of unfinished wood, scattered with scraps of paper and printouts. Beside the door that opened on the hallway stood a shredder and a large industrial-type barrel overflowing with ribbons of paper. The walls were unpainted Sheetrock with their seams bare. Which didn't much matter because a great clutter of photos and notes and sketches and printed materials and diagrams were stuck like wallpaper over most of their surface.

Long wooden tables shoved end-to-end extended down the center of the room to a U-shaped work area stacked with enough electronic devices to stock a warehouse. Several desktop computers sat side-by-side, connected by cables to a fax, a complicated grouping of devices that included a telephone and small monitor at the center, printers, a scanning device, and some photographic equipment. A stool with a wire back sat in front of an area piled with printed circuit boards, electrical components, snarls of wire, and a smattering of foreign-looking electronic equipment and components I couldn't identify. A large desk formed the end of the U, so that by sitting in the tall, cushy executive chair, the operator could easily access three working surfaces with a quick twist. On the desk, a maxi-tower computer hummed beside a twenty-five-inch monitor, its screen filled with bursts of stars. The shelf just above it held a row of small monitors.

Only at the opposite end of the room was there some concession to ambiance. There, a built-in alcove of shelves housed a large-screen television, VCR, and stereo components. One of Wolf's redwood chairs sat facing it, flanked by a small plastic folding table big enough to hold a TV dinner, but straining under the gooseneck lamp, remote control, earphones, and pads of paper.

I glanced at Eva who stood perfectly still, leaning back against the closed doors with her arms crossed and her jaw set and her eyes boring into me. I walked over to the wall for a closer look at a color photo enlarged to poster size, laminated, and stuck in the center of several photocopied news clippings. The photo was rough-grained, as though it had been blown up too large, so that the detailing became fuzzy and less clear the more closely one looked at what appeared to be a woman's face on fire. She had bright orange flames where her hair should have been and eyes that bulged in horror. Her lips were pulled back in a scream, her mouth wide, but the heat and fire had sprung there, too, so that she looked like some mythical, doomed fire-breathing beast tricked into death by inhaling its own flames. Newspaper clippings circled the poster: the FBI burns a women's collective in Indiana, killing all eighty-three women and children; Anna Lee Stone's novel *Living Down Under* cited as the inspirational model for sixties women's communities.

I couldn't imagine how all this related to Eva Blake, or whoever she was, but the clipping about Anna Lee Stone struck a familiar chord—Stone had written only that one classic work, I recalled, a brilliant feminist novel that I used to teach in my literature courses, and then she'd dropped out of sight following the Indiana fire and had never written again. Below the clippings, yellowing pictures in cardboard frames showed horses in the winner's circle and a cluster of people smiling at the camera. The people in each group varied, though in all of them three recurred: a bear-sized bald man wearing a white suit, a rakishly handsome middle-aged man with black hair falling across his forehead, and a tall, breathtakingly beautiful young woman with a cascade of dark wavy hair who could only be a younger Eva Blake.

It was then that I saw the square of blue paper tacked above. In fact, the mass of pinned-up documents that had at first appeared chaotic, now I could see were loosely grouped under pieces of colored paper. At the end of the wall, beneath a green square, was a large El Gato plat map with variously colored pins stuck on it, surrounded by a scattering of articles—newspaper clippings about an archeological dig, the suicide death of Camilla James, the recent death of Harv Benton; an excerpt from a local historical publication concerning indigenous folklore, the Cat Man of El Gato, a phantom cougar; an article from *Smithsonian* by the archeologist Dennis Stanford citing the scarred trees near El Gato as evidence of a past Ute civilization. Further on were articles about missing college co-eds, printouts of campus schedules and departmental phone listings, and portions of interviews in campus newspapers. In one of them, I recognized Professor Moss smiling among a group of colleagues below the header, "Concerned Professors Launch Student Help Line."

On the shelf above the computer, the row of smaller monitors was dark, except for the one showing the dimly lit El Gato entrance gate. Surveillance monitors, I realized, of the type used in banks and department stores, and at the moment whatever scenes they were aimed at were shrouded in the darkness of night. Undoubtedly, one of them covered Eva Blake's back deck where I'd unwittingly gone to sleep before dark, then tripped the motion detector when I'd wakened. I wondered where the other cameras were located and why.

To the right of the computer monitor, more articles were tacked to the wall. Several concerned an enterprise called merely "The Company," a Milan-based public relations firm whose CEO, a man by the name of Psichari Pasonombre, was pictured accepting various community service awards. The man was of enormous bulk, bald, and always in white, unmistakably the same fellow in the winner's circle photos. Other articles concerned a biochemical laboratory outside of Santa Fe and its CEO, a handsome, silver-haired man by the name of Simon Cruz whom I recognized from his occasional appearances on Albuquerque television. The articles had something to do with the Pecos River scandal a few years back, and I remembered Cruz refuting the allegation that his lab had any involvement in the falsification of water-testing documents in the 1993 Mexico water payback affair. A small article at the bottom mentioned the discovery of an unidentified man found dead on a New Mexico mesa.

I looked around at the walls and the room in mystification as the tall woman in black remained motionless, leaning and watching. I figured all this material must be connected in some way for her to have arranged it here, but I didn't have a clue what the connection was or how any of it related to Claire James.

On the oak desk beside me, a large spiral-bound artist's sketch pad lay open to a black-and-white pencil sketch of a group of people. I recognized Gerald and Wendy standing together with the two children. Gerald held baby Tiffany in the crook of his arm, while Wendy rested her left hand on her son's shoulder. In the bottom right corner, I recognized Claire James glancing up at the group with an unfamiliar, grandmotherly twinkle in her eye, and if I hadn't just had a behind-the-scene glimpse of these folks, I, too, would have taken them as a model of middle-class American bliss. Then I saw the other face peering out of the darkness behind Gerald, a dark-haired older woman who reminded me of the sirens of Homeric lore, her eyes shining feverishly.

I realized that I was looking at Camilla's missing sketch pad, and this was the family portrait that Wendy had wanted to frame. What didn't make any sense was why Eva Blake had it. My head stepped up the pounding, and the glare from the overheads increased. I sat in the office chair, picked up the sketch pad. Eva Blake's boots pounded on the wood floor, coming my way. She stopped beside the chair.

"The American Dream," she said, looking over my shoulder at the Crawfords.

"A beautiful woman." I pointed to Camilla's shadowy face. I thought of Marle's description, but there was no child-like naïveté in the glittering eyes that stared out of the darkness behind Gerald Crawford. A cold chill crept down my spine. "Not what I thought she'd look like, though," I said.

"Who?" Eva said. She bent forward and the familiar smell of horse and leather came with her, and something else. Something flowery and white, blooming in a southern night.

"Camilla," I said, pointing to the shadowy face. "I didn't imagine her this way at all." My voice came out ragged, a mere croak.

"That's not Camilla." She opened a red folder and drew out several photographs. "Here," she said, pointing out a woman in each—gamin-faced, mercurial, laughing in some, pensive in others. "That's Camilla. And what the hell happened to your voice?"

I told her about Gerald's attack, Wendy's battering, the terrified children, all the while staring at the bucolic sketch in my hands. Eva showed no sign of surprise, merely pulled down the neck of my sweater and whistled at the bruise. My head was buzzing with questions, but they were somehow fuzzy and distant and tangled with the pain in my head. My vision blurred, and I squinted at the portrait, asked the woman standing over me about the phone conversation, about Claire James.

An old friend of her mother's, she explained. Wanted to know more about her daughter's death, about Camilla. Eva tapped the dark woman in the sketch. "That's Gerald's mother, disappeared when Wendy was a baby. Wendy never saw her, wouldn't have recognized her. And she's dark like Camilla," she said, holding a couple of the snapshots near the sketched woman. She stood for a few moments looking at them before sliding them back in the folder. "According to Claire, there was quite a scandal. Gerald's dad came home early one day, caught his wife with another man, with the little boy in the same room. Gerald was only about three or so. Big custody battle, all that. Apparently she'd been carrying on like this for some time, according to the neighbors that testified at the trial. Gerald's father was awarded custody, and no one ever saw her after that." As she spoke, Eva's eyes remained on the woman peering out from the shadows.

I was trying to follow it all, but as she talked, the room began to blur. I closed my eyes, laid the sketchbook on the desk in front of me.

"I don't understand...who you...what's happening," I said. Each word was an effort, a heavy weight that sapped my strength. In the room around me, I sensed a pressing danger that crackled in the air, sizzled along the row of fluorescent lights, darted among the sharp flashes of pain behind my eyes. I folded my arms across the sketch pad, lowered my head.

23

I WOKE INTO THE YELLOW HAZE of the bedroom. A dangling globe in the corner glowed softly. Beneath it, a woman sat reading with her legs curled under her in an overstuffed chair, sipping a colorless drink, her dark hair wet and slicked back from her face. She wore a long sleeveless white gown of some gauzy material. The light above her streamed down, honey-colored, radiating along her edges like a full-body halo.

From between my lashes, feigning sleep, I watched her. She seemed very far away, miles away from where I lay with the black pool just below my eyes, swimming with evil thoughts that thrashed and whirled when I looked there, but with a calm surface when I didn't. So I climbed back up to the light, to the woman reading.

Her eyes were downcast, her cheekbones and jawline and lips arranged in angles of light and dark. The name *Artemis* sprang to mind, and immediately her image leapt into the air above me, rose to the ceiling and shaped itself into a cottony cloud. It floated aimlessly at first, then it lingered directly over the woman's head and began to dissolve—from behind the woman's shoulder, golden shapes sprouted into the air, feather tips of arrows bloomed, and the book the woman held between her hands became elongated, stretching itself into a bow.

"You're awake."

Her voice was smoke. Her eyes were dark and deep as the pool where the wild fish glimmered. She smiled so slowly that days passed, and her mouth rose high on one side.

"Feeling pretty good, aren't you?"

She laid the book down and stood up in one slow movement, so tall that her head touched the ceiling. She walked toward me, a column of white, her body a lean and naked shadow inside the gown. She stood above me, miles high. She tilted her head sideways and leaned over to touch my neck.

"I gave you something for the pain."

The woman's fingertip was cool as a crystal glass against my throat, and after she withdrew it, petals of a magnolia blossom floated across the air. When she sat beside me, she blotted out the globe, and the displaced light collected in a golden nimbus behind her head. My body tingled in dark places as I watched her mouth, the changing configuration of her lips.

"You're a little drugged right now," the lips said, opening and closing in some foreign rhythm. She smiled: I watched the sharp even edges of her teeth. Her hand lay across my forehead. "You'll have a pretty good time while the drug lasts, and you'll remember everything I'm about to tell you. All right?"

She stood up and walked back to the chair in the corner. The gauze swayed in long straight folds with the shadow inside. She sat in the chair and crossed her legs and took a sip of the clear liquid. Somewhere very far away bells trembled.

"I lied to you about who I am. The truth would have meant nothing to you, might even put you in danger if the wrong people were to find out where I am." She placed the glass on the dresser beside the chair and stared at the air above the bed as though she were seeing something there, though I could find nothing. "But things have changed. My phone conversation just now…you know about Claire. And unless I give you some background and explain a few things, you'll act on some half-baked assumptions that might get us both into serious trouble. So you need to listen to me," she said. She left the middle distance and pressed her eyes to mine. "I promise you this: I mean you no harm."

I closed my eyes, enfolded by an utter golden peace in a place where time had not yet been invented. Her words curled like wisps of smoke, and I understood that she was called Cordelia Morgan and the photograph of the flaming woman was someone who had died in a fire with her mother, Rachael, and eighty-two others in a women's collective in 1973. I watched the story of Cordelia Morgan's childhood unfold across a background of golden light and images that played brightly on a dark stage behind my eyes. A horse farm, a picture-book family. But the golden light dimmed, and glimmering shards in the black pool began thrashing as she spoke of her mother's escape, the women's collective, she and her mother living in a trailer in an orchard with Claire James.

When I opened my eyes, Cordelia Morgan sat next to me on the bed—closer than before. "Claire James," she said, breathing the name slowly as though it had been kept in a drawer, wrapped in lace for special occasions. "Claire is the last of it, of my mother and that time. Not a mother of the blood, but a mother still. She was in the village shopping when the FBI attacked, and after the fire, I never saw her again. Not until a few months ago.

"You see, I'd spent quite a few years working for an international firm, burned out, quit and traveled awhile." A pause, a smile. "Just your ordinary midlife crash and burn. But there comes a time when even the most solitary animal seeks its own kind, if there are any. So I looked up Claire in Nashville. That was last March."

The surface of the dark pool that had lain dormant began to move, aroused by the talk of mothers and fathers. Somewhere I heard a distant whine, a fly beating itself against a summer window.

I watched Cordelia Morgan's fingers trace a fold of gauze from knee to hip, and I reached out my hand and stroked it, too, to calm the water and still the whine, so that I could hear her speak again of the golden time of youth and mothers and their children and the orchard where they lived, and whether the words issued from Cordelia Morgan or from my own heart's natter, I held them so close and hard that they were cleansed in red, dancing a scarlet footpath across an open spiral-bound sketchbook, marching out of sight and leaving behind them valentine intaglio.

My vision blurred. Her eyes came close, and I could see behind them a movement in the darkness. A face appeared just behind her own, another and then another, each more pale than the last, until it seemed as though a long line of matriarchs sat stroking their gauzy robes, and when I next looked closely at Cordelia Morgan, her face had collapsed and shriveled like a drying apple's, and there beside me, as I had always dreamed, was the woman whose blood ran inside my veins, whose hand covered mine as her eyes reached down and soothed the darkness.

"...and so when she asked me to come here, to find out what had happened to Camilla, her own daughter she'd never really known, it was not only for Claire that I came." She raised her hand that held a fold of her gown and stroked my cheeks with the fabric, then touched it to the inner corners of my eyes. "But for my own mother, to understand the things that keep us strangers, to find some piece that turned a certain way will ease the mystery."

The creases in the ancient face melted. Cordelia Morgan leaned over me, her eyes large and heavy-lidded and close to my own, the moon-colored nimbus widening behind her head, the lips shaping a rhythm as though a heart were speaking. Her hair was cool, damp, soothing against my palms, against my fever and the great surge of heat.

Outside, I heard the sharp, yodeling nicker of the horse, and then the piercing sound of a woman's scream. I jerked upright.

"Cougar."

Cordelia Morgan sat in the corner chair, the book in her hand. She stood and walked to the open bedroom window where we could hear the horse galloping around the corral. As she stared out into the darkness, her gown billowed in the cool air.

"The cougar's cry, sounds like a woman's scream. You get used to it. They're native to the area. You seldom see them, but they're out there, watching us." she said, turning to where I sat rigidly upright, her presence suddenly terrifying as she walked slowly my way. "So solitary they disdain even the company of their own species. They stalk their prey from behind, breaking the animal's neck with a bite of their jaws, and they can jump as high as twenty feet straight up. Beautiful, solitary creatures."

I nodded, overwhelmed by a sharp stab of fear and something else. I scooted up and leaned back against the headboard, tried to get a grip on my emotions, which seemed to be careening all over the place. My headache had gone, but the back of my skull was tender and my throat felt like I'd swallowed a can of Drano. I touched it lightly.

"So," she said, sitting on the bed, "how you feeling?" She lifted her brows and nodded at my throat.

"Fine." It came out in a raspy, painful whisper, and I reached for the glass of liquid beside the bed.

"No, no." She snatched the glass away. "I'm not sure you're ready for any more of this just now." She laid her book on the bed, disappeared, and returned with a glass of water, which I drank in slow, painful sips. Whatever it was that she'd given me had worn off and left behind a powerful thirst.

"What was that stuff, anyway?" I asked, handing her my empty glass and trying to think what kind of sedative could cause the hallucinations I'd experienced. And the body heat. I could imagine becoming very fond of it.

She gave me the slow, lopsided smile of a woman with a serious Attitude. "Little something I picked up somewhere. Chemist I came across in New Mexico a few years back, trying to mix up a little aphrodisiac for the boys. Don't think it ever got the FDA stamp of approval, though. Don't think it even got close." The smile again, way high now, an eyebrow cocked. "You like?"

She was looking at me oddly, a question in her eye besides the one she asked. Whatever I was afraid of about her no longer had anything to do with bodily harm. I remembered the magnolia petals, the golden nimbus, the wet hair and body heat. I looked down at my lap and waited. She'd drugged me, and I should be royally pissed. Right, so why wasn't I?

"Look, you were hurting," she said, "and not far from shooting straight off the charts into coronary territory. Seemed like the thing to do at the time, short of tying you up and terrifying you even more."

"Well, at least my headache's gone," I said, eager to change the subject. "So Claire sent you here to find out about how Camilla died. I guess that means you know Claire well enough to know whether she would do something like, you know, have Harv…"

I had expected her to laugh, to shake her head in disbelief, but she held me with a long and penetrating stare. "I don't know much about the Claire who's the real estate developer, but I don't believe she's involved in Harv's murder. Thing is," she said slowly, narrowing her eyes, "you think tampering with someone's brakes, doctoring their camomile with hemlock, even slipping a very sharp blade between someone's ribs is an act of the aberrant mind. It's not, you know. Murder is as simple and ordinary and mundane as sipping lemonade. Only its infrequency in your particular realm of experience makes it seem bizarre to you. With more contact, a different background, you'd be much more equipped to find the villain among us." She paused. "No, not Claire. But someone here, someone close."

I didn't know what background she was talking about, and I didn't want to know. The air in the bedroom had turned frigid, and I shivered. Eva, now Cordelia Morgan, closed the window and pulled the yellow curtains across it.

"According to Wendy," I said, "Claire seems to be the common denominator for a lot of these folks. Brandenberg, for example. They used to be partners. What if they still are, off the record. Maybe Claire would like to reclaim a piece of El Gato after having pioneered its development. Maybe she's funding Brandenberg, wanting to get Harv out of the way and net four million for her investment."

"Not Claire," she said with finality. "But I did call her to ask some questions about the people here, the ones she knew way back when. Certainly Harv, Brandenberg. Maybe some of the others. You see, she put in this development not long before she lived with my mother and me at the collective. And…" she paused, eyeing my neck, "I had a few questions on my list about your friend, Gerald. You say Wendy mentioned he'd been in some trouble back there? I didn't get to ask all the questions I meant to, if you recall," she said, giving me a pointed look, "but tomorrow I'll talk to her, see what I can find out to add to our present stock. Good enough?"

"Sure," I said as she walked toward the door. I was thinking of the walls in the room next door to the one I was going to sleep in tonight. "All that stuff on the wall," I nodded toward the room, "what's it all about? How come…"

She opened the door. "Tomorrow," she said. "I think you've had enough excitement for one day, don't you?"

No shit. I shrugged, picked up the book she had left behind on the bed, and handed it to her.

"I've already read it," she said. "Be my guest."

I looked at the cover. Anna Lee Stone. *Living Up the Lie.* I stared dumbfounded—a publisher's advance copy. Anna Lee Stone had disappeared after the FBI burning of the women's collective, and she had vowed never to write again. I stared in disbelief at Cordelia Morgan who stood at the door, grinning down at me.

"Where'd you get this? I thought she—"

"Living in New Mexico. That chemist I mentioned? You might say she introduced me to him. Might have been a drop or two of that stuff you had tonight that got her moving again."

The high smile, and then the door closed.

PART IV

Crystal Springs

24

OCTOBER 20, 1997
MONDAY MORNING

I WOKE LATE. I could tell even in the muted light of the closed drapes that the sun was high. Mercifully, my head was no worse for the battering Gerald had given it or the drug Eva, a.k.a. Cordelia Morgan, had poured into it. I wore a yellow nightshirt that I did not remember putting on, and I wanted a shower badly. I drew back the drapes: in the corral, the horse munched alfalfa, and I estimated the sun at just about the 9:00 position. The sky was clear, to the east at least, and I burrowed through the suitcase full of rumpled clothes that the sheriff had packed Saturday night after the accident. I hoped this wasn't a precedent for the rest of the day—everything was wadded and wrinkled, mismatched, too heavy or too light. Finally, I pulled out a T-shirt, a long-sleeved denim shirt, a pair of jeans, socks and undies, and padded down the hall to the bathroom with them under my arm. By hanging them over the towel racks, I figured the steam from the shower would take out a few of the wrinkles.

Very few. Half an hour later, dressed in a layered wrinkled motif, I was at least clean, my wet hair braided and pinned into a hasty knot. Downstairs I found my hostess at the table, sipping coffee and scribbling on a yellow legal pad, a portable phone beside her. When I carried my own steaming cup to sit across from her, she left off the writing and looked up, giving my Designer Wrinkles a slow toe-to-collar appraisal.

"Iron?"

"Cotton," I said, sitting down and sipping my coffee.

She gave me the long look of someone who would have fit right in with the Mafia. She got up, and I could hear her boots on the stairs. When she came back, she tossed a blue turtleneck on the table. "No offense, but you probably don't want to go around town showing off that black circle around your neck."

I hadn't paid any attention as I jumped into the shower, and afterwards, dressing, the mirror had been steamed up. I went into the bathroom off the kitchen and stared into the mirror above the sink—my neck was discolored, nearly black, and it stood out like Doc Martens on a ballerina. And it hurt like hell. I shed my shirts, pulled on Morgan's turtleneck, tucked it into my jeans as I came back to the dining area. I put my discarded clothes on the table and stood in front of her, turning around in a circle.

"Do I pass?" I said.

"Jury's still out," she said, not looking up from her writing. She tore off a couple of sheets, folded them, stood up, and stuck them into her back pocket. "Let's hit the road. You ready?"

Outside, the western skyline showed a bank of dark clouds. Morgan grabbed a couple of ski jackets from the entry closet as we passed, fiddled with the touch pad beside the door, closed it behind us, and when she offered to drive, I let her. Besides, she already had my keys in her hand. She swooped under to check the brakes, opened the door with its loud twang, and we set off.

As we drove down the scrolling mountain highway toward town, my thoughts whizzed around at dizzying speed, just barely keeping pace with Morgan, who drove about the same, it seemed to me, with brakes as she did without them. I was buckled in tightly, and I braced myself by keeping a firm grip on the armrest, not looking at the cliff side. My side. Morgan had been explaining some of the items thumbtacked on the walls of her workroom, but she hadn't said much about the guy named Pasonombre, the place where she'd worked called "The Company," and Simon Cruz. And I wondered what those other monitors showed on their screens today and why she had placed surveillance cameras there. And how she had come by Camilla's sketchbook. And then I thought, as we squealed around a curve beside an open-faced cliff where I looked down over a sheer drop, that life is short, and what the hell, why not ask. So I did.

By the time we were pulling into Crystal Springs, population 3,751, I knew that Morgan had been, as she described it, a "Research Specialist," that The Company was "a private contracting firm," and that her last assignment was in New Mexico where she'd blown the whistle on her old flame, Simon Cruz, whose chemical laboratory was involved in a scheme to cover up pollution in the Pecos River. I'd heard something at the time about chemicals being siphoned into the river, but when the furor had died, Simon Cruz was none the worse for the publicity. Cordelia Morgan, on the other hand, was in deep shit with both Simon Cruz and The Company. She'd gone underground, traveling across one continent after another for several years, and when Claire James suggested a visit to El Gato on her behalf, she thought it was just the kind of place to take a break. And Claire had given her Camilla's sketch pad.

"Said it came in the mail a day or two after Camilla hung herself," she said. "Camilla must have mailed it to her the day before she died, would have been a Saturday. It's quite an extraordinary thing, really. I'll show you some of the other drawings this evening." We had taken the turnoff to the village, and up ahead was the Ford dealership, the only automobile sales lot of any size until you reached Aspen.

"And the fellow dead on the mesa?" I said. "How does that fit in?"

She glanced around at me. "Give it a rest, Symkin." She was slowing as we neared the driveway where a huge American flag was flapping beside the CRYSTAL SPRINGS FORD billboard. "I had to tell you these things because it was the only way to explain why I lied about my identity. But it's crucial that you not mention anything I've told you to anyone, especially the sheriff. I didn't say all my good-byes when I left The Company, and those guys don't play nice. Are you hearing me? You can call me Cordelia or Morgan or just Cord, whatever you want when no one else is around, but if you do that, you've got to remember it's Eva Blake the rest of the time."

"Um, okay. So which name do you prefer?" I asked, as she turned into the dealership.

"You got plenty of options to choose from," she said, stopping the truck in front of a modular office surrounded by gravel. "And if you need more, I've also been called 'The Morgue' on occasion." She shut off the engine and twisted around toward me, grinning. "Your call."

A broad fellow in a beige polyester suit with wide lapels was coming out of a mobile office, headed in our direction with the lumbering gait of the overweight. He wore a starched white shirt under his jacket, the top button undone and a string tie dangling loosely under the collar. His pale hair was clipped in a military burr, and the rolls of fat around his neck were gleaming with sweat even though the temperature couldn't have been over fifty degrees. His extra pounds hadn't hurt his energy level any; he pumped both our hands with the vigor of the truly dedicated automobile sales-man, and I knew it was going to take hours to get rid of this guy. His blue eyes disappeared as he laughed, which was most of the time, and he blustered and waved us after him as he trudged down a gravel aisle where new Ford sedans were lined up.

Morgan followed, explaining that she was interested in a tem-porary lease truck while she waited for her insurance company to replace the wrecked one. The salesman's pounds hadn't affected his thought processes either; she could lease now, he explained, and make it hers when the insurance kicked in. He punctuated the end of every sentence with a laugh that set his flesh quivering and sounded something like the pig in the backyard next door to where I had lived with my uncle. He stopped beside a top-of-the-line Lincoln Continental and opened the door. Morgan ignored him. She kept walking toward the side of the lot where trucks were lined up in front of a chain-link fence. I looked at the man, lifted my shoulders, and followed her. He slammed the car door, caught up with us, and took the lead again as he made a beeline toward a new white F250. Again he held open the door, and again Morgan ignored him.

By the time he'd caught up with her this time, she'd entered a section of used trucks near the back of the lot and was circling around a late-model F350. It was fire-engine red with a crew cab, four doors, a total of six tires, chrome dual exhausts, chrome hubs, and a chrome roll bar topped by a set of six KC lights. She opened the door that interrupted the flow of an iridescent silver lightning bolt that extended from the front bumper to the back. The salesman and I exchanged looks as Morgan leaped into the driver's seat and popped the hood latch.

She draped one wrist over the steering wheel and turned to the salesman. "Keys?"

The fellow, his mouth fallen open, turned and trotted down the gravel toward his mobile office. When he returned, Morgan had finished inspecting the drive train as well as the engine. She started it up to the sound of a deafening muffler system, listened, revved the engine as I covered my ears, and listened again. She leaned forward and pulled a narrow checkbook out of her back pocket and opened it up. She took the pen stored inside it and waited. The man was silent, looking at her.

"Well?"

"Um." I could read this guy like the *New York Times Book Review*. The dollar signs were clicking behind his eyes fast as a Las Vegas slot machine. Just as he opened his mouth, Morgan looked up at him with the matt finish on her eyes. He closed his mouth, and when he opened it again, I figured he'd shaved several thousand off his first answer. Morgan nodded and wrote the check, handed it to him, and the fellow crunched off down the gravel aisle to verify funds in her account.

Morgan sat behind the wheel, looking over the frills on her new console. This one had a CD player customized with four stereo speakers screwed into the roof of the cab and an amplifier stuck under the seat. A radar detector hung from the driver's visor. By the time the salesman had returned with the papers to sign, Morgan and I had made arrangements to meet later at her place—she insisted I had beans for brains to go anywhere near Wendy's, then said maybe she'd go along and see if she and Gerald might strike up an acquaintance. As she started to pull out of the lot in the fire-engine-red truck with several acres of chrome, I asked her what had caught her eye about it.

"Roll bar," she said, driving off with the roar of the mufflers audible long after she'd disappeared. I looked around the sales lot. Sure enough, there was not another roll bar on the place. The salesman looked a little green around the ears as we walked slowly back to the mobile office. He kicked gravel and didn't say much. When we came to my truck, recently new but now last year's model, sitting subdued and dusty with the long scrape down the driver's side, it contrasted sharply with the line of sparkling new '98s behind it. The salesman wasn't even up for giving me a sales pitch. Deflated, he turned toward his office, but I called him back.

"Do you know anything about trucks?" I said.

He glared.

"I mean, you know, mechanic stuff."

He shrugged inside his beige jacket with the wide lapels. "Like what?"

"Well," I said, stepping back from my truck, "like brake lines? Could you just, you know, point them out to me?"

I always figure, if you've got a question, it never hurts to ask. Sure enough, the guy almost turned jovial again. He seemed to gain a little air and came over to squat and peek under the truck. I squatted with him. We sat that way for a while staring at the underpinning. Finally, he eased himself down on his back and began inching under little by little. About halfway in, he stuck a short-fingered, chubby hand out and wiggled his fingers, motioning me to follow. What the hell. I slid under beside him. We inched along together until he was able to touch an article that he pronounced the brake line.

The problem was getting him out of there. It took awhile, and his beige suit was pretty well trashed with oily stuff I knew was never going to come out. I had a twinge of conscience as I pulled back out into the street, wondering if he might have taken a loss on Morgan's truck and lost a suit into the deal as well. I would have felt worse if it had been a better suit.

We had passed the sheriff's office on the highway coming in to town, so I decided to make my other stops first, catch Marle on my way out. I hadn't been to Crystal Springs before, so I cruised on down the highway leading into town until I reached a sign with an arrow pointing to Crystal Springs Business District. I turned left and followed the street, which soon widened and segued into three blocks of tightly packed old buildings made of a similar type and color of brick. Most were in good repair, their uniform bland exteriors spiced up with attractive cornices painted in designer three-color motifs. The sidewalks were concrete inlaid with small stones to emulate cobblestone, and bright patches of curbside grass were set with antique lampposts for an old-fashioned ambience. The street ended at a shady park beside a river foaming with rapids here and there. I pulled into a small parking lot across from a three-story building with an entrance inset at the center. Scrolling gold letters across the glass storefronts identified Crystal Springs Community Library on one side, and on the other, Dovecote Bookstore and Coffee Shoppe where a few people read at small tables beside the river.

I climbed out of my truck to the sound of rushing rapids, and resisting the temptation of the bookstore and the smell of fresh coffee, entered the library. It was a well-lit facility with glossy hardwood floors and an area beside the front window furnished with a patch of carpet and a couple of uncomfortable-looking wingback chairs. In one of them, a yellow cat lay sleeping. A bell tinkled above the door as I pushed it open, and behind an L-shaped counter, a woman flipping through a box of file cards glanced up and quickly down again in the manner of clerks who wish to avoid customers. I scanned the place for a computer monitor, but found only a cabinet with small wooden drawers along one wall—a card catalog, and not a computer in sight. I opted for a stroll through the stacks, among books arranged according to the long, unwieldy numbers of the Dewey Decimal System, until I found a section on local history. I selected the most promising volumes, spotted a colorful group of sofas and chairs sprinkled with animal cutouts sitting on tables, and settled myself into the children's section on a bright orange sofa. The books were disappointing, focusing mainly on the history of Crystal Springs, Old West legends, the brick-making plant on the edge of town. Nothing on El Gato, or whatever it was called before Claire James had named it. I stacked the books neatly on a table beside a cardboard figure of Maurice Sendak's Wild Thing and looked around for the ladies' room.

I found it at the beginning of a narrow, dimly lit hallway, and as I was leaving, I gave in to my lifelong fascination with old buildings. I tiptoed on down the hall and poked my head into a room where the door stood open a few inches. It was a dim, airless affair filled with the not unpleasant, musty smell of old paper. It had several milky windows on one side through which inadequate light filtered. Overhead, a naked unlit bulb dangled. A long table with several folding metal chairs filled one side of the room, while the other was crowded with tall rows of closely spaced metal shelving. Unlike the library stacks, the books here lay haphazardly stacked in untidy piles. Cardboard boxes overflowing with books, papers, and other objects were shoved against the walls. Tattered books and photographs covered the table. In the midst of the clutter lay the yellow cat, its large amber eyes contemplating me. It rose, stretched the length of its entire body, its tail high, and then sat on its haunches, waiting. How could I resist?

I entered the room to stroke it, setting off an impressively loud motor. Beside the cat, old photographs lay scattered, cracked and faded and curling at the edges—sepia prints of Crystal Springs before its sidewalks were cobbled and storefronts upgraded. I petted the cat and sifted through them. I recognized Main Street, though the brick buildings were sparser and the street was dirt. Horses stood tied to hitching posts, and there was not a cute lamppost in sight. I wandered further into the room, squeezing myself into the narrow aisle between the table and a ceiling-high metal bookcase as I sifted through the collection of old documents. The cat revved up and walked along the table beside me. When we reached the end, the cat crouched and sprang to the top of the bookshelf, barely making it, clinging with its claws and sending down a shower of papers and pamphlets. Achieving the shelf, the animal sat watching from its height as I began picking up the mess—tattered and dusty leaflets, books with missing covers, sheaves of papers sewn at the spine with colored thread. One caught my eye—*Cat Tales: Legends of Twin Rock Mountain*. The paper was old and brittle, the cover an amateurish line drawing of a cougar meant to be ferocious: red-penciled blood dripped from impossibly long fangs; the immense curling claws of its paw that struck out at the reader were surrounded by small, radiating lines to indicate sharpness. On the inside cover, a "c" drawn in with a circle around it was followed by the year 1944.

The naked bulb overhead flashed on.

Perhaps my fractured nerves remembered last night's flood of brilliant light on Morgan's deck before my mind possibly could have, because as the light came on, I leapt backward as though the cat's picture on the cover had actually screamed in the way that I heard the cougar scream last night. I hit the bookcase hard with my shoulders, knocked it backwards, and released an avalanche of books that came tumbling down from above.

Monday.

25

"THIS ROOM ISN'T FOR THE PUBLIC!"

The cat who had been watching from the top shelf had ridden the crest of the avalanche and was balancing himself nicely on the uppermost books, which slid down on me as I lost my footing and crashed to the floor, my arms raised to shield my head. My legs slipped under a folding chair, which toppled backwards. From somewhere in the stacks, a nasal voice screeched and shoes clattered on the wood floor, someone apparently chasing the cat through the maze of bookcases.

"Out!! OUT!!!! Sssszzzz! Ezra! Get out! OUT!!! Ezz—RAA!!!" The last ended in a piercing scream, and I heard more books tumbling and crashing like a series of small explosions. Something yellow streaked through the door. "Goddammit! OUT!!!!!" The woman I'd seen behind the desk dashed to the door in close pursuit with a book held high, which she threw down the hall. She stood there for a moment, then put her hands on her hips and swung around to me, fire in her eyes. The flames dimmed as she saw me sprawled on the floor beneath a pile of books and the overturned chair. I figured she was debating whether the building's insurance policy covered accidents involving public trespass and just how polite she had to be. I was involved in my own quandary: after the human brain endures an automobile crash, followed by near strangulation and battering by a psychopath, followed by the administration of an hallucinogenic mystery drug, could this textual avalanche be the last straw or a mere piss in the wind?

I lay there turning this conundrum over in my mind, blinking now and then to test the equipment, and checking out the librarian who seemed pretty much your average bookmeister if you looked above the waist. I guessed her to be in her late thirties, with narrow, sharp features except for a mouth that needed a face twice the size, the lips looking like they'd been stung by wasps and in some kind of spasm, pursing and unpursing. Her hair was dark and cut into a short cap below the ears, and a set of matching eyebrows ran together over her nose. Reading glasses dangled on a gold chain over a polyester cream blouse with round pearl buttons and a fluffy bow tied under her chin. A small plastic rectangle on her left breast said PATSY QUINTEN. But where the librarian stopped at the waist, the Sunset Boulevard hooker took over. She wore a skin-tight brown patent leather skirt that stopped just below what women of my mother's generation called Down There and brown lace stockings in a heart pattern, ending in a stupendous pair of platform heels to make a dwarf swoon.

"Hey, are you all right?"

Her voice was too high, thin as a needle, with a midwestern twang that I couldn't decide fit above her waist or below it. Outside of my ribs that ached a little more than they had before, I seemed fine, but as she stood waiting for an answer, I decided to keep that to myself. She tiptoed toward me and bent over a little, arching her back while I stared at her shoes with soles the width of a Big Mac and black ribbon laces that crisscrossed up her ankle and were tied in bows above her heels. A cloud of perfume crept toward me. My eyes watered a little, and for a moment, I was in the fragrance section at Walgreen's.

I rubbed my head and gazed around the room as though I hadn't seen it before. I blinked my eyes several times, slowly, and returned them to her feet, then up the legs. There, dancing among the hearts on the brown stockings, were tiny cupids armed with bows and arrows. I looked closely at them, moving up to the knee, the thigh…

"Um…"She straightened up and stepped back. "Can you get up? Here, take my hand." She kept her distance but stretched an arm toward me.

I considered the light bulb dangling over the table and lifted my hand up without looking at her. She grabbed it and began tugging, but without help on my part, she couldn't budge me. Even with her platforms, I had six inches and fifty pounds on her. She released my hand, and it dropped to the floor like a shot pigeon. She squatted and began weaving around in front of me, trying to get in my line of vision.

"Look! Hey, look here!" she said, flapping a hand and tilting right and left, trying to catch my eye as I looked around the walls, the windows, the edge of the table. "Listen, hey, you wait here, okay? I'll get you some water, be right back."

I scanned some of the book titles as I waited, and when I heard her clattering up the wooden hallway, I resumed the spacy look. She shoved a glass of water and a thick pad of damp paper towels at me, but I continued examining the table's edge. She squatted down beside me again. I decided to give her a break and moved my head slowly until I was staring directly at her. Then I focused on the lips that squeezed tight as though she'd bit a lemon, then relaxed. Squeeze…relax…squeeze …

"Here," she said, pressing the glass in my hand, but the hand was dead. I lip-watched: a mouth kissing air. She raised the rim of the glass and pressed it against my lips. I smiled and the glass hit my teeth. She jerked it away. "Here, *here*," she said, her voice irritable, "open your mouth, drink this." I drank a sip or two for her, and she relaxed a little, rocking back on her heels and frowning. I was happy to see she hadn't followed the Sharon Stone trend of underwear.

"How do you feel?" she said, not getting much of a spin on the compassion angle and pressing her knees together. I mimicked her frown.

" 'Sokay." I let my voice tremble a little and tried to push myself up. I tipped, and she caught me. "Really," I said, straightening. I anchored myself to the edge of the table and climbed into a folding chair. "How about I sit for a minute, that be all right?"

She frowned and puckered her lips. She stood up, the glass in one hand and the damp paper towels still gripped in the other, and surveyed the room as though she were leaving a burglar alone at

Tiffany's. In the distance, a faint tinkle came from the front door. She let out a deep sigh and clomped out. She didn't close the door, and the cat padded back in, waving its tail. I recovered the pamphlet with the snarling wildcat on the cover while Ezra leapt to the table and curled beside my elbow. His purr rippled through the room, and he turned his face up to me and closed his eyes. I scratched the fur under his chin and read.

The pamphlet contained numerous stories written by different authors with no attempt by the compiler to distinguish between facts, tall tales, and indigenous lore. The Cat Man was included with about the same details I already knew, but it was my first sense of him as a human being. The pamphlet had been issued just three years after his death, and the writer of his story had known Henry Joe Barlow, a likable fellow who made supply runs into the village once a month and had a particular fondness for entertaining his friends at the local bar with tall tales of mountain living. He swore that the bears in the area were taller than houses, and that he had learned to speak their language in order to invite them in for meals. He described the phantom cat of Twin Rock Mountain, materializing and disappearing like vapor from the water of the streams, and he explained that the cat had taught him how to cleanse his injuries by licking away the infection. Then Henry Joe would pull up a sleeve or pant leg, point to a healing flesh wound, and his friends would buy him another whiskey.

I glanced at the yellow cat who appeared to be grinning, his eyes visible between narrow slits. His purr vibrated in his throat as I stroked it, and the animal's whiskers poked out like broom straws from his muzzle. The bell tinkled in the distance.

I thumbed through the rest of the pamphlet quickly. The final article had been held back to give a sense of climax to the collection. It was significantly better written than the others, the author an amateur historian recounting the presence of the Ute Indians who had once lived in the area until the mid-1800s, evidenced by the scarred trees which the tribe used when their food source had dried up and they were driven to eat the bark to escape starvation. According to the author, when the Utes were driven from the area to seek more plentiful food, they intended to return and left their home under the protection of an immense cat who would drive out strangers. The presence of the cat was supported anecdotally, with local residents telling of sightings, describing a golden beast the size of a horse who materialized out of thin air. But finally, it was a Bigfoot kind of story: although many people had attempted scientifically to document its presence, no one had ever produced a shred of evidence, particularly the telltale bones that all wildcats leave behind after foraging on deer and elk.

"You look like you've improved," the nasal voice said from the doorway. There had been no warning footsteps; as with her first appearance, she had tiptoed down the hall and caught me and Ezra red-handed. The cat's hair stood on end, and it dashed from the table and disappeared into the stacks. This time the woman merely stood in the door, her lips drawn into a tight wrinkled knot.

"I'm feeling much better," I said, closing the pamphlet. "I want to thank you for letting me rest in here. In fact, it was just this sort of book I was looking for when I came in. This stuff looks pretty old," I said. "I bet it's worth something."

Her expression hardened. "Everything that was worth a bean, those Smithsonian people took. All they left behind was junk that's going to take me forever to catalogue." She gave the room a nasty glare. "With only me working, and nobody much interested in this stuff, I don't guess it'll get done till the zoard hires somebody to replace..." She stopped and stood back from the door, clearly waiting for me to leave.

I commiserated about budget cuts of the humanities as I stood up with several books that I placed neatly on one of the empty shelves. I mentioned my former position as a professor, lamented the low pay, picked up several more books and arranged them beside the others. "This looks like a big job, getting all this stuff rebound, organized, catalogued," I said. "Where'd it all come from anyway?"

The woman snorted through her thin nose as she crossed her arms and leaned against the door frame. "Myra—this woman that used to work here—she started going through all that stuff over in the attic at the old building where we used to be. She was kind of strange, not too good on the front desk, but she had this thing about record-keeping, history, animal preservation, stuff like that…" From the corner of my eye, I could see Patsy cutting a look at me. I kept shelving, picking up books from the floor, feeling the tension of small-town life in her voice. She was teetering between the impulse to gossip and the obligation to maintain a professional image, so I gave her a little shove.

"I just moved here," I said, "and my next-door neighbor was telling me about some kind of trouble that had happened over here. Somebody got fired or something?" I began sifting through the clutter on the table and making a tidy stack of all the photographs. The woman shot a glance down the hallway.

"It was pretty bad." Her voice was low and conspiratorial. She shook her head and walked over to the table where she began sifting alongside me, pulling out pamphlets and arranging them beside the photos. She made a little sucking sound with her teeth and tongue as she started off, her nasal, high-pitched voice settling into a sing-song rhythm just above a whisper. "Tsk, tsk. It all started when the Thompsons sold that house where we'd had our library for who knows how long. They decided to get their money out of it, a lot more than the city could pay, so the Board leased this building, and we had to move everything." She heaved a deep sigh, stacking pamphlets: *Goatherds of the Front Ridge. Miller's Study of Intemperate Climes. Ethnographical Studies of Regional Native American Migratory Tribes. Cultural Utilization of Rocky Mountain Stream Life. Nancy Crindle's Ideas about Birds' Songs.* This last was a slim handwritten affair, stapled together and illustrated with childlike, colored-pencil drawings of birds on the top sheet. Patsy stared at it. "Tsk, tsk."

By the time we'd shelved the books and organized the remaining materials into tidy piles, I knew that during the move to the new facility, Myra Jones had discovered an attic in the old house where the library had been housed, stacks and boxes of old books and documents and pictures that some thought were a great find and others considered pure burnable trash. Myra had convinced the Board to allot her the room we stood in to house the "Crystal Springs Historical Museum of Arts and Letters" and spent every waking moment on it, working the extra hours without pay.

"Just obsessed, she was." Patsy stuck the last book on a lower shelf and straightened up, pulling at her patent leather skirt to smooth the creases. She shook her head, sighed, uttered several *tsks* in a row. "It's all she could talk about. The board wasn't giving us a penny for all this, just the room here, but she had plans for making her own library cards, binding all the books herself. On and on." Patsy rolled her eyes toward the ceiling.

"So they fired her?" I still had several stops to make, and at this rate, we'd have the whole room shipshape before Patsy got to the information I wanted.

"Well, no. I mean, she was working for *free* practically." Patsy gave me a hard frown. "Why would they fire her for *that*?"

I shrugged and began alphabetizing the books by author's last name.

"No, what she got herself fired for was barricading herself in this room, saying she'd shoot anybody that come through that door." Patsy put her hands on her hips. "She even had a *gun* in here with her, can you *believe* it?"

I mumbled that it did, indeed, sound unbelievable. I was on the B's.

"Tsk. Well, it was all her own fault to begin with. She'd been the one to read about those scarred trees, then call the National Wildlife people after she found some out there where she lives in the middle of nowhere. So when somebody showed up to take a look, sure enough, turned out there had been Indians that lived there way back, just like it said in those books she found. So they got the Smithsonian into it, and then some archeologists showed up and started digging. They came by to look through all the stuff Myra had drug over here from that attic, and they decided some of it was better off in their museum in D.C."

Ezra had slipped back in and was rubbing himself against the table legs. Patsy glanced at him and kept talking. I started in on the D's.

"Myra just about had a heart attack when they told her they were taking some of it. She thought it ought to be left here where it came from, to go in her museum. But these people were big shots, it didn't matter what she wanted. They went through it all," Patsy said, nodding at the boxes, "and you see how they just left a mess of what they didn't want. Myra had it sorted out nice and tidy into groups—some old pottery and pieces of arrowheads, odd-shaped rocks, lots of pictures, that kind of stuff. Now just look at it."

I was gearing up to start on the F's, but Patsy was done talking. She eased around behind the cat, trying to head him off. "Shooo. OUT!!!! Eliot, OUT!" She stamped her feet loudly, but he dashed past her and disappeared into the stacks. Patsy clattered after him, followed by a series of small crashes as books slid off their shelves, and then the two of them emerged streaking toward the door.

"Eliot?" I followed Patsy down the hallway and entered the main room where the cat sat waiting on the orange sofa. Beside him sat his double.

"Right. Eliot and Ezra."

On my way out, I passed the periodical section in a corner where newspapers were arranged in neat formation over small poles. I stopped. Patsy had returned to her position behind the L-shaped desk, looking every inch the librarian. "So those bones," I said, "that were found a while back, those were from that dig out by where I...out there by Myra's place?"

"That's right," she said. "It was very strange, I can tell you." She had resumed rifling through the index box again, but she paused, staring out the window ahead of where she sat. "I mean they were digging up stuff that was two hundred years old, and here's a bone of somebody's *leg*. Or something. A *recent* bone anyway." She swiveled to face me, her eyes round above the reading glasses that now occupied the tip of her nose. "I can tell you, I'm just as glad Myra has gone, even if I do miss the help. It was starting to give me the willies, the whole thing. Tsk." She shook her shoulders and pantomimed fear.

I browsed in the periodical section, pulled The Denver *Post* on microfiche, and skimmed the articles starting at the beginning of the year—the new state budget, another missing co-ed, avalanche conditions at ski resorts. April: the bones had been discovered, and more recent articles cited test results revealing the bones as female, early adult, dead between six to seven years. The woman's identity was still unknown, as well as the cause of death, though traces of a nerve gas, organophosphate had been found. I sat staring out into space, cymbals crashing in my head. Six to seven years: 1991 or 1990. I remembered the day long ago, December 18, 1990—the day after I'd closed on my first multimillion-dollar deal, the day I'd gotten lost in El Gato just after the heavy snowfall. I had walked up the narrow road following the tire tracks, desperate to find help. And I had found the yellow Jeep. Harv's Jeep! With the footprints going off through the brush toward...Cougar Canyon.

On the way out the door, I stopped where Patsy was laying several library cards in a line, as though she were playing solitaire. "Tsk. Overdue," she said. On manila postcards with the federal government's postal stamp already imprinted, she was writing out the names of the library card holders and looking up their addresses in the index box. I could never quite get over how much time people who hated computers wasted. And then it struck me—

I had stopped by the desk to ask Patsy about the interlibrary loan materials Myra had received, the photocopy of my first volume of poetry. But this library had no computers, not even a database with a list of holdings and the names and addresses of their cardholders. Maybe they kept one in the back room.

"Nope. Not a single computer," she said, smiling proudly. "We do it all by hand. Everything's personal here."

"So you don't have an interlibrary loan access system?"

"Oh no," she said, astonished, "you won't find many community libraries that do, even if they do have computers. It's just mostly colleges that use that."

26

ON THE WAY OUT OF THE LIBRARY, I grabbed a Chamber
of Commerce map of Crystal Springs from the display case
by the door and looked up the location of the county office building, which was located on Muledeer Avenue, two blocks over.
Outside, the black storm clouds that had been piling up behind
the western peaks this morning were now drifting in. I stuck the
map in my back pocket, zipped up the jacket Morgan had loaned
me, then walked along the edge of the park till I came to
Muledeer. The county offices were housed in a plain two-story
stucco building with flyers of upcoming events and announce-
ments taped inside the front window: an apple-dunking
Halloween Hoot on the 31st, a Kiwanis dance, Wednesday night
bingo, a lost dog. Inside, I passed the DMV office, the county
assessor's office, and came to a glass door COUNTY CLERK'S OFFICE
printed in block letters. Inside, two women were working at
desks behind a chest-high counter piled with thick booklets of
computer printouts sheets in plastic binders. An elderly woman
with gray hair pinned in a knot and wearing a dark blue dress
with white dots looked up. The younger woman at the other desk
kept tapping at her computer keyboard.

"What can I do for you today?" she said. She had a florid com-
plexion and intelligent gray eyes behind rimless glasses. I
explained that I wanted to look up records of ownership for some
lots in the El Gato subdivision, and she bent her head and peered
at me over her glasses. "They feuding out there again?" she said,
pushing herself heavily from her chair. She walked with the rolling

gait of the tired and underpaid, opened one of the binders on the counter, and turned it to face me with a little shove. "El Gato lots. All the back-tax properties have been bought up, though." She pointed to the entries and explained how to look them up under lot number or by owner's last name.

After she went back to her desk, I scanned the entries that included date of purchase, notations of any recent changes, and the name and mailing address of each owner. There were a total of one thousand lots, and as Harv had said, Brandenberg owned the lion's share—the computer tally listed his total at 483. Second in line was John Crawford, who owned thirty-two lots in various areas sprinkled throughout the development, purchased over a seven-year period, ending at the time Brandenberg had bought every existing back-tax lot in February 1995. Together, Brandenberg and John Crawford carried over fifty percent of the votes. I looked up the Bentons—Harv and Edna. September 1971. Beneath the entry, Brandenberg's name had been entered in tiny spidery longhand in red ink with a question mark at one side. When I asked the polka-dotted woman about it, she said the title of the lot was being contested, and they were waiting for a final decision from the court on who the rightful owner was. At the moment, she said, until they heard otherwise, it was still the Bentons', though it could not be sold or transferred until the official decision came through. She shook her head and went back to her work. I used a pen on the counter and pulled out my Crystal Springs map to jot down the exact date that Harv had recorded the property in his name. I would give the Aspen attorney Wendy had mentioned a call and inquire about the statutes of limitations in Colorado and the validity of Harv's claim that using the Association money for television ads was illegal.

I started to leave and then, on an impulse, scanned the other El Gato land owners. I didn't recognize many; most were out-of-state owners with single lots. The printout had not been computer-updated since January 1997, so Eva Blake's name and address had been written in the same red spidery scrawl below the previous owner's name, recording her purchase in March. I went on down the list. Andrew Jacobs and Wolf Condidos, purchased 1996. Myra

Jones, 1985. Sarah and Felix Scott Moss, 1990. I found my own name scratched in red beneath the computer entry, recording the small lot I had bought to gain access to the El Gato roads. There seemed to be an unusually large number of recent title changes, with the computer entry names crossed out and the more recent owners' names inserted in red ink. And most, I realized, were recording new ownership to Dean Brandenberg; in fact, I counted eighteen recent purchases Brandenberg had made, not including Harv's, and the most recent recorded just last Friday. Brandenberg had apparently been contacting individual property owners and buying their lots. He now owned exactly 501 of them and no longer needed the proxies of John Crawford: he was the official lord of El Gato. I stared at the book. Whatever else it might show about Brandenberg, he hadn't needed Harv's lot to complete his grand slam. I snapped the book shut, thanked the woman, and left the office.

On the way out, I dashed into the DMV. I'd memorized the license plate of Morgan's MG, and while I wrote out the check for the new registration, the clerk punched in the number and pulled up the record. The bad news was, the clerk informed me as she looked at my check, that I couldn't just register somebody else's car, and anyway she had to see the title and the vehicle first-hand for the VIN inspection before she could issue the new plates. I guess my disappointment showed, because she softened.

"Hey, tell you what," she said, lowering her voice and glancing around to make sure the two other women in the office weren't listening. "No biggie. I'll just go on with the paperwork, have it all ready when you bring the car in tomorrow, or I can even get Brad over at the sheriff's office to drive out and look at it if you want, then you'll be all set. Okey dokey?" She cracked her gum and pushed the receipt toward me with an ear-to-ear grin. I nodded, thanked her, and tucked the paper in my pocket. I'd hoped to hand Morgan the new plates, could already see us taking the little car for spin, her driving and me in the passenger seat, but the receipt would have to do.

Near the end of Muledeer, one building had held out against the spread of the downtown business area. Placed back off the sidewalk and surrounded by a well kept lawn was a chalet-type home that had been turned into an office. A small sign placed near the sidewalk read:

PATRICIA L. ANDERSON, M.D.
Specializing in Gynecology and Women's Medicine

I paused. I'd spent most of the afternoon in the library, and I still had to pick up items at the grocery for the meal I'd promised Wendy and the kids, drop by the sheriff's office with the hope of catching Marle in, then pick up the television, meet Morgan at her place, and head to Wendy's to cook dinner. It was already after four, but this would only take a minute. I headed toward the front door, figuring that signing the release form now to have my medical records transferred to a local physician and to make an appointment to discuss the first few hot flashes I'd been having would save a trip into town later.

I pushed the front door open to a pleasant waiting room with mauve carpeting, matching sofa and chair in one corner, and a counter separating the waiting room from a bright fluorescent-lit receptionist's office. Behind the counter, a young woman with long red hair held back from her face with barrettes on each side was just lifting her jacket and purse off the coatrack as I entered.

"Bad timing," I said. "I'll come back later." I turned to leave as another woman entered the reception office from a rear hallway.

"No problem," she said. "I can help you." She nodded at the young woman who held her jacket in one hand and purse in the other. "You go on. See you tomorrow." The redhead flashed a quick smile as she rushed past me and out the door.

"Sorry, Mondays we generally close up at four," the older woman said, walking up beside the appointment book. "I'm Doctor Anderson, what can I do for you?"

Dr. Anderson looked to be in her late thirties or early forties, wearing a green cotton wrapper over a pale yellow skirt and sweater. She had fair skin, light brown hair pulled back in a hasty French braid that was coming loose around the edges, and large green eyes that didn't need makeup. She had the kind of wrinkles around the eyes and mouth that looked like she smiled a lot, and a row of perfectly straight teeth.

I told her my story—I'd just moved to the area, needed to transfer my records, probably time for a physical, wanted to discuss the pros and cons of treating menopause. She nodded, scanned the open appointment book on the counter before her, and turned several pages. She mentioned a date two weeks away; I accepted and gave her my name which she wrote in and turned the book back to its original page where large Xs marked out the boxes after 4:00.

"Are you living in town here?" she asked, taking off the green cotton wrapper. She hung it on the coatrack and removed a brown camel hair coat.

"Nope. I bought a house near the El Gato development, used to belong to Claire James." Dr. Anderson was slipping her arms into her coat, and I saw her eyes snap to mine. Then she looked away and picked up her purse and a small paper bag from below the counter. She pushed through the swinging door beside the reception window, flipped off the overheads in the office, and came out into the waiting room where I stood beside the open front door. She gave me a quick, curious look, and I remembered hearing something Marle had mentioned to me about Camilla visiting a doctor in town. Could it be Dr. Anderson? In such a small town, how many other women's specialists were there likely to be? I waited on the front steps while the doctor locked her office door.

"You wouldn't happen to know Camilla James, would you?" I asked. "Someone mentioned she saw a doctor here in town...." I let the words trail off as Dr. Anderson turned. Something in her eyes flamed for a moment, and again she looked away. The doctor knew something, and I wondered what it was and how I could find out. I didn't know much about the methods Cordelia Morgan might have used, so I went for the truth.

"I'm just finding out some things about the property I bought," I said, as I followed her along the sidewalk. She kept her eyes on the street. "For one thing, I've discovered Camilla James hung herself in my barn, and there's a chance it might be linked to the man who was killed at El Gato last Friday." I stepped in front of her, forcing her to stop as we neared the curb. "And there's possibly been an attempt made on my own life. This must sound pretty bizarre, but I'm a stranger here and I need some help. I'd sure appreciate anything you could tell me about Camilla."

I waited as the doctor studied her feet for a moment. Sporadic gusts of wind swept along the sidewalk, and black clouds crept toward the sun, creating that eerie light that sometimes occurs at the edge of a storm. Dr. Anderson looked up and nodded; she'd made her decision. I followed her across the street to a narrow dirt path among old, shady oaks whose autumn leaves swirled in the wind. She stopped at a picnic table and sat down, opening her brown bag and taking out a sandwich folded in clear plastic wrap, a container of orange juice, and a baggie of cookies. I pulled out the opposite bench and laid the license plates next to me.

"I didn't have a chance to have lunch today," she said. "Only have a few minutes, I'm afraid." She unwrapped the sandwich and offered me half. I shook my head and waited.

Patricia Anderson picked up a sandwich wedge and stared at it a moment. "Camilla was my patient, so it's unprofessional of me to tell you this, but she's dead two years now and I don't see how it matters. In fact, I kept thinking that after she died..." I waited again. She laid the sandwich back on its plastic wrapper. "Well, I thought someone might ask some questions."

"Questions?" I didn't want to push too hard. About the only thing I'd ever gotten from pushing was an equal measure of resistance. So I waited some more. Doctor Anderson frowned at the river, and in the distance, thunder rumbled. The clouds moved in, the wind gusted, and the air turned dark and chill.

"I know most of the folks around here, Miss Symkin, and given my specialty, I know a lot of intimate, private information about my patients that I would never reveal, not even in a court of law in some cases. But..." She took a deep breath.

Patricia Anderson was having a tough time of saying whatever it was she'd been waiting to say. I figured that she wasn't going to back out now, all I had to do was wait a little longer. I was right.

"She came to see me about two weeks before her death. She was bleeding badly. She was one of those extremely thin, tiny women who often have trouble with their cycles—heavy bleeding, painful cramps, that sort of thing. I'd seen her a couple of times before. But this was different, this was..." She glared at me with green, angry eyes. "She'd had rough sex, she was torn to pieces inside. She would have bled to death if she hadn't come in. I tried to get her to say who did it, but she refused, and I couldn't talk her into returning for a check-up. Of course, it could have been consensual, but...It was vicious, like someone had tried to kill her by..." Her voice trailed off, and she looked back toward the river. I didn't want to hear the details; the thought sickened me—and scared me. Camilla had been seeing the sheriff.

She wrapped the sandwich back in the plastic and put the food into the brown bag. Her hands were trembling. "I'm afraid I have to get going. This is my afternoon at the women's clinic, pro bono."

"How long had you been seeing Camilla?" I asked, as Patricia Anderson stood up.

"Oh, since not long after she came here, that would have been a year or so. I could look it up. I gave her a pelvic her first appointment when she came in complaining of cramps, irritability, irregular periods. Classic perimenopausal symptoms. I ran some tests, gave her a prescription for hormone replacement. That seemed to work."

"So after the first pelvic, you never gave her another until she came in hemorrhaging?"

"That's right." She looked very tired, and I wasn't feeling all that hot myself. I thanked her and watched her walk slowly out of the park with the paper bag dangling from one hand.

I bought the hamburger, buns, and condiments at a local grocery and asked the clerk to pack the meat with dry ice. By the time I pulled into the parking lot in front of the sheriff's office, a small modular structure with two large picture windows in front, rain was falling in long straight lines. Just as I shut off the engine, the clouds suddenly released a deluge that hit the metal body of my truck in a deafening racket. Although lights shone in the sheriff's office, Marle's Bronco was nowhere in sight, so I sat in my truck, waiting for the rain to let up and staring out through the windshield where water washed down in waves.

My mood had darkened right along with the clouds, and I felt deeply depressed. Everything I'd come across today added to the confusion and unrest that had been building over the last few days. I had thought Harv was poaching when I'd seen his yellow Jeep the day I'd gotten lost in El Gato, but now I wondered if he might somehow have been involved in the mystery of the bones discovered in Cougar Canyon. But why just a hand? If there were actually a dead woman, where was the rest of her body? Were Harv's death and the bones connected? Was Brandenberg involved? Just the thought of the beefy man made me burn: he was now in a position of absolute control over El Gato. I had spent most of my life professing the virtues of individual freedom and the evils of tyranny, yet I was now living next door to it.

And Camilla. My stomach lurched when I thought of what Patricia Anderson had told me. I didn't know how it fit in with her death, but first Marle and now Dr. Anderson had expressed doubts about the suicide, and though Marle had been her lover, I couldn't believe he had been her tormentor. And then there was Cordelia Morgan... she walked across my mind like a dark shadow, deepening my anxiety.

I was so lost in thought that I didn't hear the Bronco pull up or see the sheriff till he tapped on the glass. I jumped—the rain had stopped, and my windows were fogged.

"That how they do it in the big city, curb service law?" he drawled as I rolled down the window. He bent over and squinted in at me, his gray eyes dancing a little.

"Anybody looking for curb service in the big city is most definitely *not* looking for the law," I said. I jerked the handle on the door and rammed it with my shoulder. It popped loudly as I got out, and the sheriff eyed the long scar across the side, his eyebrows raised. I must have been carrying my mood on my face because he took a step back with his hands up.

"Looks like everything I been hearing about you today is true." He lowered his hands and gave me a curious, probing look. He was still wearing faded Levi's, but today he had on a dark green crewneck sweater topped by a leather jacket like the ones I'd seen highway patrol officers wear. It was unzipped, and it hiked up a little when he stuck his hands in his jeans pockets. "I been calling your place, Eva Blake's, too, but no answer. I was about ready to head on out there when Brad called on the mobile, said you been sitting out front here awhile."

"What's wrong?" I looked around a little wildly, trying to think why the sheriff was looking for me.

"You tell me," he said, as several fat drops of rain splatted down. "Had a complaint this morning, accusing you of aggravated battery. Sounds like you're getting into the spirit of things out there."

"'Aggravated battery'?" I stared at him in confusion. "What're you talking about? Says who?"

The sky suddenly opened up again, and a stinging blast of wind and rain swung across us like an ocean wave.

"Says Gerald Crawford."

27

I DASHED THROUGH THE DOOR that Marle held open and stood dripping and shivering in a large room with two desks on each side facing the door. Behind one, a young man looked up from a newspaper. Marle disappeared down a hallway and returned with a roll of paper towels, and I wiped the running water from my face and squeezed it from my hair. It was a tantrum of a downpour, beating and spitting and thundering while we watched from the cocoon of the office, its gray windows blind with rain, the air steamy with the smell of wet clothes and leather, the crash of rain on the tin roof making talk impossible. After a few minutes, the rain stopped as quickly as it had come. Outside, the ditches beside the highway boiled with muddy, rushing water that spilled down the mountain. My mind, just as turbulent, returned to Gerald Crawford as I followed Marle to his desk.

"Are you telling me Gerald Crawford is accusing *me* of attacking *him*?" I said, as the sheriff pulled down a blanket from a shelf and handed it to me. I slipped out of my wet jacket, hung it over the back of a chair beside the desk to dry, and wrapped myself in the thick, woolly fabric. Marle hung his coat on a nail, and we sat down, staring at each other across his desk. He tipped his chair back, his hands clasped behind his head, his gray eyes aimed at me down the spine of his nose.

"Yep. Said you accused his wife of being in cahoots with Harv and setting you up to buy that property for twice what it was worth, not telling you somebody had died there. Said you attacked her, and he happened to drive up in time to stop you from doing something worse. Said you sideswiped his truck when you left. Didn't file charges, just said he was thinking about it. Probably figured you might be coming by here today. Wanted to get his side in." The sheriff's eyes were in laser mode, waiting. "Also said he thought you had it in for Harv, thought you might know something about cutting brake lines."

"I presume you know that is pure fucking horse shit." I nailed him with one of my own laser stares and pulled down my turtle-neck to show the black bruises around my neck.

"Gerald's specialty," he said, though I couldn't tell if that was a response to my words or my neck. The fellow at the other desk was staring over his newspaper. I let the turtleneck snap back up, and the deputy rose, saying that he was going to see if the rain had set off any alarms downtown. He was a nice-looking guy with a square chin and the kind of wide body that had probably made him the star of his high school football team. When the door closed and the room was quiet, Marle listened while I told him about the inci-dent at Wendy's place yesterday, the get-together in the kitchen, Gerald's attack, and my following talk with Wendy.

"And that scrape down the side of my truck was just the final kicker. If anybody's pressing charges," I said, banging a fist on his desk, "it'll damn sure as hell be me."

"Just settle down," he said. "He came in here this morning, had Wendy and the kids with him, had her make out a restraining order. They're all three backing up his side of it."

"The *kids!?*" I looked at him in disbelief. "So you saw Wendy? What he did to her?"

Marle nodded. He clasped his hands together on the desk and looked at them.

"And he's saying *I* did *that*?"

Marle nodded again.

"That son of a bitch!" A finger of sunlight slipped from between the surging clouds, moving across the parking lot. "You don't believe him?"

"Not saying you're not capable of doing some serious damage, but most folks know the story on Gerald and Wendy. Seen her like that before you showed up."

"And you just sit by and let it happen?"

He frowned as the sunlight crept in through the window, moved across the dusty wood floor, and then disappeared. "She's not going to bring charges against Gerald. You probably already picked that up from talking to her."

I looked at the sheriff, at the set of his jaw and the hard muscular hands clasped on the desk in front of him. I thought about Camilla, how she had felt those hands on her skin. I thought about what Patricia Anderson had told me. My headache had begun nibbling around the base of my skull, and I felt tired and faint.

"You okay?" the sheriff asked. He disappeared down the hall and returned with a cup of water, a loaf of bread, and a Tupperware container. I sipped the water while he untwisted the end of the bread and pulled out a handful of slices. He pried the top off the Tupperware and peeled the plastic wrapping off some bologna and a stack of processed cheese slices. "You want to take this restraining order seriously, Sym. Gerald said you had some idea of going over to Wendy's this evening, taking a television for the kids and bringing dinner. Ordering his wife to clean her house." He shot a glance at me. "What he's saying with this restraint is a warning to you. Don't even think of going over there, you hear me?" He slapped a couple pieces of cheese and bologna between two slices of white bread and handed it to me.

I stared at it, trying to decide just how hungry I was. Pretty hungry; I took it. Jesus. I nodded as I bit in, but I felt bad about promising the kids. When I told Marle, he offered to take the television over himself. I chewed, drank the rest of the water, and went down the hall to the bathroom for more. I came back with two cups full and set them on the desk where he had another sandwich waiting. I ate and drank, and then I started in talking. I felt about like that cloud must have when it dumped all that water it had been carrying around. I told him how I'd felt like selling out after the accident in Eva's truck, and then I told him about my new resolve to stay. About launching my own investigation with Eva—our visit with Wolf and Andrew, going to the professor's house and to Myra Jones's. I told him about all the information I'd collected from the El Gato visits as well as from the library and the county clerk's office. But I withheld my conversation with Patricia Anderson for the moment. And Cordelia Morgan.

The sheriff leaned over his desk, listening as I talked, the muscles around his jaw working and his features hardening. By the time I finished, the sky outside was black with storm clouds, their bellies rippling with threads of lightning, and the sheriff's face was stone. He leaned back in his chair and stared at me. I chased the last of the sandwiches with water and started to work on the stack of bologna. I chewed while blue shadows deepened in the corners inside the office. On the wall behind the sheriff, the clock read 5:15. I listened to the rhythm of the second hand and watched it chuck along. The sheriff stared.

"What?" I said finally.

When he still didn't say anything, I shrugged and finished off the last square of processed cheese. At last he shook his head, not taking his eyes off me.

"You really need a caretaker," he said slowly. I was so relieved that he said anything at all, I smiled. I wondered if I looked as goofy as I felt. "And just so you can set what passes for your mind to rest, Gerald couldn't have messed with Harv's brakes. Brandenberg started an all-night marathon party Thursday after he nailed down that last lot and knew he had control of El Gato. Brandenberg, Gerald both—lots of folks saw them Thursday night during the time that grader was setting at Harv's waiting for somebody to work on its brakes."

The sheriff pulled the empty Tupperware container toward him and set its plastic lid on top. He glared at me. "Professor Moss was teaching a class, so you can mark him off." He gave the lid a karate smack on one side. "The Gillmans were also at Brandenberg's bash, so mark them off." Still glaring, karate smack to the other side. He stood up, grabbed the bread by the neck of the bag, held it with one hand, and gave it a hard smack with the other, sending it twirling. "Myra Jones was at the party till Mrs. Brandenberg drove her home at midnight. And, sure, I suppose she could have walked several miles in the dark, across canyons and streams, but why would she? She was one of the few people Harv got along with." He steadied the bread on his desk and twisted the wire several times around the neck of the bag. He crushed the plastic wrap from the bologna and cheese into a ball and hurled it at the wastebasket in the corner with the conviction of Kareem making a slam dunk. Then he crossed his arms and walked over to where I sat, towering over me. "And Brandenberg's in the clear, no motive. He's got investments up the kazoo, financial records show him well-off without any help from the Association or selling the El Gato lots. So you want to talk alibis, let's talk. Where the hell were you that night? And Eva Blake, for that matter?"

He was standing so near that his knees were touching mine. He had a nasty look in his eye, and the dark mood that had been gaining on me all day exploded into anger. I shoved my chair backward, its legs grating harshly against the wood floor, tossed the blanket off, and faced the sheriff, nearly as tall.

"I was sleeping in the room next to my contractor, if you want to ask him. And what about you? Maybe you knew about whoever was raping Camilla, ramming the hell out of her and nearly killing her. Maybe you found out it was Harv. Maybe those rumors circulating about him and his hands-on approach to women were true, and maybe you've just been letting some time pass before you got him for it. Or maybe—" I stopped, my mouth still open. "Maybe it was you doing it, and Harv found out about it."

The words flew out my mouth, and the blood left Marle's face. I knew it was crazy, my anger speaking. I didn't really believe he had raped Camilla. I wanted to call the words back. I hadn't planned it this way, hadn't planned it at all. I hadn't even known the idea was growing there until the words found it. He stepped back as though I'd struck him.

"What the hell are you talking about?" he said, but now his voice was low. He sat down in the chair and put his forearms on the desk and looked at me with hollow eyes.

"Marle...I..." I took a step toward him and touched his arm, but he recoiled. I pulled the chair back and sat down in it, leaning toward him. "I just found out," I said. I told him about my conversation with Patricia Anderson and tried not to see the look in his eyes as he watched the rain come down again and the day lose its light, slowly, like sand ebbing from an hourglass.

He sat for a long while staring out the window after I finished, and then said, "Just for the record, if I were going to kill a man for doing that, I wouldn't wait two years to do it, and I wouldn't cut his brake lines. I'd do it face-to-face, so he knew who was taking him out, and he'd know why."

"Sounds like you've put some thought into it."

"Might have." He shifted his gaze back to the window where the rain spattered on the porch.

"I'm sorry," I said, rubbing my temples, which were pounding at about the same tempo as the rain on the roof. "It's been a long week."

Beyond the window, the street and the trees and the parking lot had turned into shades of gray. I was relieved that I didn't have to visit Wendy, but I would have to go by my house with the sheriff to get the television. The driveway was newly made; the mud would be deep, maybe impassable.

"It makes more sense now about Camilla," the sheriff said, "why she didn't...why we weren't closer. But it still doesn't explain why she said she was leaving that day and didn't."

I remembered that Patricia Anderson said that Camilla refused to have a follow-up pelvic exam. "I think it had been going on for some time," I said, "that it had maybe escalated, and that's when she went to see Doctor Anderson. I think she was planning to leave to escape whoever was doing that to her, that she didn't want to tell you for whatever reason of her own. But maybe she'd changed her mind and decided to stay, maybe she was thinking of blowing the whistle and whoever it was panicked, killed her and made it look like suicide."

"Could be. Still isn't getting us any closer to who cut Harv's brakes, though. I've only asked preliminary questions, still got to do the follow-up, but so far, just about everybody's accounted for Thursday night and Friday morning..."

Not quite everyone, I thought, as Marle was talking. In fact, the sheriff had said it himself: where was Eva Blake? According to her own story, she'd come to El Gato for the very purpose of looking into Camilla's death. She had come in disguise, and if she had discovered that Harv had been raping Camilla, maybe even killed her,

I didn't have any trouble seeing her fix his brakes. She had the expertise, that was certain. What had she called herself last night on the phone to Claire, a *hit man*? She'd explained that it was a personal joke between her and Claire, but maybe it wasn't. And she'd cautioned me against revealing her identity to the sheriff, of course she had. I was just getting ready to tell what I knew of the fictitious Eva Blake when I heard Marle.

"...not sure how that fits in with someone tampering with Eva's truck, though. I did a background check in Hollywood, and she's clean. Husband's running all over town with other women, just like she figured. Besides, Eva only knew Harv in passing. So I'll check into her whereabouts that night and the next morning, but I doubt there's much to find there. As far as your idea about the husband sending somebody to cut her brakes and take her out of the picture," he shook his head and grinned a little, "been reading too many murder mysteries."

I looked at him, dumbfounded. How could Eva Blake's story check out if she were Cordelia Morgan? My headache had climbed up a few floors, and I heard Marle talking through a staccato tapping of rain and tom-toms.

"...figure the bones in the canyon are probably a separate issue. The lab results came back; no DNA match. And the bones showed markings to indicate the hand had been severed at the wrist with a circular saw."

I stared at him.

He shrugged. "It's not all that uncommon. The perp removes the hands of a victim, no prints. If the entire body had been dismembered and the parts dumped, other bones would have shown up, what with coyotes and all. But we can't match it up to a body that's been found anywhere at this point."

"What about missing persons?"

"You know how many missing persons there are on record every year? It's like finding a gray hair on a pale dog." He fanned though several pages of names, then put the materials back in the folder, slapped it shut, and leaned forward with his arms on the desk. He sat looking at me with his fingers dancing on the manila folder and something working behind the gray eyes. "It's not a game, Sym. You've done a pretty good job of detective work in a short amount of time, and I'd rather know what you're doing than not, so I've shared this with you. But there's a lot of questions unanswered, and somebody's killing people. I think if you're planning on staying out at your place, you ought to get somebody out there with you, somebody that knows something about protection. If you're thinking of staying at Eva's, you want to keep in mind somebody either tried to kill her or you. You might be headed in deeper by staying there."

Lightning glimmered outside, and after a moment, a clap of thunder. The sheriff collected the Tupperware container, the loaf of bread, and the mugs, and disappeared down the hall. The thunder crashed again, closer, rattling the plate glass windows and sending a tremor through the office. I had sat outside in the parking lot today thinking of the El Gato puzzle, but also thinking of running away again. Talking to the sheriff had cleared my mind. Now I was determined to find out why all this was happening, and for a start, I had a few questions I intended to run past Eva Blake. Or Cordelia Morgan. Or whoever in hell she was. In fact, after the sheriff followed me home and we loaded up the television, I planned to give her a call, invite her over for that dinner I still planned to cook, and try to get some straight answers.

I stood up and folded the blanket I'd tossed on the floor, while the sheriff made motions of shutting down the office, switching off the overheads and fiddling with a timer on the coffee pot in the corner, putting on his leather jacket. I slipped on my own, which was still damp but drier than it had been, and as we were walking out the door, he paused.

"I want to thank you for telling me about Camilla." His jaw flexed and his lips compressed for a moment. "Some things, you have to know before you can... go on."

The sheriff was holding open the door, and I was standing close enough to see, in the half light, the way the rain had left his hair springing in curls above his collar, close enough to smell the damp leather of his patrol jacket. Close enough to hear the sound of the leather shifting as his arm came up to circle my shoulder, to feel that other shifting just below where Gerald Crawford had left the dark rings on my neck, the wings that opened and closed at the center of my chest. And below that—the rush of heat that brought my face to his.

At that moment, a blast of wind tore through the trees and blew back the door. Outside, the rain had turned to a rolling mist, and I shivered as the cold shot through the office. The sheriff and I stood awkwardly in the doorway. Night was descending; inside the dark clouds overhead glimmered brief pockets of lightning. I looked away, walked out across the porch and down the steps toward my truck as he locked up, and discovered my window rolled down and the seat soaked.

"Shit." I rummaged behind the seat, pulled out a wrinkled blanket, folded it over the wet seat. Beside me, I heard the sheriff's Bronco start up. I looked around, and he leaned over, rolled down the passenger window. We stared at each other as the seconds stretched out, and then he said he would be at my house after he had made his routine pass through town.

I stood alone in the parking lot and watched the Bronco disappear down the wet street. Overhead, lightning skittered soundlessly through the clouds. Thunder rumbled in the distance, and my headache pounded.

Somehow I had imagined the sheriff and I driving to my place together.

PART V

Payback

28

Morgan

I place the cages along the sides of the barn, leaving one foot of space between them, adjusting the spring latch on each. When the first animal is caught, the others will be wary, but then as all species, they will adapt to the afflictions of their captured brothers—and ignore them. Twenty cages. I do not know the number of cats; it does not matter—a week, a month, six months, the Symkin woman's cat problem is eradicated. I tear open the bag of cotton balls, open the small package from Rocky Mountain Outfitters that I picked up at the UPS drop station in town, uncap the bottle inside, pour one drop of mixture per cotton ball as I walk along the cages and toss one in each. Already the males are attracted by the smell. Several of them sit watching at the edge of the sunlight by the open door.

I have pulled my truck inside the barn to unload the cages. After each contains a cotton ball, I close the barn door, carry the larger box from the veterinary supply to the loft. I push open the heavy plank door. The sun streams in through the clerestory windows. I carry the shipping box to the back of the room and set it on the kitchen counter. In a drawer near the sink, I find a knife, slice open the box, arrange its bottles on the counter beside the sink: Texazol, Ketamine, and Xylazine, which I will combine for the anesthetic, Atropine for stabilizing the heart rate. I lay out the surgical gloves, peroxide, needle holders, mosquito hemostats, suture, scalpel blades, syringes, needles, the long-sleeved leather handling gloves. It is a simple operation, one that the Symkin woman can perform easily once I have demonstrated.

As I stand beside the clerestory window arranging the materials, I see a movement in the distance, a shadow floating among the trees. At first, it is merely a moving darkness. I watch it hover from tree to tree, a human shape carrying something, nearing the house, the windows, then disappearing behind the house. Time passes; the figure does not emerge.

The western clouds move in, a low gray ceiling. Inside them, light quivers, a spasm silent and incidental as a horse's muscle repelling insects. The clouds have begun to release a perpetual mist, not yet a rain. I leave the barn, edge through the moist shadows, beneath the trees where the mist collects among the branches, creeping along the ground. I approach from the north, choose the kitchen window where my silhouette will not be backlit as I peer through the glass. The living room is gray and empty; the stove sits cold at the room's center, the chairs still grouped as when the Symkin woman and I sat there Friday late during the full moon. All the same: the books, the corner shelves where Garbo waits, the long dining table in the glass solarium. One thing different: beside the far window, tied at the top, leans a fat black bag, the plastic kind used for trash.

Time passes. A man comes down the stairs with another black bag, empty. He wears gloves and a long gray rain slicker, streaked with red. He drops the empty bag, unties the other, pulls out an object. A dead animal, a cat, its yellow fur matted with blood. The animal is limp, recently killed. He holds it by the torso, squeezes it with one hand as he catches the blood in the other, as one might squeeze toothpaste from a tube. He walks along the windows, squeezing and smearing the glass with his hand. He works his way with slow deliberation across the room till the windows are red from the floor to as high as he can reach. He uses the rhythmic, circular strokes that one might use to wax a table, pulling the bag after him, removing cats, squeezing, rubbing the glass with gore. When he finishes with each cat, he pauses, looks around the room, takes aim. The stove, the stereo, the chairs, the rafters above. I step back as he nears the kitchen, receding into the trees and the darkness. I stand watching the round circling smears of his gloved hand against the glass.

I recall earlier, as I returned from town, the sounds of gunshots in the forest. I had thought poachers had entered the open gate, removed today by the Brandenberg man. In my mailbox, among those lined by the entryway, had been a notice of a meeting to be held late this afternoon—an explanation of the gate's removal, of new policies, the new covenants. But this is no poacher with his bags full of cats.

Cats: the Egyptians considered them divine, prized the animals so highly that to kill one was a crime punishable by death. The Egyptians—who, till this day, value their horses enough to give them free roam of their homes.

The front door is unlocked, the front room dim—from the rain clouds, from the blood smeared across the windows blocking the light. The odor of metal, blood, a damp primeval stench clogs the air. The dead animals litter the room with their eyes filmed over, their fur bloodied—everywhere, their bodies hanging and scattered and wasted. The large vaulted room is deserted. I climb the stairs slowly, testing each before trusting my weight. The second floor, too, reeks of dead, fetid air, the windows smeared. I climb the narrow staircase to the third.

The Crawford animal sits in the sunken tub, vapor rising from the water's surface, the liquid gone red so that he appears to be sitting in a steaming bath of blood. The slicker and gloves, clean, lie to one side. His eyes are on mine as I climb the stairs into the room, as though he has been waiting. His hair is wet against his skull, making his pale eyes appear larger, sunken. A smile quivers around his lips. His naked arms lie stretched along the marble edge of the tub, and his fingertips jerk spasmodically. Resting beneath the right hand is a Smith and Wesson .38 revolver with a four-inch barrel.

I understand that the Crawford animal is not someone who will shoot without extensive preamble. I sit beside the open stairwell, leaning back against the wall, and I wait for his performance. He begins by holding the silence; we stare across the red steaming water at one another in the style of feline standoff. I look away in order to allow him the illusion of dominance he wishes in order to begin.

"Nobody ever taught you manners?" he says, his words slow and honed in the Old South. "Taught you to knock before entering a man's house?" His upper lip curls faintly, and the silence spreads again.

His left hand slips into the water; the fingers flutter on the surface above his chest, above his pelvis. His eyes are almond-shaped, the color of running water. They glitter in the crimson light of the smeared windows. His hand sinks into the water, the muscles of his left shoulder begin working, the water shifts rhythmically. His eyes darken with the expanded pupil, the lids drooping slightly.

I avert my gaze; he interprets this as submission: I have known riders who make this mistake with a sly horse, thinking they have the reins when the horse has kept his teeth just so on the bit.

"You like my decorating?" he says, his words thicker now. "That Symkin, that Symcunt, she don't know fuck about decorating. You? You know fuck about it? You want to show me how you fucking decorate?" His breathing quickens, the surface of the water moving with the rhythm of his shoulder muscles. "'Cause I'm going to give you that chance, see what you know, see if you as long and tall inside as you are outside."

I wait and watch him through the steam, the rhythm of his breathing the only sound.

Finally, I speak: "Like Camilla?"

He smiles in the slow, casual way of those who enjoy the discomfort of others. His shoulder moves; the eyes darken. "Yeah, like Camilla. She took it every which way." His words are slow and uneven. "What was she going to do? Tell her mama? Her kid? Not fucking likely. Ole Camilla, this was her last stop. She had nowhere left to go, and she wasn't about to say jack shit." He stops speaking for a moment, the muscles of his shoulder still moving. He breathes heavily, curling one corner of his lips into a sneer. "And she wasn't nearly as long and tall inside as I bet you are. She wasn't long at all, that ole girl. She bled like a stuck pig, she did. I don't mind telling you, I was real sorry when she hanged herself."

His eyes slowly close and then open again. Distant thunder, a drum roll of unfolding sound.

I say: "Have you ever killed anybody that way, Gerald?"

For a moment, confusion passes across his face. "I didn't hang her," he says. "She hung herself."

"No, not that. I mean by battering them inside, killing a woman by fucking her to death."

He smiles. I knew he would smile. I would have bet money on it.

"They're cunts. Them ones like her. They like it that way. They say they don't, but they just waiting for somebody to shove it to them. I can see it in their eyes, the ones like her. They don't even know they want it like that, but I know it. I just give it to them they way they like it. The way they like it so much they scream for more."

"'The ones like her?' Do you mean the ones like your mother, Gerald?"

I remember Claire's voice on the phone after I have called her back this morning, telling me of her son-in-law, the boy who had nearly killed a prostitute in Nashville the night of his graduation from high school. Not battering her almost to death with his hands, though that too, but sexually, during intercourse. A painfully thin, dark-haired woman, Claire had said, describing the prostitute. And she told me of his mother—the thin, dark-haired woman whom his father had banned from their home when he had returned unexpectedly and discovered his wife in bed with a stranger, the three-year-old Gerald watching, the boy and father listening to the mother's screams of pleasure.

Claire's voice is low, sad, tired. "Wendy was pregnant, crazy about him," she says, "and the prostitute he attacked agreed not to press charges. We, John Crawford and I...we gave her money. We talked with Gerald, put him into therapy, and the property out there..." Claire pauses, sighs. "I hoped that getting away from the city, the memories he must carry around of his mother, that it would be all right. I promised him the land on the condition that he stay out of trouble. I thought...I thought everything was all right. When he left Wendy this last time...he had done it before, but this last time John flew out and put Wendy and the kids into the A-frame. It was a bad winter. John came back and told me...how Wendy had looked. She'd been beaten. I felt our bargain had been broken, so when Ms. Symkin approached me about the house, I sold it." Her voice rises. "Damned right I sold it, and would sell it again! I tried to get Wendy to come back here and bring the children. I offered to buy her a home, but she refused." I could see Claire staring off past the telephone, shaking her head. "She cried. She said she loved him. What can you do?"

Many things. Anything. One fits the punishment to the crime.

"Tell me, Gerald," I say to the grown boy in the tub. "How often do you meet those bone-thin, dark-haired women who look like your mother? Are they rare birds, just the two of them—the prostitute you battered in Nashville and Camilla? Or do you meet them often, Gerald? When you're away from home in the winter? How many of them have there been, Gerald?"

Gerald's eyes, almond-shaped, narrow. I see the madness in them, the disturbed child behind the angel's face. He flips the drain latch, and the water level begins falling as he sits again with both arms stretched along the marble edge of the tub. When the water is nearly drained, he still sits,

*his penis enormous and roused between his legs. He lifts the revolver and
stands. With his left hand, he takes a spray nozzle inset into the tub, draws
it up to neck-height, rinses the bloody water away. He keeps his eyes locked
on mine. After he has rinsed, he steps out of the tub, onto the tiled floor,
and dries himself with one hand using a white towel lying near the tub.
He strokes himself with long sinuous motions. He enjoys being watched,
having a woman see the size of his organ. I look at it a long time, and then
I look back to his pale eyes and give him a high sideways smile.*

He mistakes my smile. I knew that he would.

*"Can you take that, baby?" He flourishes the revolver toward one of
the three rooms, the one that is empty except for the figured carpet. I enter,
stand at the carpet's center, turn and face the barrel of the gun. The windows here are also smeared, and when the lightning flashes several times
in rapid succession, the air is a red strobe light.*

*I begin to undress as he watches. I pull the black body sweater over my
head. I unfasten my belt, unzip the black jeans, pull them off over the
boots. I wear no bra, no underpants. The lightning flashes, a brilliant red.*

*"The boots," he says, grinning. "Leave the boots." The thunder cracks.
Close.*

*We stand naked across the room from each other. He moves the barrel
of the revolver in short gestures toward the floor. He wants me to lie down.
That is what he thinks he wants.*

*I lie down, and in my mind's eye, I see Camilla sleeping in the loft: the
Crawford animal coming late to her door, raising the handle that can only
be locked from the outside. Camilla, her eyes filling with terror, lies in the
bed where the moon turns her naked skin silver. He undresses and stands
over her, letting her terror make him hard, then lowers himself, forcing her
legs apart, covering her mouth with one hand as he guides himself into
her, forces himself into her with the long, pounding strokes. And Gerald:
seeing not Camilla but his mother spread wide on the bed below the
strange man. Gerald: hearing her screams. Seeing and hearing all this
with joy, plunging himself into a woman with the applause of righteous-
ness in his ears.*

*Hatred is a cunning emotion, wedding the hater to the hated in a most
diabolic embrace. I look up at him as he stands above me. I still wear the
boots, but I do not need them—nor the small silver gun inside the left one.
I need nothing but to touch him with my hands. There is no danger in*

him, only a great anger, an unrelenting pain. Hatred has burned away his life, left a smoldering void where something might have grown. When he kneels, his knees spreading me apart, the gun bobs in his right hand as his left descends to cover my mouth.

Child's play, a simple matter of timing. A quick roll of my head just as his hand touches my lips, an instant's imbalance. With my left hand, I twist his wrist and take the gun; with the edge of my right hand, I hit the occipital bone behind his ear. Unconscious, he slides from me. I take the cord from the mini-blinds, tie his wrists behind him. The thunder shudders in the distance.

I shower and dress before going to work.

29

WHO WAS IT SAID, "THE WAY UP IS THE WAY DOWN"? Heraclitus? Or, "The going up was worth the coming down"? Kristofferson? I was pretty sure neither one of them had been to El Gato. The going up was pure hell, with the rain a drifting mist one minute, a thrashing torrent the next, coming down so hard in places that I inched onto the narrow shoulder, praying no one was behind me because visibility was zero. In between deluges, I drove.

When I reached the turnoff to my house, I hesitated. I had a quick glimpse of myself stuck in the mud, mired for the night if the sheriff got tied up in town, having to hoof it home through the mud and the dark and the rain. Besides, I reasoned, driving past the turnoff, I needed to pick up my belongings at Morgan's, tell her the visit to Wendy's was off and I was moving back to my place, find out when she was planning on coming by with the cat cages. Invite her over for hamburgers in person... The truth was, I realized, that I hoped she'd follow me home; I didn't know how long the sheriff would be, and I was nervous about walking into the house alone. There was something very reassuring about the presence of Cordelia Morgan in precarious situations. Whatever her role in Harv's death, strangely enough, I felt no menace—I'd believed her when she'd said last night that she meant me no harm.

As I neared El Gato, the rain thinned. I noticed small realtor-type signs had sprung up alongside the road: "EL GATO! Lots for Sale!" with "Brandenberg Enterprises" and a phone number printed at the bottom. A larger sign was attached to the floodlit El

Gato sign at the entrance road, contrary to a covenant forbidding advertisement on the grounds, and bright red arrows pointed toward the entry gate. I slipped my gate card from above the visor, but I could have saved myself the trouble. The crossbar had been removed, and the entrance was open. I didn't live here, and it wasn't going to affect me, but I wondered how some of the residents would take this. I thought of Myra Jones, whose proprietary attitude about the wilderness was going to receive a serious jolt—the area would soon be overrun not only with Brandenberg's prospective buyers, but with drive-by tourists, hikers, RV campers, teenagers looking for a secluded party spot, and hunters who often sought out protected areas where deer and elk and bear gravitated. The night had fully descended as I drove around the lake with my headlights cutting through the misting rain. The very air seemed black, as though the sun had been extinguished, the darkness charged with more than the imminent threat of another downpour.

I could see Brandenberg's place long before I got close to it. His castle was lit up like Disneyland, with cars crowded in the driveway and parked along both sides of the road. I recognized the Gillmans' GMC and Harv's yellow Jeep. And Morgan's fire-engine-red 4x4 crew cab with the fluorescent silver bolt of lightning down the sides and the chrome light bar across the top. It was the kind of truck you couldn't miss, even on a night like this one. I nosed in behind the bumper that had been customized with a solid strip of tail-lights between bands of silver reflector tape.

In spite of the rain, the double front doors of Brandenberg's house stood open. What the hell, I knocked anyway, just to keep in practice. The entryway led into a long hallway toward the back of the house where I heard voices and saw a wedge of light lying across the high-gloss hardwood floor.

I followed the hallway and poked my head into an immense room, the size of a basketball court. It had been divided into two sections: one end held a couple of green-shrouded billiard tables with green-shaded lights dangling overhead, an impressive collection of body-building and exercise machines, a Ping-Pong table, and a shuffleboard diagram painted onto the floor. But the action was on the other side. A crowd of people sat on metal folding chairs or stood behind them. I saw several I knew, more I didn't. They were listening to Dean Brandenberg, who stood at the front of the room behind a long wooden table stacked with tidy piles of papers. Behind him, the entire side of the room was solid glass, overlooking an immense patio lit with enough floodlights for late-night baseball and illuminating a prolific garden and a freeform swimming pool with interior lighting. The wind had begun to accelerate again, ruffling the surface of the pool and driving the rain in diagonal streaks across the windows.

"...never should have been separated from that hundred acres, and we're going to get it back. All we need to do is..." Brandenberg saw me in the doorway and suddenly stopped speaking, his mouth open. The room grew quiet; heads swiveled in my direction. Janie Gillman's eyes met mine and slid away quickly. Edna's lit and switched back to Brandenberg. Wendy and Shawn and Tiffany stared with round blue eyes, and I noticed Wendy had applied her makeup heavily enough to conceal most of the damage to her face, though there was little to be done for the swollen lip and bloodied eye. Light from the overhead lighting glinted off Professor Moss's glasses. Myra Jones stood at the edge of the chairs, near the front; she glanced around briefly, then turned back to Brandenberg. Leaning with her shoulders pressed against the wall beside me was long, tall Cordelia Morgan in her black jeans and sweater, boots shining in spite of the mud, the toes tipped with silver. She looked at me, pulled her mouth back in a High Attitude smile, cocked a brow, and turned back to Brandenberg.

"...uh..." The fat man had a sheen of sweat popping out across his face, his small eyes darting from me to the others and back again. "Um, this here's a meeting of property owners, Miz Stymson. If you'd stop by some other time, I'd be happy to see you."

I shrugged, stepped inside the room, and leaned against the wall, shoulder-to-shoulder with Morgan. "Looks like you forgot to invite me, Mr. Brandenberg. I own property here, too, you know." I glanced at Janie. "Mrs. Gillman, didn't you say just the other day you had my address? I guess you forgot to send me a notice. No problem. Sorry to be late." I smiled encouragement at Brandenberg and felt the heat of Morgan's shoulder touching mine. The heads swiveled back to the fat man behind the table; Morgan's swiveled my way, blinking her eyes slowly in the way of musing cats.

"Well, uh, sure. I guess our records aren't as up to date as we thought, say, Janie?" Janie Gillman scowled at him, sticking her lower jaw out. "So, uh, the next issue is the gate." He flipped to the next page of the packet of papers he held. "The new gate policy is that there won't be one. I believe we're being way too exclusive here, shutting out the local folks that like to drop in and bring a sack lunch of a Sunday. No reason to have a gate, we got nothing to hide here. In fact, we'll set up some picnic tables—"

The crowd surged noisily. A voice rose above the others.

"Dean, you know damn well you took that gate down to invite in buyers for your lots. We're going to have people stampeding the place. We're surrounded by national park lands, for Christ's sake, where the government spends hundreds of thousands of dollars every year just for picnickers." It was Wolf Candidos speaking, standing with his elegant figure erect and his dark hair pulled back in a ponytail. He looked around at the crowd with a droll smile. "And the parks service has already got their picnic tables set up." The crowd tittered, and several cheers went up. Wolf resumed his place beside Andrew.

"Glad to have your input, Wolf. Janie will make a note of it in the minutes." He flipped another page in the packet. "Okay, here's the new policy on upkeep of grounds and water allotments—I'm throwing all those restrictions out. You want a garden, folks, why you ought to have one." He smiled broadly. Behind him, the plate glass wall stretched like a giant movie screen, showcasing the elegantly manicured grounds, the pool's surface dimpling with rain. I figured Wolf wasn't going to argue with that one. Heads in the audience were nodding in agreement.

"You must stop this immediately!"

Every head in the room turned to where Myra Jones stood like a block of wood. She had on a long, rain-spattered khaki coat with the attached hood hanging loose. "All of you know that the water situation here is desperate," she said, facing the crowd like an experienced rabble-rouser. I watched her in wonder, her speech suddenly articulate and the words no longer painful and clotted. "What streams come out of the mountains empty into Crystal Springs, and on into the Rio Grande, just as they should, and it's illegal to leach off them, as everybody here knows." She glared at Edna for a moment. "And if everybody here, and all the new folks buying lots, start using their wells to pump up ground water for gardens and...swimming pools," she said, fairly spitting the words and glowering at the scene behind Brandenberg, "then the water source will dry up for all of us. And when the ground water is gone, the trees will die. Anybody can tell you this. Go into town and look at the geological studies, the location of the fault line, the point at which the water is no longer able to recover. If you do this, there will be no way to live here unless you cart the water in. How many of you are willing to do this?" She looked around at the faces in the audience. "You must see that these policies are a disaster. And the gate—just since it came down today, I've already heard gunshots and seen strange vehicles cruising past my road." I felt Morgan stiffen beside me. Myra raised her voice; it became shrill as it filled the room. "Poachers! Hunters! You must not allow him to do this!" she screamed, pointing at Brandenberg.

Passion and loud voices, outside of churches in the deep South, will send people fleeing to the opposite side of wherever they're standing in both body and mind. The faces in the crowd turned away from Myra Jones as though she were an embarrassment. They looked anxiously at Brandenberg, who visited on Myra the kind of benevolent, mindless smile reserved for the homeless, the mentally impaired, and the very young.

"Now Myra," he said, playing to his audience, "Armageddon is not on the agenda anytime soon. There's no water problem here, and if any records say there is, then somebody's been tinkering with them. This place, look around you, is Eden itself." Brandenberg was working on his showmanship skills. Standing in front of the illuminated background, he threw both his arms wide, as though to indicate the bounty behind him. Just that moment, as luck would have it, the rain suddenly escalated, and a great torrent of water driven by a passing gale hit the floodlit glass. He jumped slightly, then turned to watch the deluge. He snatched the occasion and lifted his arms high as though he were God revealing his Creation: "There is no lack of water at El Gato."

The crowd laughed, and for a moment, the tension in the room evaporated, the people heaving a communal sigh, nodding and talking among themselves. Morgan leaned sideways, so close that I could feel the velvet of her cheek. She lifted her chin but kept her eyes fastened on Brandenberg as he leafed through his packet and broached yet another topic. Her voice was low, musically southern as aged Kentucky sipping whiskey.

"Man up there says El Gato by rights owns your house and that hundred acres Claire sold you. Says Claire mapped it out as part of the original plat when she took her idea to the bank. Says it wasn't hers to sell. Man says he'll go to court and get that property back for El Gato, that everybody here ought to be happy as pig shit." She rolled her head around on the wall toward me. Her eyes were large, the color of dark chocolate, looking full into my own. She grinned sideways. Her voice was a purr, slow and filled with one-hundred-proof Attitude. "That right, Symkin, you happy as pig shit?"

My mouth fell open, and I stood stark upright. Brandenberg noticed and faltered again. On the patio behind him, the wind had been steadily increasing. Suddenly the rain began hammering against the glass, and a blast of wind smashed through the trees near the pool, striking with such force that the water rose up in waves and slapped out over the sides. The enormous plate glass wall shuddered, seemed to bulge inward for an instant, and the lights flickered, then recovered. People stood up and began milling nervously about the room. A blinding flash of lightning lit the window; almost simultaneously a deafening clap of thunder followed. Everyone became silent, stared out the huge window as though it were a movie screen: we saw an immense bolt of lightning shoot from a cloud, crackling and sizzling, hitting a tree beside the pool. The stricken tree shuddered for several moments, then began to split, one side leaning slightly, suspended, then shearing off from the mother trunk with a great rending splinter of a sound, its furthest branches swiping the power lines as it toppled to the ground.

And the lights went out.

There were screams in the darkness, a stampede of footsteps. A hand clamped on my shoulder.

"Easy, Symkin," Morgan purred in my ear. Her other hand found mine, and I followed where she led. Down the black hallway, leaving the voices behind. Across the porch, her arm circling my waist. Down the stairs, into the driving rain. Surrounded by darkness—thick and absolute and unrelieved. There were no voices now, only the howling wind and rain. Behind us, in Brandenberg's house, someone had found flashlights; small darts of light glimmered in the massive darkness.

"I think we need to take a drive, you okay with that?"

I felt her breath against my ear as we stood leaning together in the black rain, which had begun to subside as suddenly as it had begun. Voices from Brandenberg's house rose in the darkness, then a scream. I smelled the odor of magnolia, had a memory from last night, the image of white petals drifting above me, the press of Morgan's breasts.

"Good," she said.

Her arm circled around me again, guided me toward my truck parked behind hers, and when she opened the door with its loud creak, the cab light came on. She eased the door closed till it went off. "Follow me to my house. Use your parking lights." She disappeared, and I stood alone. The dark was absolute, impenetrable. I heard her truck door slam. I fumbled for my door handle, got in, both our engines starting simultaneously, and followed her as she said, with my parking lights on. While the faint light from them hardly lit the road, they bounced off the reflective tape on her bumper ahead as she drove slowly along—without lights. At last, we pulled into her driveway.

I sat in the darkness with the engine running, trying to figure out what to do next, when the door opened. Morgan pressed against me, leaning across me, into the cab to switch off the light, smelling of rain and wet hair and this morning's shampoo and last night's magnolia. The cab light was extinguished, but she didn't move. She might have been invisible to the eye, but she was fully present to my other senses, still pressing against me.

Once, as a child, I caught a hummingbird and held it, felt its tiny body pulsing in my palm. I could feel the same pulse in the weight of Cordelia Morgan's body against mine. When she withdrew, the bird stayed.

"I came by to pick up my stuff," I said. My words swam through the darkness, a stranger's voice, a little breathless. "I...I decided to go back to my own place."

"Not a bad idea, under the circumstances. Mind if I join you." It wasn't a question. "You stay here, I'll get your clothes and suitcase. You can follow me over. I'll fill you in on Brandenberg's little coup when we get there. Lock your door."

Ten minutes later she was back. I heard her truck door slam, and this time she switched on her headlights. I followed her along the gravel roads. When we passed Brandenberg's, the crowd was churning around outside, engines starting and people yelling and headlights coming on, vehicles jockeying for position in the yard to light the house, but Morgan drove on.

By the time I was on the highway, following the blazing strip of rear lights and reflectors on Morgan's bumper, my mind had started operating again, if just barely. Forget Brandenberg; I was thinking about the dark house ahead, about walking in the door and going straight up the stairs to where I kept the .38 in a bedside drawer. I was thinking that I would attach its leather holster to my belt, double-check the locks on all the doors, and double-damn-dare anybody to come through a window.

When Morgan turned off the asphalt onto my driveway, I followed the resplendent bumper until the gravel gave way to mud, and my truck began to fishtail, slowed, and stopped with the tires mired and spinning.

"Shit!" I smacked the steering wheel and watched Morgan's bumper twinkle and disappear in the heavy mist. If I'd been thinking of my driving instead of my .38, I'd have stopped on the pavement and turned my hubs, and I wouldn't now be trudging through a mud bog that came well above the tops of my shoes. By the time I climbed back in the truck, mud clung from calf to shoe like weights on both legs, and I was soaked to the skin. I took the blanket I was sitting on and wiped the water out of my eyes and blotted it from my streaming hair as well as I could. I flipped the heater up another notch to take the chill off. Lightning flashed and dazzled the night, followed closely by thunder that shook the ground. I shoved the transmission into low four-wheel-drive, gave it some gas. The tires grabbed and began slugging through the deep mud like a tank. It was slow going, but as long as the truck kept moving, I wasn't complaining. Still, I reasoned, as the wipers slapped the rain away and the headlights reflected back off the thick mist, Morgan was just ahead. If worse came to worst, she'd come back for me. What the hell, I thought, if worse came to worst, I wouldn't have to worry about it. Who was it said, "Nobody gets out alive"? I thought it was Jim Morrison, but he'd probably never met Cordelia Morgan.

The truck growled on, fist-sized clumps of mud flying from beneath the tires, splatting on the windshield. The road wound uphill for three miles or so, snaking among the trees, with water flowing down the grooves in the road made by Morgan's recent tire tracks.

I leaned forward, gripping the wheel in both hands. I was going home, pushed forward by the rain and the night and circumstances and whatever force had laid claim to this forbidding mountain and was shoving me along whether I wanted to go or not. The truck fishtailed and slipped and dug in and growled its way inch-by-inch through the mud until finally, in the distance, the house loomed ahead.

30

WHEN I PULLED UP INTO MY YARD, the rain had thinned. The red truck sat like a neon sign in the driveway, gleaming and twinkling, as subtle as a hooker in a choir. My headlights cut across the front porch where Morgan stood with her arms crossed, leaning against the front door. I killed the engine, left the lights on, slipped the keys out of the ignition, and flipped on the cab light to find the house key. I hefted a grocery bag in each arm, glad that the worst part of the storm seemed to have passed.

"Thought I was going to have to go back and pull you out," Morgan said, as I fiddled with the key. The door swung open, but the room was black as ink. While Morgan returned to the yard to shut off my headlights, I stepped inside and flipped the porch light switch, but nothing happened. Either the bulb had burned out or the power outage did not stop at El Gato. Praying it was not the latter, I crept along the entryway, grocery bag in one arm, the other outstretched and feeling my way: the chair, the table, the lamp. I switched it on. Nothing.

The place was cold and damp, and an odd, unpleasant smell hung in the air, perhaps a residue from the months the house had been absorbing cat shit. I edged my way into the kitchen with the groceries, felt my way to the bottom drawer beside the stove and retrieved a flashlight, a box of candles, and a lighter. I switched on the flashlight, set about lighting the candles and anchoring them in saucers, as Morgan returned and made a fire in the fireplace. It felt like years had passed since I'd been here, and an atmosphere of desolation had moved in—I could feel it everywhere around me. I pushed the thought away, set the candles strategically across the room so that the room filled with a golden glow, spotted with a veritable witches' coven of tiny flames. I took one of the candles upstairs to light my way, shed the wet clothes, and wrapped myself head to toe in my white terry-cloth robe. I braided my wet hair into a long rope and pulled it across my shoulder. When I returned, Morgan stood drying herself in front of a roaring fire. The room was toasty warm, and the air of desolation had gone. I forgot all about getting my .38 from beside my bed.

"Jesus. Mondays are a bitch." I sank down in the chair beside the fire, feeling numb from exhaustion. Outside, light rain tapped gently on the windows. Occasionally, the darkness glimmered with distant lightning. The storm had passed. Morgan had taken the other chair, stretched in horizontal position, eyes closed. A large, green nylon shoulder bag with lots of zippered pockets sat on the floor beside her, and she'd put my suitcase by the stairs.

I didn't know what her day had been like, maybe trying out her new truck on the mountain highways, but as I began to sift back through mine, I found that I was speaking aloud, telling her about my visit to the library, the county building. When I related what Patricia Anderson had told me about Camilla, she merely nodded.

"I stopped by the sheriff's office on my way home," I said, wondering at her silence. She hadn't moved. I looked at the way the tiny candle flames in the room lit the dark wing-like brows, the high cheekbones, the sculpted face. I had a sudden urge to go kneel beside her chair; instead, I told her about the information I'd learned from the sheriff. Then: "He said he checked out Eva Blake. Says you're telling the truth." I waited for her to respond, but she didn't move. I sat forward, my elbows on my knees. "So what's the story? I don't get it. You said there was no Eva Blake."

Finally she answered, but she seemed preoccupied. "No, what I said was that *I'm* not Eva Blake. Morgan's Law, rule number twelve. The best lie is no lie. You choose an identity by matching up your description with someone else's—height, physical appearance, that sort of thing. You want someone whose background experience feels comfortable, not too much of a stretch unless you're into lots of research and acting. Someone who's out of town, can't be reached. Simple enough. Eva Blake's just one of thousands of women I could have chosen—anybody calls Jack Blake, he gives them a verbal ID over the phone; maybe somebody even pulls her DMV photo. There's a good resemblance, close enough. Go ask her friends or her husband, they'll tell you she's somewhere in Colorado, not exactly sure where. They don't spend much of their time thinking about it." She rolled her head in my direction. "You thought I lied about being Cordelia Morgan? Nobody would lie about something like that, Symkin."

I'd never heard the haggard edge in her voice before, never seen the burned-out look in her eyes. She turned back to the ceiling, closed her eyes.

"I picked up vet supplies at UPS, got the cat cages, set them up over in your barn. Twenty of them. I closed the barn until we decide when to start. The cages are set and baited. All you have to do is open the barn door, give me a call. I'll show you how to do the operation. The supplies are..." She paused, and when I glanced over at her, she was watching me with that long, level look I'd come to associate with trouble. I didn't want to hear it; whatever it was could wait. I sat back in my chair, positioned my head carefully so that the part bruised by Gerald's battering was cushioned. My side was still sore as well, with a dark bruise from his parting kick.

Morgan talked about the fireworks at the homeowners' meeting before I'd arrived, said she'd stopped by early, before the meeting started, and found the professor railing at Brandenberg about the gate.

"I thought Moss was going to have a coronary. Yelling about the gate being gone, that strangers would be coming in and he wouldn't be able to concentrate on his writing." She paused, and the fire crackled and shifted. I opened one eye at her. She jiggled her brows and drawled, "My, my, he sure does get his leather elbow patches all in an uproar over a little traffic. Who would've thought academic writing would require such concentration?"

Gallows humor. I ignored her and closed my eye.

"I wouldn't worry too much about Brandenberg's little plot. He probably figured, with all the melodrama going on around here, you'd be easy enough to buffalo. In fact, I...heard somewhere that he wanted Gerald to give you a hard time, figured his suit might stand a better chance in court if you weren't living on the property. From what I understand, Gerald had been borrowing some pretty serious money from Brandenberg, in so deep looked like the only way to get out from under was to sign the property here over to him, and Brandenberg would let him keep the house and a couple of acres, but the rest would be his."

I sat up. "You're kidding! Where'd you hear this?"

"I get around. All those winters Gerald had been going off to 'work' for Brandenberg? Turns out he was vacationing down in Florida. Borrowing from Brandenberg on this property, writing him out IOUs for when Claire James put it in his and Wendy's name. He'd take off for the winter, leave Wendy with the truck and enough money to get by on till he got back. But last winter Brandenberg put on the brakes. Thought Gerald was into him for too much already. That's when Gerald struck up with Willa, apparently formed a habit of taking a winter break, but this time he didn't have any money to leave with Wendy, and that's when Gerald's dad showed up and took Wendy and the kids over to that A-frame he'd bought for a song a couple years ago."

"I guess you went somewhere besides UPS and the barn since I saw you last," I said. "Who told you this?"

She raised herself in the chair and stared at me, that bone-deep look that gave me the willies. I looked away.

"Rumors. But it makes sense, doesn't it?"

I thought about it. Gerald would have been pissed all right—not only about losing his house, but about being into serious debt with Brandenberg and no way to pay. If he could scare me away, he'd have at least cleared the way for Brandenberg to file a suit on behalf of El Gato and claim the property that way. How far would Gerald go? Would he resort to murder? Gerald had been at Brandenberg's party when the grader's brakes had been cut, but he might have paid someone to do it to get revenge on Harv, then cut the brakes on Morgan's truck if he'd seen me stop there that day, thinking she'd drive me home.

"Doesn't compute," Morgan said. She rose from her chair and stood with her back to the fire, facing me. "He *could* have paid somebody, sure, but who could he trust with that kind of job? And where would he get the money? He's totally broke, from what I hear." She narrowed her eyes, let them follow the damp skein of my hair where it hung across my shoulder. She walked over and stood looking down at me. "You can mark Gerald Crawford off your list of things to be afraid of, Symkin. He's not a player here anymore." Her voice was low, the rustle of dark wings against a moonless sky. Somewhere a summer evening sighed; a hint of magnolia circled the room and brushed the veins at my temples.

I looked up at her face illuminated by all the golden, flickering candle flames. "But how—"

"And while I'm thinking of it, you can mark Brandenberg off, too. Claire filed for bankruptcy back in 1970. That's twenty-seven years ago, long past the Colorado eighteen-year statute of limitations deadline. Which goes for the Benton property as well. Brandenberg's whistling in the wind, probably thought intimidation was worth a try. For sure, it would have worked on Harv, and what did he have to lose by trying it on you? Anybody can hire a lawyer, spend a few bucks initiating a lawsuit, gamble that the other guy will disappear. Most people, especially those like Harv who can't afford legal fees, just head on down the road like cattle, without looking back." Morgan knelt beside my chair, slowly unbraided the long, damp rope of my hair, spread her fingers beneath it, and drew them down through the damp strands, the back of her hand sliding down my shoulder, over my breast, her eyes on mine.

I leaned back in the chair, closed my eyes, felt a delectable ache flooding like ether through the very center of my bones. The firelight danced against my lids, as the hand slid along my ribs, down my inner thigh.

"Funny," I said, feeling the seconds soften, expand, "if it hadn't been for Harv's Jeep parked near the waterfall that day, I probably never would have moved here." The day took shape again—the entry into El Gato, the labyrinth of roads, the deep silence and interior mystery of the land; the rise and fall of drifted snow, the curving hills and forbidden crevices.

"It was the falls, really, that drew me," I breathed, "following his tire tracks up the road, seeing Harv's Jeep, hearing the water. It triggered the memories of the waterfall where my mother had died, of course. I never could forget that day, this place." My voice sounded distant, someone else's. I opened my eyes, vaguely feeling as though I'd been talking in my sleep. Cordelia Morgan knelt beside me, her eyes burning on mine as though she had been watching the images bloom inside me. Suddenly she withdrew.

"Wait." Her voice had hardened, the automaton's voice without inflection. "Tell me what you said. About Harv's Jeep, at the waterfall. Tell me when."

I sighed, swimming to the surface from a deep place, back into the room. "It was…December," I said, trying hard to concentrate. "Before Christmas. I'd just closed on my first big real estate deal…December 8, 1990." I shut my eyes again and saw the fresh tire marks going up the narrow road. "I followed the tire tracks, thinking someone must live up there. That if I just kept walking, I'd come to a house. I got to the top, nearly walking into Harv's Jeep, a box of shells on the seat. Hunter, poacher. Trash bag behind, on the bed. Footprints leading off toward the canyon's edge, above the stream…Cougar Canyon."

I thought of Myra Jones when she had appeared on my way to visit Edna. She knew I'd been in the canyon because she'd warned me about cougars there. I sat up, suddenly wide awake. Morgan was looking off past the windows, her face in deep concentration.

"Listen," I said. "I read a bunch of stuff in the library, about this phantom cougar no one has ever seen. But Myra's seen it. Don't you think that's odd? She worked at the library, called the Division of Wildlife people in to look at the trees, yet she never mentioned to them anything about the cougar."

"No," Morgan said, her voice distant, "she wouldn't have wanted them to know. She may not have realized the Smithsonian people would take the historical materials from the library, but she's a nature junkie. She'd have known that once the Wildlife people discovered the presence of a cougar that close to the subdivision, they would want to tag it, maybe attach a radio tracking collar. The last thing she would have done was report it."

"But, from what I've read, the way most cougars are detected in an area isn't that you see them, but that you see where they've been. What's left of the deer, elk…" Morgan wasn't listening. She looked around at me as though she'd received an electrical shock. "What—"

"I'll tell you later," she said. From the green nylon bag, she took a pair of black gloves and a black stocking cap and put them on. Then she drew out the handgun I recognized as the one from the glove compartment of her truck. She grabbed her black leather jacket, began putting it on as she walked fast to the door, and slipped the gun into the inner pocket. "Two hours max, I'll be back." And then she was gone.

I sat staring at the door, hearing the soft click of it in the room for some time after it had closed. The atmosphere of the room had darkened: the black windows caught the edgy, ghostly tremor of the candle flames, multiplied them, and threw them back; diagonal streaks cut like silver against the outer glass where a light rain had begun again. I walked over to test the door behind Morgan to make sure it was locked, checked the other doors and windows downstairs, then took a candle and worked my way through the upper stories until I was sure every door and window was secured. Desolation had crept back into the house. The odd, unpleasant odor hung thick and sharp in the air upstairs, and I noticed several faint smears on the walls, wondering if there were leaks on the exterior of the house where moisture was seeping behind the drywall. I would examine the places more closely tomorrow, but just now I was recalling Gerald's comment—his reference to my library, the implication that he'd somehow gained entry. My heart pounded in my chest. I went into my bedroom, lifted the .38 from the bedside drawer, and began searching for its leather holster. From the window, I saw the nearby treetops light briefly as an arc of approaching headlights swept across them.

31

Morgan

*Camilla's barn: I wait beneath a tree for shapes to flower in the soft rain.
I wait as the passing minutes brighten the pine branches, the bar across
the barn doors, the hordes of cats gathered around them, waiting for the
doors to open. I wait.*

*Remembering the Chicago summer before the fire, when I lived at the
Women's Y, down the hall from a student at the Art Institute. Her room
was papered with sketches and paintings and collages done on any surface
she came across at her part-time job cleaning construction sites—pieces of
lumber, bricks, broken portions of drywall, squares of ceiling or ceramic
tile, Masonite. In her art, she was avant-garde, dashing headlong from her
past into the future, into the latest fad—back then it was "environmental
art." She had adapted it to create her own system; I adapted hers to create
mine.*

*The walls of her room carried her life's history so that she was con-
stantly immersed in herself, in remaking the person she had been born into
the person she felt herself becoming. When I walked through her door, it
was as though I walked into her body, felt her spirit vibrating on the walls
as I browsed them from beginning, full circle, to end—paintings and
sketches and collages of her parents, her horse, the family ranch; scraps of
newspaper from the small town where she was born, local events, the
strawberry festival, the greased pig contest, the two young children trampled on the rodeo grounds. Her senior graduation, pictures of classmates,
yearbook clippings, portraits of intimates and enemies, their subsequent
misadventures. When I touched the walls, I knew this woman intimately.*

Yet I came to see, too late, that the secret of her was not in the carefully tabulated years, or the way she sometimes reconfigured them when the mood struck, but in the occasional miscreant gaps in sequence, those recurrent shadowy portraits of a boy and girl tacked first in one year, then aged a year in another, moving restlessly through time. And when I discovered her dead in the bathtub, her wrists cut, I stood looking at her walls after the medics had gone and the room was empty, and I saw that the day of her death coincided with the deaths of two children on the rodeo grounds, and that it was their shadowy portraits that the woman had aged, had shifted year to year, as though trying to find a point in time where they might re-enter. But though the two children were named in the rodeo article from the newspaper, none was listed for the rider of the rodeo horse under whose hoofs the children had been killed. And I thought then, as I did years later during a difficult assignment for The Company, that if my neighbor had only been able to read her walls as clearly as a stranger had finally read them, she might have predicted her own fate. Or maybe she had.

It is her system I use in my workroom: to avoid the killing gaps, one must know a situation as intimately as one knows a lover, must listen patiently from within till the silence speaks.

And the darkness blooms.

I can now make out the colors of the cats, their motionless bodies and their restless thrashing tails. I follow the path to the stream that is swollen over its banks. The trail nearby is well traveled by deer and elk, churned to mud. I keep to the grass, entering the mist that lies in the hollow of the meadow. Ahead, the barrier of tangled underbrush separates the meadow from the rocky, seldom-traveled road to the falls, the northern boundary between El Gato and Claire James's hundred acres. The Symkin woman's hundred acres. I turn east, walk up the road, toward the falls.

The year was 1985. Brazil. One of my first assignments: targeting a man notorious for behaving so unpredictably that he had eluded several previous surveillance attempts. It was then I formed the habit of researching my assignments in immaculate detail—not merely the target himself and every aspect of his former lives, but the situation surrounding us, his every speaking acquaintance, the nuances of our location, the geography, the very air of the city. I would paste the information on the walls of my hotel room, sometimes using chronology, sometimes rearranging the materials categorically, sometimes letting the chaos of it consume me until the materials forged a shape of their own and thus presented me with the key. My room became the body of the assignment, the target, and like the room of my neighbor in Chicago, I could walk into it and inhabit the man so that when he turned abruptly down a corridor one day and seemed to disappear, I knew exactly where to wait as he emerged.

I can tell you that this is as close as one comes to becoming the other.

As I near the falls, the immense sound of it, I stop along the road and take the small plastic container from an inner pocket, smear the dark oil-base makeup across my face. Above, clouds scud across the sky where a faint radiance lurks behind them.

Of late, I have been adding myself to my walls, in the manner of my Chicago friend. For these days, with the loss of Pasonombre and The Company, I am at the center of my assignment, my history in this case linked with Claire's, with Camilla's, the three of us related in some bloodless way. As though they walk with me.

For there is something else, an obscure refrain, playing in El Gato, a motif which is a mystery and which has kept me here, has gathered volume over the months so that now it strains the room where I work. At the computer, at the windows, I feel it singing along my spine. It invades the peripheral vision, evades the quick spin of the heel. I pace the walls, review the choreographed images. I absorb the information, feeling it trickle inside the bone, feel it begin its inner hum, its demonic hiatus, until…the orchestration falters, impaled on a jarring gap in rhythm. A most damnable, unpresent refrain. An ellipsis of the soul. It gives the ear a stumble: it will not play.

Not even after I have performed on the Crawford animal a suitable justice. Taken him back to the shambling trailer, further down the county road beyond the A-frame, to where the woman called Willa opens the door as I deliver her the still-anesthetized body. And leave it there.

In my room, I pace the walls, but the symphony still bloodies the air. I go to the homeowners' meeting thinking to discover the missing note, but it is not there. Not quite. Only the Symkin woman. And the loss of electrical power which brings darkness to El Gato, to my room. To my surveillance cameras: it is my turn to stay with the Symkin woman until the darkness, the danger of it, passes.

The falls are close as I walk the road just as the Symkin woman walked it that first day. Somewhere in the wild music of the water, a refrain: "...nearly walking into Harv's Jeep."

Harv's Jeep as it appeared in the Symkin woman's story: a yellow vehicle on a high back road in the December snow which had fallen the night before, the roads freshly graded, the bright red Porsche circling like a bright beetle inside the labyrinth and parking below the road; the Symkin woman stops her car in the road, walks up, discovers the Jeep on December 8, 1990. It is then I see the walls of my workroom, the clippings. And the gaps are filled, the extravagant symphony at last complete.

The rain has subsided; lightning plays in frayed, silent threads in the bellies of the clouds just above. The darkness is alive with images: the news articles, the women reported missing always in the fall—the missing woman in 1990 who worked at the animal grooming shop, who bathed the animals without gloves, whose hand bones would have carried traces of organophosphates.

I enter the clearing which is filled by the sound of the waterfall, its water gushing from between the twin rocks, flooding the dam, sending the water crashing over the cliff into the canyon. I locate myself among several large rocks giving a clear view of the path, the dam, the crack leading to where the waterfall lives. The clouds above are moving, boiling; the moon is momentarily revealed and then covered behind a fine, rolling mist.

Sitting on the path is a shape—a black plastic trash bag.

From between the twin boulders, a small cone of light appears, blurred by the mist. Behind it, a moving shadow climbs down the ledge, through the water, toward the bag and where I watch hidden among the rocks. The shadow stands close enough to touch, lifts the bag, swings it across the shoulder, then lurches away toward the crevice where the waterfall crashes.

The water that had once moved in a thin sheet toward the dam, now courses over the stepping stones, reaches almost to my boot tops. I follow the shadow across the water, through the mist, up the ledge. It disappears into the crevice where the waterfall is engorged from the rain, deafening. The cone of moving light is nearly lost in the black interior where the water slides from the sky, disappears in the cleavage of the cave's floor, sending up a backlash, a thick flume of mist which fills the cave. It is very much like breathing underwater.

The shadow drops the bag, unties it, picks up a corner so that the contents spill across the stone floor—the body parts tumbling out in a pile, frozen hard. As I thought.

I step forward, nearly upon him before he knows I am near. He looks around, leaps back, the flashlight in one hand, the empty bag in the other. He removes a gun from his jacket pocket, aims the flashlight at me. I do not move. I stand in the cone of lighted mist, the blast of his words lost in the noise of the falls behind him. I wait.

High above, at the zenith of the two leaning obelisks, the clouds dissolve and a sliver of light streams down. The moon: her face nearly full as she peers into the cave. And slipping into the moon's silver blade, on a shelf of stone just above the man's head, the black shadow of the cougar's head emerges.

The animal bares its teeth, emits its sound—a woman screaming.

The professor turns.

32

WHEN I OPENED THE DOOR, the sheriff stood dripping, his shoulders drooped and his hat collapsed with rivulets of rain spilling down across his leather jacket. He looked like an animal too tired to limp the last quarter mile.

"Don't reckon you got anything stronger than tea?" he said, stepping inside. When I told him the power was out, could maybe drain a glass of water from the pipes, he went back into the rain and returned with a bottle of whiskey. "Emergency supplies," he said, handing it to me. "On the rocks?"

Exhaustion is relative, too. Just looking at the sheriff put mine in eclipse. What the hell, I felt fine. By the time I brought Marle's drink into the living room, he was standing in front of the fire, his soaked coat and hat spread beside it, his hands stretched toward the flames. He took a healthy swallow of the whiskey and sat down.

"You look a heartbeat away from roadkill," I said, sitting opposite him. "What's going on?"

"You don't want to know." He stared at the fire and heaved a great sigh. "After all these years, it's still amazing to me what folks can get into. Phone lines are out, or I'd have called you and canceled, but it wasn't that long a drive. I was already in the neighborhood. I might as well move on out here." He shook his head and downed another slug of the bourbon.

"What's happening?" I sensed the proximity of crisis in the air. "Morgan took off like a bolt a little while ago."

He stared at me. "Who?"

There's a reason I've never been high on the CIA's list of potential recruits. "Um, you know. Eva Blake. Morgan's her middle name. She said her friends in L.A. call her that."

"That who belongs to the rig outside? Hard to miss that one." He squinted at me, then shrugged. "So where'd she take off to?"

"I don't know. I just thought...what's happened?"

"Well, I guess she wasn't at Brandenberg's when the fireworks were going on. That place just keeps challenging the imagination for meanness." He was shaking his head at the fire again. "Myra Jones went off the deep end, stabbed Dean with a letter opener after the lights went out at the homeowners' meeting."

"You're kidding! I was there when they went out!" I remembered the hullabaloo as Morgan took my hand and led me down the dark hallway, and then again as we drove back by.

"Must have been in a hurry." The sheriff shaped it as a statement, but it wasn't.

"Well, I wasn't in the best of moods. Dean had rewritten the covenants—"

"So I heard."

"I'd decided to go by Eva's to pick up my things before I went home. I saw her truck at Brandenberg's, so I stopped. Turned out he'd called a secret meeting, deliberately kept it from me to get support for claiming my property, disputing Claire's title and her right to sell, based on the existence of a prior plat."

The sheriff's jaw muscles were working as he listened. He'd apparently not heard this story. And I didn't want to think about it right now. "What about Brandenberg?" I asked. "Is he...?"

"He'll be all right. Takes more strength and night vision than Myra's got to kill somebody as thick-chested as Dean with a letter opener in the dark. She left her mark, though; he'll be in the hospital a couple days. But that's just for starters. Mrs. Brandenberg used a cell phone, called the ambulance, called me. By the time I got there, the Gillmans had Myra sitting out with them in their car. She'd calmed down, but she started up again once I got there. Said somebody had to stop what was going on out here, and since nobody else would, she had to. Felt it was the responsible thing to do." The sheriff drained his glass and set it hard on the table. Then he leaned back in the chair with his eyes closed. "Confessed to cutting the brakes on Harv's grader. Said she'd caught him cutting down those old trees, those ones with the Indian markings that she'd called the Wildlife people about. Said she heard a chain saw, went to check it out, and there he was, felling one. That's what he's been using to make those burl tables out of, I guess. Said she warned him, told him to stop, but he said he had a living to make. Brad drove her on back to the jail for the night."

"Jesus." I tried to imagine Myra slipping under the grader in Harv's front yard. I realized that she must have done it early Friday morning. She hadn't been following me when she spotted me in Cougar Canyon, she'd been coming from Harv's, sneaking home through the forest. "But why did she tamper with Eva's brakes?"

"Says she didn't do that one. I got to believe her. Why would she lie at this point?"

"But who, then?"

"I'd just as soon save that one till tomorrow. I reckon it'll keep. I don't think I'm lucky enough for this place to disappear overnight."

"So she, what, ordered books on cutting brake lines?"

"Said she went through several vehicle repair manuals. Said it was easy as cutting anything else. Went inside the cab and wound some wire around the blade control lever so Harv couldn't lower the blade to stop that way either. That's probably what you heard Harv yelling that day. When he found the brakes were gone, he went to lower the blade and found the lever jammed. He probably knew then, just before the crash, that somebody had done it deliberately."

I shifted position on my chair to avoid a damp spot behind my shoulder that had soaked through my clothing. I looked up to see if the rain had somehow seeped in above, but I saw nothing. "I wonder how she decided to do it that way. I mean, with her interest in nature and all, you'd think she'd have found some exotic herb or something. Maybe planted a brown recluse."

"She wasn't quite as forthcoming about that, but sounds like the professor might have given her the idea. She said he once mentioned watching a television special about how easy it was to kill people, cutting the brake lines being somewhere at the top of the list. Seems like it was the professor gave her that copy of your book, too. She was starting to get a little teary there at the end, just as Brad showed up and she was climbing in the car with him." He sat up and leaned toward the fire, his forearms propped on his knees. He raised his eyebrows at me with as much humor as he seemed able to muster. "Asked me to give you her apologies. She thought from reading those poems of yours that you were somebody that tortured animals. But said you come by her place one day, something about you going out of your way to step over a beetle on her porch. Said she knew right then she had you pegged wrong."

I stared at him in amazement. "A beetle? The professor? But why…?"

Marle picked up his drink and sipped at the cubes that were left. He stared into the fire, talking at the flames. "Can't say as I got the answer to that one either. I did take a run by the professor's place before I came here, nobody home. Place locked up tight. Power's out all over, but I'll be right interested to have a talk with him."

I remembered seeing him at the homeowners' meeting, and Morgan's description of his quarrel with Brandenberg over the gate. I wasn't having any luck at all piecing this together. I let it go and looked over at the television I'd brought here to watch Garbo tapes, figuring it would be put to better use with Wendy and the kids. The sheriff looked like he was having trouble just lifting his glass, not to mention the television.

"I don't think you're in much condition to be making deliveries tonight. Looks like Wendy's just going to have to wait for the TV. Maybe tomorrow—"

"Wouldn't worry too much about it. Think she's got her entertainment back on track. Hadn't got to that part yet. Willa Hanks, that woman Gerald's been living with? She come flying over to add to the party atmosphere. The ambulance had just took off with Dean in it, Brad had just pulled out with Myra. I thought things were winding down. I should have known better. Here comes Willa flying up the road in Gerald's truck, jumped out screaming and wild-eyed. Said your friend Eva come by this afternoon, carried

Gerald into her trailer, dumped him on the bed unconscious. Said Eva told her she found him out along the highway, thought he was drunk or on drugs. Said she was dropping him off so somebody wouldn't run over him. Willa figured he was drunk too, let him sleep it off. He woke up a while later screaming like all hell broke loose." The sheriff looked over at me. "Found a bottle in his shirt pocket, some pain pills. Willa said they helped a lot, calmed him down. Said Gerald wasn't saying much about it." The sheriff heaved a bone-deep sigh that sounded like he'd pulled it up all the way from his boots. "But she wanted to know what kind of psycho was running around…'operating on people,' is how she put it."

" 'Operating on people'?"

Marle gave me a long, level look. "Appears somebody went and castrated Gerald Crawford."

Marle and I stared at each other. The tiny candle flames flickered. The fire snapped, and a log settled. The rain still came down, but slowly, the drops tapping across the windows.

"Appears Gerald wants to let it pass. Which might be the most amazing thing of the evening, considering Gerald, but there you have it. Willa had come over to get Wendy, wanted her to get Gerald out of her trailer. Then the two of them entertained everybody for a while, going at it like a couple of wet cats. Last I heard, Joe Gillman and Andrew and Wolf were headed to Willa's with Wendy, going to carry Gerald over to her A-frame." The sheriff grinned a little, the gray eyes crinkling. "Wendy seemed right happy about it," Marle said, clinking his ice cubes. I went to the kitchen and brought the bottle of bourbon with me and handed it to him. He poured the glass full again.

After the sheriff had gone, I sat numb and utterly exhausted before the fire. At least, I thought, Gerald Crawford wasn't lurking outside my house in the rain, waiting to crash through the windows. Apparently. I looked up to see the rain had stopped, but in spite of exhaustion and the late hour, I was wide awake, anxious. I lit another batch of candles, added them to the ones already burning, so that the room was bright with a flickering galaxy of tiny flames, yet I felt my anxiety increasing, circling above my head with the high, thin whine of summer mosquitoes.

I paced around the living room, wondered where Morgan had gone, why she wasn't yet back. I noticed several odd patches of moisture throughout the house, but no leaks. The windows that Tony had left sparkling seemed to have acquired a dull, smeared finish as the candle flames reflected off them. On the dining room table, I discovered a cardboard box of the type used for mailing. Inside were several bottles, scalpel blades, needles, thin rubber surgical gloves—the veterinarian supplies Morgan had picked up today. I pulled out several of the bottles, read the turgid scientific names. Materials for operating on the cats, for—

For castration.

You can mark Gerald Crawford off your list of things to be afraid of...he's not a player here anymore.

I went back to the fireplace, sat on the floor cross-legged before the fire, my arms wrapped around my shaking body. I closed my eyes, but I kept seeing the shipping box, the bottles that had been opened; kept hearing Morgan's voice joining the high mosquito-like whine: *he's not a player here anymore.* My head swam. I leaned it back against the chair, closed my eyes. I dreamt of walking through a surreal landscape, through a rubble of rocks and diamonds and rivers of molten silver.

33

W HEN I WOKE, Morgan lay horizontal in the chair. She sipped at a drink of clear liquid with ice cubes, and somehow I didn't think it was water. I sat up and looked around in the firelight as memory returned. The sheriff's visit. Gerald Crawford. The box of veterinary supplies on the table. The locked front door.

Morgan smiled faintly, her dark eyes catching the flames of a hundred candles. She set down the glass beside the sheriff's, stood up, stretched her arms, rolled her head back, flexed her spine, lean and supple as a cat.

"Looks like the sheriff made it by," she said.

When I nodded, my neck popped from where I had fallen asleep propped against the chair. I massaged it and told her the latest update at El Gato, but I was thinking about the box on the dining room table, about Gerald Crawford, about my locked front door she'd come through. She walked over to the windows and looked outside where the rain had passed and the moonlight lay in bright patches.

"That's right," she said, without surprise. "It was Myra. She had a couple of mechanics' manuals in her book collection, fairly new acquisitions, not the library's discards. Why else would she have had them? And the photocopy of your book—difficult to find, though I didn't have all that much trouble," she grinned around at me, "her copy with the Interlibrary Loan stamp, where else but from the professor? But why?" She pushed herself from the wall of windows and paced along them, as though moving were a necessary part of thinking. Her deep voice was low, speaking as much to

herself as to me. "Myra and the professor: they seemed to be...
close. In fact, insofar as Myra Jones was capable of love in the
romantic sense, that's probably what she felt for him. She must
have told him about Harv cutting the trees. She wanted to stop
Harv, but how could she forget how the law had failed to stop the
Smithsonian people from taking her museum artifacts? The professor must have realized this, too. Sensed that Myra Jones was one of
those committed fanatics who would mete out their own justice.

"But the professor had his own agenda." Morgan stopped pacing and faced me. "You see, he'd been busy on campus. He'd vol-
unteered to staff the new off-campus Help Line. An ideal place to
come across women in trouble. He'd watch for just the right ones—
lonely, parental problems, alienated, friendless, misfits. He'd pick
his mark during fall quarter, somewhere around fall break offer to
give her a ride, drop her off home on his way to wherever he might
have told her he was going, or maybe he'd just suggest a casual
drink to offer a sympathetic ear. At some point, he'd put something
in her drink, easy enough these days, bring her to the cabin—"

Morgan stopped talking, and I looked up at where she stood by
the fire.

"The cabin?"

"I believe he's abducted at least six women this way, starting
with when he bought the cabin back in 1990. My guess is that he
brought them here, raped them, killed them, and I think we'll find
a workroom set up in the garage out back. Probably a circular saw,
certainly a freezer. He would dismember them, put them into plastic bags, then fit them in the freezer, come back in December and
finish."

The flickering light illuminated her face from below, cast the
hollows in darkness. She was eerily beautiful, and it struck me that
she was perhaps mad as well. My heart raced. She smiled slightly
before continuing.

"December, the cold month. The month Moss's college closes
down for the holidays. He waits until after the fall quarter, waits
until snow is predicted, drives to his cabin the night before. As was
always Harv's habit on a morning following a snow, he drives his
Jeep to the subdivision's garage, which is just to the rear of the pro-

fessor's place. Harv parks his Jeep and gets on the grader to plow the roads. He knows Moss likes to visit during the snows, knows he drives the small Volkswagen useless in such snows. He offers the professor the use of the Jeep if it's parked at the garage, always leaves the key in the ignition. If Harv happens to come by after grading the roads and the Jeep's gone, he knows the professor has it, drives the grader on home, gets the Jeep later. That's what happened the day you walked up the road that December afternoon and found Harv's Jeep—"

"But I thought it was Harv, that he was poaching."

"Yes," Morgan said, "but according to Edna, Harv drew the line at killing animals in the protected vicinity of El Gato. He might apply for a hunting license and use the BLM land which is all around this area, but never El Gato. It couldn't have been Harv.

"It could only have been the professor. He froze the bodies in October, waited until the snows came, took the frozen bodies of the women, dropped them over the embankment into Cougar Canyon, a place so difficult to get to in winter that it was impassable. You see, frozen bodies meant he could choose the time to dispose of them, and he did it after a snowfall so there was never any decomposition, no vultures to tip anyone off, no odor to attract anyone. And the final stroke of genius: he knew the cougar would carry away the body, that there would be no bones for anyone to discover. It was foolproof."

Morgan paused, looked out through the black window.

"He might even have heard of the old legend, maybe that's originally what gave the professor the idea, but it had to have been Myra Jones who told him that it was more than a legend. She spent most of her time in the woods, she'd have run across the trail of the cougar, known it wasn't just the paw prints of a passing wildcat. She'd probably seen it herself, had warned you about it. She knew it was there, never mentioned it to the Division of Wildlife in order to protect it. No, she was scrupulously careful never to tell anyone at all about what she knew—except the professor."

"Tell him what?"

"About the cougar, where it lived. You see, the reason it had been thought a legend rather than an actual cougar was because it never left behind bones to prove its existence. And, of course, it wasn't the same cougar all this time. Over the years, as one cougar died, another would take its territory, live in that same cave behind the falls where that first one had lived long ago. The cave—the eating place where the cougar always took its prey to feast, as cougars do. Not in the deepest part of a canyon, as other cougars would have, but in a cave hidden behind the water. The professor was dumping the bodies in Cougar Canyon, knowing they would never be found." Morgan turned to me. "Except you caught him doing it, saw where he'd parked Harv's Jeep that day in December."

"But I didn't. I thought all the time it was Harv."

"True. But how long was it going to take you to put the pieces together? Hadn't you already been thinking about 1990, the missing co-ed, seeing the Jeep there? How long would it have taken before, in talking with Harv, he mentioned letting the professor drive his Jeep? The professor figured you'd put it together sooner or later, because he knew it was you who had seen the Jeep that day. He couldn't have missed seeing your footprints in the snow that day as he came back to collect that second trash bag you saw on the flatbed, following them over to the cliff and looking down. How could he miss that bright red Porsche parked directly below on a snowy road? And then he saw it again, the day you drove by his place with Harv, the same day you drove past my place. You can be sure he asked Harv who you were, found out as much as he could about you.

"Then you moved next door. To be safe, he had to get rid of both Harv and you. That's why, when Myra was in such a rage at Harv over the trees, he started slipping her information about ways to arrange accidents for people. And she bit, just like he hoped. He was setting you up, too, figuring it was just a matter of time before you started putting it all together. In fact, he had no way of knowing at that time that Harv might not already have mentioned it to you, so—"

"—so he tracked down an early volume of my poems, photocopied it, gave it to Myra, thinking she'd be so incensed by the animal cruelty in them that she'd want to do the same thing to me as she was wanting to do to Harv."

"Exactly. And then he happened across you in the woods that day, on your way back from Edna's. Maybe he was just out for a walk, more likely he was following you, waiting for a chance to get you out of the picture without raising suspicion. But when you stopped in at my house that day, he figured it was going to be too late to walk back to your place before dark. He must have been pretty sure I'd offer you a ride, so he crept around to the far side of the garage, cut the brakes. That's what had set the horse off that day as we were talking. As luck would have it, when I came down the front way and let you in, I'd shut the alarm system off, so the surveillance camera didn't pick him up; otherwise, I'd have had him on tape."

"You don't mean you actually made a mistake?"

An actual transformation from chrysalis to butterfly, I read somewhere, takes weeks and even months; Morgan's, we're talking microseconds. I could have sworn that long skinny shape of hers could have doubled for that cobra in *The Black Stallion*. She had it down pat, everything but the tongue.

She turned back to the windows. "So you can imagine why the professor was nearly hysterical when Brandenberg took the gate down today, knowing every hunter and tourist and wilderness backpacking junkie that came by would be driving into El Gato. He knew the canyon wasn't going to remain private much longer, not with all that activity. He had already heard the gunshots going off this afternoon, thought there were hunters around when it was actually..." Morgan gave me an odd glance over her shoulder, then continued. "But he couldn't change anybody's mind, which simply meant changing Brandenberg's, so he knew he had to get rid of the body he'd brought up here with him this time before the winter snows. Who knows how many people would be nosing around by then, and sooner or later, someone besides Myra would figure out where the cougar lived and come across all those bones. He had to work fast. He'd already frozen the body, probably was in process when we happened on him that day and drove him back to his house. He didn't want to risk going to the canyon in daytime, given what he thought was the presence of hunters, so he waited till dark, but instead of dumping the body in the canyon where someone might come across it, he knew this time he had to take it directly to the cat."

"But...how...where did you find all this out?"

"I've been doing a little walking of my own," she said. "I saw the cougar the other day, and tonight—when you mentioned seeing Harv's Jeep—I knew it wasn't Harv driving it, had to be the professor."

"And that's where you went tonight, up to the waterfall? So where is he? Marle was just here, you couldn't have called him. And anyway, the phone lines are out. Where...?" Her eyes had grown hard; it was the gaze that the professor had seen that day in his yard, staring at me.

"The cougar, its cave. Leave it private for as long as you can," she said. It was the voice without inflection, where all emotion had been pressed out. "As for the professor..." She paused again, looking from me out to the bright silver patches across the yard. "Whether by accident, or whether by moral intent, on occasion the universe steps in. Call it faith."

I think I'd gotten her gist. I watched Cordelia Morgan stare out the window as though I were seeing a madwoman talking about sawing people into pieces, a woman whom I had reason to believe may actually have castrated a man a few hours ago. I heard her, I nodded, but I was also hearing another voice at the same time, the one that I had always called Common Sense. It took the shape of my old buddy, Margot-the-shrink, and it was screaming for me to stay calm, to pretend I was talking to a rational person. I felt the blood leave my face, my skin grow clammy. When the sheriff had driven up, I had put down the .38 and come downstairs; now I wished it were beside me.

"So the professor took the body parts and froze them and threw them into the canyon?" I said, standing up. I walked into the kitchen, slowly, trying to appear natural. "And the cougar was getting them, taking them into its cave?" Much as I tried to control it, my voice sounded as though I were placating a naughty child. Morgan didn't seem to notice. She followed me to the kitchen, still talking, sitting on a stool at the bar while I picked up a cloth and wiped off the perfectly clean counter tops.

"Right, and that's where you'll find a pile of bones going back into the last century, as well as the more recent bones of women who have disappeared in the Denver area during the last few years. Always in October, bodies never discovered. Except for the bones of the hand of the young woman who worked at the animal grooming shop, the one who disappeared in 1990. The only one who would have had traces of organophosphates where she bathed animals at the grooming shop. There's no way to tell why the cougar left it behind. Maybe it smelled the chemical. Maybe it fell from the cave and some small creature carried it out into the canyon." The candle flames caught her expression, absorbed with the nuances of her tale. "Who knows? According to the old Indian legends, the cougar was some kind of intelligent life form, a resident mascot left behind by the tribe to protect their mountain home till they returned. Maybe it left that hand on purpose." She shrugged, her chin propped in her palms. "I guess it's one of those mysteries you have to live with, like questions of the soul," she grinned.

Part of it made all the sense in the world, I suppose. But not my world. I found it bizarre and foreign and insane. My hands were trembling so badly that I put them to work, taking groceries out of the bags, putting them away. Then I remembered the registration receipt. I dug it out of my pocket and handed it to her, forcing a thin smile. I still wanted to please her, but not for the same reasons as this afternoon.

"It's for you." I said. "For the MG. All you have to do is drive it down, show them the title. They'll give you the new plates."

Morgan stared at me as though I were holding that .38 upstairs, aimed straight at her heart.

"What?" I stared back. "Look, if you're not comfortable driving it down, they'll send the deputy out to check the VIN if you want. I thought you'd be pleased. I wanted you to be able to drive your car while you're here. You know, when there's no snow. No salt."

But she was still stone. I wondered how a person who'd just a few hours ago castrated a man, could now be so unnerved about the thought of salt on her MG. Go figure.

"Look," I said irritably, "you don't have to get the plates. It's okay. Just forget it."

"When, what time? You used my name when you paid?" she said. "Morgan, Cordelia Morgan?"

"Well, sure. I mean, it's not registered to Eva Blake, is it?" For a smart woman, sometimes she seemed a little dense. "I did it this afternoon, somewhere around four, I guess. I memorized the number of your old New Mexico tags, and the woman used it to pull your record up on the screen. There was your name, an address in New Mexico. It was easy. Look, no one around here is going to go in and check the name on your license plates."

Then she was moving fast, talking fast. She went to the chair by the fire and grabbed the green nylon bag still leaning there.

"It's later than you think, J. S. Symkin. Listen up," she said, coming back to the kitchen counter and rummaging through the bag as she talked. "The people I used to work for? Pasonombre, The Company? And Cruz, the guy I lived with in Santa Fe? The DMV registration's going to send a flag up for them, high and bright. Couldn't have given away my whereabouts any quicker if I'd gone on national television. Paso, he'll let it ride maybe a day or so, but Cruz, for him it's not a game anymore. It's life and death. He wants me off the planet, and he wants it to happen before Paso shows up."

She pulled a book out of the bag, Stone's *Living Up the Lie*. She laid it on the counter. "Your personal copy. Bookmark. Anything ever goes wrong, Gerald comes around, anybody strange comes around," she said, giving me a hard look, "drop it in the mail. Doubt Gerald will give you any more trouble, though. We had a little talk before he went under the knife. He won't press charges, approach you ever again, or slap his wife around. I'm pretty sure of that. I can be real convincing." The Attitude smile, way high.

She pulled a folder out of the nylon bag, slipped it under the book, headed for the door, talking: "About the cats, meant to run you through it in person. Simple operation. Open the barn doors tomorrow, take a few of the cats in, make notes while your local vet does the honors. Supplies are on your table, directions inside the folder. Trust me on this, Symkin," she said as she stood in the open doorway, the slow-breaking smile easing its way up and my heart doing its hummingbird number while I suddenly remembered an image I'd forgotten: her face last night in the moonlight when I'd wakened with her body against mine: "No solution was ever easier."

She crossed the porch, her boots loud. When she reached the bottom step, she paused, turned back.

"You okay?"

I thought about it in that last split second she gave me.

"I don't suppose you've got any of that sedative you could leave behind?"

I stood on the porch and watched the bumper twinkle out of sight, heard the mufflers of that red truck long after the tail-lights had disappeared. When I had closed the door behind me, the living room with its two-story rafters and glass walls had the kind of emptiness I'd felt walking through graveyards. But there was no longer danger lurking anywhere, just a hollowness the size of a continent.

34

Morgan

*The El Gato gate is still down, the power off, the development dark. I
cruise through: silent roads lit by the moon, cut with shadows.*

*I have stayed here too long, distracted by the personal. One pays for
such folly. I drive slowly, watching for signs, recalculating the time window: the Symkin woman visited the DMV in Crystal Springs at four
o'clock. Give or take. Information giving my Colorado address would have
been fed into the computer, the New Mexico point of origin updated elec-
tronically with the new address. I know Cruz's methodology, as well as
standard DMV procedure. When the information is received in Santa Fe,
the removal of the old DMV number from the database will have been
programmed to trip a blocking device, setting off the Code Red alarm.*

Somewhere around four o'clock Mountain Time, at the
Department of Motor Vehicles building at 915 W. Alameda, Santa
Fe, New Mexico, in a back room with a fluorescent ceiling and no
windows, the twelfth woman in a row of fourteen data input clerks
stared at her computer screen. Her eyes burned like hell, and the
blue veins running along the inside of her wrists filled with sharp
jabbing pains when she tried to rest them on the lower frame of her
keyboard. She glanced up at the industrial clock chunking its second
hand along like a heavy load: 4:12. She'd give it till 4:45.

When the flashing red square sprang up in the center of her screen, Merilyn Martinez was thinking about the fifteen minutes it took to drive to the junior college for her five o'clock evening course in Basic Marketing Strategies, wondering how long she could keep leaving here early before her supervisor wised up. She stared at the screen for a moment before registering the red flashing ALERT, thought at first the new computer network had crashed again, then thought she'd stumbled on some nerdy programmer's idea of a joke and struck a sequence of keys to jam the program. Then she saw the message in the lower portion of the screen:

THIS INDIVIDUAL HAS BEEN REPORTED MISSING AND IS CURRENTLY UNDER INVESTIGATION. CALL (505) 431-7281 IMMEDIATELY TO REPORT ANY UPDATE OF EXISTING INFORMATION.

Santa Fe to El Gato: five-hour drive, straight through, no delays. If Cruz received the message at four o'clock, someone could be here by nine—that's if the universe is traveling on rails and the wind is at your back and goodness and light are following you all the days of your life. Not a chance. So I figure for the real world, figuring fast and driving slow, cruising El Gato and thinking of the Cruz I know, the creature of habit who eats out, home by seven, heads for his study. Workaholic, big time. Thinking of how entropy sets in, sand jamming the gears; thinking if the sandman's on my side tonight and Cruz doesn't get the Alert till after dinner, let's call it five hours from seven o'clock. Let's call it midnight. Give or take.

Merilyn Martinez slipped a glance right, a glance left. There was no audio alert with the message, no one had noticed her flashing screen. She hit the minimize button to hide the program and thought about it. There was probably a shit load of red tape ahead, a cop to be sent over from the police department, forms to fill out, god only knew what else. The Marketing instructor had warned her if she were late for class one more time, he'd drop her from the roster. That meant she'd lose three credit hours, and that meant the end of her monthly financial aid check. This part-time job at eight bucks an hour wasn't worth it, definitely wasn't worth it. Still, there might be a way to manage it, keep them both. Merilyn figured it was worth a shot, what's to lose. She called up the word processing program, spent the next half hour typing in copy for the latest driver's manual, waited for 4:45 when she maximized the license update screen, told Betty Jo sitting next to her that she was sick with the flu, and did Betty Jo know what that flashing red square meant. Then she took off.

At Brandenberg's house, scattered rectangles glow dimly with candlelight, and the yellow grader still sits stuck in the wall, a pale smudge in the dark yard. When the Symkin woman opens the folder, she will find the information she needs to stop Brandenberg if she chooses to use it: confidential information and documentation provided by Claire, photocopied ledger sheets, the kind of double-bookkeeping system that will get you a choice between bankruptcy court and jail time. She included her signed proxy, just in case. According to those creative bylaws Claire had written up and had court-approved way back then, as the original developer, she kept the right to force a vote of the landholders at large in special situations, one vote per individual, which could override an existing vote, even force the dissolution of the development entirely. The signed proxy is Claire's method of payment to me, a gesture made at my request. In return, I have put together a narrative for her, detailing the information I collected on Camilla's life, the affair with the New York artist who is Wendy's father, Camilla's penchant for the bohemian life in Paris and other places, my speculations concerning her death. It is the most complete biography of her daughter that Claire is ever likely to have. It is a positive rendering; it captures a truth without telling the truth. After spending a significant amount of thought in selecting and arranging materials, I could find no reason to include Gerald and the rapes. None: the truth, like any potentially lethal serum, should be administered in small doses, a vaccine for the soul.

At 4:55, Frieda Glendinning sat in the outer office adjoining the one belonging to her boss, Simon Cruz. She didn't need to look at the calendar to know it was Monday. It had started bad, and it was ending worse. She blamed it on the full moon, because that's when her period had come last Friday, and at first she'd even taken it as a positive sign, feeling tuned in to the Great Earth Mother's lunar cycle, even though the hormones the doctor gave her were supposed to have stopped that part. But they hadn't, she was bleeding heavier than any teenager, and they hadn't stopped the hot flashes either, and instead of drying up, she was heating up and dripping like a Louisiana willow in spring rain. She wore a Tampax Super Plus and two napkins, just to be safe, and as Simon walked out of his office swinging his briefcase in one hand and holding his cell phone to his ear with the other, her desk phone began ringing just at the very moment she felt the blood start to trickle out of her, then gush like a Texas geyser between the sides of the napkin. The reason she knew it was Monday was because she'd worn the white raw silk Armani suit.

I turn off the main road and drive past my house. It is dark, as expected. I take a left at the next side road, circle back to the lot behind mine, park the truck beside the road, shut off the headlights, pull the green nylon bag over my shoulder. I get out and fold the seat forward, sift through the jumble of items retrieved from my wrecked truck, disentangle the ESN Reader, and take it along. The underbrush is soaked from the rain, and the stream behind the house has overrun its banks, rushing wild and loud. I set up the Reader behind a thicket of bushes, curious whether Cruz will come himself or send someone. I check the display readout, adjust the antenna and controls, then settle down to wait, figuring if it doesn't intercept a cell phone transmission signal within the next fifteen minutes, chances are good no one has arrived yet. Cruz, or anyone else assigned surveillance in a remote mountain location, will be using a cell phone to maintain contact— standard operating procedure. I scan the tangle of moonlight and shadows as I wait, calculating the risk involved in trying to rescue the hard disk drive from my computer against the safer course of driving away, leaving it behind.

No contest: if Cruz finds the hard drive, I can count the hours on one hand before he breaks through the passwords and codes, has all the information he needs to locate and access my bank accounts. Without substantial financial means, chances of evading both Cruz and Pasonombre are significantly reduced. Try nil.

*After fifteen minutes, I pack up the Reader and head for the house. The
water has reached above the bridge, and I wade through the ice-cold rapids.
I stop by the stable where the horse stands waiting for dinner.*

Just before they reached the door, the lightning exploded and
the thunder crashed behind them. It shook the ground and
pounded the windows, and they hit the front door running,
nearly blinded by the flash. A deluge of water let loose from the
clouds again. He wasn't calling it rain, he was calling it a fucking
flash flood, hauling right straight down out of the sky. And that's
when he knew why he'd been tormented all through dinner by
thoughts of The Bitch from Hell. It was the weather (wasn't it?)
touching something off, keeping that last day playing in his mind
over and over again like a bad movie, the worst rain since she
stole his Mercedes four years ago (wasn't it?), left it in the fucking
arroyo to see (what?) whether it'd swim or float in the fucking
flash flood she had to know was going to come along. Knew she'd
put it there because she'd left The Company's custom-issue
Heckler & Koch behind. *Her* HK, one-of-a-kind, signature
weapon that you don't fucking go around leaving in a stolen
Mercedes, *his* stolen Mercedes for Christ's sake. He couldn't think
of anybody else except Cordelia Morgan who would do something like that, would have the balls to do it. So it had to be the
weather (didn't it?) that brought her slipping in and out his head.
You can't have bolts of fucking lightning trying to nail you in
your own front yard and not think of The Morgue. Hell, the smell
of sulfur in the air would do it. Cordelia. Cord. Fucking Cord
Morgan. He slammed the door harder than he needed to and the
room shook and the windows rattled some more. Gayle stopped
in the hall and looked back at him. He ignored her, turned and
went up the stairs.

When he walked into his study and saw the red light on the
answering machine flashing, he didn't even have to push the Play
button. Well sonofabitch, he was thinking, so this is how it feels.
This is how she felt all those times when she knew what was happening before it happened. Sonofabitch. But he went over and hit
Play anyway, listened to the message. He was expecting it to be her

voice (wanting it to be?), but it wasn't. It was Frieda, giving him the info from the DMV.

Gayle was watching him from the end of the hall when he left by the front door. He checked his watch. 7:12. He didn't know how far it was, sure as hell couldn't fly it in this shit. Didn't matter. He was on the cell phone by the time he squealed out the driveway, getting somebody on the stick down at Transportation, getting him the best directions. Getting Frieda to call Herm and Jack, meet him in Española, follow him up to Colorado, to El Gato whatever the fuck that was, for backup. This was D-day, this was Christmas, this was fucking Fourth of July, all wrapped in one. He'd been waiting for it. He'd been dreaming of it.

Odd thing, though. He downshifted, slipped the Mercedes up the I-25 ramp, took the Pecos Trail exit and down the back way through Tesuque to miss the traffic, trying to figure why in hell somebody like Morgan had gone to the fucking DMV and registered a stolen MG in Colorado. Any nickel-and-dime car thief had better sense than that, and we're talking Cord Morgan, Paso's Número Uno, for Christ's sake. Hotshot big-time international Specialist. (Proud, Cruz? You're sounding *proud* of her?) By the time he hit the four-lane through Española, he knew she wouldn't have done it. By the time he took Ojo Caliente, he was starting to worry a little (paranoid?), thinking maybe it was some kind of trap she was setting up for him. Because no way in hell would she have expected to register that MG, *his* MG, under her own name and not have it send up a red flag; no way would she have given her actual address, the actual VIN number, not a chance. No, if she wanted to risk registering the damn car at all, and he couldn't believe she would have at this point, she'd have created a phony bill of sale, just like she'd done it back in '93 on her way out of the States, use her own name, a new SSN, a fictitious address, figure out a workable VIN that wasn't going to send up any DMV flags. Okay, he thought, heading into the rolling hills with Tres Piedras coming up, so someone else (who?) registered the car. Without telling her? Or maybe it wasn't Morgan, he thought, maybe somebody else had come across his car, didn't know the history, trotted down to the Crystal Springs DMV (Jesus, "Crystal Springs"? She was really boondocking now). Or maybe it was Morgan, after all, her kinky kind of in-your-face brand of communication (sounds right, doesn't it?), wanting to talk, tired of running, wants to deal.

He was streaking through the night, making good time in the flat lands of the San Luis Valley, the alkaline fields spooky in his headlights, trying to get her face out of his mind, the touch of her, the musky voice. She was looking right through the windshield at him with that fucking smart-ass smile you wanted to slap right off her face, stuck there in his headlights stubborn as an old song you can't quit hearing no matter how high you jack up the volume on a new one. So he started erasing her, thinking about that time four years ago, had thought about it as many times as there had been dollars, millions of them, that that fucking Cunt from Hell had lost for him when she blew the whistle on his Pecos River deal. Walked off and got herself put on Paso's hit list, and sure as hell was holding steady as number one on his. He thought of how he just about hadn't pulled his reputation and his company out of the fire after all the publicity she'd arranged before she drove off and trashed his brand new Mercedes S500. The last thing he thought of before he got past the Valley and started up Highway 17 toward Aspen was what he wanted to do to her while she was still conscious enough to remember where she'd put those papers she'd been holding over his head for four years now, papers that were his death sentence guaranteed if Paso ever saw them. And then somehow, he couldn't figure out how he did it, but somehow he had missed the fucking turn off Highway 82, had circled around looking for it, Herm and Jack following. What the hell. He picked up the cell phone, put in a call to Transportation.

I cross the yard, staying in the shadows, sensing the night, the humidity still thick in the air, the odor of pine and earth and night fragrances. I enter the house by the upper deck, slipping into my workroom where the moon lies bright across the worktables, the walls. I check the electrical system: the power is still off, the phone line dead. I set up the Reader, switch it on, shift into high gear: slip the cover off the computer, remove the hard drive, drop it in my shoulder bag. Add various items from my walls, the stack of folders on the table, the picture of me and Paso. In the bathroom, I grab the bottle of chemical that I had given the Symkin woman last night. Just as I secure it inside a zippered pocket, the Reader emits a series of beeps. I check the display which is registering the phone number of the mobile unit. I slip my head through the strap of the nylon bag, anchor it firmly over my shoulder, then watch the front entrance of my home from an upstairs window. In a moment, a glint of metal flashes in the moonlight. It is moving, very slowly, stops. I draw my own cell phone from the nylon bag, wait. When I see a figure enter the shadows beside the garage, I dial the number that appeared on the Reader's display.

When he answers, I wait for a moment, watch the shadow below me stop beside the locked garage door, the phone to his ear. Wait until he suddenly turns, looks up at the house. And then I move, stand directly in front of the window where the moon pours through, so that I am caught in the light above him, perfectly visible with my phone held in one hand, the Sig Sauer 210 in the other. There is something particularly lovely about what moonlight does to polished steel. I didn't expect Cruz to appreciate it.

"Cord."

"Cruz."

I have seen the other shadows too, two of them edging now from the rear and toward the front yard, toward Cruz.

"You're slipping, Cord. Leaving your truck parked in the middle of the road. Paso would be disappointed in you."

"Good point, Cruz. Maybe you finally got something right. Maybe it's time I had a talk with him, go over some past history. Maybe I ought to hang up and give him a call. You think?"

He lets a few beats of quiet time pass. Then: "I think you ought to come down here so we can talk, Cord. Nothing's happened that can't be fixed. I give you my word on that."

"Your word?" I laugh, then match his beats with some of my own, counting the seconds, hitting twenty. "Thing is, nothing's broken, Cruz. Nothing needs to be fixed. So we're clear on that, let's get clear on something else. Just so you know, just so your buddies over there know, you're not in the bargaining seat, in case you haven't noticed. What you are is one dead son of a bitch if you move one muscle, one inch, and you know what?" He doesn't answer. Of course not. I do the twenty beats again. "It would be my pleasure."

"Cord—"

"And so your buddies know, so you don't subject them to unnecessary danger, I think you better tell them, Cruz, that by the time I get three shots off, it's not even a ballgame anymore. You know that about me, don't you?" I step back out of the moonlight, into the darkness. "Maybe you want to let them know that, too, Cruz, maybe you want to let them know now, because if you don't, I'll have to make my point another way, then that will leave three of us."

"Jesus, Cord, for Christ's—"

"Now Cruz, do it now!"

"All right, Jesus, just calm down. Shit."

I can hear him talking to the men through the receiver, but I can hear him talking even better in the clear night air from the rear deck. There is something quite magical about the way sound carries in the mountains if you are not careful. It is possible to follow your neighbor's private conversations with just the smallest amount of quietude on your part.

By the time Cruz is back on the receiver with me, I have reached the corral where the horse stands saddled in his stall.

"All right, Cord. You got it. So let's talk, all right? So you've got the upper hand, that's all right. I didn't come up here for a fucking shootout, okay? I came up here because I wanted to talk to you. I—"

"Cruz." I ease my boot in the stirrup, slip the Sig back in my jacket, mount the horse.

"Yeah."

"Thing of it is, Cruz," I say, guiding the horse out of the corral, toward the stream, taking my hand from the mouthpiece so he can hear the sound of the rushing water filling the receiver, "sometimes a girl just doesn't feel like talking, you know?"

"Shit, son of a..."

I toss the receiver in the yard, just when he gets to the good part.

By the time the first man, and then another, rounds the edge of the house, the horse and I are galloping toward the stream. By the time they have taken aim, we are in the darkness of the trees, my body lying flat against the horse's neck, leaning into his gallop as I feel him gather his muscles, rise up and over the water.

By the time Cruz and his men discover there is no way to follow us into the forest, we will be out of El Gato, climbing the eastern ridge with the moon behind us and the dawn just ahead.